I0706450

Toward Him Still

Michael Okulitch

Fomite
Burlington VT

Copyright © 2024 Michael Okulitch
Cover image from The Monk by the Sea (Der Mönch am Meer) 1808-1810, Caspar David Friedrich

All rights reserved. No part of this book may be reproduced in any form or by any means without the prior written consent of the publisher, except in the case of brief quotations used in reviews and certain other noncommercial uses permitted by copyright law.

ISBN-13: 978-1-959984-43-6
Library of Congress Control Number: 2024932054

Fomite
58 Peru Street
Burlington, VT 05401
www.fomitepress.com
08-14-2024

Merely, thou art death's fool,
For him thou labor'st by thy flight to shun,
And yet runn'st toward him still.

—Measure for Measure

Prelude

They make way for him, some adults, a cluster of students. By their attitudes, I expect they think his manner odd, anomalous his zigzag course. I do. He pushes a broom down the main hallway, lost in thought, apparently; at some remove from the others passing him this way and that. I can't see his face. His blue cloth hat is pulled down low—typical—its brim turned up all around. Quietly stylish. I wonder where he got it? He will be brought to a sudden stop by the foot of the stairs if he doesn't soon come to. I hope the principal doesn't see Jimmy like this. That's what he calls himself, anyway. I lose sight of him.

The first bell has rung—I'm tired already—and the corridor crowds with people. So many. Friendly some, some impassive (as if best just to get on with it); and then there are the troubled. More troubled, I should say. There is a pretty one; not too troubled yet, it seems; the likely cost of prettiness still to come. People. Their eyes (much to be read there). Some see you; not all. Eyes dance sometimes, glittering eyes, as the poets say, gaiety for a moment, freedom from whatever dampness hangs on the spirit; and then the coda, a moment later or many years on, truth in the turn of a mouth.

Patterns of identity—smiles from this one and that, the usual greetings. I don't know all their names—even after some time—and yet how good they can feel, these daily exchanges (I can smile and nod at least; raise a friendly hand), brief encounters scarcely varying, a series of small pleasures in passing. I remain pleasantly surprised and sometimes should like to stay the chemistry. Pleasures that can almost get the better of caution. Over and over. I catch myself about to speak. One day—who knows? My mouth opens and I manage, just, to hold back a sound.

I once had a beautiful voice, or so I was told. Coy, that. I did, I do, but don't tell anyone. Anyway, morning greetings, good morning, comity, social scaffolding. Pretending to have marched on beyond distrust, past the pale's limitations: the tribe. Standing up to nullity, in effect. Futile in the long run, I know. But yes, pleasure. What tenderness am I missing to so value the ritual, I wonder? Jane. Of course.

On the other hand, nothing from that one or this: look at those eyes, turned in on themselves as if. It is not only me she doesn't see. A janitor, after all. Others too, as if invisible. What does she see? And here, for this other—his face signaling displeasure at all affect but his own— these social niceties are an irritant, or so I imagine he believes; how else account for that face? Petulance. I wish I'd missed it. Small minded notion: I should like to greet him effusively. Of course, I mustn't. That he wears a frown to signpost his position: cast off your useless, bourgeois leavings, he might well say—shout rather—overcome by impatience at some hapless soul wishing him a good day (I don't speak, of course); or no, something simpler: Fuck Off, I would guess. Well he is angry about something. Who cares?

Jimmy has since disappeared and I have come into possession of his diary. His diary and some. Just wait. The three paragraphs above are two of his entries. School District exercise books filled cover to cover— taupe, blue lined, a great many—with writing in a usually legible longhand, often in gray fountain pen ink, sometimes in pencil, occasionally in blue or black ballpoint. Here, at the top of this page—there is a generous top margin—he has drawn a tree in gray ink, branches extending this way and that, some leaves still remain here and there, one is falling, just detached he'd have you believe, the image rhyming with its roots shown below ground: as above so below. Nice. Is that a worm? Yes. He tried to give it a face, has spoiled some the effect of the rest.

Even before coming into possession of his notebooks I had come to doubt, more, disbelieve with an almost unbecoming certainty, that Jimmy is his real name; convinced of the likelihood that he pretended to be mute; and that by working as a janitor he meant, in effect, to make himself invisible. This suggests that Jimmy is to some degree a man skilled in the ways of contending. Some degree because, for all his obvious intelligence—canny, he is, with godly intuition even: you'll see—he makes mistakes. His manner for one; his style for another, in spite of himself I should think, if his intent was to disappear. Who is he hiding from?

I remember the first time I saw him. The period one bell is chiming. He reaches his janitor trolley and leans on the broom, tall, slim, clothed in a boiler suit in mother-of-god-blue; a figure improbably chic, if you have an eye for such things. Where did you come from? How did you get here? I confess, if you've not already considered it, that I find him attractive. I imagine certain things about him. Without shame, by the way. You can just tell sometimes; and it's not just one thing. No, it's something beyond the whole, more than the sum of his parts. Notice— because I will share—how in the diary he sometimes writes of himself in the third person. It takes getting used to. "Je est un autre" again (I remember this from college). Jimmy is a reader, it's safe to say. I stud- ied literature, incidentally. I recognize some allusions in his writing and suspect there are more that I miss as I make my way through the notebooks; but certain turns of phrase—you just know: the goddess is betrayed by her walk, as it were. I'm not showing off to make my point.

That's from one of Jimmy's entries. I looked it up and have already forgotten the author: Propertius by way of Pound? Virgil? You just know sometimes. He expects—or so I believe—a level of literacy I am no longer used to. Expects of who, though? My husband, for instance, is an attractive and intelligent man but in no way resists the dissolution of culture in our time. Immune to the frisson of it, I'm sure he would admit. So no, he, Jimmy, doesn't expect it. He just can't help himself. Sometimes, while reading him, I find myself wishing that I'd kept up my studies. Anyway, who would he have imagined was going to read his words now that those who had done so in the past are all dead? How could he have anticipated me? Should I be worried? Perhaps only himself, lonely Jimmy: "*Hypocrite lecteur,—mon semblable,—mon frère!*" It's contagious. Words. Once you start. My husband remarked recently that I am speaking differently these days. More fancy, he said. I expect he was teasing some. He can be sly. I teach learning handicapped children in a learning handicapped world.

Not all brooms are created equal, Jimmy thinks to himself. A girl is approaching him on her way to class. Handsome and self-possessed, Jimmy thinks. How well she carries herself: upright posture, the limbs' motion in concord. He imagines her successes to come as the years pass; apportions a qualitative advantage to her family life. And some socio-economic advantage too: the elegant austerity of the haircut looks expensive. He leans on his broom. His lips move, as if he were about to speak. I catch myself. Eyes meet; faces lift in smiles. Knowing almost, those eyes; but knowing what? His pretense at dumbness? She makes a point of holding his gaze and passes by. A friendliness and grace beyond her years; and nothing more, he adds, to temper this secretion of enthusiasm; but intelligence has a special attraction. I like her parents already. This scene plays most days. I enjoy seeing this young woman, Jimmy says to himself, happy for this passing moment, wondering at his own children, remembering his dear cats. A little thing, this passing by; and yet. Some say Jimmy is mute, others that he is possessed of a speech impediment and consequent shame.

I once had a beautiful voice, Jimmy writes, says to himself and pushes on. The period one bell is chiming. He reaches his janitor trolley and leans on the broom stick, contrapposto, one leg relaxed, the weight on the other. Note the opposite turn of the hips and shoulders, S-curve, the line of beauty. Unselfconscious, I assure you; but once, you know, the word for something. Original sin. First there was the word; then self-consciousness, Nature's vulgar stepsister. Bitch. Jimmy shifts his weight onto both feet, stretches the long fingers of his right hand in an elegant feline gesture, suddenly chagrined to notice that as well. Insidious, the self. I daresay we need others for distraction; but unfortunately that doesn't work for everyone. The young woman. How I should like to chat with her. To what end? Still. He turns to look over his shoulder, to see her again, but she is already gone.

Don't be like that, Jane admonishes, not willing to let me off the hook with any hint even of self pity. A beloved ghost, Jane. To what end? she repeats mockingly. Jane, my metacognitive other. Yes. So many years since Jane died—in Venice and it was snowing, I remember—and then later in the Pacific Northwest the young woman on the island, come from the opposite shore, found me there, on my island hideaway. And even while loving her, and I do believe she loved me too, I had to learn how to protect myself from her as she tugged on this and that string, never having had to acquire that skill while Jane lived. As if I didn't have enough to contend with. And poor Martin, dead. Father Martin, Catholic, my friend. The dead crowd around.

Jane still makes her way to me, if less frequently, the distance arduous for her, I suppose. Or could it be the destination? My hiding place. A high school in America. Imagine that. Dare I say where? They may find me yet. Pushing a broom. Years of mistaken identity. Might that be a universal title for autobiography? It's natural to expect more from them, yet the powers that be disappoint so, don't you think? They pursue me for what came into my possession by accident. I will never willingly surrender. My intransigence. Jane. Murder. Pushing a broom. How she laughed till she cried when finally, recently, she tracked me down, accompanied still by the god, her cavalier servente with whom I have better relations now after all these years; polite at the least; older of course, but ageless still. Still beautiful. (We did not enjoy friendly relations in the beginning, the god and I. Besotted by Jane, he was not happy to witness her love for me, dead or alive. We are used to each other now.)

This place. Temporary to be sure. I thought it would surprise her. This new place to hide from them: don't I belong here, Jane, after all? Jane's laugh. So wonderful. She remembered these words of mine, from so many years ago, first spoken as we descended a perfectly proportioned stairway in Avignon. And the boys' bathroom still to clean on this floor. The stink and the impudence go together. It's not funny, Jane. The god turns away. Embarrassed on my behalf, Jimmy thinks. Divine empathy. Naked, no matter the season. Good figure. Wings beat at his ankles.

I have Jimmy's diaries. My husband asks me why I spend so much time at my desk, what I'm writing day after day. (I keep Jimmy's notebooks hidden). Memoirs, I say; but that's not really true. It's not good to tell lies. I am tempted to quip that Jimmy is getting between my husband and me. I watch him pass by and wonder—where do such thoughts come from?—if Jimmy would fancy me. He notices things, discerns what is attractive in us, if we're so lucky; and the not so attractive too. To see: not so common a trait as you might think. I'm not sure, given what I know, that I would trust myself alone with him. "Her eyes, the turn of her mouth, the way she can surrender to passions of all kinds and then carry on …": I imagine him writing of me in this way. Each time I turn the page I half expect, no, hope, to find myself there. "Did I mention her scent?" he would write. Or, "Her deep-throated laughter." He would notice all this and more and god knows what I've been missing. It's not funny. I feel I have a responsibility to Jimmy, to the contents of his dairy; to you, even, whoever you may be, because I have come to understand that they are more than simply jottings about him, and, through this commentary, now me, for that matter. I have indeed entered into this. Thanks to Jimmy I see more, appreciate many things that I was missing. And want, almost cry out, I must admit, for more. This is a bigger concern than what you might be thinking about me at this point. To say nothing, at this time, of the creepy twins I am seeing here and there—brothers; early middle age—who I imagine are watching me. Jimmy had recorded in an early entry that twin brothers murdered the Inspector to whom Jimmy addressed his long missive at the time of and following his wife's death. Father Martin came to believe Jimmy, though it took time. He resisted at first: tried to stuff the manuscript back into its package after a page or two, cut himself on a staple and bled on it. It's all here. He is now dead. Think on it: I have children.

Father Martin's resistance at first is understandable; lasting for some time after he received the first bundle of words that arrived by post wrapped in a brown padded paper envelope, colorfully stamped with a multitude of images and denominations (a handsome subfusc Arctic image the largest and most valuable that Martin especially fancied), stapled shut and further bound with twine knotted elaborately as to frustrate a saint—thus Martin writes in a margin of one of the first pages, smearing it with blood from a finger cut on a staple and cursing in a legible hand his old friend, noting too his own failure to resist, stuff the bundle back into the package and send it back without more ado—, in frustration (poor sad Martin disposed to melancholy as it was), transitioning from anger, sadness, and even nostalgia, unable then to resist, turning page after page, finally creating in him a need, a need for commitment, no longer a pastime to while away the hours reading, spurring him to leave the comforts of routine in some discomfort (a rotting hand from a burn gone wrong: he had tried in a fit of pique, insulted by a reference to him amongst the pages, to burn the manuscript and then reached into the flames to retrieve it; and then the pain off decaying flesh assuaged by his growing fascination with morphine), to voyage out by sea to find his old school friend. It is true, the diaries do at first suggest the sufferings of a paranoiac. And then, trust me on this, the initial dissonance begins to resolve, first into a distant assonance about which one cannot be certain, and then there comes a crucial moment and there remains no middle ground.

My husband tells me I'm neglecting the children; and it is clear he means I am neglecting him; but so far he is too restrained to be direct about his own feelings. I see what effect I'm having. It's not a good thing to do to one's spouse. To any intimate relation. Dinner is ready. And I am feeling, I must confess, a stirring within me, something of Martin's need to abandon all else and set forth and find the man. This man. I can't. I mustn't. I have to. No, I don't.

The order of notebooks can be difficult to establish. They are not numbered, dated, sequenced in any way I have noticed. For example, at the end of one notebook, on the last page, dense without paragraphs, there is penciled text crowding the space above the blue lines at the top. I have to admit he has an attractive hand. Who writes in cursive anymore? An incomplete sentence apparently, it continues nowhere in this notebook if you follow the looping arrow directing your eyes to the edge of the inside back cover. Now where to? Impatient, I gestured in frustration—my mother once called me a diva after some such similar display—and knocked a stack of his fucking notebooks off my desk. One fell open, only one, folding back its cover on impact. And there, I find the continuation of the sentence. Am I not lucky? Not really. After all, how much of the stuff is apportioned us in this life we're bound upon? To be used up in this way? What a waste. I'll never win the lottery now. There, on the first page of the splayed exercise book, my allotment of good fortune spent, he, Jimmy, continues in pencil for a dozen lines about heading toward the noisome boys' bathroom—there's a smudge where the lead must have broken—and then scribbles on in *Nuage Gris*, his French ink. Somewhat mannered, don't you think, to be bothering with a fountain pen these days? How do I know the brand of ink? There was an almost empty bottle of it at the bottom of the bag he used to stow the notebooks. Handsome bag, if battered; a section of the strap not bound to hold for much longer. Antique leather, a fissure crudely stitched with string, makeshift as if for a war wound on one side, the hide shiny there from use. Greek postman's bag. Greek letters stamped on the flap. And as for the recovered sentence: as if a high school boys' bathroom should smell in any other way. Very frustrating this. My luck spent on retrieving a commonplace. No refunds.

Jimmy resigns himself to the task at hand, frowning some, one eyebrow raised; starts off toward the boy's washroom, turns the corner anticipating the stench. Should he expect it to be any different from yesterday and yesterday and yesterday? Of course not. Oh, but look, here she is, in this spot, with that same boy, her beloved. Blooming in the miasma. Perhaps she doesn't even notice the stench. Every morning at this time. The first period bell will ring. They will be tardy. Set your watch by it. Priorities. Pretty, petit, she stands close to her beau, looking up at him happy as can be. She wants babies, not good grades. What does the boy want? Imagine such a state of being lasting indefinitely: such promises have been made. Are made.

Vex not the atmosphere Jimmy, Jane says. She calls me Jimmy now, sometimes. I don't like it but she loves to tease. It's not a name I especially want to have attached to me either, you may as well know. I am feeding on this, Jane. And not as you might imagine. Slim adolescence, shiny sable braids twitching over her shoulders, moist dark eyes turned up at the boy, himself admittedly attractive, yes even handsome. Such affection, Jimmy says to himself. His lips move. He'd have choked on tears to say it aloud. I'm not well, he whispers. The girl: She sees nothing else. I am not here, Jimmy dares says to himself under his breath. He looks to the boy, almost says aloud, almost: Fool,—thus does he address the youth smiling back at her, Jimmy wondering at his presumed ingratitude—I hope you deserve all this. He reads the tumid confidence of the young man feeding on adoration, taking it for granted, Jimmy has decided, pushing onwards toward the filth and stench waiting for him. Jane steps in his way. Do you remember? I do, he says. I do of course. Well then, she says. And that is that.

Red wine stains the cover of another notebook. *A delicious Bourgeuil, he notes. I should like to be able to say I can tell what I was drinking by the different colors swatching these covers and pages; but I can't.* Jimmy writes that Jane, with the authority of the dead, speaks affectionately of Martin's guide in his quest to find him, the girl Carolina, whom shortly after setting out he met on the ferry, she: so self-conscious, sometimes awkward, and very beautiful. *Theresa is my confirmation name, Carolina had said. Martin laughed when he told me. Near his end as he lay dying. Martin. He insisted that Jane and Carolina were in the same room with him as he lay dying and Jane actually long dead by then. How can you say that, Jane asks. You know what I mean, Jane. The girl, he mostly called her. I finally wore away the childish sanctity that coated her strength and daring and so I'll continue to call her by her legal name, Carolina. And the awkwardness too, by the way. Her mother was an extraordinary person. I'll get to her. Anne her name. Good people, Jane called them. Approbation from beyond. Jane's god, naked, beautiful beyond belief, eyes me. Kindly. I am truly grateful we can get along now. I'd feel a fool to ask, but does he never feel cold? Jane rolls her eyes.*

There is a letter from Anne tucked between the pages here: beautiful stationary. It explains much. I am reluctant to share it. She saved his life, you know. Jimmy's. I am getting ahead of myself. My husband is calling me. Before I go, once again: who can possibly be surprised by the stink of a high school boys' bathroom? Christ. Wait for me. I'll be back. Read a section of Jimmy's diary while I'm gone, why don't you? He lived on his own island somewhere in the Pacific Northwest. Don't ask me how he came to possess his own island. He is somewhat coy about an inheritance. From what Martin is said by Jimmy to have written in the margins of a letter he had sent him, the girl (no, not Carolina), see below, is suspect. More, dangerous. Not a girl. Neither then or now. Very much a woman—twenty years later, incidentally. Twenty years roughly speaking. I've managed to sort the passage of time out here and there, I say to myself, and then the whole thing gets turned upside down. Time not what it used to be. I can't quite explain why she in particular and even his beloved Jane have come to irk me so. I, a woman with two children, an attractive if not quite dashing husband, a woman moreover who has kept her figure and who enjoys fucking. Yes I do. Anyway, I have become possessive of Jimmy. I confess. You've already surmised. And I entertain questions such as, did he ever, from beneath the brim of his hat, did he ever notice me? You know already that he remarks on school girls—I don't say objectionably—and I can add as much as it pains me some, that he spent an inordinate time on one floor of one wing of the school. Oh I won't go there: an attractive colleague—perhaps a little younger than I, had a room on that floor. I couldn't help but notice his cart, always parked near her room. She never seemed to pay him any attention, noticed me more, to tell the truth (I believe she has a wife); and I admit I never saw him peering at her. On the other hand, it's not as if I ever actually saw him paying court to anyone. What he noticed, and he does notice, I know only from his diary (I almost wrote confession). And it's not as though they could have a conversation without him blowing his cover. Still. Still. Might that floor have been especially in need of custodial attention?

A disheveled blonde in a baggy, oversized sweater. Almond eyes. *Mine, she said, when she reached for me and fumbled with my belt. And I was. All that time ago.*

The woman from across the inlet, visiting again today. *See the Dutchman on a broad reach across a choppy sea, jib and main sails full to bursting. My belly alert: that visceral sweetness of sensation. Incomparable. Do you remember the first time you felt it? There, at the first sight of her approach. Free will: what's that? Lunch together. I'll roast a salmon. A gray day. Old rocky faces staring back opposite, pine green and cedar black, mottled here and there with autumn color. These faces not indifferent, somehow. Not this morning. Nor friendly. Odd. It will rain later. I watch her make her way for another beat or two before returning to the kitchen: slim still, it appears, perched on the port gunwale, legs stretched out before her, she is as if flying toward me. This time I am not reaching for my gun. Why not? Champagne rather. What am I missing? Dead Martin protests still. Fool, he says. I hear you Martin. His visits continue, as does his predisposition to worry. Not Jane, in this instance. What do you know, Jane? Tell. That Martin had reason enough to worry, she says. That doesn't help.*

Carolina and her mother Anne both urged me away from her all those years ago, too; and Martin never trusted her. Questions remain. Unexpected meetings, sightings here and there. Beyond coincidence finally. A distant, if uncertain, glimpse in Corsica. Late spring. Wild boars everywhere—the babies adorable, suckling their mothers—; tiny owls singing in the night-time; a giant full moon the night we arrived. You might well ask what I was doing there with Carolina. Not long after Martin died—Carolina weeps silently, leaves a final kiss on dead Martin's cooling forehead, the chill lingering on her lips she told me, Father Martin manifest there, on lips so pretty, accompanying her away from his carcass, not unpleasant, she said to me, takes with her Martin's bag with all my writing, herself now in thrall, her word, to the bundle of papers she had started to read, spending day after day in his hospital room as he lay dying; herself falling under their spell, she brings me to her mother's home, where Martin—did words of mine…? I can't go there—had stayed before finding me here. Hurried me away, the girl did, abducted almost from my island home, unexpect-edly, more, completely by surprise, arriving in the motor skiff one day. The Boston Whaler in which she'd brought Martin to the island. I could have shot her: She, standing perfectly still behind me one morning, standing there without notice as I tied my laces. The cats no longer alive to warn me. I miss them so. We found some fuel—she had neglected to calculate—and left in a hurry. At her home on an island some hours distant from mine I was given Martin's old room to use; not too long after that the mother's bed. I am getting ahead of myself. How much time remains for me to leave a record, after all? I'm beginning to see signs of them again. The threat. Jane.

Jimmy and his cats. A love story in itself. I've never liked cats much, I confess. Not a cat person. My husband and I have a Labrador, choco-late brown. And this Corsica business with the young woman Carolina who had guided poor Martin for whom I developed affection and some pity. What is that about? Wait. Not all the notebooks are in Jimmy's hand, incidentally. There is an extraordinary trio that have sections that unfold, fat bellows they appear to be when tied, bursting with desire to be opened as if, or so I thought—really, I could not believe it when I found them, wrapped in parchment paper, bound with string, accordion like instruments with a feminine music all their own. There is a scent coming off the pages. Unmistakable. Woman. I sorted the voices very quickly. When I share I expect it will be apparent even to a less than perceptive reader, that within those pages is a woman's story, page upon page bound with a fine hand and by several means: tape glue staples thread and paper clips. Admittedly, there is no name or other form of identification. I have my own ideas. I will share. I will. Not yet. Cold Heaven, the writer put at the top of the first page and underlined it once. There is a poem by that name that I'm very fond of. This is something else. It's like a script. Mother of God and her daughter: you can have no idea. Fountain pen by the way. Affectation? Don't bother. But both of them? Jimmy and the woman now? What clue is this? I've got to go. My husband is preparing dinner. I hear the sound of a cork pulled. But what if Jimmy authored it, dictated it, unable for some reason to write it down himself?

The cats were holding me together. They would not survive without me, I had argued; then admitted I would not likely survive without them, or so I believe. Without them I should not exist. I miss them so. I was tired. Jane was no more of this world. I know, Jane. I know. What remains? says Jimmy under his breath daringly, as a blind girl passes in the opposite direction, flinching at the sound of his words, to her at least louder and more startling thereby than they would likely be for a sighted person, Jimmy leaving broom and cart behind and not bothering even to pretend that he has a job to do. The blind girl turns a circle in the middle of the hallway: as if in a holding pattern—tick tick tick sounds her stick—then continues on her way.

I've got to go. My husband's getting angry waiting. I can feel it through the walls between us. I don't blame him. He takes special care in the kitchen. Read this. Start here. May as well begin with this mystery. Thomas—see below—must be Jimmy. Don't you think? I would hate for you to suffer my earlier confusion. And now look at this: who is this woman writing in one of his notebooks, as if?

When we became involved I didn't think of the difference in years between us. I didn't notice. Beautiful we were. Now I think of that difference in years: fourteen, between me and my son, the boy they took from me on the dock, and I realize they number the same. The boy nine and I then twenty-three. Fourteen years. On the Russian dock. Rough they were. The pair of Soviets. Poorly suited. Coarse featured. They said to me, Go, go, but not your son. Whore, one of them exhaled at me and then looked away and stumbled back a step. My escort from British Intelligence: outnumbered and hamstrung by diplomacy. His nervous breakdown came soon after. And mine? Breaking still. I am, however, of a stronger disposition. Still standing, anyway, after a lifetime. Fourteen years. Thomas just out of university and I in my thirties, recently divorced. My second son staying with his German grandmother for a couple of weeks. A Greek island. A decade since my boy is walking away, holding the trembling hand of the Englishman who, not long after, left for Canada, and following some sensitive years and a predilection for Scotch whiskey that he at least did not consider an affliction, became a diplomat for his adopted nation. My son—long-legged, stumbling once to keep pace with his escort, strained to keep looking back at me, eyes fixed on mine, still too confused for tears perhaps—walking toward his new life with his Russian grandmother and my dear sister. Years later, Thomas long-legged and naked and tanned, walking toward the water on the Greek shoreline, glances back and his eyes meet mine for the first time.

The dog beats his tail against the door, percussion to his gentle whining. I can't deny him. In moments of sadness he cares for me so. Such golden eyes—oh don't be so sad, darling—nuzzles and gentle whimpers to accompany my tears. I can't concentrate. My husband is cooking so well; and the wine… I am sated. I must rest from this now. I can't go on. More wine. Thomas you are wondering. Jimmy, yes.

Painted ladies migrating. A wet spring. I stop to watch them, staring through the windows, toward the northeast. Mountains in the distance gouged in afternoon shadows blue and grey. The butterflies undulate against this backdrop, composed within the grid of the window. Preparatory drawing, as if. A fluttering cloud rising together to clear the brink of heritage brick building before them. Children here and there on the quad below. Palm fronds rattle. Weary Jimmy leans on his broom and stares.

Mother in the kitchen. I can hear her at the sink as I enter the house, home from school. Early teens. In the fall my shoes damp and carrying a wet leaf on one toe. Quietly I make my way to her and seize her from behind, cupping her small breasts. And she laughs. Imagine. I would have been so angry: you understand, from being startled, provided I survived the shock; but she laughs, calls me a fool in her mother tongue and twists free of my embrace, turns the water off and offers me a raspberry tart and milk, happy to see me. I can tell. I have been looked at like that since. Over the years, from time to time. It has been a while. Come on Jane, how often do I indulge myself thus.

I'll leave you with something. Here is a page heavy with attachments: old photographs, a drawing, letters, a postcard, fixed variously with glue, paper clip and staples. Handsome artifact. A black and white closeup of a beautiful woman; in faded color a Mediterranean landscape of rolling hills and spring flowers in bloom: young Jimmy, oh Thomas then, Christ, with a young woman (I wish it were me), both just turning toward the photographer, the two standing gorgeous on top of a hill, the sea blue beyond them, a corner punctured by cat's teeth (trust me: I know). A pastel drawing on dark gray paper: two cherry tomatoes on their stems: one tomato really. Transit. Memento mori: green fruit, red fruit, no fruit—a bare stem. A trinity. Well rendered, smudged here and there. And a postcard, Sienese Mother of God recto. Anonymous. Verso: in a beautiful hand, smudged brown ink, "You were here and did not come to me."

Wave upon wave of painted ladies rise and fall. Mother sits in her easy chair. Crossword puzzle—her English teacher—and tattered loosened Webster's at hand, the newspaper folded in quarters. Tea with raspberry jam cool by now on a metal side table. A Haydn piano trio on the radio. Her first son will die before her. Far away. Prostate. She will see him once years before he dies, traveling to Russia.

I can't say I understand. I repeatedly return to these last and try to sort who Thomas/Jimmy is writing about. A mistress shares details that I am certain belong to his mother. Or is this Thomas on a literary jag, trying out a feminine persona? Go fetch Tertullian then, or a psychologist, to sort the matter out. I have not yet managed to unravel this. Perhaps neither has he. Mother. A love interest. Not Jane, by the way. I would like to mother him.

Bushtits: too vulnerable we thought. They construct a hanging nest in the near branches of oak just out of reach from the balcony railing. Back and forth, both birds engaged. Days pass. They are tiny, seem accustomed to us; even to the cats, for the most part. The cats less so. The nest a miracle of design and unstable beauty. Jane stares out to sea. White caps and gray lowering out of the east.

Mama told me. Carmen in Tashkent. On tour. She a factory girl in the chorus. She opens the album, a loose photo drops out. A little boy. Circles under his eyes. Sad. My brother. She tucks it away. Here, another. A small black and white photo, border jagged-edged. Look, definitely not Spain: palm trees, toreadors and soldiers notwithstanding. An especially friendly looking couple, musical as mother used to say: Don José and Escamillo, the latter a tad swollen in the thighs; and there, see, the cigarette factory girls, each young woman with a cigarette in her mouth, all brandishing a fan. And there: Carmen. That one smiling with a flower in her mouth, a saucy friend who makes mama laugh even now to remember. So many years passed. I picked mother out. Right away. I'm about six. She in the back row just off center. Unmistakable. Mother remembers. Admired, she was. Persik, Peach, the handsome native said, an older man. Lined brown face. Neatly clipped salt and pepper mustache, she remembered. Loose trousers, tailored tweed jacket. Speaking Russian with an accent. Good voice. Camels! Camels walking down the street, chewing, lidded eyes, no illusions about mankind. Chort vozmy: the devil take you. All of you. Almost. And especially wonderful, she said, smiling: two mules galloping together down the main street, their handler left cursing far behind. Escaping. They'd had enough. Legs don't fail us now. And melons, she remembered. Market stalls. The perfume of them, she said. The flavor.

Behold. Here is the Carmen photo, neatly fixed to one of the accordion like folds attached to a notebook. Next to it another photo, a woman— not mother—in winter garb, standing in a cold St. Mark's Square. Blurry tourist photo. Meaningful juxtaposition or haphazard? Thomas, I want to turn the page and see that you've attached a photo of me. Let me into this collage.

The bell rings. Jimmy leaves the cart outside in the hallway and enters a third floor classroom. No-one is there.

And I in Aix with Jane a lifetime later: Carmen set in a therapist's clinic. And next day we share a beyond delicious whole Saint Pierre, over looking the sea near Cassis.

An elderly woman walks the twilit streets of Uzes searching for her cat. She is well dressed. Hours later I see her in the night still searching, stopping at gateways, peering into dark courtyards.

In Arles, the Alycamps, a man is singing in a crypt, his voice resonant. We go in. Lovely, I tell him, Jane next to me. Thank you, I say. He sings again. With even more feeling than before.

My husband's cooking is delicious. And the wines he serves. But back to this other business: these accordion bellows constructs with writing and photographs, pastel drawings even and an especially good pen and brown ink: two wine glasses and a dish of fruit, writing to one side: "My love," etcetera.

Piss. Circus. Mother. Son. At the circus a man exhorted mother as a young woman to piss on him, she told me. We were watching a Hollywood classic on television. "North By Northwest", "Sunset Boulevard"? I don't remember. I'm preteen I think. I'm ready for my closeup. I don't know if she did what he asked. She never said.

Sisyphus, Tantalus. Same old fucking thing.

I've got to go for now. Read. Go ahead. You sort it out. I'll try to catch up.

Part One

Words without end. Snow falls in another world outside mine. Limned through the weather, the flaky palimpsest, a hand holds open a shutter ogee-framed in pockmarked stone. I wait for the face at the pane: her young face opposite and a story above. Eloquence in an open hand. And here is my Jane: dead and still warm. There will be no excusing lies, Inspector, but truth free of value's touch? Undiminished, as if, by attempts to shade it so and so and so; her life nothing more finally than a duration occupying the space between two dates? The truth of what it means to see her so—ellipsis swollen by the understanding incumbent on my witness.

Tears overflowed her eyes as she had a last laugh—laughing, laughing—loitering even now on her upper lip. I dam the flow with a fingertip, raise to my lips a salty drop: jewel of the dead; shamed to self-consciousness in an instant. No more of it. God help me I'm panicked. Images of a lifetime swarm bee-frenzied; my hive shattered and queen dead. Memories furious to be undermined so. Sting and die. I look around me, and once again: apparently nothing to blame, nothing to draw to your attention and with your witness call out to it to take my challenge. My life in fragments, unbound, free to fall apart for want of a center: she, who laughed until the tears ran and died picturesquely sprawling—see the gentle curve of her instep—by these tall Venetian windows on the other side of which snow flakes fall.

There is that young woman in the upper story opposite, watching me and smiling. (She has seen how I notice her these last few days.) It is as though she sees the humor in the whole scenario. Heaven protect her: look away, young lady. I had no idea Jane would find this whole business so deathly funny. Humorous, yes; perhaps I miss the point; do not see that the joke is over some other thing. Who now remains to tell me, trembling as I am, frantic with intuition of a mistake on such scale there can be no remedy?

Jane lies dead and still warm by these tall windows overlooking the canal on which snowflakes continue to fall, stay a little, melt. We two—I cannot shoulder all the ensuing blame—will tell the truth and pretend it is just a story.

The temptation to explain one's self to others should not be indulged. I exhort you, Inspector, especially you, to take my lead here and forestall for yourself the bathos of causality. Experience suggests that personal time is not unlimited, and if I am forever qualifying myself what shall I have achieved? There is a record to be made and I am pressed for time, as you will come to understand. There is a train to Paris tonight. Of her death, at least, I am innocent. I declare this lest circumstances, consequent of what I hope to detail here, make it appear otherwise. Jane was going to help me get it all down. Incidentally, she would never have taken this time to stop and explain herself, nor allowed me any self-indulgence.

I won't answer the phone. (Could it be the lovely young woman I have seen in the window opposite calling me here in my hotel room? There is no sign of her at the window. Haven't I spent half a lifetime counting on, hoping for, such distractions to take up my time?)

Here is my love, more immediate than hope. How beautiful, even after spending her last breath; still warm to the touch; no matter the mutiny of flesh, surrender of muscle. The grand design of her lingers. (If you have seen the dead you will know that it is not always so.) It is as if she provoked it into lifelong attendance, and some, by apparently not caring. I shouldn't think, however, that insouciance—is there a night cream by that name?—will work for everyone. Better I attend to this other business. It will not keep indefinitely. (The warmth is leaving her; then I too will have to go.) Apparently there are limits after all and I've many things to tell; but look at her. Beauty will not leave her alone. (I resist joking about her soul; only just; she would not, herself wondering earlier if congestion and constipation might block the soul's migration at both places.)

So many years together. There is a smile on her lips. I am not imagining it. She had caught her breath to laugh when it happened. Her final exhalation a little laugh, fragrant—for I bent over her, saw in her dark eyes that something else was happening—fragrant with licorice and a combination of her scent, something I can only call womanly, and something pungent, uncharacteristic, faintly underlying the whole. Her smile. Perhaps I was her experiment. I can't help but wonder sometimes. I may be having the last word, but something behind her smile promises somehow to outlast that.

It is snowing here in Venice. She has chosen well to die today, if depriving herself of the rare enchantment outside: snowflakes settling onto the canal for the duration of a breath, jade-green water thick with cold; was planning to drag me out for a walk before lunch, a risotto, she had had in mind, and roasted sea bass and salad and lots and lots of wine, she had laughed, so deeply, crinkling her large eyes, last night's kohl smudged some, so randy this morning biting my fingers and hand as I pretended to sleep, and lots and lots of wine, she had insisted—and then yesterday that business with the pigeons in the square. As if Nature herself were compelled to signal by way of emphatic portents what was to come. Half an hour after that weird business with the birds—are you still with me? I had gone for a walk on my own as she bathed—I met Jane outside our hotel and we went on, ducked into a museum and I, amazed if not shaken, chattered over it as we wandered round our favorite room until she asked me to shut-up before Giorgione's "Tempest" and threatened to pinch my balls, delivered this in a voice of natural cultivation as though offering a detail of connoisseurship to the smiling ghost of Lord Clark, earning for herself an appreciative smile from a handsome Chinese leaning knowingly toward the painting, the only other person in the small room. (More of him later.) What complexities await me. The formalities enjoined by the body when it dies to say nothing of the hauntings of memory and whatnot else besides. The dead weight. Smiling still, I think; yes, and still warm. I can reach over and touch her from the little desk, run my fingers lightly over the high brow, trace round her eyes, caress the cheekbones. It is true the skin now hesitates a little before returning to its place over these bones, envy of many a woman. Not an hour ago she asked me to help her move the chaise longue on which she liked to lie and stare at the canal when she wasn't rereading her favorite, closer to the tall double windows that overlook and open over the side canal and from where she told me she could better hear my story. I can touch her by leaning. Damn my foot, though. It would hurt now, vying with kamikaze pigeons and aberrant weather for significance. She is still warm—her nose, such a nose, is cold, but so is mine—and still smiling, likely amused at having known me all these years and kept from me her knowledge of my perfect moment. Why would she do that?

For the first time, this very morning, she showed me the photo, after so many years together. Imagine. This photo. The evidence. One corner punctured by cat's teeth. A small print, black and white, seen through the eye of her father's Leica that allowed for no improvement (he wondered himself silly as to when he could have shot this excellent photograph—his camera a forbidden thing, as the daughter knew—which to his chagrin then mysteriously disappeared, along with the negative, so that he came to doubt his own eyes). She confessed that it was dumb luck after looking at me with such a glance as to wonder how I might think she could do anything less than perfect. I fall for her over and over again.

I had believed for a lifetime that no one saw my perfect moment. As of this morning this is somehow inconceivable and Jane providentially my witness. We had not yet been introduced, but there is something occult, as if inevitable and perfect, about some meetings. Her lips are still colored and shapely, lasting promise of her beautiful discourse. Look there. Look there…

I am falling like an angel. Yes, that one, the pride of etcetera. Imagine myself frescoed on ancient church walls. So perfect was my fall I sometimes wonder, doubt even, that I ever hurled myself from the edge, made the high dive at all. No one sees, for all that the photograph belies this so long after the fact. Coach has a mote in his eye, he says. Mother wipes at my sister's painted lips with tissue (I am having my apotheosis and my sibling is perishing of shame). Father must be at work; and yet now I wouldn't be as surprised as before if someone presents me with photographic evidence that he is enjoying just then a completely other life than that of husband, father and provider; that during my lonely exultation he is sharing his own perfect moment with someone more like him than mother. My father a secret sensualist? I don't know. Had he been a public man perhaps we'd have photos and scandal and I open the brown envelope, see these projected in black and white before my mind's eye. Look, the woman in the underwear of the time—how her disabused eyes know and understand me, fill me with longing and all the rest of it—and then more pictures flash lit and bright with detail in variations on dishabille and hunger and the tumid consumption of one another and I remember and almost smell and taste and smell again… So I am falling—and the lifeguard saw, I'm sure, but did not want to believe his own eyes, so as good as blind, and instead, glandularly racked with the inherent meanness of his species, begrudged me its excellence, nary a splash as I broke the water, incidentally—until pricked into self-awareness, a sudden blushing of detail, infusion of ecstasy, I slowly rise to the surface prolonging for as long as there is air in my lungs the remains of the moment, the escorting bubbles reluctant to break then sighing with a lambent fizzle into the air, expiring into the whole and already the exultation at the remove of consciousness: bird song, broom smell and scraping leaves, murmur of voices, crowding into my diffusing clarity as I search blinking water from my eyes for acknowledgment from my dear family, the chance regard of strangers, a scudding mackerel sky, the shiver of swaying poplars, retreating eagle yonder. And all the while something is very wrong, hump-backing my lonely and fading deification; and as a warm breeze ruffles the water, anesthetizing me from the rest of the world for an extra moment with the perfume of Indian summer air layered with North Wind, assuaging my pain with broom's perfume, it is upon me. I feel my foot cramp up never to relax, know that I will carry the golden moment forever, that I am now possessed by something beyond me, something perfect. My foot gimped by perfection and I to limp for the rest of my days.

The doctor who had attended my birth, unplugged my long-suffering mama, a gruff Yorkshire man who in his eyes betrayed a barely withheld affection for mother as I knew from the start went out of his way at first to cure my deformity and later salve my understanding and his blameless failure with tales of Byron, angel deformed Jacob and jokes about the Fallen One's limp. (How many doctors these days…? No matter.) So I was to understand that I was deformed in no ordinary way. A divine touch, he managed, mumbled with a straight face, some now forgotten quatrain and turned from me as his eyes filled with unforgiving memory. Connoisseurship thus began with myself as object somewhat early on. Later some women were stirred by the effect of my comeliness accented by this imperfection, this caesura in the freshness and vitality of my line, accent to the something more than the sum of my parts. That same something that envelops Jane now, the accent of death maybe, looking a little stiffer as it happens. Anyway, how I should have loved to have had this years ago, this photo that lies to my left before me now—see her ghostly gibbous thumb print on the bottom, the whole cropped without a margin, how from this oblique angle and the tall windows directly before me the contour lines of her thumbprint are suddenly rainbow lit like a letter from Kells' Book, a palette brought to the surface and a monk's eyes plankton-parceled on a cormorant's back, fading within seconds in the air, here alive by the alchemy of her skin and the borrowed light of passing snow flakes. I can lose it or bring it back by the tilt of my head… And Leni Riefenstahl's, Kurt Reichert's, have nothing on the photo or the falling figure, their rote perfect divers nothing on my one dive printed here. How I'd have liked to show those well-meaning (and those not so, come to think of it now) doubters—everyone doubted; though perhaps not father who humored me when I tried to tell them of my moment—how I passed from air into water and in the process…

That was long ago; but with lasting consequence; though I insist that it was less debilitating than you might think, despite the gibes of cruel schoolboys from time to time, with whom I also got along notwithstanding, and despite the bent foot's barometrical sensitivity to the weather. Weather satellites have nothing on me. The consequences of which I speak are more those of reliving the fall, against which nothing else very much matters. The precious moment living on with every cramp in my twisted foot, more, even with each uneven quotidian step toward the market checkout counter. Not an easy way to get on in the world. I sometimes find myself having to translate my sensibility from that of the moment's abiding eternity, falling, perfect, alone, to that of flowing social convention. Imagine eschewing a tittup and taking hold of a moving train from a standstill: thus am I jerked into the world as if out of dream to the bemusement and sometimes amusement of check-out girls, passing friends on the street, motorists in a hurry. I'm not complaining. The doctors all think I suffered some kind of stroke for want of anything better to say. There is no evidence of this; but they had to come up with something.

That business with the pigeons, by the way, the frantic birds' repeated passing, till brought up short before the sudden brutality, bloody and stupid, and not a spot of gore or feather left—for I have been back this morning—to suggest that what I have to tell is true. The birds. Pursued by what? Flying side by side, up and down the square, Campo Santa Margherita, as if with no recourse to the sky. The screeching little gulls are flown, escaped from here. The madness and no accounting for it. I tell you, I took my hand out of my coat pocket, leaned on my stick looking about myself, keeping an eye on them, wary, flinching as they neared, even ducking once and then self-conscious about it, imaging faces behind the sky-reflected panes, eyes squinting between the shutters' slats. But there was no time for that. The racket of wings. The overwrought resonance within the square. Now again, the bug-eyed pigeons, starting red-eyes, horrible, the blurring cry-blood effect as of emblematic red streamers trailing alongside, so many pumping hearts, flying fast and low in such numbers the air washes after in pursuit, sweeping up in its wake fish scales and shrimps' whiskers from the morning market, whirling dust over cobblestones, whipping fore-locks tickling over eyes, mine, those of two startled children, a little girl crying, pony-tail panicking over her nuque—it's far too cold for it to be bare—running in a red cardigan sweater unbuttoned and too short, MacGregor plaid skirt and tights, shod in oversized, shiny black gum boots pulled after her brother dressed in tweeds like a little man ducking into an alley, and there a cat low to the ground making its escape, here again a trapped air wave stirred up to slam end to end over the square, empty arctic grey and cold, the wild beating of wings whipping up at each stone constraint, wild currents of winter brittle atmosphere again and yet again… this the vermin infested, plague-driven portent of the pages of malignant spoor the hapless professor unloaded on us, pull up, pull up! Making sense of it all; the habit of thought to be indulged now and again… but first let me tell you how a chance meeting in a Parisian restaurant not so long ago—I still can see a whole roasted duck steaming on a platter, almost unmanageably smothered in green olives—is brought to bear on our, my circumstances today. I say chance. But who knows? Subsequently, in Vancouver, the Mounties insisted on three interviews—when I wanted a quiet day or two with an old friend—and quizzed me on biochemistry. I failed easily and they let me be, or was it they simply passed me on by way of free trade to the American agencies who thought I was playing them for fools—thus my cosmopolitan airs, and one of them let slip he thought I was not long for this world after forcing their way into our Los Angeles home and frightening our cats—while the French quietly got to the point when we returned to Paris and simply threatened to deconstruct me. Eyes follow me everywhere still, untiring, unblinking; though I am no longer physically examined. I have passed onto the next stage, perhaps. Graduated to what? But in that lovely restaurant not so long ago, I remember, the visiting professor of German Literature in the fine grey suit with the hand stitching I had admired, and now I wonder: what if his suit had not been so well made, not draped just so over his distinguished form? My love smiles in answer, looks as though she is dreaming. Would we have continued after an exchange of pleasantries if the fabric had tugged, unseemly here and there? And yet he had been so cultivated, and enjoyed at the same time such an easy manner.

(A manner that I tried some, I confess, by not being as serious as he had need of that night, nor as quick as was imperative to him at the time. Later that same night the manuscript was unpacked before us at his hotel not so far away. The bundle unpacked in a small salon off the lobby (why not in the greater privacy of his rooms?), a fragrant oak fire burning, tended by a porter, and more eau de vie, the thick handmade paper singed and still smelling of smoke two and a half centuries later, which should have been one amongst many tells; on the other hand the wine and drinks that preceded and followed, the enduring charm of the restaurant lingering with us, his conversation, and what had I to do with Global machinations... ?)

He possessed, he said, later carefully untying the twine wrapped thrice round the bundle, part two of *Dead Souls* and what with my Russian... (but I do not remember telling him anything about that). That which wonderful Gogol had supposedly burned at the insistence of a priest, but which he had come to possess, the professor explained not right away of course but really so very soon after making our acquaintance, at his initiation by the way, turning to look at us sitting side by side at the end banquette under the window. Ours a lovely table with a view down the length of the small restaurant, the battered zinc bar to our left. A young woman with dark eyes and hair and a porcelain complexion enjoying attention unworthy of her beauty, I remember, at the opposite end of the room. Things as I say moving quickly, launched from his beneficent smile and appraisal of us, then his comment (as he turned down a cheap paperback edition of Brecht whom he knew, as it happens, and I asked of him, curious about the dirt with which it was said by Mann, Thomas, he made up his finger nails), saying after he sipped from his wine that here we eat as people have eaten for three hundred years, and Paris has few places such as this remaining. Thinking back, I shiver at certain implications and try to remember how it was we came to eat at that restaurant that evening. This is not a healthy pastime. Everyone, every one, becomes a suspect in an interminable concatenation and everything, every thing, then implicates itself. Is this a chain of being? My head will start to ache.

If only I had known what he was up against, I would have engaged him from the start with more of the seriousness which now I know was warranted; or more practically politely nipped the whole business in the bud and returned to my love and my dinner and later offered him a friendly smile and a nod as one or the other of us stood first to leave. So the charred bundle, one of three of which he would come to show us in his nearby hotel. Which the professor explained, rushing over these details as if to get them over with, told us with the patience of a teacher who, except for the occasional twitch or shift in tone, has long gotten used to traveling at a more leisurely speed than that which he should have preferred, but at the same time without so far as I can recall any hint that what he was about to tell us was a code to a matter of Life and Death, that the manuscript was saved from the flames by an illiterate (highlighted by a double arching of the brows), aristocratic (and this he emphasized with noticeable delectation that had nothing to do, I eventually understood, with snobbery), girl child (photo of a charming girl provided and I not wondering at all about the significant dates, Gogol's chronological bracketing, that of light chemistry and what a well-bred child would be doing in the chambers of a sublime madman), on the verso of which were all kinds of for me indecipherable equations which the professor's thumb twitched over repeatedly in time to his clearing his throat also repeatedly and looking into my eyes with such significance, an increasingly theatrical urgency (if only I could apologize for my daftness; I simply did not get it), that I would have been embarrassed had I not had my capacity to feel shame for others numbed (a well-deserved rest) by drink. The girl in the photo perfectly lovely, by the way, and with terrible burns to her hands, the professor told us in marked and significant detail for which he then apologized to Jane (it was assumed that my mettle was up to the horror), what with our dinner before us, the duck's carcass, the delicious crispy skin in shreds here and there, the professor barely stifling what I thought at first to be a sob—taking me aback;

madman I thought, though charming certainly—but was, I think, a sigh and swallow and gasp of exasperation with my lack of progress toward understanding what he was getting at all the while, the arcane allegory, the pagan mystery coding the advanced science he was being so coy about between helping himself to the olives scattered round the carcass of our bird.

I don't altogether blame myself. Later I would make my way through delightful but unavailing volumes of esoterica trying to unscramble the mystery. I think that he could simply have whispered to me what he had in mind. (I should have put a couple hundred Euros on the table and left immediately.) Jane all the while quietly watching, resisting his evident but silent appeals to her to understand the point of it all. She did, as it turns out. There was not time enough for us both to be dull-witted. How she enjoyed the process unwinding, stalling, unwinding a little more, as might a cat playing with a skein of yarn. Not everyone thought this quality in her as engaging as I. She wanted to see him work, she said to me back at our apartment; and, too, that if he had wanted her assistance, he should have addressed himself to her from the start; and with a certain hungry look proceeding then to initiate a desperate embrace from which we would as if turn each other inside out.

Inspector, were I attempting a literary entertainment rather than this chronicle, I would put to use a vision I had this morning before I woke. Start with what I saw just before Jane inserted her fingers into my mouth and with her tongue and quickened breaths compelled me to love her again. The vision somehow lingering despite her urgency, imprinted on my eyelids as I stirred to her overtures: shadows fleeing a wave of light over the earth, myriad cries of birds and animals wakened by the encroaching day, myself in motion, witness in a place neither exclusively of light or darkness, heartbreak of countless dreams scattering with the light and then the sweetest surrender to gravity and I, unafraid, am falling again, perfectly falling, as in my one dive, as in the photo, my foot offering a voluptuous reminder of sensation, waking to taste her fingers and her mouth, to blink at the sight of large snow flakes falling, a momentary glimpse through the drawn windows, the flakes settling on the window sills of the palace opposite.

I have called for coffee and biscuits. The tall and handsome waiter who brought the tray did not appear to notice anything odd, nor the protruding butt of my 9mm automatic; quietly went about his business, a little crestfallen perhaps that he would not enjoy his customary exchange of banter with my wife, whose Italian is so much better than mine, apparently sleeping on the chaise by the window. He tiptoed out and gently closed the door after himself, sharing with me an understanding glance of appreciation for her beauty that skillfully remained within the bounds of propriety. There is the young woman again. It is the first time I have seen her walk outside. She is talking to herself. I imagine I hear the sound of her soles crunching the snow. I have need of company. I must dash. I'll leave the *Do Not Disturb* sign on the door.

Hearing the exhortations of the god on my way out the door, even so I look back. He has turned around, I hear, an anguished cry. Who, she said? Jane still smiling and yet it hurts some that she should joke this way. I told you not to look, the god said, his voice full of sadness and some disappointment in me that he was unable to hide. What a comedian. Mutterings of the god. I left. Will she be there when I return? She will keep, I told myself when I shut the door and hung the sign. I had no idea for how long.

By the time I am outside… but stay a little: it is something to behold… and he stops here, does Thomas, at the first step of the bridge, grips the snowy railing with his free hand, leans heavily on his stick—it is so quiet—turns to his left looking down the green passage of the small canal, eyes squinting and tearing through the falling snow, pauses along the way to look up at their windows, blinks the image of his Jane away from there, the smoky image behind the pane, Jane smiling at him through the glass, remembering as well when they first had come here all those years ago and all the years since rushing after, the first time, she a teenager in a djellabah softly lit by the dawn as they ferried along the Grand Canal after no sleep on a train from he has forgotten where and Jane hooded, the young Mother of God before the annunciation in the first light, and Thomas blinks to return her to the chaise longue, and closed her eyes and she smiled still and he blinked once more and sent his eyes off again, out along the side canal to the boarded-up and flooded palace that faced him back at its end (the plywood tagged with graffiti in the American manner)… this wonderful city in the snow… And for a moment I am alone in this wintery impression squinting past outsized flakes that settle and melt on my lashes, am—it is so quiet—as if the last of our kind, the only flesh and blood remaining here, this mud sunk plumb-measured marvel of factored stone and wood and metal turned to account by souls whose numbers and hands haunt the worm eaten curve of arches, rust-blighted leaves and filigree, masses of air-eaten stone raised to the sky, turned, gilded, carved to call out, What about me? And how about this? I will brood on this some, thrill to the affirmation of daring, against both the little certainties and the larger thing, that constant sigh of monumental silence. Stillness a counterpoint, an improbable music in a hidden register, while a heartbeat signature sounds in the ears.

Here everything is patinated with age, the bygone. Who will blame me for my pursuit of the living girl? I have a ghostly sensation, apart from my love who has caught up with me, Jane smiling, a mischievous glint in her eyes, oh, accompanied by the god, incidentally, tagging along like some cavalier servente (makes me cold to look at him goose-bumped and skim-milk blue and he pretends the arctic air is as nothing to him, his talaria meanwhile trembling, feathers puffed up and bunched around his finely turned ankles). I free myself from this apparent jag, was off for youthful companionship and a drink or two.

But first this silence, the answer to his felt query about a missing person, an impossible tomorrow… and then Thomas returned to himself and turned from the railing, the leather finger tips of his left hand glove dampened and chilled, urged on to find the girl… and I, limping and poling with my stick at the speed limit of dignity have crossed the small bridge over the canal beneath our respective windows, and the young woman nowhere to be seen. Still I heard with persistent resolution—and I am not possessed of cetacean hearing—echoes of her boots crunch-crunching the snow, as if resonating within the prints themselves, just as I had indoors. As I can even now and I ask you, what happens to sound? Prove to me that the waves, like god discoursed on for too long, finally diminish into nothing. If only I had the time to ask my Uncle the scientist (how as a boy I coveted his Copernicus Society crest), for whom—we are the last to share our name—I have been tragically mistaken. What an error. Engendering all this and our relationship, yours and mine, Inspector. Fifty years between us, my uncle and me, and those in error the prime earthly movers, the powers that be, the power that is the Global Reach. How does it sit with you that such mistakes can be made? (It has occurred to me that my Uncle, although he loves me, I'm sure, who lives in my gestures, the set of my mouth, a particular friskiness, might have thought I could use the challenge since being fired from my job at the university; and he could, it is possible, have put me up to all this without knowing what it would entail. If only I could reach him now.)

I easily picked up her trail. Somewhere in the blood a hunter, the last of my tribe: I will find you, I said. Her spoor admittedly the only one leading from the palazzo with the angled tower—how often I stared at it until it seemed to give way from the point of greatest stress, to my imaginings about a third of the way down from the top and the masonry crumbling forth—in a single upper storey of which she daily appears, the tracks beginning suddenly as though without history, no past, from outside the green wooden door that was noticeably pressed from within by a neglected garden that manages through this chink and that, and several overreaching boughs, to inquire of the outside world, silent but for its tiny berry-eating birds, feathers puffed up into parkas, arrived with the snow this morning scratching and twittering and hopping about the gnarled branches of a tree unknown to me, its fruit already dead and shriveled for months.

Her trail marking the snow in even steps, at one point a heel imprint cradling the expelled seeds from one of the berry starved birds, the husks red and black with only modest signs of having been processed through the meanderings of a tiny intestine—imagine its little twists and turns. At the young woman's window a handsome tawny cat watches, head cocked and nose flexing to test the air. Vainly I tried to follow the steps after the promise of the first lonely series that lead along the small side canal turning onto a more traveled way, managing for a time to see the shape of her sole amongst the increasing number of others imposed above and pressed below hers and here she slipped and there turned round and once again. What, to see if I was following? Finally I lost her in a confusion of tread marks.

I am in no mood to relive my perfect moment, what with the cold and disappointment and Jane no more; yet I was falling again, over the edge willing or not, stopped before the window of a travel agency, its windows urgently stuck with colored strips, each bearing the name of a place on earth, Babel of place names that were, for all that Jane and I had found joy in many, as nothing to me then, the deep end drawing near; and where normally in passing I remember this or that place, picture a snapshot from any number of years ago, see a suitcase on a station platform, Jane trusting me, slim in a striped dress, hair cropped short, or myself bobbing in the sea off some other temporary desti-nation, instead the dark shade drawing near and the wondrous city itself become as nothing, and nothing either passers-by, who doubtless flinch from my eyes and step away, and who can blame them: don't chance it citizen; though Inspector I have never hurt anyone who was innocent of intended harm to me or my Jane and I can explain the handgun.

Snow-blind with desire, I stared at the many footprints at a cross-roads and endured a snowball square in the back (just try coming within range of my stick, fiend); left off trying to sort out where one shape ends and another begins, when two young women inquired if they could help me, one of them boldly dusting my coat of the snow adhering between my shoulders. I could not bring myself to answer straightforwardly, thank or tease them for their concern, smiling and failing to say what I was doing reading marks in the snow, myself passing from one world into another, object of a tug of war between what I cannot begin to say, for I don't know. I need an interpreter to translate myself to myself and now that my love is gone—as I had thought, anyway—and picture for yourself my figure bending slightly at the waist and neck and staring at the slush… anyway they were kind enough to smile and make gracious their quick escape and only from a safe distance laugh and look concerned at the same time. I thought they might even turn back, for they were sweet, and try to lead me safely home or to the authorities, and laughing, yes, still laughing despite themselves as I can see red mittens brought up to one chortling mouth the front teeth engagingly gapped, while the other's leather fist serves to choke back her mirth, and I am waving urbanely, now raising my stick and smiling, partaking in the joke as well lest they feel guilty about laughing at such an unfortunate. My dears, I do understand. I cannot blame them. I would be beside myself too. How will I get on with the everyday? How manage to buy groceries or order lunch and I was getting hungry. I walked on thinking how increasingly difficult it is now to go out into the world without humping the language of my private concerns, forgetting how to change tongues, unable to leave behind a language related to that understood beyond my threshold, yet distinctly inapposite to its concerns; straining to adjust to normalcy as though suddenly woken. Jane so used to enjoy my purgatory between waking and sleeping, my attempts to converse as if perfectly sensible to this world and not held back by succubae tugging on either ankle in the other.

And so I headed to a favorite bar following a wiggling track—amber-colored the trail to Hyperboreas, Apollo wintering there—of frozen piss for most of the way, despite myself, eyes tired and patience frayed with disappointment in my chase, and I saw the poor cur my brother with woebegone eyes limping round the corner still dribbling piss. I entered the prickly warmth of the bar and sat down to take a hot chocolate and a grappa and managed to order with surprising ease, what with my self-conscious musings, and while waiting explored the pockets of my overcoat, which I had not removed, only unbuttoned. I turned up nothing and then my chocolate and grappa arrived and I drank the latter in two easy stages and, as the warmth spread, noticed sitting at the other end of the cafe two women who may have been pretty I thought though could not confirm this for my eyes had not adjusted yet from the cold outside and their close-focused concentration on tracking. I busied myself with the chocolate, thick and dark and creamy and I ordered another drink to which I owe being finally able to focus on that distant corner, on an unknown blonde, one woman now, not two, with engaging pouches under her eyes, as if buoying them, and a tired and well-traveled look—most engaging I thought and for some reason considered that these were eyes that had seen many things, the things these eyes have seen, they seemed to say, cradled, these knowing windows, by the fleshy half moons tumid with ripening promise, don't ask why. I thought her very attractive. I had thought myself immune by then to the thrill of such things, despite hankering for my neighbor, even as I had this morning with my love lying dead but smiling still, at least she was when I last closed the door to our room (and the god's disapprobation), hanging the do not disturb sign after and for a moment then at the cafe a thought nagged: Did I hang it with the correct message facing out? And what if a draft of wind invited service?… and I stared out at the falling snow, watched a billy goat with a fez and rain cape (MacGregor clan plaid in plastic) bearing a monkey on its back—they had played for Jane and me beneath our windows three days ago—pulled after a lean man in a long green coat; and I wondered where they find them, where and how whoever runs the show recruits the other players. I speak apropos of what the professor inadvertently involved us in; inadvertently, Inspector, for by then I shared a name with only one other, the dear dying Uncle, a great authority on biochemistry and much else besides, who decades earlier in Belgrade, not yet out of adolescence, I was later to learn, put two shots into the heart of a man with a 7.65 Browning and redrew thereby a certain map, people said over a woman. Where do they find them? The young woman across the canal, for example, such soft looking lips, and some hours later her stomach would grumble ever so slightly and she would place a hand—beautiful fingers—to comfort her belly and smile, knowing and candid this smile, promising that we should find much in one another, hinting at obstacles the world places before all such feelings, intimating what must come whatever we make of one another. As in a story—a sin in a story, I almost said, Inspector. And speaking an accented and formal English, occasionally halting at an Italian, French or German possibility that she whispered or mouthed, she called our encounter a story from the start. Our story, she would come to say tenderly and with no hint of irony, and as you can see Inspector, this business with destiny has set me to doodle on the upper half of the page as if I have all the time in the world, and what you have here in brown ink—I've changed pens: picked up Jane's Pelikan—is a pile of bones, mine, beneath a tree—notice the rendering of the roots beneath the earth corresponding with the branches in the air (initially winter bared but to which I later added the dry remains, once cruel and heady promise of a long past leafy spring, as well as suggesting a gentle wind, here and there daubing an unconnected leaf, with a squiggle that trembling of withered leaves barely attached to the wood, their promise to fall) and to that skull I tried to impart myself, please note the arched brow and the pleasant smile, undermining the objective point of a memento mori (so you might for a moment indulge yourself with the thought that this won't happen to you—*to him, to her, not to me*). That is a hunting dog, still in mourning. I tried drawing a lugubrious brown Labrador, my first dog, with big paws and thick, long tail brooding over my old bones and have made a perfect mess of it (Jane drew very well, had a wonderful hand. What couldn't she do?) and I remembered where I knew her from, this young woman, so keen to talk and laugh over serious matters and some not so serious, that an image of her was hanging in the Louvre and I wondered at it as we sat in a favorite restaurant later that afternoon: *La Vierge Et L'Enfant,* fifteenth century, by the hand of the *Maitre de la legende de Marie-Madeleine.* You will appreciate this correspondence, Inspector, and I will attach a post card of the painting that I happen to have somewhere amongst my things (we had bought several). Jane did. She saw the remarkable similarity from the first sighting: the young beauty weeks ago petting her tawny cat, cat's eyes golden, squeezing shut with each caress suddenly fixed, open on me, the girl standing by the window in the upper story of the tower, window open to the cold, her breath and the animal's clouding the air, her eyes on Jane, or so it seemed and I remember thinking, what about me? Jane never told me how much the coincidence moved her until after she died. Don't worry this necromantic notion—as I must tell you the young woman would soon worry my hand with kisses and laughter and more, and this last in a way that had Jane's rare signature of pleasure (make of that what you will for I cannot afford to surrender to its potential for significance), shades of the sinister, I thought: her sudden low laughter and the rest that followed my having told her that Jane my wife lay dead, though smiling, back at the hotel—for you will do better by not vexing it between the jaws of your reason).

It was Jane who left that post card propped against the window that looks out over the side canal that we share with the leaning tower; and how many times in these last weeks did she and I put our books, our magazines, our refreshments down to look up, or first thing from our tangled sprawl between peaks of morning linen, raise our eyes to the rotting ogee of the tower opposite, in that quiet before the day begins in earnest, glimpse her passing to and fro. Later each day the maid with dark eyes will read our sheets (her ripe lips move; she murmurs), make the bed, change the towels. She too looks up to the tower, sometimes sees the young woman there, wonders, leaning against the molding, standing still by the tall windows dust rag or pillow case in hand, wondering as did we, eyeing up the pock marked bulges of masonry, through the tall windows to the upper story of the little tower. That tower so often besieged by raiding parties of little gulls, black-capped and lovely. Hear them: discordant, sorrowing voices. Day after day wasting away, they exhort us.

Her forehead is high, as if shaved back in the manner of long ago one might think and perfectly shaped like the girl's in the painting, her brows as long, thin and arched and that smile and with no intention to blaspheme but it is of a certain knowledge in addition to that conventionally befitting the Mother of God. Let me sin that I might be saved—ah, the old stand-by, I hear Jane's voice—but she, the young woman, knew of my wife, of course (and there is no telling what from her aerie she might have glimpsed through unheeded gaps in the folds of our drapes), and answered prettily a suggestion, two of her long fingers for a moment pressing fitted between my knuckles, that we shouldn't do something I might regret and I almost—and here was my first inkling that something was going on for I heard Jane's voice as clearly as I heard my own, heard her voice, Jane's, goading me to say it, don't be daft, and I almost did as I was told but think I was still in shock, what with her lying dead back at the hotel and doubtless becoming stiffer and colder as I sat warming myself with beauty, youth and wine. . . almost said: But don't worry about that, my wife is dead, as of this morning, for you see I told her the story and then, etcetera, I almost said, caught myself and thought I heard a murmur, the voice of the god (and I think he is in love with my Jane), something along the lines of, What have I got myself into this time? Greek, it sounded like. Mutterings of the god, then, in a dead form of a language foreign to me and somehow understood all the same.

Strange things are happening and more to come, just wait, Inspector, and let me say now that we have finally met how I should so have liked to have had your companionship instead of having to keep a step ahead of you and all the rest of them, all your purposeful pursuits based on misunderstanding. The more I think of it the whole business predicated on mistakes, as you will see, touching us all more or less, my portion quite suddenly and haphazardly more, an accident grown so out of proportion to its origins, merely mistaken identity, as it would seem; while on the other hand you, Inspector, have based your life work on looking for such trouble. To what end I wonder? Where finally does such curiosity lead when whisky in hand you an old man, stare from your terrace into the distance and just as your eyes accustom themselves to the necessary focus for such long shots your wife is calling you into dinner and shaking her head at the sight of you, old fool she will think, wondering if you haven't had a little stroke, you sitting there holding your amber drink, looking so far away, looking so sad? So the whole, what, a chain reaction of error and variations on a lost theme, the original pattern of which yet survives palimpsest-like in fragments through miracles of intuition: little gleaming gists, sun-kissed motes dancing in the corner of a still hallway, blink and they're gone, moments of abiding understanding? Oh Inspector, the smoky manuscript the professor passed on like a malignant chain letter with its threats of dire fate to the breakers of the concatenation proving to be true… Jane, is that you? It is. She shakes my arm and thinks it funny that I will go on so at a time like this. My pen leaves an elegant squiggle, a flying bird, wings curved on the uptake. What of the train to Paris? I hear her laughing, so nicely. The dead can laugh and the god who coveted her for years before this morning I now suspect, her grousing cicisbeo, now amongst the shadows until I join her there, is proba-bly fighting back a grin. She says: Thomas, come in for a landing. All right. But I now know I'd like to have had you, Inspector, near at least from the time of what apparently happened since Jane's and my fate-ful meeting with the professor whose beautiful suit I so admired—the oddest things stay with one and I still think that if he had not been so beautifully dressed…—and thereby enlisted your help, entangled you rather and now that you do know, don't you wish you didn't?… and the Inspector, as Thomas wrote sometime well after lunch and their first meeting standing around the still smiling though no longer warm body of Jane, is a sympathetic and attractive man who is not a police-man as Thomas had at first been led to believe, being thus introduced by the weeping hotel manager; and he felt a particular affection for him. Is there any wonder? Jane declared, as he scribbled beside himself and stopped only to sort through her words, addressing her, saying aloud but sotto voce that as yet she seemed to be enjoying herself, and was death such a lot of fun as she appeared to be having, and was she just trying to lure him into that next world with such promise as her playfulness and mischief would suggest, and I miss you so, he said and swallowed, straightening up some with a distinct and spine-tingling sensation as if Jane had taken hold of his right ear, pinching it between her thumb and forefinger: Ere Babylon was dust, he heard her say, The Magus Zoroaster, my dead child, met his own image walking in the garden. She let go his ear and before tearing up and staring out the window for minutes that seemed so long as to finally defy his sense of passing time, he wondered if he weren't still a shade more handsome than the other; and as if Time itself felt there was little percentage in existing for poor Thomas any longer, the works of his wrist watch became eccentric, ticking round and round with the second hand and yet refusing to move the others, frozen at twenty past five—the other hands, and on the other hand he said to himself—as if abandoning him to the awful shape of eternity if he was going to continue behaving in this way.

As it happens, the Inspector is an Intelligence Operative, so-called, as Thomas records without giving up his sources, posing as an Italian police detective—and here the Inspector was accidentally derailed from Thomas's train of thought (it fascinated him to read of himself) inadvertently shut outside for a time as Thomas chased a gadding digression, and so the Inspector locked out, as it were, left to tap on a window, become opaque on the other side of the glass for a time, peering under the awning of one hand raised to ward off his own reflection, a visitor to an aquarium, the Inspector may as well have been, Thomas, now a sea creature (fascinating and bemusing the Inspector), swishing his tail amongst caressing tendrils of drowsy tresses of kelp, this way and that with his tail and thoughts of sea change and such matters stirred up in little clouds, puffs from the ocean floor, deep sea eyes seeing no more than vague shadows, if that, on the other side of the glass, not deigning to lip read the silent mouthing of his subject just now, the handsome Inspector who had preoccupied him so, to whom he had the need to explain and confess the business, the deadly business of the Dead Souls; and here Thomas must have grown impatient with himself, so thought the Inspector, pausing for a lasting coughing fit, picking a thread of tobacco from the tip of his tongue, promising and withdrawing his promise in the next gasp for air, wiping his teary eyes, that he would quit-cut-down-carry on, the handwriting here wild with impatience, lighting by now another unfiltered Gauloise for which he had a self-destructive weakness, and he continued to read.

And oh that snowy day with the young beauty—her exhalations lightly suffused in garlic he has become heady with her, as he will record, absorbing her, then coming to, thinking of his own life even as she talked to him of many things, of China (of all things), the gentle rise and fall of her words. See now the autumnal garden of a small villa, poppies long gone to seed, flowers withered, weeds and golden salt hay scraping, falling maple leaves, an ancient carp, golden chain-mail broaching the black pond, proffering its snout to be rubbed at the young mistress's approach, a tawny cat, like hers, she said, knowing he had seen her, the cat hopeless now for the sound of familiar steps, and her father dead these many years and he heard most of what she said, later wondered at her beau discourse, thrilled as he himself first set foot in that marvelous garden, a step ahead of those who intend him harm, to the realization that the Cathay of which she speaks is her home across the canal, thinking, as she talked, of his many spring times all there in the freshness of her face. His past time found—and poor, poor Thomas, in such a lot of trouble already, even before he knows the extent of it, forces gathering by the train station as he sits by the girl full of wonder, contending with little skill as yet against the powers that be. Some little advantage there is in that they are only men; some more in that he is not normal quite, not as predictable, or as vulnerable as he might otherwise have been. Later: you must become skilled or fall sooner than is becoming, he will hear the god intone in his ancient tongue, the god reluctant as he imagines, then a somehow flip-sounding quotation in German—not the god's first language he thought, somehow able to understand another language he could not speak, as with the Greek—spoken facetiously, as if the god felt self-conscious, not prepared to commit himself to him exactly but for Jane's sake: You must change your life. As if I haven't enough to deal with, as he thought. Yet Jane is on his side and the god, too, if reluctant, (thus Jane's effect even after life as we understand it; and the god will come around).

Here the wind of his wings beating on his cheek, scent of rosemary, and Thomas recording the sensation of being a fighter in his corner between rounds and the trainer—a beautiful young man (he has to admit) nude but for winged sandals, the god for whom he feels a little embarrassed but without the strength just then to offer him his robe—fanning him with a towel as he surrenders to blackout, temporarily loses himself to despair, doubting that he can actually go on without Jane, now coming to, blinking into a blazing white light. And the god, talaria beating the air in audible, measured breaths, hovering off to one side, and Jane's breath in his ear whispering to him in another language—all Greek to me punch happy Thomas responds and receives a cuff on the cheek from her, admitting then that he understands her, but not knowing how that could be, something Jane says about relying on self and the Other and that she will never leave him. Can't you be more forthright? Mightn't we rely less on nuance just this once? Do the dead really have to be so mysterious, so sphingine, speak in dead tongues (How else, the god muttered witheringly, exasperated, not a patient creature)? Come on Jane, this is me, Thomas, after all. Rules are rules says she and kisses him on the mouth, that kiss and the lips as before soft and delicious plus something else, and he remembers that she had been speaking of that Inspector before she pushed him back toward the center of the ring, put 'em up, where a dark amorphous thing slouched forward to meet him. The Inspector, a handsome man as Thomas notes repeatedly, worrying at an idea of disembodied intelligences, even though there is a train to catch. Shape and psychic intent, he remembered from young Gaudier: the girl's tawny cat, winter birds pecking at the freeze dried berries, berries, boot prints in the snow, wind, even; and last night as they walked deserted streets, their resonant footsteps parading after, he and Jane for the last time, the last walk with Jane in the accustomed form in any event, and disembodied intelligence, he scribbled and his head started to ache.

The Inspector despairs; reads that he is a sympathetic man helpless to save Thomas. My beneficent Doppelganger, he will read of himself. (Except for school reports, when had he ever read of himself, he wonders?) Had indeed known as early as in Rome that there was little hope; compelled to try, somehow, all the same.

Rome early in the new year, late on a winter afternoon, he steps out of a broad sunbeam shoring up the sky. As glimpsed by a bored child fogging a pane from an upper story, a shade appears out of her dissolving mist and passes through a buttress of light, now gone and darkly footing onto a quiet street, a tenebrous peace there, the Inspector shadowing Thomas wandering just ahead. Where the Inspector happens to live alone (how many years now since she has gone her own way he wonders and calculates?) Here the fissured archway to his home that he passes by with a quick look in, waving to a neighbor who would have liked to talk, the hope in her eyes, the Inspector careful to quickly turn away and carry on, his apartment within, across the courtyard and perched high up from the street at the end of a zigzag of stairs and passage ways where Jane and the reluctant god trespass.

The diffident god—he has been keen on Jane forever—behaving like an estate agent, showing her around the alternative reality before the fact (Jane napping, in a heart-stalling deep sleep), never having thought he would be called on to snoop, the unseemliness of it, as he thought, emotion suddenly rouging his cheeks with unwonted color. Having lately arranged to meet in her recurrent dreams, the time in their sequence to be an interval after the appearance of three little nuns in the hotel corridor whom she spies from above, who are to Jane's swelling trepidation just about to turn around, and just before being chased out of sleep by the charge of a handsome wild boar whose meat she will eat for dinner this coming night.

The god had had no idea to what use she would put him. He is surprised, too, at her ease in and familiarity with his world. She will not cease to amaze him and he will forever be jealous of her love for Thomas.

So see you at siesta (and he was there early), she had said in that low voice of hers. Where in the hotel she lies half-dressed and breathing death, the taste to be left in her mouth when with such difficulty and unwonted confusion she will passionately awake and the god turn away as Thomas kisses her on his return, her breath ripe, moving him to kiss her over and over; and she will come into her own again, for a time.

But for now, on that day late in the afternoon their oneiric presence, Jane's and the god's, is manifest to two gray hounds in the apartment below the Inspector's, sprawling on a couch in conceited languor but with snouts half raised and ears cocked, jaws open that they might hear better; the interlopers subject as well to the curiosity of a crow perched on the metal railing of the Inspector's terrace, fixing the pair first with one blinking eye, then the other, affecting periodically to be sharpening a fine ebony beak, flying off at the god's threat to turn it into a nib should word of any of this get around. Far below them on the street, the Inspector looks up and trips over a raised cobblestone, filling with a familiar sadness to which he is unwilling to attend. He has an inkling that something is up, and a roiling in his bowels, but tries to concentrate on the figure leading the way before him, even as he is undermined by an indefinite shame—poor everybody, he whispers to himself—and the compounded loss of half a lifetime, a sense of the whole business being a process of sustaining losses, one kind after another from the start.

Jane meanwhile, in effect, drags the surprised and outmaneuvered god after her. This will set a precedent; but again, he loves her so. They are there in order to determine just how efficacious their only mortal ally will be, about whom she and Thomas were told by the German professor who, after asking if he might have a few more of the olives heaped over their roast duck, apologized for not being able to tell them anything about this Inspector but that he exists, as Jane in turn quietly explained to the naked divinity accompanying her, talaria folded neatly around his ankles, who is not convinced that there is any good reason to trespass and for whom Thomas is a mortal nuisance and little more. His godly cheeks remain tinted with shame at the use to which he is being put, and love for the woman, and for whom, contrary to his reputation as the patron divinity of thieves, snooping around another's home uninvited was not comme il faut.

You can, she said, learn so much about someone from their home— oh the saddest vulnerabilities tell there, she added, to take away with her only two, here not the pathos of unformed taste, rather an old photo tucked into the frame of a mirror on his dresser, the only photo displayed, of a pretty young woman whose face is the very pattern of trust and love and joy in the world, Jane thought (and her throat constricted, and the sound of sobbing reaching her from where she sleeps and soaks a pillow several blocks away, crying in her sleep, she knew even then, as she stared at the picture, later with no idea why), the young woman, sitting on a suitcase by some tracks in a train station, and the other a small eucalyptus pip placed before the photo—and we are not here to steal anything exactly. Well, she admitted, just some privacy that might help us later. Just, the god answered, but didn't go on, had waited so long for her; for which admission he would pay dearly as a certain suspicion falls on him as to why Jane should in the prime of life have died so suddenly. "Lay aside fear, the god does not harm lovers," Thomas would later recite in Venice, quite without irony, though the god was sensitive and sulked for the remainder of the day.

Jane moved about the small apartment appreciatively, hesitating only at the tug of waking that pulled now and again, passing in and out of indefiniteness in those moments, an agreeable visceral pull, knowing this home very well she thought, knowing the man, approving of the combination of spare comfort, warmth and fineness she found there, as she later reported to Thomas who in turn passed on her compliment to the owner, who in turn remembered as he read the passage in Thomas's pages a scent of fragrant asphodel when he returned home later that night, as well as an indeterminate sense that he had been violated. He saw dark reflections playing in the round convex mirror in the hallway when twice he rose—admittedly without his glasses—to piss that night, passing images of an eye that blinked or winked at him, then the fading image of a beautiful face caught hours earlier cheating to the last light in the west, an image of the very woman he would see lying dead and smiling less than a month later, in addition to well-turned male buttocks filling the round glass, a god's or young hero's rump it looked to him, one that seemed more marble than flesh, then more flesh than marble before disappearing. None of which troubled him inordinately. The round, termite-mined oak frame, glass thick and bubbled within as if with frozen champagne, eerie, much loved.

So the book-lined home with fine light and vantage westward to the panoramic beyond, far past his tangled potted garden, over the edge of the terrace bounded by leafy metalwork, past rooftops, distant cupolas and painterly skies. Where he is haunted, Thomas has written, the Inspector starting in recognition as he reads Thomas's record. The home where he is whelmed in his westward looking. Where he is possessed during the happy hour, lonely witness (not always, the Inspector protests) to the gorgeous vainglory of the westering sun; but especially so, he went on, in that dark hour before the dawn when alone he watches (some of my friends prefer to sleep, he answers, a little piqued at the unqualified implications) the at first gentle lightening of the western sky, sun rising unseen behind him, tender darkness fading then rudely thrust off earth's curve before the sweeping wave of light: overwhelmed the dreamy signaling of snails' antennae, leaves pulled scraping after over the Borghese Gardens, dousing him in day, curtain rising, again. The Inspector remembering, as Thomas wrote and addressed for a second time now (what's with him? the Inspector wondered and lighted another cigarette), reviewing a host of details, all of which, irrespective of past joy or grief, repeatedly deliver a sting of regret. Oh my brother, the Inspector thinks a little bitterly and turned the page and lit another cigarette even as one still burned.

So a month earlier in Rome, a month or so before the morning when the story was done being told and Jane lay dead and smiling, and he is walking close to home in the midst of purposeful continuity from which he imagines he is estranged; as he follows (himself followed as he is aware) the strolling figure, tall, hands in pockets, well-wrapped in a fine dark overcoat against a cold January sunset. So the shady way of the street fragrant with burning oak and the rest of the city as if at one remove in its reawakening, the distant sounds of clattering shutters, locks turned, the accelerated tempi hastening with renewed purpose. He looks up. The upper stories, tops of the tall walls and umbrella pines beyond touched in late afternoon gold drawing him up to imagine a place for himself and a loved one there. Instead of on a favorite rooftop apartment his eyes settle on a neighboring row of windows he has somehow never noticed before. They are blacked out along an upper story, broken he realizes, and a face appears framed in the first blank space on the left, ghastly, fixed on him, he imagines, gone as

soon as seen, and he chills of some awful vague imagining, an emptiness at the core of the sun-banded stories at the top, all the others
signposted with flowers, statuary, laundry, while after the terrible wan
face, the blacked out row remains an imageless sequence of frames.
He glances back down to street level, passing by a craftsman in his
shop working near his fire. Where he has been hours and days and
years before, a constant working his old furniture, his door open to
the street and the Inspector almost loses Thomas who has half a step
before adjusted his scarf and suddenly turned into a courtyard pre-
sided over by a moss-bearded Green Man drooling water into a bronze
basin, quite outnumbered by small-faced cats. Here and there, poised
atop walls, perched on weathered statuary and hunkered beneath
untended boughs of potted shrubbery, they huddle against the winter,
following Thomas with their eyes (pupils swell at the double apparition moments later; some bound from their places, just in case; all will
scatter when another figure unlike these two comes trailing after the
as yet single entity, one of Thomas's advantages for a time). Most still
hold their positions as Thomas follows some well-known way across
the courtyard, through the cat and smoke-fragrant arcade and up the
stone stairs to the apartment near the top where the woman waits, her
hair drawn back, uncolored, as promised, since she turned forty, years
ago now, to reveal such a face as had caused joy and complications half
a lifetime ago, now waiting on him to laugh and talk of sad things, care
for him with choice refreshments for a winter day; and the Inspector
followed almost all the way, catching a glimpse of her before she closed
the door and she, pausing to stare back, accustomed to sundry appa-
ritions, smiling ever so slightly before squeezing her eyes and shaking
away the image of the love she had admitted, easy enough for her to
do without fussing over eyesight or sanity, this goddess betrayed by
her walk, Thomas will record later, still like that after all these years, he
wrote, and the whole world trembling with portents and wonder. So

the Inspector standing by a knuckles up marble hand the size of a large armchair with a gesturing index finger in the vomitory of the arcade, provided with a glimpse of the woman: the years, he thought, exhaling through his nostrils, eyes prickling, coveting her arms around himself, that he might weep cheek against her bosom, warm with tear damp-ened wool, as she embraced Thomas, kissing his cheeks his mouth and the Inspector outside, seeing in his mind's eye, glimpsing as she moved to close the door, what must have been a book-filled room, piles on the floor next to a piano and the door closing after. He lighted a cigarette and turned back the way he had come, not a cat in sight, adjusting with an adrenal rush for the shadow slouching behind him as he crossed the courtyard.

There is evidence that Thomas is observant, even acutely so, Jane whispers, teasing that his sensitivity to detail is both a symptom of ref-erential mania, and a valuable weapon against the hostility of the world. Observing not only that the Inspector and some others are following him in Rome, Thomas records details of being shadowed remembered from an earlier time. As early as the day after the fateful dinner of duck and olives and the meeting with the German professor whose suit had hand stitching and a particularly fine drape. A day during which it seemed too many people bumped into him. A day on which too many people noticed him for something other than his good looks, as he put it. Including in these numbers several faces that he insists continue to reappear, one just having passed below his Venice win-dows in a gondola, scolding the gondolier, as it seemed to him. How unseemly he thinks and lifts his pen from the scrawl to see the troll, as he would write, turn suddenly to stare at his window with the most ridiculous pretense of just looking (at him illuminated by a candle, the framed image that in this dusk would look lovely, too lovely indeed, from across the way.) Faces, so many faces. Yours, Inspector, being the nicest of the lot, incidentally, a consolation I can tell you, for the others grimace and jeer out of a gallery of madmen and vile Calvary oiks, dunning me for a debt not mine. Here in Venice where I write before the window with the smallest of snowflakes floating here and there on this day too full for me, what with Jane gone and the meeting with that girl, why should I busy myself with war?

It was a day—that day in Paris after the night of the duck smothered in olives and all the rest, about which Thomas had started to write before being distracted by the fussing outside his windows, that scolding creature in the wobbling gondola, a being, as he thought, in grotesque contrast to the gondolier who continued his formal poling, eyes front, posture rather fine for all the abuse from below, as the Inspector read—a day during which he rued intemperance, provoked too early in the morning when he noticed that a hotel clerk kept eyeing his singed bundle of Dead Souls Part Two that he had thumped down onto the front desk while he tied his scarf and found his gloves. She seemed to stare so much that he made a show of tilting his head as if to concentrate on it too. This had no effect on the clerk, a pleasant young woman who could be forgiven for thinking it a bit odd that a burnt bundle of papers should appear to be bleeding, soaking a corner of the manuscript, and who in all fairness showed an admirable degree of sangfroid. And let me emphasize, as Thomas recorded months later, having taken up his pen again, with a tone of formality that the Inspector found endearing, blood was ponding on the table top where it lay eyed by the young woman with interest if apparent dispassion that had the opposite effect on the blanching Thomas, his eyes widening so as to bring a smile to the face of the clerk who asked if he should like a bandage or a doctor perhaps for his bleeding manuscript; telling Jane of the incident later, fact and fiction by this time interwoven some and he unable to distinguish where the clerk's dialogue broke off and his invention began to embellish, about an hour or so later, as they sat in a bistro hiding in some passage near the Bastille, as it poured rain outside, and with a bottle of delicious red Graves working its magic and Thomas's headache all but gone and himself again taking pleasure in entertaining Jane with a story that had quite enough natural extravagance without his addendum that took him as far as a synthesis with menses and the holy grail itself before Jane decided that enough was enough and that it was a good idea to visit the dying Uncle as soon as possible and here, what does this say for feminine intuition and isn't there just such a thing to be accounted for as the Inspector read with interest and heartache, agreeing all the way—for as he knew there was just such a thing some women surely had for Jane seemed to know and didn't she always that there was a mistake being made here of a more serious nature than normal, one that would average out in the grander scheme of things she was impassively sure, but one which would involve them at the disadvantageous end of averages if they didn't try to do something about it. Jane is so smart, the Inspector read, touched by Thomas' ingenuousness and love and unlike the especially sensitive god never for a moment thinking that there was any ironic intent in the exclamation. Thus the Inspector read, willing to concede that Thomas was observant as Jane said but impatient to know why the bundle of old singed paper was bleeding, flipping ahead with some frustration and no luck, lighting a cigarette before retreating to where he had left off to read that after their first introduction in the hotel room and Jane lying there cold but still smiling, he, the Inspector, had been recalled by Thomas from a passing glimpse in the past. A time before even Rome, as far back as Los Angeles, in fact, a time shortly after the adventure in Paris, remembering… the Inspector running in the opposite direction around Lake Hollywood on a perfect afternoon in the springtime several months earlier, the mustard in bloom and red-tailed hawks soaring their feathers shot through with sunlight with each turn and this man—could it have been?—in the same color jersey shorts as me, you Inspector, the same shorts, imagine, only moving at a greater speed with such a graceful stride, in better condition and sure to be younger… as he went on to concede at some length before focusing again on the trouble he was in. And think of it: all because of such bêtise. Not a mistake just anyone could make; rather a perfectly stupid mistake, cosmically stupid, of which only God was capable, this mix-up of identity, his with that of his genius Uncle who lay dying, who would tell Thomas, sadly and as sympathetically as he was able, for how sad can you be for others, really, when painfully dying yourself, that he was in an impossibly bad situation, a situation promising him, as he put it, the stations of the cross without any of the perks, and smoothed his mustache, first on one side of his distinguished nose and then the other, like a villain Thomas thought and smiled for that was the intent of the mischievous old man who so enjoyed showing off some still… and, Inspector, had I called on you from the start you would only have been subject sooner to the very powers that pursue me, those that covet the professor's singed and malevolent manuscript, you a knight move and nothing more in this terrible game and what did I ever do to deserve the burden of Dead Souls and the last word on this particular recipe, that as Uncle said with too much pleasure I began to think for all that he was entertaining, too much pleasure I say in the perilousness of the whole business from which he soon expected to be free—this business of what will return us all to the bacterial compound of our origins from which Uncle couldn't resist saying we have not evolved all that far and he saw the look in my eyes as I smiled appreciatively at what I took to be his wit, quick to tell me that I was something of a buffoon (he was in terrible pain, the cancer in his bones, every movement, and I unthinkingly had just dropped onto the side of his bed) and he meant what he said, and here I am inadvertently possessed of death's scythe, the prerogative of Dis—mightn't Jane, surely Jane: "Dis' bride, Queen over Phlegethon, girls faint as mist about her" is now in a position to have a word with him on my behalf?

And the meeting with the girl, my neighbor, Inspector, earlier on the day Jane died, she and I getting along so well (tell her name, Jane says, this beauty, this more than disembodied intelligence, she teases. I hear Jane and feel her breath, smell it as it was before she died, without that something other, that pungent something other, sweet Jane as if at one ear and then playfully at the other, the god near but out of sight: Helen, I said aloud), so well were we getting along—how she looks at me, our eyes exchanged in that way I never hoped to know again—it was as though it cost her dearly to say that we should be careful with what we give in to; so as to not regret it later, as she had said. Such technique. Jane is laughing again and promises to make this something of a challenge if she continues thus. Jane! At the same time it is as if Helen hadn't said it at all, for she looks at me with such a look, has reawakened the best part of me which Jane concurred with right away, breath in my ear, saying how I was at my best in love, be happy, and too how she should so have liked to share some of that lunch before us, my neighbor and I enjoying lunch, the dead hungry, something we have forgotten and how was that risotto, those delicious little clams?

How I jump about, so much to tell, so little time; but we were finishing up at the restaurant when I remembered where I had seen her, the spitting image of the young Mother of God; and I have since found the postcard in my valise. You, Inspector, may be holding it in your hands now. Very like, the Inspector thinks, looking from the card to a photo and back again, before returning it to his file. Very like it's true. Later we stepped onto the street as I thrilled that such things can be, making no effort to ask how or why, stepping into the cold, and not another soul about now. In the distance the cries of those little gulls. Strange. How to explain such things as continued between us? She was laughing and serious in turn as we made our way left and right and here and there, and I reassured somehow to see imperfect teeth, off-white and jagged (evoking as well, I confess, a strange carnal promise), how the slush on the ground darkened the skin of her boots, spoiling the leather some, relieved that her feet must be a little chilled at least, able thus to both come to some and still maintain the spell, just the right tension between self-consciousness and nature, a tempered exhilaration: we two gaily setting forth; and yet as though already grieving in anticipation—of what? the Inspector impatiently to himself—making our way to that unsafe place to be tided by compulsion, a poignancy itself beautiful, in the Japanese sense, as I have read: mono no aware, the sadness of things. Inspector, there is an implicit high seriousness to my date.

My date! Imagine, I come to say to myself now, my reflection dark in the window before me, the candle low (and I have surely missed tonight's train to Paris) and the young woman's light in the tower opposite. Her laughter today. As it happens we lunched at the trattoria where just this morning Jane had been so eager to eat. It would seem there is no getting away from apparent significance. I have come to discount it, however, for all the pleasure I take in some kinds of coincidences, these inevitabilities as I see them, coming as they do from out of our too common grab bag, for all the wonder that we make of them, for all that I continue to see and sort through them.

You, Helen, were in Rome, too, Thomas addresses the window across the canal. Amber ogee in the darkness. Cat's shadow looming behind the light, bent out of shape, passing, gone. Trastevere, he remembers. His nostrils flex. On the sill before him, a full ashtray of twisted filterless butts left from the Inspector's visit. He has been alone for almost two hours now. He is not used to it. Jane is no longer stretched out smiling on the chaise longue. She's in the fridge, Thomas thinks and shivers. Cooler, Jane quips with little enthusiasm, and I must say I don't like the thought of it much. Terrible, the god concurs, and shoots Thomas a look as if to say that he's wanting in tact.

Shouldn't you put something on, Thomas asks him? The god nude, knees up and back to a corner by the windows. His talaria shiver and flex, then are still. Jane to be sent off—please Thomas, the body, she corrects him, lightly tracing the tips of her fingers down his neck—by train to Paris tomorrow morning. In Paris, imagine, she used to say, thrill to the thought of being planted there years before they made the city their home for several months each year, inheriting from her aunt who had married rather skillfully on the third throw a lovely little plot for two in Père Lachaise, a bosky corner where I one day will join her if I'm not minced into little pieces by the powers that be and my remains kept without burial, fed to mongrel dogs so that I will have no rest, imagine passing through a cur's bowels—they think of everything, do the villains—and my spirit wonders for eternity where it went wrong (I think I know), wander the earth for a sympathetic ear only to find one that is ill cared for, too late for a swabbing to do it any good and I would choose then to keep my stories to myself rather than mire them thus. But really: haunting who? Complete strangers? Who that I know and like might be left then? Eyes to the cutout of light across the way. Flourish of Islam, daring carnal expression in the bodily curve of an ogee. Gull's cry. Thousand and one nights. Some of them, the villains, are old enough to know of such things. The unburied (Palinurus), without rest. Four a.m. forever. So Jane's body, I stand corrected, has been removed. How careful they were, with what deference did they finally lift her onto a gurney that they had made up with a spotless white sheet bright to the eyes, and a fine looking blanket (Italian woolens), all tucked and turned so neatly with perfect corners and certain decorative touches, the blanket folded back to a point with a trim of sheet evenly showing underneath, that reminded her of Japanese gift wrapping. The unoccupied gurney rolled a little on its own, I swear, Jane had whispered to me at one point, pulling on my ear. I thought so too. Saw it roll out of the corner of my eye, everyone standing around uncertain, weighting from one foot to the other, some sniffling, another looking handsome and somber and fighting an urge to smoke. Why ever did you resist? Respect. I understand. Still, even Jane urged me to tell you to light up. Anyway, how about you Inspector? Did you see the gurney roll first forward then back? No one else seemed to notice. Inspector, are there earthquakes in Venice? I ask you now and almost did then but felt already as though I was not making the best impression and was more a suspect in my Jane's death. My concern with appearances for otherwise I am fairly shameless is due only to the importance of my mission and the need to be left unimpaired to do what I must do. I can ill afford time lost being interrogated. There is a whole world to see to as you know very well. What ails you world? Thus begins a chapter in the infernal Part Two of this so-called Dead Souls. I have read a third of the text so far and can make neither head nor tail of it from the point of view of biochemistry. Uncle told me that its meaning would insinuate itself to the initiated. I didn't think so at the time, but now I really think he meant it. Fool, with all due respect. There's so little time. That I make the time to leave a record for you Inspector is admittedly questionable under the circumstances. But you may find something of use herein when I am taken and you are on your own. As is inevitable if my uncle is to be believed. As for my role in Jane's death? I could almost become indignant if she weren't shushing me even as I scrawl these words to you now. Ask instead the god where he was, et cetera. Harder for a god to have a convincing alibi I should think. I'd like to see him on the spot. He sighs in exasperation at my mortality. In all fairness I must record this. Even his naked put-downs. But where were we just a couple of hours ago? A lot of sullen fellows standing around looking somber and Jane giggling and quip-ping, the only woman, enjoying the attention and it's not everyday… and I suppose she even can be wound up some and look at the god, after all, who Jane assures me would like to be my friend, appearances notwithstanding. And the weeping manager who flourished an over-sized hanky in the manner of Pavarotti, even put a pillow from our bed down where her head would be, with your permission sir, he sobbed at me, and plumped it up. And when they lifted her dead weight as if heavier and her stomach grumbled a little and when they lay her down and a cat's purr rattled from her throat she continued smiling pinching my ear some and barely able to contain herself, meow she whispered in my ear, meow, even as the god wept in a corner unable to look and it must be quite something to see one's self dead and about to be carted away, handled with the respect, as it appeared to me, accorded not just to the dead but to a distinguished loved one, and there in the doorway again the tall dark and handsome waiter blubbering and dabbing his eyes, his hanky soaked through and I stoic what with Jane so enjoying herself by my side. I didn't want to spoil her fun, heartless or in shock they must think me, time enough for me to cry and the Inspector, you, sir, standing and reaching repeatedly for your cigarettes but refraining from taking one and yourself looking very thoughtful more as though Jane stood for the loss of all the dearest things, the passing of every day and Jane meanwhile whispering with a sweet giggle that she hoped she didn't fart when they moved her, then imitating herself with a sexy kitty cat purr-growl to follow her corpse's purr, prrr deep from her throat, I buried a dear cat that did that as I lay her in the ground a last purr, then take my ring she told me and I stood then, hesitating, and everyone looked away pretending to have business for their eyes elsewhere in the room—a nice room it's true, still: a nice room and nothing more—all but you dear Inspector who watched as I took your hand, Jane, quite cool by then and it came fairly easy, and what a hand am I right Inspector? How often does one see them like this, and took from the beautiful fingers her three rings a-jingling and slipped them onto the little finger of my left hand bent to kiss your forehead cool now, coolness registered on my right front tooth, Jane, and then returned to my seat by the window and escritoire and looked up to see you my dear, my new young friend, standing there and my god I waved, couldn't help it, and everyone saw all eyes up and looking out the window as the girl turned away, petting her cat then all eyes on me, and Jane had a laughing fit and the god only continued blubbering not noticing anything. My God (and the lachrymose one has the nerve to look up, as Thomas notes even as he wonders…). It occurs to him for a moment that everyone knows each other, that everyone, the young beauty across the way, even dear Jane, is in on the business but him. Don't be foolish she whispers.

Now I remember. Jane, I said, this is not America, as we made a diagonal across Piazza Santa Maria in Trastevere over a month ago, to which she answered: Then why are you gripping the gun in your pocket? And it is true I was as we continued over the square, clip clop our footsteps in the quiet, a dark and almost deserted place on this night, oddly abandoned I thought, veering off our line to stop before the steps of the unlit church Santa Maria which I had hoped to be open (to pray, doubtless, muttered the god. How can he see my text from across the room? I wonder. The god evincing something of an attitude toward me, increasingly facetious lately whenever Jane attends to my existence—you are a jealous god I offer, mustering a neutral tone, shhh says Jane—as she is doing now with her affectionate touches, oh her familiar touch, and the eyes, hers, that accompany me everywhere— imagine if these were lit with reproach instead of love—and she says: I see a winged heart equipped with my eyes, brows and lashes included, and see them now with glasses, they'd have been squinting without the specs (a heart's erratic flying, she said, and isn't love supposed to blind? She said then: don't you believe it, unbecoming for a heart don't you know, seeing so clearly now, so watch your step I'm only joking she said; somehow feeling the little squirt of anguish in my belly, guilty conscience piped in the god and I tell you I shan't be able to ignore him indefinitely), and she was nervous that night and squeezed my wrist as we stood before the locked iron work gates before the black church, and that she is nervous is unnerving; nerves not characteristic of her, and so a little contagious, so much so that while discounting her fear out loud, I too was keeping an eye on the position of the stocky figure, at a distance a cartoon jailbird in the flesh zigzagging this way and that behind us, then inexplicably before us (we did not know the neighborhood well), his shaved and polished head a beacon of our mistrust that curiously found what little available light there was, such a dark quarter, charming in parts, drawing on such faint sources as stars even, as Jane said, this polished head, this ignis fatuus, fallen friar's lantern, will-o'-the-wisp that went this way and that, appearing to be as aimless as we apparently were, but for the bearings he was taking on our position, admiring eggplants here, an Adelphi window display there (such serious books given prominence of place, I said, watching Jane's eyes in the window following the reflection behind us, which paused for a moment as if about to effect his deed, join us at the display, no, change of strategy), taking bearings or so we both had come to imagine and I pushing the safety off and Rome itself melted in the Tiber, eternal city, no longer a place with any but casual significance, and Jane and I agreed then and there not to play our existential game where we each take turns using the material at hand with apt allusion permitted in cruelly describing the absoluteness of dissipation and despair in evidence, the whole story underlying the seemingly most innocent object: whether costume, twitch in the eye, or nail trim, provoked into giving evidence against it. An orange, innocent of us, having rolled off a stand to color the cobblestones, oh… as we walked around the quarter with time to kill, unhappy phrase, before our rendezvous and finally practical Jane had had enough of cat and mouse which we had started to play instead of the despair game that tended to laughter of an enervating kind eventually and might have endangered us with distraction in these circumstances in which we imagined ourselves, and she saw a rhomb of deep yellow electric light cast from a doorway at the other end of the square to which we had been returning again and again and to this we made our way as she challenged me on something I had said about Lear who had ranted wonderfully in Italian the other night and made bastards or naturals of us all when he divided the kingdom and that maybe just maybe, Cordelia refused to make ceremonial obeisance just for the excuse of coming back with France oh traitor to invade the kingless kingdom and be Queen of all three parts and Jane still won't buy it, and our strides across the square were long now as we headed past a group of Japanese who had gathered around the dead fountain at the center of the square to which as I say we kept returning and were squinting into their shared guidebook until pausing to observe our passing toward the bar from whose light was beamed the yellow rhomb, our next position. And as it would happen, just as we stepped into the light, a chicken foot flew out to land before us, as if we should be in need of more juju, and you don't know half of what has been happening since the professor passed on that infernal bundle, the chicken foot rather nicely positioned in the framing of the yellow rhomb I had to say later, and we both smiled and giggled a little I remember, such significance, well Rome just the place the city eternal and solid again one could say, unmelting from the river in all its substance, asserting its place distinct after all, and then the cat black and the chicken foot still with a wiggle or two left to it, a sinister claw foot and the cat careful to play it just right, she a beautiful feline in the Roman cast with little face and green eyes fairly close together, and we stopped to observe the show, not having found evidence of who might have arranged it for us. Who could have thought otherwise? (Honest employment keeps such thoughts at bay, I'll bet. And yet I still see an honest-looking man on a bicycle momentarily losing his balance, wobbling perilously as he pedals home from work, turning to stare at and swerve round this sinister magic, and count yourself lucky sir that your wife doesn't show you enough affection and that you are somewhat underpaid relative to your intelligence and culture, for there are worse brunts to bear I can tell you—though for now I can't think of one—thus I call after him in my imaginings, after the fact at the memory of him, the bicycle bouncing and rattling across the dark square now and don't look back lest your wheel catch between the stones.) And we remembered what the Professor had told us not so long ago in Paris: discount signs, especially the melodramatic ones, at your peril. All right. So we were suitably impressed and carried on as we entered the working class bar, looking for the one person who might have taken the trouble to arrange for us such significance, pandering with meaning on our behalf, and nobody and nothing suggested itself, not a feather in evidence, nor a misshapen crone or kola nut voodoo man. The quotidian holds its secrets close. We found ourselves a place to sit in a corner with a view around us and an ally in the wall at our backs, and I had no sooner ordered two glasses of wine than the jailbird and murderer who would have done unspeakable things to us, kept us alive masterfully that we might bear witness to each other's agony and slow death, passed through the rhomb of light with a girl child holding the little finger of his strangling hands, looking up, adoring him while he cradled in his free arm a sack of groceries and smiled and made kitty-kitty talk to the cat who batted the claw while the girl stared and eyes wide shot her dad a look: is this okay? A lovely child with white ruff overflowing the collar of her coat and foaming beneath her chin, she looks back to see what follows, and dad, his beautiful green eyes and refined mouth loving the mystery, easy for you I thought remembering how it had been timed to appear before us and not this family man walking home hand in hand with his daughter, the mother must be quite something I reported to Jane who had been watching through the open door and after agreeing with my observations described you, Inspector, rather well as a man we had seen too many times already for coincidence to serve as anything other than foolishness. In the wake of the father and daughter I glimpsed no more than a lifted heel of what looked to be a well-made shoe and the tail of your gabardine with the raglan sleeves you wore the day you trailed me to my friend's. I had no sense of you yet. Jane, though, was noticeably uneasy and intrigued and that was the first I heard that you resembled me to an unholy degree, as Jane put it, our terms of reference increasingly flavored by religion as we lingered in Italy and I must say I didn't like the idea that there was an other so similar to me that Jane could be moved beyond a quiet observation and then a necessary qualification to soothe my sense of self; and in this instance Jane actually disturbed, and how now after a lifetime of self-confidence am I to deal with you, Inspector, my ally it would seem, so far? My specialness, after all: my foot, the perfect dive. Pull down thy vanity, the god mutters. What a smart ass, I thought, this lovesick divinity whose attitude was beginning to surprise me some. After all, we expect of gods a certain aristocratic behavior, an effortless high civility, when not bent on destruction. (And so is love not always ennobling? I wonder, a little too facetiously, my words echo back harshly on my sensibility. He turns away at this. Really I should prefer to be friends with him, too.) Who are you, Inspector? Just the question Jane asked, whispering her words after you into the night; then she and I with appetites that thus far mysteries could not dent speaking of how hungry we had become, and we drank our wine and ate olives and quizzed each other on what we might eat for dinner, never that I can remember prepared to sacrifice the time for a meal to other exigencies.

You won't, Uncle intoned during my last visit, have a chance. Thus he had spoken waking out of a narcotic catnap, eyes suddenly open wide, Uncle acting the soothsayer, playing the fool again, weren't you?

And I shouldn't wonder too much if, sponsored by another god, he joins the cast later to take some more pleasure in the travails of my continued survival, should I manage to last a little longer. Our bane, Uncle said, is our self-confidence. Just ask the women in our lives who so come to believe that we must, by virtue of carriage and our manner with headwaiters, be able to provide a safe place, a better place in the scheme of things, a magic circle with which to surround them. This, no matter how we try to disabuse them of the notion that there can be any such thing. So you see, poor nephew—poor nephew he called me, Inspector. I didn't like that much under the circumstances—you are in for it, with your manner and expectations of the vile forces against you. You will make the mistake of crediting them with more understanding and control over themselves and their empire that is our world than they could ever hope to have. But I am so tired of them. Never could bring myself to vote, and was rarely surprised by the shamelessness of their partisan stupidity. Enough of them. They are your problem, nephew, I am sorry and I admit it also amuses me to say. How could a private person such as yourself have ever... he started coughing then, Inspector, and that assuaged a great deal of my anger for I think it was almost fatal, that fit of his, and yet when he recovered his face the color of a plum he was still smiling at the idea of it, my plight. Do you think compassion diminishes with the years? Or is it a coping mechanism as I once heard someone refer to my sometimes-uncontrollable laughter? What do you think, Inspector? The Inspector stopped here and took a long pull from a whisky, felt extra protective of him: fool, he thought, angry suddenly at the burden of responsibility he had started to feel.

Thomas looked up across the canal to the leaning tower (toppling masonry, he blinked, replaying it: bricks giving way, the top of the tower remaining upright a moment longer than the rest, chin up, no blindfold, vertical even as all below it fell away). Did I really see you there in Rome too, he asked the window? You did, Jane answered on the young beauty's behalf. Remember? Later in the night. Only you didn't know it of course even though I told you I had seen the young mother of God from the Louvre, your favorite, blessed creature with eyes for you already in the back of the old Citroen. You were sorry to have missed her, you said, even while having such fun flirting with me in the back of the taxi. What got into you anyway? Jane said sadly and scratched the back of his neck in the manner of his father, and Thomas surrenders for a moment—it has been a long day after all—to fatigue of emotions and body, weeping quietly at loss after loss and sundry other things over half a lifetime. So many things, he marveled, smudging the ink some, that he found himself wishing he had not done or said. The Inspector, when he came across such pages, thought not for the first time even as he lighted another cigarette with a hand that he became aware of then was shaking, that Thomas was too hard on himself; then thought again, maybe not.

The bells tolling, already nine and I should be on my way to Paris oh Christ, but am to meet Helen in an hour. (Jane tugs my right ear, Inspector. Do you know I actually feel guilty about it? I'm still going to do it but I thought I'd put it down for the record.) Anyway the woman in Rome. Uncle had made arrangements, choosing the restaurant even, charming place, lively, and the food delicious. The lamb, I tell you, a tender little leg, and the creature taken from its mother's teats having fed on milk and nothing more, taste of innocence. I shall say nothing about the artichokes and fava beans we started with Jane especially beside herself over them having been hungry all day it seems. It's true I was, she said, playful again after her moment's sadness, and I'm hungry now. The dead know hunger, Inspector.

The woman with whom we met that night did not conform to our dark imaginings of the previous hour: in place of Hecate a jolie laide, middle aged professor from Turin. (When I asked her about what I had heard was the most evil spot in Christendom, a square in her city with sinister trees leering around its perimeter—I thought they were sinister—she fixed me with a look missing even a hint of a smile and said that my uncle had warned her about me. Oh I remember, Jane laughs again and hugs me and the god shot me a look, oh I can tell you, feeling quite left out he was, pretending to take interest in yesterday's news.) Only after the accident did I realize that the woman's control over her features—the ability to effect a preternatural stillness—was in the same manner as my Uncle's: both driven to perform and she too spurred by the ludic, making her demise before dessert (a tasty Monte Bianco) all the more awful. Of average height and quietly well groomed, she did not conceal that she was meeting with us at some risk to her person as a favor to my uncle, whose theory of bacterial conspiracy had changed her life. She took the time, however, to tell us about her own research. More to Jane, it seemed; and I recall that I questioned my manner then, self-conscious if only for a moment. (Become all too human the god would wish to bait me here, clears his throat to make certain I see how he tires his eyes with rolling. You might think gods would by now have developed antibodies to such contagion: the inherent malevolence of our species that even friendship will not contain. And what if he should return to where he comes from, spread it around, and all the gods become thus diminished? So much so that we can no longer tell them apart from us? Flushing some—I must say, the beauty of his skin and turn of his limbs befits his identity, and I too was young once with a certain something to my form—he feigns unconvincing interest in a particular snow flake which with some few others is challenging gravity on the other side of my greenish image, lingering just beyond the glass.) Anyway, I remember now that I was a little hurt and the only one still drinking as the performance got under way. As if I've no right to some charm of my own, Jane pipes in. (Exactly! says the god, untouched that I make as though he weren't there. And by now why should he be? He will come to define my self-consciousness; there is method in it. He will resort to anything in his pursuit of Jane.)

She's quite right, of course, though I never begrudged her the considerable effect she had on others; and yet in retrospect, because of the ostensible importance of what this woman who my uncle had arranged for us to meet had to tell us, and then the horrible thing that happened to her half way through a plate of especially delicious grilled mullets, I feel all the more how I had not connected with her as much as I should have, now want to, and wonder how lost opportunities are ghosts that know no rest, no matter how splendidly we realize the others; lost opportunities founded on much less than mine with this woman in Rome that dark night not so long ago that I stop to address here, no more substantial, say, than the passing of a person with whom one's eyes connect for an instant, a fleeting but dead-on connection never to be realized, and yet with lasting resonance. (For those with time on their hands, perhaps, the naked one interjects. You are less divine by the second, Thomas mutters, unable to ignore him. His cheeks tint. What do you make of that, Inspector? For which of us does he color so?)

So a most tenuous thing, these momentary exchanges; yet in rare moments striking deep, then running off a seemingly endless spool that over a lifetime must for some constitute a veritable web of connections, and for some others an unwieldy tangle. Before she stood to go she took hold of one of Jane's long and shapely hands in her own, handsome hands good for everything, accustomed to function, powerful, wrapped round Jane's to emphasize a point: about our relatively gradual demise. Which for the most part, as she said, escapes our notice. And then she started to sing, her voice surprisingly lovely, burnished, low: *Itsy bitsy spider...* And I thought her mad, charming but lunatic, missing the point of her at the time. Now, having come to understand some the burden of the bundle of sheets the professor passed on to us, I intuit in memory of her a larger web than my own tugging network. One that is not simply an apparent chaos of lines, but rather a rarely glimpsed symmetry of splendid and awful indifference. This issuing from the terrible abdominal beauty—thus did the poor woman describe it, exchanging understanding eyes with Jane and suddenly gripping my wrist and giving the skin a little twist, an Indian burn we called it as children, and I was grateful for the attention feeling suddenly accepted by her—of a cosmic (don't forget the s, mutters the jealous nudist glowering in the corner) spider nesting inside us all and consciousness the tangled web in whose work we tremble. Our relatively minor differences (here I admit to suppressing a shudder at the gross implications of this measurement which I prefer, personally, to think of as more substantial) in the degree of mobility and the time we take throughout our twitching on the *sticky invisible* to look around. The god is coughing. Yes, this time, yes. I forget myself Inspector; but the woman was making some such point, a very like point, Inspector, regarding a bacterial nous as being the Universal Mind. Though for the purpose of illustration, she was singing the children's spider song, in German yet—you tell me—and talking of the web of mind and memory and yearning as characteristic of a germ. A germ as Prime Mover. A spider germ, as if, for that was what it happened to look like, she told us, these the fruits of her learning, that could be modified at a molecular level by pulling off (cruel image) a leg here and there. A modification with the potential, should it be set loose to evolve in amputated form, to turn us all into Dead Souls. I have a headache.

(The god will squinny at me from his corner as if to make a point. And now he speaks (his voice beautiful, admittedly, with something of an accent to it that I can't quite fix): He will return again to his sticky invisible. Thus the god announces. He means me. And so I probably will. There is purpose here to be found yet. Jane understands; that's all I need). I feel the tug of lines again and return to these anonymous passings on the street: hear their steps forever receding. Unrealized destinies. And you, god in the corner, tell me, do they, all this time

after, remember too? Inspector, he deigns to answer, and his look soft-
ens: Sometimes, he says…

We are getting somewhere. I think I have actually dozed. Or so it
seems. I may have fallen off for a time. Speaking of which, I cannot find
my watch. There it is, on the middle of the bed. I cannot bring myself to
look somehow. Excuse the smudges, Inspector. A real gouache, what?
Tears of a clown. What do you see in it?

And months later in Paris, the Inspector admitted to a baby
dragon and a gorgeous female bottom, should one squint a little and
look just so at the paper; and as he tilted his head to an accompanying
click in his neck, which sound was more adverse than the sensation
but which sensation subsequently became consequently more pro-
nounced, he blenches at a sound heard or imagined: a difference he no
longer acknowledges in the interest of staying alive. He knows these
two pairs of footsteps; heard them more than once in Rome, frequently
on the street that passes by his home. He turns off the small bedside
reading lamp and rises, though it seems hardly necessary. He parts a
curtain and sees the ugly Geminis barely troubling anymore to stay
in the shadows beneath the awning of the shuttered bakery across the
street from his corner room one floor below Thomas's, whose steps
he hears now and again in addition to those more occasionally of two
others who he has not seen for all his vigilance, and about whom he
has not allowed himself to speculate.

The Inspector's presence in Paris is unknown to Thomas, who
wonders onto the page over the taking of another's life; something he
now knows about. Who would have thought, he writes. His conscience
does not trouble him in any conventional way. He worries the point in
his own fashion. He is alive still, much to the surprise of everyone. The
Geminis will make no more substantive move tonight, the Inspector
knows, and he returns to the bed picking up the bundle of paper, pad-
ding in stocking feet into the bathroom to run a bath and continue

reading, marveling at what he cannot help but consider being the miracle of Thomas's continued existence.

So this woman, as Thomas continued, with whom my Uncle had arranged for us to meet on that dark night in Rome. Do you recall that chicken's foot, Inspector, that handsome black cat? She was explaining to Jane matter-of-factly that she had gone so far in her research as to find evidence that consciousness is bacteria, (I am a good listener, usually, and can dress my face with empathy and accept what would for many be cause for flinching with outrage or fear; thus am I prey for the mad who see in me something of a companion for commiseration), bacteria swept by afflatus, solar wind carrying it to earth; bacteria that under a microscope is a marvel metamorphosing in stages of resolution (stay your questions doubting Thomas, she said, gripped my wrist to gave it another painful twist, with affection I thought). Under further magnification the arachnoid creature burns like the emblematic fires of Hermes's chiton as understood and rendered by the divine Sandro, she said. Impatient with excitement for a moment I parted my lips to speak; and I blush at what expression I must have worn then; but oh Inspector, hers was not a discourse for daily wear, and I sorrowfully thrill to it now. But she would not allow any interruption as I chirped in remembrance of Edgar Wind: that the flames were of the Underworld; though now shared her eyes with mine and Jane's as she went on to tell how the flaming bug (and from here it was only a small leap back to spiders) conspired on earth—conspired to what end, I asked? She didn't flinch—conspired in the minds of men disguised. Disguised, she said, as their ingenuity. *Oh, Invention*, she intoned, *Cultura*, she tongued, was an act of desperation. She would not stop here; no matter that my brows were cocked and mouth open to speak. Vanity, she raced on, the carapace of the bacterial army, the whole—and I include your choice of neck wear she said and pulled at the end of my loosened knitted tie, bearding me in effect like some

Goneril, I thought—the whole *business*—and she gestured nicely with a large and handsome hand—a bacterial conspiracy. Your uncle must have told you, she exclaimed raising her voice some. I must suppose in surprise once again at my facial expression (I'm only guessing, but perhaps this time my eyes were like twin blue saucers or some such things), conspired she said again in English, then Italian… and that the Dead Souls et cetera et cetera… and for my inadvertent smile—I blush still, I wince Inspector, at such bêtises—I received only a look slightly less scornful than when I smiled at the idea of Mr. and Mrs. Bacteria, as she had adorably called the fiery and spidery bacterial sexes, speaking English for our benefit but resorting to this childish idiom at one point. I'd not meant any harm. Moreover she expressed candidly that she had better things to be doing back at the university just then than amusing me here.

She was a woman of idiosyncratic charm. Perhaps if I speak her name thirteen times into a mirror or at my own reflection in the window she will join the host of revenants and divinities that crowd around me now. I could use her expertise, Inspector; I'm filled with dread. You too are in danger; and though we are both armed there is not ammunition enough in the world for what must come. It is as my Uncle said, I fear. The Inspector drew a finger from his whisky and lighted another cigarette. He forgot Thomas and the transplanted shadows from along the street that ran by his home, and the beautiful Jane whose corpse he so well remembers lying smiling on the chaise on the very day that corresponds with the entry that he reads. He remembers instead his wife and cat, and stared out the window. Then from somewhere far away bells tolled an unknown quarter hour and he read some more.

She did not look the type that one would arrange to have run over by a car (what type is that? thought the Inspector and drew heavily from his cigarette, picturing a succession of types that could be imagined typical, one of whom he paused to reflect would be run over conventionally and then backed over for good measure). Neatly framed by the picture window, beyond a glistening tableau of staring sea creatures frisking over a bed of seaweed, ice and split lemons, she stepped out of the restaurant and onto the sidewalk, looking back at me over her shoulder to smile, I remember with disbelief. The ugly thud, and I am helpless with embarrassment recalling her vulnerability, disorder of limbs, her learning counting for nothing.

She left us early to return to the university, availing herself of only one of the mullets that she stripped of its flesh and rendered a skeleton like a cartoon kitty. Very good, she had said and the oil… she'd added appreciatively. In her leave-taking had suddenly become friendlier, stroking Jane's hand, gripping my wrist and giving it more painful little turns, her implacable mien softening with concern as she wished us well.

No, Inspector, it was not an accident. She had grown increasingly worried over the time spent with us. Didn't I already say that she repeatedly checked the hour and grew impatient with me? For I was making conversation when I really ought to have just let her get on with what she had to say about Dead Souls. This is not a social visit, she finally told me. And if I had kept my mouth shut? Something else now to consider at four a.m. Fully booked for quite some time to come, the god said, but this time in a kinder way and with something of a gentle smile. I think he wants to be my friend now. Smart move, for he'll not get anywhere with Jane by being my enemy. I'm sorry for any misunderstanding between us, he says. I repeatedly forget that he can somehow read over my shoulder without standing behind my back.

Several months earlier a bird cried out. Ardor, my Uncle said, finally breaking our prolonged silence.

(Which somehow reminds me, Inspector, I have a late dinner

date tonight. How this record will possess me at the expense of time. Helen—there: her shadow passing opposite against the amber lighted wall—wants to take me to a favorite place… but look at this: reflected in the window the god, with narrowed eyes yet; so soon after seeming to want to be friendly. He will snoop over my shoulder, as it were, and dare to be huffy at the same time; and yet I am sure he'll be happy to be rid of me. So long as Jane doesn't come along, whereupon he will follow after and pine for her attention.

Sitting on the floor in one corner the god shifts around on his buttocks and squeezes his eyes shut. He is easily piqued, sighs in exasperation, Inspector… Thomas closes his eyes and lifts his pen from the page, opens them and talks toward his verdigris reflection in the glass. Are you coming tonight, Jane? Her hand on my shoulder, he scrawls. I might, she says, her voice warm with gentle teasing. I might surprise you at the darnedest time. I can live with it, he says, lips trembling; tears stream from his eyes. Oh Jane, I must confess… shhh she says and strokes his nape.)

So the bird cried and Uncle spoke and I yanked back from distraction, memories of Jane and me as teenagers in her parents' home, ankles tangled in blue jeans—stirring, these remembrances—my uncle's sonorous voice, hastening me back from the past with a jerk, returning me to his living room on a sunny afternoon, an Indian Summer in the last fall when as yet I did not know the full extent of what I had become involved in. Leaves from his maples and Lombardy poplars yellow and red, falling to the ground in listless turns, crackly underfoot on the dewy lawn over which earlier uncle had led me to see an owl perched within the shadows of an old pine, the air warm but layered with autumnal cool, seasonal mists veiling the day here and there, the fog horn reporting off the point. He had spoken, fixed me with his blue eyes; sharp though rheumy with what might have been emotion for all I know. He was sick to the bones. Ardor lingered. The word remaining warm, informed with his beautiful voice. A fine word, I thought and hastened to make the connection. Suzanne, his favorite wife, held out a rescuing glance, signaled with a smile and roll of her almond eyes. What about ardor? I asked. Far away a bus shifted gears, stillness of the afternoon. I wonder now if it wasn't the bird to which he was calling on to stand in for one of his swelling points. I remember how with a slight tilting of his head he directed my attention to it, over my left shoulder. Ah Thomas, he had said smiling as I turned my head to look, what are you reading these days? he enquired without waiting for an answer and I don't know why: I had to contain my pleasure. There was the blue jay puffing up his feathers on the railing as Uncle resumed his talk. The old man picking up his earlier thread in which the name of the unfortunate professor from Turin had come up for the first time. One of the funniest people he had ever known, he said of her (I sadly imagine now how that might be), and one with whom I should meet for help with a section of the Dead Souls; if, he said, I wanted to postpone the inevitable, and he lifted both brows as if in enquiry. After this we sat quietly for a time, sipping our drinks, looking out our respective windows. Like this for some minutes, which under the circumstances is longer than it sounds. I sat up more straight. (Sometimes I feel like a mere receptor jerked this way and that by stimuli. All these years later even, Inspector. A mere thing despite my sense of a well-dressed self, draped in finely tailored and relaxed urbanity. The Emperor's clothes, what?) The bird called again and honed its beak on the railing, cocking its head to look inside or perhaps at its own refection in the glass.

Uncle had been talking before our silent interval, holding forth on the Bacteria, a Mr. and Mrs. whose life he had been describing anthropomorphically, sentimentally I thought, turning their life, then all of Life (his leaps and bounds exhilarating, sometimes; and there was nothing for me to do but follow; Uncle after all a distinguished scientist), turning then this whole life into a single creature, larding it with subversion all the while, a patient chef preparing his pet for the oven even as he stroked its head, his eyes looking well past my shoulder, beyond the bird, suddenly fixed on mine once more. Innocence has sharp teeth, he said. As I'm sure you know, he added. You are graying some I see, he said. He smiled and looked through me: drawn perhaps by a memory, perhaps in anticipation of my fate. It struck me then that he was quite mad.

Did I think it aloud? I flinched within. For he said as if on cue, nipping at the tail of this thought: I know you are; but what am I? I started and colored some then noticed that he was looking past me at the bird that had cried out again, chortling quietly. But what were you saying about ardor? I asked, thinking that I had made it sound similar to the way he said it. He carried on as if I had no more than coughed.

Life he said, all life, he reminded me… He was on to Life, as you will remember Inspector, apropos of the charred manuscript, incidentally; and I may as well add that because of some expression that passed across my face he felt it necessary to let me know that the platitudinous nature of this part of his discourse, that I had signaled an impatient awareness of from the perspective of my well-advanced sophistication, as he kindly put it, was necessary in the context of the hidden formula of the manuscript, the power of which, he reminded me, I had no idea. Mooncalf, he had said, you are in so much trouble. I was abashed and wonder how many times I may have pained or angered someone with an inadvertent expression of impatience… I was wondering then if he hadn't had a drink or two before tea. He paused to acknowledge the bird again with something of a wistful look I thought in his blue eyes, a cool shade warmed a little as it moistened some. A thing back here he said apropos of nothing and made as if to grip his own and then the cat's medulla oblongata, pinching her scruff, answered with a loud purring, a squeezing of her beautiful eyes as she looked back at him from his lap and then fixed her gaze on the bird and chattered. There is he said a knot of such unrelenting complexity that will yet unravel on a single pull, and he fixed me with a handsome serpent stare from which I, little bird, as I called myself to Jane when I told her of this, could not tear myself away. This all a little theatrical I thought, not yet having read the burnt manuscript with the attention it demanded; realizing that the theatricality was perhaps the only way to speak of such things. Inspector, I wouldn't care to cheapen it by labeling it a mere coping mechanism. I confess I was slow on the uptake. Even as I write, I wince at missed opportunities to derive advantage from the knowledge of others.

Uncle did not tell me until later, when he was hospitalized and had become significantly more Baroque in his manner, that he had given a précis to three of the most clandestinely powerful beings of the time, only one of whom still lives, and that they were the last of a worldwide Intelligence network disbanded by the Global Reach that has since been subsumed by an underground, in fact criminal, organization called the Shanghai Reach. Only this so-called criminal organization, he would come to say, wore the white hat in the scheme of things. Very interesting, I thought at the time. Then he tied in the subject of maggotry, as he came to call his unifying principle that afternoon—this, toward the end of the first drink, our first drink in any event—to which principle he attached his cancer—tin cans to the tail of a dog, he called the fuss made over it—which he said was no pathology, rather an integral function, part of the process which he said we could call a form of digestion: the whole of life in a perpetual peristalsis. Beaming then with infant pride: passage, he happily informed me, as the wonderful James brothers Henry and William liked to call the infrequent movements of their bowels. Imagine Thomas, he said smiling, that you and I are elements in the Universal Bowel, polyps hanging on for dear life as the tugging flow, the universal mess, passes us by. He caressed the cat's nose, tickled the beloved creature's belly. In my mind's eye I could see well enough his cartoon of the world and, too, how he was visibly enjoying his own voice, and an amber beam that settled onto half his distinguished face, the light of which was comfortable to his eyes for he had no need to squint, uncle sitting back with his legs intertwined, crossed twice (a sign of my patronage, the god has just informed me, Inspector, fixing me with a sympathetic look from his corner, caduceus on the floor by his side. Where is Jane?), a beautiful old man, as some will be, smiling some.

At this time I enjoyed his Manichaeism with the ineffable shiver of pleasure afforded by any adequately told tale of darkness, not yet having taken very seriously the burden of the cursed bundle that the Professor had mistakenly passed on to me. Uncle, however, already knew what had happened to us in Paris and much more, it transpires, and I am overwhelmed by almost a physical rush, a hectic of helpless rage and intuitive shame: that everyone is in on something, complete access to which is being denied me, me alone. Foolishness, of course— don't be so sure, the smart-ass in the corner (the god and not my uncle, if you please) offers, thinking himself amusing I would guess from the expression of his admittedly divine face, and Jane is tickling my neck, back again. Hello my love. Where were you? Just dead, she replies and pulls my ears.

In Rome the woman from Turin had used the same storytelling device as my uncle; and it combined with her accent, the darkness of the story itself, and especially the sudden remembrance of that after- noon of ardor to make me smile, inappropriately, I confess, which she, you remember, misunderstood as mockery even as I had for the first time become aware of a universal concatenation: that I possessed an unwanted, esoteric schematic to it in the form of the Dead Souls. By that time there was hardly any point in asking, why me? (*Why* an irri- tating word in any event. *Because*.) So, contingencies and coincidences repeatedly vindicating my Uncle's ancient and unpopular worldview in the face of the order more commonly placed over the whole, the template of causality and balance. Such a precarious thing, this so-called order, he said, slowly releasing the word as though itself a frangible, somewhat smelly object, the whole business so fragile he said, and finished his drink, a crumbling rotted tomb's lid as he called it before relishing the excuse this presented for some Gothic excess, more of his maggot extravagances.

This the last time I saw him before he was hospitalized. When he presented me with the gun that he had already brought into the living room in expectation of our get together. Thus are we by necessity always returned to the right of might. In effect, anyway. Can we ever escape the coarseness of this? He reached under the chair in which he was sitting and drew out an old, olive drab gunnysack. He laid it on his lap, stiffened some, and I watched as he found the cloisonné pill box that he carried with him, looked away as he turned to stare out the window and went through the process of trying not to hurry the desperate movements, extraction of the tiny nitro pill, placement of it onto his tongue, trying all the while to dispel any sense of urgency. I had seen the routine before in the last year, and continued to look away anticipating the second when he would resume his talk as though nothing had happened. I turned from the window again and saw how he manifestly ignored the concern I could not hide from my face. You should try these some day he said and shook the little box like a tiny rattle before dropping it into his breast pocket.

Himself again, he undid the straps of the sack and extracted a bundle of oily rags. Suzanne entered, sat down with a cocktail and quietly watched. He unwrapped the rags and stuffed them back into the sack, holding in his right hand an automatic pistol. This was the one with which my father insisted his brother had redrawn the map of Europe, a Browning High Power with which I had been familiar since childhood.

You will want to keep this with you now, he said, held it out to me for a moment, then slipped it back into the gunnysack reeking of gun oil and neatly packed with extra clips and several boxes of ammunition. You unlucky fool, he said. Thus my gun, Inspector.

We lounged in his living room opposite one another, each with a sweating tumbler of vodka and soda in hand. He had been teasing me in an affectionate way. Making fun something of an intermezzo with uncle between rounds, between the acts, as he'd sometimes say. And I came to be inappositely distracted by the pleasure one can take in such flirtation when it is just right, recalling past times when I was the object of such playful, amorous attention, which has as its boundary an emotional flash point, just beyond the savor of frisson, at any significant chipping at identity's flinty cornerstone. I said as much about my sudden intuition into courtship, I recall, Uncle holding my eyes, taking pleasure, I think, in what I possessed of my dead father, resuming a vintage fraternal banter with a dear ghost before he countered with the truth of the matter, that I was simply too old to be considered for such attentions.

I can't recall what he teased me about at the time of levity, earlier that afternoon; whether it bore any connection to the single word he'd spoken in one of the rare times when he had appeared wistful, romantic even. I was used to a less emotive man. Ardor. We were enjoying more drinks by then, the first having followed on the tail of tea and cookies that hadn't all been cleared away before the tune of ice against large tumblers sounded from the kitchen, Suzanne watching him from the kitchen as she prepared cocktails.

That bird there—a blue jay stood on the railing of the terrace on the other side of the picture window fronting the large backyard— reminds me of my mortality, he said.

What about ardor, I had asked? The bird scolding; then suddenly silent. He gestured with both hands, neatly but with expression, a delicate and elegant blooming, a gestural aphorism in comparison with the extravagant, sometimes cruel way, he would later perform from his hospital bed. He looked toward the kitchen at Suzanne, then back at the jay that had remained silent, the coarseness fallen away with the last echo of its crotchety voice, as if itself struck by an immense stillness spreading after the waves of its last harsh call, as if from the center of a stone dropped into a pond and the concentric circles widening, the bird having created a center at the core of which we happened to be as if in suspension, the bird motionless and perfect, an emperor's bird resplendent in opulent blue. I dared again: Ardor, Uncle? He narrowed his eyes and looked almost as though he would smile, as though he were about to tell me something intimate. Pleasing himself still more, however, in that he knew that he would not be sharing any more of it than he already had with his rebus, that conglomeration that was his self, word, gesture, the happy accident of his physiognomy, his face tinting as his eyes broke away with the slightest, unwonted suggestion of shyness, and the bird suddenly calling us back to ourselves, the emperor long ago dust, unsustainable silence rebounding to knock the strutting instrument of cacophony off the rail and into flight.

The way all experience accumulates, all the years, Jane said. Unbearable… Almost. When I lived, said Jane… Will you hear me?

Yes, he said, barely feeling the awkwardness of acquiescence, alone and as yet unaware of it dying in the Paris room. Here in this corner room where he had spent cherished times—and he imagined that he smiled at the familiar fissure in the acanthus molding over the windows—over so many years at the crossroads.

A pair of footsteps, their resonance growing more faint with each beat, the steps in time—faintly annoying somehow—click-click down the dark avenue. She waited for them to fade away before continuing, he thought, and he too waited patiently for their metronome beat to disappear, ineluctably lingering, (his hearing fine to a fault, he declared silently to himself; imagining the steps walking in place, the diminishing sound effect a trick to fool him, a promise of their return: You cannot hurt me now…) a monotony against which he had strived, he declared to himself with a sense that he had come to understand something, as he waited for the voice to take up from where it had left off, for her to go on, the comfort he felt belied by his awkward sprawl.

Forget all that, she said, and the Inspector attended to her voice, sound of footsteps fading while yet staying in place, he was certain, marked them even as she spoke.

The years, she said… with pleasure he thought, thrilling to her voice, sweet and low, full of promise even as against the circumstances, she somehow smiling still, he remembered, even as Thomas said she'd done, smiling, gently smiling as the weather changed before the window over the canal.

There was a mirror so ancient and become so crowded with images it shattered in a slivering burst of silver, Jane began again, but he still thought his own thoughts, still at one remove though drawn closer by the voice, her spell, the Inspector thinking, his hand turning pages, as though despite him, as the steps apparently diminished, lingering with intent even as his body willed itself on in spite of his weariness with contending, and here now the warmth and promise of her voice to which he was in thrall as at no other time during this long case… How long now this case? He interrupted, asked of himself, conceding to her answer that it was a lifetime in effect, and still some, as she went on to say. She teased, he thought, nonetheless, yes, quite, and I have never not been assigned to it, grateful in his belly that she had in effect pointed this out to him—willing to surrender to her entirely should she want, only one small part of him hearing still the malevolent twins, the very same who had dogged him to his doorstep in Rome—and she came closer, he felt—and who knew where else over the years, he heard her add, the Geminis dogging him to his destinations on that afternoon in the winter, the long shadows and the smell of burning oak as he himself doubled after Thomas to that woman's door beneath the wall of the Borghese gardens. The neighbor living just down the block from him beneath the ancient yellow walls, opening the door that afternoon, cats everywhere, smoke in the air and the craftsman before his fire, framed by the open door, bent over the same chair hours later… and Jane went on to say that it was there, in the woman's home, that this mirror hung still, having lost the better part of its ancient glass, having burst on a winter afternoon, Inspector, you remember, she said, as he thought over the pages, flipping back, flipping back. Those pages still coming. Tomorrow. Inspector, she repeated with a little reproach, attend to this, for there's not all that much time, and he passed through long fragrant shadows, you remember the woman—so beautiful—who opened the door at the top of the stairs. She had waited for you for years. What can she mean, he thought? But she just went on and he considered: she will answer if I address her but he heard a car pass, and voices from the street, and his hand brushed over the metal of his gun then back to the pages and he flipped back further, turning and turning as she spoke… You could have entered after Thomas. She wanted you to on that afternoon where your image, even from where you stood on the landing outside, your eyes fixed on hers from a distance, was the last the mirror could hold, and it shattered as I have said with such violence that I later plucked—and the Inspector felt the puckered tissue on his own neck—a sliver from Thomas's neck, hours later coming out of my dream, and it was already dark and he standing at the foot of the bed with a thin black line running from under his left ear that I could just make out in the light remaining, and my breath heavy with warmth and sleep and so wanting him I remember, and do you think it somehow shameless of me? Plucked the sliver of glass that had bled him and drawn a line of blood to soak into his collar. Scent of asphodel. All this you know, I know, she said taking up from wherever she left off, no matter when and where he may have lost her. Began again. Always that. No end. World without end, he thought.

Part Two

I am dreaming, Father. I wish I could scream. Stay awhile. In this hand are the deep places of the earth. Oh Martin, I'll tell you what and some.

The bright and windy fall day, alone at home listening to the wind howl, four years old and knowing what (with inarticulate certainty; certain nonetheless). That fall afternoon, running from the house I drop two at a time down the entry steps calling for mother, for father. No one hears. Mother and Father who must not hear me calling. A sudden blow lifts me from the walkway onto the rough. Torn leaves spin from groaning wood into fallen others, scraping in a red and yellow tumble along the boulevard and I, ankle deep in foliage, choking on scream, am trying to wake.

Do you see, writes the priest and confessor Father Martin in his diary, addressing himself, as was his habit, and in effect someone other, what I am up against? I want to ignore my calling, yet again; have done so before; had I not loved him once would probably not—God forgive me —be bothering with this now.

Where to start? How begin? If I could help it I should probably not tell my story, constrained by the tact of the wide-awake. For whom, really, but jealous lovers, are others' dreams of any interest?

Amen.

Thus the confessor. Three hours now since he tore open the weighty packet, curious (his birthday still months away), innocently admiring many dollars worth of colorful stamps decorating the brown wrapping: from the bottom, row upon row of dogwood blooms, three lines each of pterodactyls and cowboys, a vertical line of atomic models closing the right side, then one top story of hopeless splendor, a row of subfusc Arctic beauty, the dearest and largest stamp, and he shivers, cutting his thumb on the staples suturing one end.

Don't be daft, Martin. No cause for alarm. A conceit, merely: the everyday persists, in spite of me. I dream the everyday, and some. [The confessor sucks his bleeding thumb, scans the first page of the neatly typed bundle looking for some explanation for this intrusion on his acedia, at a loss at what to make of this urgent conceit.] As my need on that fall afternoon of tree bending gusts bright with motley color, loud with howling, as my need to call for my parents overcame me, untethered panic—overwhelming, Father, an autonomous thing—gripped my being, took hold of my throat and I fought, struggled to wake, yet the world all softly golden, and this song, listen, not of promise, but of what is: eerie, terrible, beautiful, a song breathing strange contentment while I, full of wonder, am straining to break free, as so many times before and since without success, managing finally to call, become practiced after the initial paralysis at disengaging the chokehold of fear, shouting into the wind for mother, father, the words hurled back like spit; crying out shyly at first (after all, Father, the neighbors), desperate all the same, knowing this time they will not answer.

Saturated with intoxicant fear, I panic even more; but then, perhaps only for those for whom the dreaming never ends, Martin, for those who must ride it out without the expected relief, there is a bonus. A sudden appreciation—is it true, Father, that the Devil knows how to turn all sorrows into pleasures?—that all along there is an accompanying sensation, pleasure underlying the whole drama. Could I do without it now? As I call out for mother and father who, as it happens, have not left me forever, are in the lane back of the house prattling with a neighbor, I am already somehow sorry for them. Sorry for how they would ache with love and helplessness, hurt on my behalf if they only knew. They did know, of course; but more practical than I, knew as well not to dwell on such things; and I knew then for the first time of terminal helplessness, but of that something other, too. Something new, then, while calling out again and again into the wind, turning this way and that on the walkway leading to the leaf-frenzied boulevard, dancing on my long legs, caught up in the whirling gusts, footing about with such impatience that one of my sandals folds violently to one side, adheres to the concrete while the thong of the blue rubber flip-flop disengages from the sole.

This is making more than reasonable demands on a man, even of a priest, Martin writes. This priest, at least, he pencils in after. Stuffing the many pages back into their wrapping, breathing heavily, crabbed and fussy, he opens and slams desk drawers in search of a stapler. He finds it lying empty on its side, later explains to his dear diary that: With something like conscience I overcame my initial impulse to return the manuscript. Professional conscience, I confess; quite unfelt. But by its example I became reacquainted with my feelings, my one time love for him (though I never thought of it like that then); re-experienced through his confession the pleasure in heartbreak. It is this that unbalanced my doubt, my hesitation. Perhaps, too, the absence of staples, string or tape, and the sight, in contrast to the neat white bundle of paper, of dusty layers of unanswered letters, personal and commercial solicitations and exhortations, all this crumpled rubbish on my desk. Pulling the pages back out of their package I somehow guessed that in them I would finally find the motivation for my long postponed resolve, God forgive me.

So the priest wrote of how he pulled the manuscript back out from the envelope, his thumb throbbing, reminded of the simpler pain of the body as he noticed his dark red thumb prints smudging the first two crisp white sheets.

While I must tell you my story, little of the urgency to explain myself remains: that predicament, this life of somnolent imprisonment in which I am both subject and object, my consciousness a panopticon affording incessant viewing, myself as prisoner and warden, the nature of my crime, the duration of my sentence, so highly confidential as to be unknown to either. I no longer bruise myself from pinching; nor draw the questioning, amused, or fearing looks from others disturbed by the spectacle of myself muttering: Wake up! Wake up! Sometimes I think I've returned from the dead; returned, just not quite all the way. Father, it might be possible that some complication other than metaphysical resulted from my head becoming stuck as I was squeezed from my beautiful mother's womb, and I the consequence of a fateful hesitation on the part of a young doctor, forceps trembling in his hands and he in something of a funk for which my mother never forgave him or the family doctor who insisted on finishing a round of golf before attending to her. A professional failing then, which, in the ensuing period before the old man arrived and seized me—finally—bawling bloody murder, might have caused me some harm. Mother screaming: Pull it out! Pull it out! Ghoulishly imagining that I was finished once and for all and she plugged with crow bait. The theme unnerves: that I should suffer a lifetime as a result of another's incompetence? Swine. This is speculation, granted. It may lend itself—I certainly won't—to those of a psychological bent, Father, but I have other ideas; and yet, as I recall, that is a bent in your way, down which I will bet you are still wandering. I've not forgotten your periods—so long ago now, it seems, that I last saw you—of waning faith and how you tried to account for them by pointing fingers at your kind and unfortunate parents. In any event, I hope to avoid the subject of my possible natal damage. It simply does not go far enough in my opinion. (I don't like the idea besides; grates me, for all of a minute or two; momentarily diminishes a keen and necessary sense of my particularity. Quite intact, quite perfect, even. Not damaged goods. Imagine that, then, if you will.)

I imagine you are a perfect fiend, scribbles the confessor in his diary. If only his old friend could have chosen a more merciful, a more succinct means, he continues writing, still detached, for the most part, tired and cynical, fanning the pages lying before him as he fills another of his own. He went on: However, I will fulfill my duty; but I fear, fitting as it may be, that somehow in the process he will exile me forever from the God from whom I have shamelessly sought only favors.

In the event this falls into the wrong hands, I won't disclose my exact location. This island from which I write to you will be any island. On the other hand I cock a snook at my pursuers (mercy is most times wasted, believe me; I should have dispatched them all). Go ahead: try to find me. I'm here: a compass shudder north or south of the forty-ninth, west of one hundred thirty. God's own little archipelago. A family of whitetails grazes before my windows; salmon fight one another to leap into my pan; an otter joins me for the happy hour, floats on her back just off the jetty, understands the gloaming with me. Father, perhaps you shouldn't keep this bundle lying around after all.

On our arrival here I look back with such pleasure: spring, my birthday. Jane with me, stronger, no longer pale or always leaning on her stick; keen again in the morning, keen for the day in her own manner; sometimes quiet, sometimes mischievous, somehow gay even in repose; never imposing her inherent melancholy on the atmosphere as so many children of Saturn do, mistakenly compelled to display, as if they are the first to see the way of the world, as if it made a bit of difference to fret and beg attention to expressions of hope and despair, the thematic variations, Father, of your vocation. Please Martin, by mentioning her charm, strength and character I don't mean to underline your past failures. I have forgiven you your trespasses and besides have more important concerns, believe me. I know you tried. Besides, she was special, one of those for whom a certain knowledge of the world is not so much a burden as a foundation. I miss her so. When I dream her there is no need to wake. I am displaced by her death. In Venice. Did you know? I can't remember, Martin: how did you, so very sensitive, impatient for reassurance and explanations, stumble into the priesthood, anyway?

First Martin's ears, then the rest of him, burn a painful crimson. Blotchy red islets drift out from behind his dog collar to remain there for the rest of the day. (Father Amaro found him some aspirin and burned his fingers on his brow; felt very good about having forgiven Martin for sending him to the Devil; promises himself the daring pleasure of looking in on and serving him the next day.) When finally Martin's breathing becomes more regular, he groans and forces himself up from his chaise longue. He finds a great, heavy atlas that had belonged to his family and which his sister had presciently trimmed of various Imperial pink maps around the globe for a school report some half century ago. He strains to make Thomas's coordinates from a Mercator map of the world at the front of the book, flips through the large pages and finally locates the Pacific Northwest, into which he digs a yellow thumb nail, fissuring the page as far south as California, then bursts into tears.

Congenitally rich with expectation, a sense that destiny has something special in store for me, here I am targeted on my island, expendable after all. (This is not a confession of mid-life crisis, Father. Remember your calling. Abandon all hope of using your years of student psychology.) Specialness is potentially repellent; yet combined in just such a way (as in the delicious redolence of sex peculiar to some) can be inexorably compelling. I have been mercilessly spurred by it myself; and Martin, even you were once keen on me, for all that you later came to see me as a serpent. Anyway, despite being bound by an oneiric consciousness, and glandularly coaxed, alas, I was born with a nagging certainty that something was up in which I have a part; no mere secondary role. Nature's puffery, Martin. She has her way with me, no doubt about it. Do you understand Father? [The confessor scribbles in the margin, Yes: that you are mad with conceit, a shameless megalomaniac without an ounce of humility and genuine self-consciousness.] Jane was drawn to me with the same intuition. [Martin smiles.] Fundamentally we both knew better. Still, one should a few times in a life test the hypothesis of expendability some, make nature work a little harder to have its inevitable way, pique it into displaying its amazing ingenuity before surrendering to the scheme of things. Martin, no offense intended, and you are by no means alone, but you surrendered early, possessed the emotional equivalent of the sagging mien and paunch of a suburban forty year old by the time you reached thirty. There is no blame attached to this phenomenon. But here I am going on about my sense of self, that I knew the big trick all along, when I wanted by way of something like an interlude to calm you, relieve you of the inevitable strain from the seriousness of my situation, give you at least some sense of how beautiful my island is. Something like the intended effect of those sheets of wallpaper printed with photographic scenes of nature somehow never laid quite flush which you must have stared at once or twice at the dentist. (It is true your teeth were neglected.) But of course you know. We shared the same doctor. He had an autumnal forest of beech trees, as I recall. Anyway, I especially wanted to tell you about the whales.

His large red ears twitching at the sound of sobbing, groans and curses from behind the door, observed by three brother priests at different times to be tying and retying for at least half an hour what must have been a devilishly recalcitrant shoe lace, Father Amaro crouches in the shadows just outside Martin's rooms. He has almost given up his vigil when he hears the cry.

There is too much excitement. Martin comes to, pulls the smoking manuscript out of the fire with severe burns to his left hand; raises a blistering fist at Father Amaro bursting in at the sound of his cry, Amaro trying to seize hold of the burned paw, chattering all the while that he must be permitted to determine what salve to apply. Struggling for possession of the blackened manuscript—now missing a page— Father Amaro—asthmatically gasping the Lord's Prayer, bravely taking a box to the ear from the archfiend—pretends to be persuaded by Martin's reassurances. Imagining himself to be more or less safe outside the possessed and smoky room, Amaro runs (a fast tip-toe) to see the Bishop, forgetting that his Excellency is on vacation, later telephones several lay friends and acquaintances instead. With the passing of all this excitement Martin locks his door with a last curse for Father Amaro. Grimacing, he lays himself down onto the chaise longue to read about the whales; to try, at least, to calm himself before vespers.

Harvest moon rising, a pod of Orcas fished alongside me in the twilight yesterday; the cat and I in a skiff. The grilse were running, Martin, ruffling the sea, stabbing at the air. Quivering they leaped, red stained with moonshine; and the piebald whales, four adults and a calf, arching with patient, well mannered rhythm, fed on the frenzied young salmon, one of which tugged at my trembling line long before I finally started from this vision to reel it in. Abreast, we ran along the wrinkled moonbeam until with a fish for myself and one for the cat, the time came to struggle against the tide and swells of the straight to return home.

Father forgive me—I mean it—but this would be the way to go: with the tide on a moon beam, companioned by Orcas; and somewhere far from shore and hours into the night weight the pockets and tip oneself backwards over the gunwales. For now I am with second thoughts, as if hanging onto a long drowned bowline trailing alongside the hull. Not yet. I'll holler into the wind now for effect, Not yet! I have scared the cat. Come back, pussy. Just think of waking under such circumstances, Father, full fathom five. This calls for hot tea.

Father Martin wakes, hand swollen with pain, and roughly tears out two dense pages from his notebook. They are not of a generous nature. As the confessor's notebooks fill, along with certain of the margins and blank spaces between the lines of the manuscript, he cares proportionately less to erase, black out, in any way excise his spontaneous comments and outbursts. After his sad end some of the notebooks, his favorite oilskin scribblers from the now defunct Chinese Magic and Stationary Shop in Chinatown, were noticeably tampered with by another hand. Here and there a page neatly removed (I tell you, he could never have brought himself to be so fussy), precisely razored along a straight edge. Although Father Martin did not regularly date his entries, it is quite certain that one notebook, the penultimate, is missing.

Martin can't bring himself to visit a doctor, sloppily bandages his blistered hand and goes about his duties relieving anxiety, restoring hope in various measures, forgiving on behalf of the Lord an above average number of souls bussed in from all over town. Sins are allowed to multiply with monthly excursions for penitence to Martin's diocese. Transportation is sponsored by the bottlers of some soft drink ever since a number of churches, one with a charming, ivy-festooned dome modeled on the Pantheon, another with generations of bats in its belfry, have been deconsecrated and torn down to make way for mini-malls financed by these same pop bottlers; whom, one could be forgiven for thinking, might have had an anti-papist bias, despite their bussing program, if they weren't financing a condominium development within the shell of a former synagogue as well. On this day the evident gratitude of a good number of those who confide in him for a time makes him accept his lot, touches him with intoxicating belief; but by late afternoon, when he returns to the bundle of paper locked in one of his desk drawers, emptied unceremoniously the other day to make room for it, he is himself again. Lifting the burnt offering onto his desk, blackened, sooty on the edges and smelling strongly of last night's fire, Martin sits down with a groan to read before supper.

Father, am I wrong in imagining that you would prefer not to deal with this? (For all that you may not be able to help yourself.) There is doubtless something entertaining on the television; but stay a little. I imagine you lying in wait for souls, camouflaged like some terrible ocean predator, dead still against the background. It was this hungry passivity that made you an indifferent reader, as I recall. Your papers were so dull, if solid, and so insufferably well received. You would not actively engage the text. You wanted all the answers to swim on their own into your hungry maw. I'll try to drive some your way. There is so much to tell you.

No one could accuse you of not being curious about the lives of others. You would, I remember, earnestly, and I'm quite sure sincerely, ask the same questions over and over again; listen to the answers (like a tender wife indulging the enduring nostalgia of a callous and back-ward-looking husband, for whom the good old days don't include her) as if for the first time; faithfully listen as though there was something you must have missed in all the other tellings. A storyteller's dream, in a way.

You offered little of yourself. I had the feeling—though sometimes ignored it, as I recall—that it would somehow be untoward to question you. I used to try. Your embarrassment was my petty reward. I admit it may be unfair—I am sure it is—but after a time and for all that I liked you, I never expected you would have anything to tell me. As for your curiosity (your present reason to be, if you're searching for one), I'm almost certain that only diffidence kept you from peering into windows (did you ever?). Oh, I'm sorry, Martin. Really I am. I should be more careful, too; for all that, I trust you can't resist going on with this. You see I have an obscure but genuine need to engage you. Father, bear with me just a little more here. I'll rid myself of any but the most intermittent need to drag you behind my chariot soon enough.

For my purposes I need at least to imagine your duty to attend to me and provide the signposts of your cosmology; and as I write and remember, I need your personal failure as a man to locate my own position; show me the way, if you prefer. Do you see? I really do not want to cause you undue pain, but you deserve a little. Here, for example, I'll never forget the trouble you once made for me at the expense of young Jane's trust. Jane, by the way, forgave me very soon after. You did little harm, as it turned out; relieved us of our naive expectations, or at least of what is too easily accepted as friendship, a useful push toward informed cynicism.

Do you remember the way she laughed? I admit, she cried some too; but she loved and trusted me so much that she could not doubt my own for her. Our love was a life sentence, she used to say.

A part of you had to know it would make a difference to betray me. (Betray sounds so self important a word for something so reflex, subordinate in nature only to breathing.) Which brings me back to my task at hand, I hope. For I want you to know, you Father Martin, my friend, what has become of me over all these years. Now that Jane is dead who else will take the time? And there is not much of it left. I will wake one of these days; soon, soon. And while you probably do not read now any better than you used to, if I keep grabbing you by the ear and compel you to pay attention by touching on your vanity—I need you Martin—and your curiosity, I may yet take some little satisfaction, perhaps even manage some on my tormentors. More of this later. Words can run away with me. I am compelled to dramatic utterance from time to time; compelled to express myself in a prolonged and tempered howling, not without some musical value sometimes. I try to catch myself. There is so little time for self-indulgence, so little time before the harpies catch up with me. I hope you won't post those coordinates I offered in anger, Father. I need a little more time. My bravura's on the wane of late. I think I am found. A particularly fancy powerboat slowly making its way across my bay, from the bridge of which four searing white disks flashed, two binoculars focusing on my island, my home, for the duration of its passing, chased away my breakfasting deer, made the kitty cry, quite unnerved me this morning.

Bells for vespers ringing, Father Martin wakes, sniffing at his burnt hand. He rises in the dark and makes his way to prayers. The injured hand has begun to give offense, soon filling any room he might be in with an unwholesome reek. But Father Amaro passionately sniffs at the corruption with something like devotion. It is to avoid him and his flexing nostrils that Martin now takes his meals in, and rarely leaves his room, not any concern that he might be repelling others, not the catchy reference to Philoctetes by the librarian, mischievous, Greek-loving, Father Stephen. Martin, venturing out from his room to look for a more detailed book of maps, overhears him mutter the epithet, quipping unawares to himself this first day of autumn, fine, misty and warm. Stephen wrinkling his nose, frowning, standing hands in pockets, compact and attractive, alone in a mote-full sunbeam of late afternoon light. Through the stacks, Martin watches how he stares at the proffered bottom of—Stephen sighs the name aloud—a veritable Ganymede halfheartedly feather-dusting a lower shelf of encyclopedias, an almond-eyed seminary student whose help in the library Stephen now regularly enlists; the boy plump and rosy-cheeked, of the kind so beloved by Caravaggio who Stephen passionately reveres, probably not entirely as a connoisseur, although his monograph on the artist's "Youth Bitten By A Green Lizard" is much respected, if some-what provocative, and whose pictures in a large volume lie open on a nearby table. Martin—dreamily absorbed, fixed to his place and peer-ing over the tops of assorted atlases—watches him ardently explain a painting to the novice, the librarian's rousing interest in his subject overcoming the malodorous intrusion by the voyeur.

Martin pulls himself away, taking with him a detailed and descrip-tive book of charts of the Gulf Islands. (His Excellency the Bishop is an avid yachtsman.) Holding his bandaged hand to his nose and mut-tering under his breath, he hurries back to his room, foregoing the customary tea. He reads now, sitting at his desk by the window in the umber shadows, the ripe autumn twilight.

May we go somewhere and kiss? My first words to her. Here was witch-ery, Father, with your permission. A sudden force mastering our youth with intolerable pleasure, catching us up—belly, throat, seized by sweet sensation—and she colors some, looks positively hungry for me, Father; for me. My eyes contract with hers, the narcotic loading, her eyes green and gold-spoked, reflex contraction by appetite—that must be it—and she takes me by the hand, how I remember, pulls me after her. In shared moments with Jane, especially with her, I forgot my struggle to wake from in-betweenness. Pressed together, or even with a room between us, we were a perfect fit. Somehow she knew how to slip into my dream world, make it more comfortable. I was lucky in my trust, that our desire to surrender to one another, leave instinctive wariness at the door, was shared. When we had to battle with the world, and the world be damned, Father, we were as if back to back, and our confidence, attraction and power trebled and trebled again. You might like to think that Nature would not have brought us together if it hadn't some inex-orable inspiration to be realized. You would be forgiven for thinking so under the circumstances. We kiss outside, in a car parked by the gray river on the muddy and grassy dike, on the very river's edge in the fall smelling of wet leaves and mud; and over there, the last light of day, pale yellow, torn in the windy blue and gray; and she, her face before mine, confirms my sense of destiny because it will include another such as her; and as well, although at first I was too enchanted to pay it any heed, that, just as in the old stories, one ought, if only as a matter of taste, to temper some even the most justifiable self-confidence; but ought is fraught with snags. Is there hubris, Father, in simple animal pride: a cat's regal languor, a striding horse's snorting pleasure in his design? If in fact I had caught the attention of the Gods—rather than just the spawn of your resentment—they set me up grotesquely. What with that sleepy-eyed, disheveled hot dog girl (what childish, plump feet she had; what hunger… and mustard under her finger nails) and you (still spotty-faced as I remember), as their unknowing agents. And to think that at first they had come up with nothing more imaginative than an instance of haphazard lust and your purposeful meddling with which to humble me by way of Jane's pain before eventually pitting me against the supreme power of Pater's Global Reach. Now that was more like it. Here, then, is the story of resentment, Father. Its cosmic range extending from the failing of your better sensibilities to the all-powerful machinations of the Global Reach's hegemony. Is there a relationship between things of such inconsequence as, for example, my biology or your moral failing, and an imagined larger scheme of things? Are these really parts of the same design? Have we found a first principle? Not yet: mere reflex, a twitch, plain consequence of mind. But I do intuit something trembling near the horizon. I feel, I smell, something. Just wait. And for all its familiarity, as if all this mental plague were not enough, I still struggle to come to grips with my con-dition, struggle to wake, strain against myself in this mental isometric exercise. Father, it wasn't very long after your impulsive meddling that I came a cropper for the first time, having let my appetite get the better of my consideration for another's feelings. But I got right back up into the saddle. Aren't you ashamed of yourself for telling on me, Martin? Character is destiny, you know.

Martin looks up from the pages, glances heavenwards for a little sympathy, then at his dark reflection in the window. He rubs his eyes and yawns. Outside his door the floorboards groan in disapproval, will have none of Father Amaro's eavesdropping. Martin seizes the nearest solid object, hurls his hymnal at the door with such force as to startle himself; with some satisfaction, listens to the signature sound of Amaro's retreating footsteps. When he no longer hears their shamed and sham tact-tact-tact, he hears himself breathing heavily, as if from over-exertion. Keeping double time his heart, too, beats hard, the pulse resonating in his ears. His cheeks burn. He turns toward the windows. A fog is coming off the sea, decking the maples in soft gray suspense. Martin aches with melancholy pleasure. Crows caw and croak, calmly forage among the scattering of orange and red leaves; a tawny squirrel staring at the handsome birds is fixed upside down, spread-eagled halfway up the trunk of the nearest tree. It scolds the crows; they pay no attention. Rising with a groan, grimacing at the rising stink of his bandaged hand, Martin walks to the leaded glass and stands pressing against it with his brow; squeezing his eyes shut, he turns his cheek to the cooling pane and weeps.

Oh Martin, revenge, as the Italians say, is a dish that a man of taste prefers to take cold. Me too; but time is running out and I've so much to tell you, so much revenge to take. In the expression of remembrance, particulars take the upper hand and I, still warm with memories, make hissing contact between a warm heart and cool head (steaming up Verdi's prescription for the ideal conductor); yet in the execution of fate, fate as I choose to make it, Father—no moral divertissements will enter from my side—I remain cold; cold as can be. Do you doubt me?

The two assassins in the once splendid powerboat of which I wrote the other day would not disagree. I wonder if you will understand. With your forgiveness quotient at seventy times seven, at least I have a margin. I will tell you of my life of protracted revenge; how I became targeted, then harried, by the powers that be, the power that is, Father, with which I am in bitter collision. Jane. Oh, I understand. She was the only effective weapon against me. I was willing, resigned even, to keeping my speculation to myself, letting everything be, living out my years. Will you believe me?

Stay. I will tell you how I have become urgently expendable; know something that is none of my business, first a mistake, subsequently a consequence of time on my hands, a mere accident of nature. With the sole purpose of punishing me—for what I will tell you—I am pursued still. First they went after my love.

Their chance swipe half-crushed her. I brought her to my island, spirit still intact, nursed her (and she me, as always); but thwarted, they flayed about again in a frenzy of spite and caught her in our favorite Venice hotel room, snow beginning to fall past the ogee windows. Father, this organization is one big stick with a life of its own. Its nature is plain and simple, counterfeiting purpose. I should never have interfered with this confidence game. An imagined conscience—time on my hands, I say, really nothing more—moved me to prick the conceptual bubble of the hegemony. Martin, Father, attend to this: you know that, for all the rest, I am not mad.

Such confidence in his sanity! Martin jots, smugly tilting his head and pursing his lips, as if to admire his handwriting, ashamed right after. He is not troubled by madness so much; more by a disturbing sense that Thomas, for all the extravagance of his somnambulant conceit, is telling the truth. At first this applies more to the painful commentary on himself than to the worrying—but, he thinks, surely notional—quality of the other disclosures. Continued exposure to the insidious bundle, however, begins to have another effect on him, urges him beyond the excruciating realization that his life is interlarded with ethical failure, that he is more helpless than he ever imagined, to flinch at least half away from self—no matter if at first only from an instinct to survive—and accept that Thomas, in his characteristic arrogance, had in fact taken on Heaven, as the Global Reach, the universal communications empire, is known.

He is going about this as though he expects a new testament to be devoted to him, Father Martin writes, grimacing as his oozing bandaged hand begins to throb again. One written by him. And what does he think? That I will sanction it? That I, a coward and a failure, will run the risk to my already battered self by making public his desperate musing? He slides a small glass vase toward his blotter, bends to sniff the fragrant bloom bought this morning. Jane used to keep a sprig of white freesia in a small ancient glass on her desk. He remembered her earlier while chancing to look at a green plastic bucket of freesias at the stall next to his favorite bakery where he stopped to treat himself to a dark chocolate Florentine. She does not yet exist for him in a nearer to contemporary way. He has difficulty imagining her as infirm, leaning on a stick as in Thomas's evocation, now dead according to these ravings, hasn't even been able to picture her in connection with Thomas's nostalgia (envenomed nostalgia, as he notes in his scribbler) about their time as friends so long ago, is confused, made unhappy remembering Thomas's manifest love for her in contrast with what he believes to have been a mere acceptance of his friendship within an eclectic circle. He sniffs the flower, Jane revenant suddenly, become a presence; and he aches, painfully thrills in her immediacy, shuddering at his foolishness for imagining that she was, could ever have been, his rival, and she was gone.

Martin stares out the window, concentrating, can just make out the slowly drifting movement of the fog. A mass of gray slowly passing across the frame, past the grid of leaded panes. He glimpses an apparition of the nearest tree, the shadow of a crow, a spare cluster of leaves still holding on to a bough here and there. The telephone rings. He lifts it from the cradle, says hello once, twice: silence, a seashell-like resonance as he presses the receiver to his ear and strains to hear. This is the second time today, the third day in a row. He isn't yet prepared to give it another thought.

He thinks again of Jane, of missed opportunity for friendship. Now full of tenderness, he returns to the manuscript lying in darkness before him. Reaching across the desk he switches on the goose necked lamp, resisting the sudden ghoulish apparition of himself in the glass and starts to read.

You must remember Wu's Magic Shop.

Of course he does. In front of its small display window filled with a mixture of genuinely wonderful curios and mass-produced junk, Thomas once doubled over teary-eyed with laughter apparently directed at him; the reason a mystery to Martin still. Within a minute his jolly friend had prompted the hilarity of several others, passers-by, all Chinese, men women and children who saw the humor inherent in the situation right away (the collective preposterous) and joined in the cross-cultural fun, surrounding him, pointing and guffawing until Thomas, still howling, dragged him, irremediably mortified, away. Of course he remembers. He continues to buy his favorite oilskin scribblers there, braving, with quite mixed feelings still, the memory of his humiliation, considering it something of an exercise of character. Bastard, Martin prints as a heading in his commentary, then continues to read.

We had fun in Chinatown, Father. Do you remember? I could eat some dim sum right now. One autumn afternoon, I became certain—as much as possible—of Heaven's plot against me. Jane and I had just finished lunch upstairs at Sun Lock and were walking in front of

Wu's—I think I may have been recalling for her that time you attracted all those people to us so many years before—when suddenly Wu himself appeared, deigning to put at least one foot onto the sidewalk. This was something to see: old Wu reaching out with unwonted alacrity and drama, pulling us both inside and slamming the green door after. Remember, he wasn't even young when we were students; and so imagine old Wu then, without his stick—the first time ever I saw him so—dressed in neat gray flannels, white shirt and buttoned charcoal cardigan, with one liver spotted hand reaching out as we passed before his shop and actually taking hold, first of Jane (I still can hear her surprised chirp), then me with the other. Old Wu clutching at the sleeves of our raincoats, then dancing backwards on the toes of his felt-slippered feet, and we surprised but compliant, dutifully in tow and shuffling after. He did not stop tugging until we were well into the dark and narrow space, incense and dust fragrant, cluttered with the stuff of wonder and just stuff. Wu motioned for us to wait and balanced his way back to the front where he had hung his stick between the raised and blessing fingers of a worm-eaten Buddha with a perforated and fragrant rotted belly. Hours before closing time he locked the door and pulled down the shade. Never had I seen him behave with such purpose, as if something could actually matter.

We did not dare speak, exchanged eyes and neat smiles of anticipation. (Jane's mouth, her Koré smile, knowing, charmed with a subtle mischief. I never managed to resist the need to tell her so. She was kind enough to appear at least not to have tired of the compliment. You must remember her smile, Martin.)

It was lore, habit of childhood become adult hopes, to imagine Wu to be any number of things: a dragon in disguise, a Tong godfather, the Miraculous Mandarin; imaginings chaperoned by genuine respect, even a little fear. To me he was the very pattern of knowing, at the center of the storm. I picture him now: the gentle mouth, with yet a

hint of irony; a patrician tilt to the head; gaiety in his eyes, yet the saddest eyes I have ever seen.

So imagine, Martin, our surprise at being shanghaied with
unprecedented earnestness by courtly and aged Wu. Uncharitably I
wondered—only for an instant, but still, still—if he had lost his mind.
[Look who's talking, Martin scribbles in the right hand margin.] An
unbecoming lapse on my part: that I, of all people, should momentarily seize on the suburban explanation for whatever does not accord
with expectation. A shameful stumble. I still wish I could blame it on
something I had eaten. Father, stuffed with delicious dumplings (I
make myself hungry as I write remembering those lunches), could I
have been tempted at that moment by the Noonday Devil?

We waited. I squeezed Jane's hand, become myself again, and
watched him. He stood facing his counter, actually a tall ebony escritoire, an odd Chinese variant on the clerical double desk, outsized with
drawers, pigeonholes and secret compartments on both sides, at which
one would have either to stand or sit on a very high stool to work. Wu
stood leaning on his stick. It was very still, more so as muffled city
sounds from outside reached us and set our perfumed space in aural
relief, with one's pulse beating a tom-tom, a persistent low percussion.
He stood very still and we watched him there, unmoving at first, in the
usual position of a customer, an anomalous customer without expectation or desire, a dark elegant shape in the shadows backlit by the front
window through which a rhomb shaped beam of dusty amber light
penetrates as if to buttress the unseen sky. Wu was a little stooped, but
not humbled, nor leaning against the edge as he dexterously flipped
open what I couldn't see from where I stood, forgetting to breathe, but
knew to be a quincuncial cloisonné pill box.

I imagine at this moment Wu's eyes widening, his lips parting in
uncharacteristic, purely physiological astonishment as the nitro dis-
solves under his tongue and rushes through him; hear a sigh, see the

settling of his eyelids in keeping with the stabilizing pulse, the resetting of his lips as he turns to approach us, more familiarly cordial now, but still purposeful, an addition to his manner with which I was not familiar.

Father, although you proclaimed not to take him seriously, nor to be interested in him and his odd wares, something of you was captivated. I am sure of it. This was clear from our many discussions. You fretted over this business, but kept a brave face. Nothing, you consistently said, was to be taken seriously outside the riches of Catholicism; and I argued that there is so much in your own church, so marvelously fulfilling are the ways of paradox Martin, which you avoided for the same reason you eschewed Wu. I thought it was clear all those years ago, when I used to compel you to accompany me to his shop, exhort you to allow me just a few minutes there (which I admittedly stretched without excessive concern for your feelings), that the evident discomfort before him and reluctance even to enter his place, proclaimed your instinctual knowledge that he was someone, manifesting something, outside the range of your experience and, alas, your curiosity, something which you were not prepared to reckon with, that teased and undermined complacency. In all fairness, maybe you were simply bored; or maybe from irritation resisted my enthusiasm for what I imagined of him. And yet, perhaps this certain something has, without my gadfly prompting, caught up with you on its own, Martin. Or you with it? I do hope you're still reading.

Martin pushes himself out of the white circle of light into the shadows, away from the desk and two uneven piles of paper over which one of his notebooks lay spread, densely filled with brown ink scratches, his barely decipherable scrawl. He tips the chair back onto two legs, leaning against a bookshelf with his shoulders, staring at his own dark movements in the window. A cat meows between foghorn blows from somewhere outside in the dark; he yawns, momentarily losing his balance, suddenly wide-awake again.

His hand stinks. With the exception of Father Amaro, whose eyes Martin is certain are becoming proportionately brighter as the corruption of his paw worsens, his colleagues, given up offering tactful advice that he should see a doctor, have taken to avoiding him. It is simple to do. He takes his meals alone in his room—Amaro passionately serves him—and, as was his right, had formally absented himself—temporarily as he thought—from his duties. For his part Martin doesn't notice that the others avoid him. His hand doesn't smell abnormal to him any more. Occasionally he catches a whiff, starts aback, gags a little from the pungency; but even so, it seems somehow natural, such is his preoccupation with the testimony of his old friend. The pain has, for the most part, assumed a uniform dullness and become acceptable. What he struggles with at the moment, aside from urgings to murder the unctuous Father Amaro—this morning Martin snatched and raised a long sharp bodkin of a letter opener above the offensively lowered head (Amaro attempting to kiss his bandaged hand)—is his competing fascination and repulsion with the text. An uncharacteristic willfulness to accept his old friend's testimony finally takes the upper hand, as he himself records in his notebooks, adding, rather drolly for him, as Thomas would have been the first to remark, that the upper hand is for the moment the one that does not smell.

Harpies, Father, harpies: grudging, rancorous, under the aegis of my own conscience this time. I've killed two more men. Two men without bitterness toward the thieving dogfish at the end of their lines, nor toward the nagging wife whose voice scolded over their radio as I struck. Decent enough men, probably, and probably satisfied with the way of the world which is natural to many who take the time to look about them—Martin, these mountains, this sea, the sun rising and setting over this extended, this splendid Indian summer. These were sport fisherman innocent of my fate except for my blundering vengeance.

The not so innocent pair that I killed rather neatly in their boat the other night must have been lucky (as it were), chanced on my island. Or so at least I like to think. I've thus far given away no very good hints, except in these pages to you; and one would have to be a very fine seaman to sort the matter out. Heaven knows there are amazing mariners. Superhuman, they can seem: able to read shifting patterns of texture, of tint, identify idiosyncrasies, characteristic variations inherent in an apparently anonymous sea.

Mantled by an apple and sea fragrant fog bank that has still not burned off as I write, I scuttled their ship in the dead of night. All went well. The equipment and two men secure, a network of strong currents to tidy up should the need arise. The inlet is very deep. My remorse lingers through breakfast, still abstract for the most part. There is little consolation in that one of them is at least now free of that shrew whose voice intruded on their calm and so evident pleasure in taking part, in sharing this miracle of place. As I looked on unobserved at their last minutes of quiet affection, their sympathy for living—quite as simple as that—she suddenly wrought such evident grief, despite the twisted smiles and the knowing eyes exchanged. I believe the resentful voice almost broke the spell of my misdirected vengeance, so much did I want to turn the radio off, commiserate with them over a drink.

Oh Father, the smell of ripening apples is delicious. There is a hint, too, of fermenting fruit. I smell it through the fog, the ceiling of which is lowering, streaming above me as if self propelled, no hint of a breeze; and now, the last veils tearing away, here is blue sky and sunshine for another October day. I've so much left to tell you.

Father Amaro taps at the door like a preciously solicitous woodpecker, Martin scribbles in his notebook, smiling. He lets him tap some more. If only Amaro would wander onto Thomas's island, he scrawls after, then scratches it out before rising to unlock the door, considering on the way, as he yawns once and then again several others whom he might like to send there, probably not yet having taken Thomas at his word.

Amaro stands holding a dinner tray. Radiating humility, he stands humbly raising his eyes to Martin with a picture perfect look of piety that to the delight of his mother and disgust of his father he has been able to assume at will since childhood. Martin, peering at him over his bifocals and scratching at the stubble under his chin, hazards to suggest as much. This look, he said, not only reassures those with whom you come into contact that you are a sanctimonious toad, but God himself, who has no difficulty reading it from even so far away as heaven on a cloudy day. Thus Martin offers, bursts into unwholesome laughter as Amaro quickly flinches from eying the manuscript fanned out on the desk that he might look on Father Martin with forgiveness. Martin continues laughing (sign of the Devil), quite beside himself. No offense intended Father Amaro, he manages before another outburst of laughter overcomes him, conscious even as he howls, that his nervous state is not at its best.

Amaro stands holding a tray with dinner, describes in an eager whisper tonight's menu which closes with fresh lemon sorbet and Italian biscuits dipped in dark chocolate. A real treat, Father. Martin flushes—despite himself a little shamed over his treatment of Amaro— and bites the inside of his lip; manages, just, not to give in to more laughter. Contrition flies. His little remorse is overcome by impatience as he watches Amaro tip-toe to his desk with the tray, laying it with very special gentleness to one side of the manuscript and the notebook, his neck twisted by an invisible rope, eyes ricocheting from side to side as he attempts to read the typed sheets and Martin's annotations at the same time.

Martin—somewhat fiendishly, he later considers—gives him time to whet his appetite before seizing him by one of his extra large ears and leading him (Amaro, eyes to Heaven, complacently surrendered to being tugged along) to the door. You must learn not to snoop, Father Amaro. You must resist temptation. You know whose, don't you? It's not becoming, which won't trouble you; but neither is it right in the eyes of God, which you must at least pretend matters some, he added in that especially understanding voice he sometimes takes the trouble to assume for children—budding Satans, as Baudelaire says—suffering from hyper-piety and unoriginal sin, the sort whom he particularly wants to get rid of in the shortest time. Unfortunately his usual matter-of-factness further piques these soul sufferers to try even harder for an extra benediction which Martin is loath to offer; and so he learned to keep his distance, to puff them up with just the sort of encouragement that makes it shameful, if not impossible, for them to ask for more. Tone of voice accomplishes much of this for him. It almost doesn't matter what he says with some; and, God forgive him, he had more than once to resist the temptation to experiment and read from the business section of the local paper in his special voice just to prove it. The assumption of this voice is at the expense of his patience which, when it finally snaps and he finds himself representing a more savage God and startling some poor sinner, requires a self defense; and he would excuse himself, think of his anger as candor pure and simple, honesty before a God who, like a cheating heart in a country and western tune, he cannot help loving still. But how he was tried. Often now he grows impatient in confession. Especially when faced through the fretwork not with the sweet hopefulness and sorrow which the passion of Christ evokes in certain souls, to whom he is quite capable of giving of himself in an attempt to temper their emotion, encourage them with the richness of life, make it possible for them to practically face the world, but with instead an unctuous self-scourger feeding on castigation. At times like these, quite unknown to the self-centered prattler, Martin would feel himself become dangerous.

I know it's not right of me, Father Martin. I know it's bad to snoop. Just as you say, Amaro says as Martin pulls him out of his room and into the dark corridor. I haven't told anyone about your friend. Amaro's face sneers in the shadows. Martin does not see, but he pulls and twists Amaro's ear with all his strength.

Amaro resisted, no, Martin later writes in his diary, he relished his pain until he fainted and collapsed onto the faded oriental runner stretching along the corridor. Only at the second before he fell—rather dramatically, but drama is part of nature as Thomas in his student days was often eager to point out—only at the last moment did he piteously scream and some of the doors along the hallway open. In a moment several priests stand around asking what the matter is; and while bound to be solicitous and certainly curious, trying also not to breathe or stand too close: a black-clad spectacle of alarm as they witness and smell Martin standing over the fallen Amaro whose ear he still pinches and twists between the thumb and forefinger of his good hand.

Martin finally lets go of the ear, offers a courtly nod to the others. Good night, Brothers. Father Amaro is just a man, after all. Let's not judge him; at least not too harshly. Good night, he says without looking at anyone and then, as an afterthought, gives Amaro a solid kick to his ample rear. Father Stephen, who happens to be one of the party, smirks and can't help liking Martin a little more now than before.

Amaro grimaces with something like passion from the blow, stirs dramatically, as if waking from a trance, and slowly stands up. He asks everyone to forgive him in the softest of voices, not missing a chance to exchange eyes with each of them in turn (all of whom—except for Stephen, who looks at him with amused contempt—turn away embarrassed), then slouches off with the sin of the world on his shoulders, which evokes a quiet chorus of God help us, sighs and muttering, some sympathy for Martin, but a note to the Bishop nonetheless.

Father, I don't remember when last I felt so good, all things considered. Instead of the usual four a.m. thralldom to bladder, dark fretting and despair today I opened my eyes at half past six feeling nothing less than cozy: pillows in place (smelling of fresh air and bleach), knees tucked up, quilt under my chin, at truce with the world. There is no fog this morning and lying on my side I stared through the undrawn windows past the near pine and eucalyptus all the way down to the inlet. The sea barely stirring, deep blue, just beginning to lighten with the sky, mirror the granite crags and slopes dense with fir on the shore opposite, its unruffled plates of varying temperatures and currents tethered still to the night. Even kitty appeared content to forego her usual demands for a pre-daybreak meal to stare with me out the window at the dawning of color; at least until I more or less came to my senses and, both startled out of a narcotic spell of complacency, we let appetite have its way with us for yet another day.

Oh Father, when will the killing end? Kitty caught two mice today and brought them most purposefully to me for inspection. I couldn't lie to her. They too were, both of them, innocent; but she meant well, certainly, and I stroked her for well-intentioned effort and she settled squeezing her eyes shut, purring with contrition on my lap. She'll soon get over it though, looked haunted when later she returned to where she'd left them side by side at the foot of my chair on the deck—both quite plump and gray and each with two deep ruby drops to bead the necks of their handsome coats—and found them gone. My favorite pair of ravens (I watched from the window above the kitchen sink) had taken care of the evidence while I prepared lunch and kitty, beside herself, pestered me for anchovies and tuna.

As I sit here writing now, sipping on the last of my deliciously stinky Montrachet (youthful inner thighs, straw, mint, apple, hint of cow pies), the fog starting up the inlet, loon crying, my place is oasal once again. I would like for you to know my place here, if only for an afternoon. It might do you some good, balance some your fits of solemnity and fervor. I am indulging in passing contentment with place and time, this autumn, this island, trying to share with you some moments of good will toward the world (the world and I and not a grudge between us); should you be hurt and angered by my candor, my killing (which I doubt you have yet come to believe or understand), you can (though such bitterness would be unbecoming, Martin) be assured that my pleasure is persistently gouged away for the high relief of Jane's absence.

Flinching, Martin pushes himself away from his desk, realizing that he is digging his finger nails into his palms, leaving red crescent imprints in his good hand, generating charging, throat seizing pain in the other. He gags, swallows back a sudden rise of bitterness; pulling off his glasses dabs at his eyes with the back of his good hand, stares at the tear damp back of his hand and thinks he sees incipient liver spots, thinks he is coming undone, that he doesn't want to let go; thinks all this in words such as these, breathes in deeply, exhales loudly several times, self-consciously reminding himself of a diver about to go under, mumbles, shivers, pulls close over his black suit the oversized burgundy cardigan with mixed buttons and darned elbows, bunching the fraying open front together in his clenched fist. He is no mendicant priest. The sweater once belonged to Thomas, who twenty years ago called him twice to ask if he happened to have picked it up accidentally and taken it away with him.

It is another foggy day. Out on the inlet an incoming freighter is signaling its passage in anxious tenor blasts of its horn; while from the lighthouse the basso profundo sounds with steady, paternal reassurance. Martin's room is comfortable and warm. The electric fire glows. A pot of tea resting on the tray with five butter cookies to the right of the pile of paper is still warm. He drags himself and his chair forward toward the desk again, seizes a fountain pen, holds it poised above his notebook, thinks of driving the nib into the page, imagines the sudden splatter of brown ink over the half-filled blue-lined paper, pictures it taking on the face of Christ smiling as if at a half-funny joke. He scares himself sometimes, imagines Thomas's japery should he be somehow monitoring these thoughts. You can never be too sure, he thinks, adjusts his posture, reflects that he is the one who has become mad. I wouldn't think so then, he considers; and as if to reassure another, smiles; more a grimace really.

Martin gazes out the window, half-watching the fog slouch by, focuses and stares at the crows suddenly arrived out of obscurity, hopping amongst uneven piles of soggy red and yellow leaves, thrills to the sight of a squirrel flying out of the gray to land on the delicate ends of a maple branch where, chattering all the while, it hangs on as the damp wood bows and sea-saws with its weight, Martin touched by the intense little animal that waits for three beats, then dexterously grapples along the still trembling branch until it finds its legs and scrambles away. Twice the telephone rings; no one is there. Martin replaces the receiver. He no longer says hello more than once or bothers to strain for a clue as to the meaning of this.

Resting bent over the manuscript, weighted on his elbows, having reentered the yellow circle of light with another lurch forward atop his chair, he picks up his glasses with his good hand, rests them on the end of his nose and reads some more.

Now Father, it was through a wonderful gentleman whose name must be omitted, the man who best fits for me the Master's description of effortless high civility, that I was first introduced to the possibility of realizing great wealth from my mistaken identity and accomplishments as a geologist. Material wealth, Father: sleepwalker or not, my soul had already struck gold. This gentleman who worked for Intelligence making trouble for Heaven, brought me together with the Shanghai Consortium and the redoubtable Du Yuesheng: ascetic, tall and thin, with terrifying (if legend's to be believed; I kick myself for never remembering to look), inexplicably terrifying feet. In the nick of time, too. The Geology department, excepting the wonderful old dean, was not responding well to my literary and philosophical bent, even when I presented a simplified—and very neat, I must say—equation for first principles which could be followed by an above-average undergraduate. I was a Doctor of Science, they said, not a skirt chasing (really, Father, I am not joking), pipe-dreaming humanist. My tricks, as they called them, with, just for example, Dysprosium (the impervious), finding a way in and out of its illusive complexity; with Lantanium (the hidden), delicately parting the veils of its miraculous accident, its component elements, to provide a glimpse, exhilarating and elegiac both, of elemental mystery; these tricks, they said, were the legerdemain of a carnival barker—one wag couldn't resist calling me a mad dog, behind my back —, a country fair magician's dexterous deception. When I published a prolegomena to my technique for approaching Gaea (purposely leaving her mystery intact, needless to say), I had Seurat's Sideshow reproduced on the cover. Beautiful. Perhaps I was over-evoking the elemental way of paradox, the coincidence of opposites, the distant resolves of dissonance and such like; like a guilty man repeatedly ducking behind the Fifth, you might want to say. Someone did. Well I don't really blame them, on the one hand— that hand again, Father! [Martin's bandaged paw is throbbing here. He has firmly sided with the department in regard to this blasphemer's hermetic, Rosicrucian hocus-pocus]—but when I held the matter, as it were, in the other, well…

Anyway, Father, I sold my telluric secret, the Gaea formula and the Dead Souls, and became very wealthy. Don't even think of judging me, Martin. By their acquisition the Shanghai Consortium, whose business interests tend to be conventional, if not always exactly respectable, claimed not to want to profit from its power, a responsibility arguably beyond the ken of public men and best left to the realm of the imagination, as Du Yuesheng said, motioning to his secretary to hand me the envelope, smiling with his splendid eyes. He was amused, he explained, in an effort not to be an inscrutable Chinaman—his words, honest—and moved as well by the instinctive distancing of truth characteristic of the species, the need to consign such knowledge to the Arts and the mysteries of religion: touching, exhilarating and inutile. An old story, and I confess I was thinking about other things, even praying—you know what I mean—that I would not wake without having first deposited this bank draft stamped with its dreamland series of noughts. What about science? I asked him, pinching myself through the lining of one of my pant pockets; but he was done philosophizing and commanded his secretary to call for the car; a little embarrassed, I imagined, for indulging in the pointless.

So, Father, by making me rich, the Shanghai Consortium, whose criminal organization is the last bastion of independence, of ostensibly free enterprise, effected to keep the secrets of Gaea and the Dead Souls from falling into the hands of the Global Reach. And if Du lied about his intentions with Gaea (which I doubt; as I also doubt anyone's ability to actually realize her mystery and profit from it with impunity), it is still better that there should be some displacement of power, no matter how uneven. Heaven is a domineering bully, a very clever, very heavy fat boy on one end of the teeter-totter; Du's consortium is a quick-witted, dexterous and merciless trickster, if only a trim lad by comparison.

Martin lifts his eyes from the text. He uncaps his pen and holds it poised above the page, pushes his glasses further down toward the end of his nose where they stop against a small blemish; glimpses himself in the window's reflection and suddenly looks around, scanning the cluttered room for the illusive alternative to the word his pen is already tracing in the air above the page. He searches the ceiling for it—playing to the gods—where only the dusty remains of a spider's web waves tiredly at him from one corner; then the bookshelves, from which there is no apparent inclination to do anything other than distract him with the associations inherent in their titles. There is no helping it, he decides, even while imagining Thomas's scorn: sees the lips curl into a grin, the eyes flash with derision. He scribbles the word anyway. Rather he scrawls it angrily, bending his nib, pressing it over and into the last paragraph itself, defacing the neat typing, his first graffiti ever. Later, with a sinking feeling, he wonders if the mad man would ever see this pile of paper again, then feels a little ashamed when he sees that he pressed so hard on the paper that PARANOIA has seeped through into the page underneath.

Oh Father, what a morning it's been. Twice Martin reads the sentence and twice looks away. He had skipped vespers and hardly touched his dinner, having managed only one sand dab, with which he could not help associating—had it been left to thaw too long?—the fingers of his bandaged hand; and more, as if his imagination had sided with Thomas's, he would not touch, even averted his eyes from the Brussels sprouts: unwholesome, flayed little glands, as he saw them, rubbing his eyes with a thumb and forefinger, and aching with obscure anxiety. The mashed potatoes he somehow dented and dug at with a trembling fork, without any further intrusion of unhealthful thought until Father Amaro, having entered the study to take away his tray, predictably encouraged him to eat and assuming a motherly tone, was foolish enough to spear one of the sprouts and try to feed him.

Ears boxed and penitent, Amaro takes the tray away and gently closes the door after himself with a solicitousness that infuriates Martin, who is grimacing from having used his bad hand, and from realizing that he has perversely come to need Amaro, disgusting Father Amaro, just the way he is. The Lord in his wisdom, he quips to himself, and swallows some spit. His face reddens, and he painfully clenches both hands. For a dozen up-tempo heart beats he appears to want to hurl something at the door, his good hand poised and shaking, passing over a stainless steel letter opener, his fountain pen, hesitating over the telephone, his claw retreating back over the desk top without a suitable missile. He exhales noisily, breathes deeply once, and once again, picks up, fumbles, and hooks his glasses over his ears, and returns to the text, color draining from his face except where it has pooled, lingering in the corner of one eye, and at the top of the other, red puddles gathered in the reticules of veins that appear to be straining to hold the weary, weighty eyes themselves in their sockets. Martin is not looking well at all; which, given the opportunity, Thomas would have been the first to tell him, he thinks, having again looked away from the text to stare at himself in a small finger printed shaving mirror that had been lying face down in an open drawer. He puts the mirror away and pushes the drawer in. He clears his throat; is anxious, actually sick with anxiety, and yet curious. He adjusts the lamp. Curious like a bystander, he self-consciously admits to himself, witness to a gruesome accident.

Oh Father, what a morning it has been. But before I tell you of a visitor to my island —she's an extraordinary girl, woman, I should say—let me continue from where I left off with Wu having pulled Jane and me into his shop. Just so you don't imagine that I'm paranoid. That is something that has occurred to you, hasn't it Father? Once or twice, perhaps? Yes it has. Oh Martin, I see you blushing and shifting to and fro from one ample buttock to the other. Don't worry now. Wait until later. Fuck you, Martin whispers, uncaps his pen to write it in the margin before sighing, embarrassed by the impulse, a terrible anxiety roiling in his guts that is beginning to frighten him.

When old Wu finally regained his equilibrium, fitted a cigarette into an amber holder and lighted it with a battered gold Dunhill, drawing heavily on the strong and fragrant tobacco, he approached us, as I said, with a purposefulness, something in his manner with which

I had no familiarity. Standing before us he smiled slightly, and then motioned for us to walk past the dusty clutter: a sentry of blue urns, a frangible reclining Buddha (which Jane liked very much), ancestor portraits, rolled up carpets tied with string and standing on their ends, onwards through a short avenue between stacked cedar chests, three, four and five chests high, around a tall, worn and discolored screen, white with stylized blue bats, to where there was a sitting area.

This was an illuminated circular space dramatically surrounded by darkness, as if stage lit, lighted by a single twisted brass standing lamp violently festooned with curved spikes at its base, and topped with a silken shade that gave off spokes of wine-colored shadows radiating out from a rosy, comfortable circle of light. Tea was brewing in a Brown Betty set on a tray of blonde wood that had had much of its varnish worn off, resting at one end of a low black lacquer table on which three mismatched china cups and saucers of European design stood ready. Passing into the light I flinched, hearing, then glimpsing, I swear, in the deeper shadows beyond, a roly-poly Chinese, doubtless a serving man; but after hearing a door close I neither saw nor heard him again. (Jane later said I was seeing and hearing things.) On either side of the table there was a sprung brown leather couch, scuffed skin burst here and there, and three odd cloth-upholstered easy chairs.

Frowning, Wu settled slowly into the heaviest of the three chairs facing us, we sitting opposite him on a sofa, somehow remaining quiet through our initial bemusement, resisting what was for me an unusual urge to break the silence, make small talk in this interim, some reassuring noise. Martin, the stillness, the suspension: like dreaming that I was dreaming. (Jane, incidentally, was simply intrigued and had felt no such compulsion to speak, or wake, wondering, she later said, how much Wu might let the reclining Buddha go for.)

Smoking elegantly all the while—now I'm certain this was a period of highly charged seconds only—and staring at the coils of blue smoke rising from his slightly trembling cigarette, Wu appeared a grave caricature; yet no less real for seeming so. His form was not as if assumed for the purpose; it was the pattern of it; and no more affected to my eyes than ocean waves in a storm, as those rising before my eyes now as I write: a sea gone dark gray under a lowering sky against which in the middle ground between myself and the water—Martin you should see it—a golden grove of shivering aspen has soaked up all the light. I must carry on. A thing of nature, then, but naturally artful too, Wu now a glyph in my mind's eye, a pictograph of one reluctantly considering how to deliver himself of a matter of great consequence to another while struggling to remain one for whom there is no such thing. He sat staring into the shadows over our heads, sitting well back in an easy chair, left arm lying over his lap, the right poised upright on the armrest, blue smoke uncoiling from a raised hand, the amber holder fitted at the crutch between index and middle fingers, legs crossed twice, first at the knees, then one foot bent further around and propped behind a calf.

Is it, do you think, any wonder that faced with his novel behavior I should have felt an uncharacteristic impulse: to talk about the weather, say, or admire a vase aloud? He smiled, suddenly vulnerable, like a loving father, I thought, the resemblance to my own striking me even at this distance; like a father powerless past a certain point to be of any more assistance beyond his own example. And so I am moved now, in remembrance, by the ultimately helpless love of some parents for their children. So Wu, usually detached, aloof, touched (Jane thought maybe just inconvenienced) by our fates as he might be—bear with me—by that of a dying sparrow. They eat little birds in China, Martin thinks, rubbing his right eye. Thus was Wu's overall empathy with the way of the world particularized by the threat against us. Maybe old Wu was growing soft. It is hard to imagine any good reason for him to be attached to us, as deserving of affection as I believe we were. But I think maybe Wu, excuse the blasphemy Father, was like God—remember Matthew, or your Pope. Alexander, you fool—"who sees with equal eye… A hero perish or a sparrow fall". In any event, he was moved by what he had been asked to tell us, by what he had to see as the inevitable consequences of Heaven's wrath. I'm certain that were it he who possessed the Dead Souls and Gaea formula, himself threatened by a contract to obtain them at any cost, he would have faced it with the stoicism becoming his strength of mind. Whether Buddha, God, or even the Devil himself stands before you, fight to win, he had once said matter-of-factly, smiling inscrutably. (What do you make of the order and emphasis of threats, Father?) Then, however, that afternoon when he pulled us into his shop as if there were such a thing as purpose, he was like a parent anticipating a profound sorrow for a child. Jane later confessed to seeing little difference in Wu's manner, and attributed my understanding of our meeting to conjecture, a vivid imagination, perhaps digestion.

Father Amaro farts loudly and startles himself. He rubs his nose, shivers and looks around, to the left, to the right, peers around the window sill again, pressed between it and the rustling foliage, a wet and prodding laurel bush actively disapproving of his behavior. He peeks through the window of Martin's study, wishing, even praying that he could hear inside—he sees Martin's lips moving; as it happens, Martin is promising himself, aloud, a visit to Wu's tomorrow—or somehow catch a glimpse, even just a page or two, of that text. Oh to see, to hear what is going on and to have worn an extra sweater too.

Martin is trembling. Martin, who for years has not prayed, except professionally, and then with increasing reluctance and only by rote, starts, tentatively at first, to pray again; for himself, for Thomas, is his intention. At first Martin prays as he had done as a child: with unquestionable sincerity. The philosopher, the psychologist, even the theologian all exhausted sleep within him at this moment. Sincere as when himself a child, he prays with devotion, self-admittedly for profit, with self-conscious goodness (eyes peeking at heaven: nota bene Dear Lord, see this lamb, your lamb, oh dearest God, and further my way in the world), and out of profound fear. Genuinely, all the same, Martin calls on God. With helpless devotion and hope he calls to the old Controller. Devotion most intricate, a mixed weave of tangled odds and ends mocked to little purpose by the indifferent or peevish or those with a nose for sniffing out definitive motives, the imagined first causes for the endless range of possibility—the whys and wherefores of the altruist, serial killer, compulsive nose-picker (finger already up to his second knuckle), the laughing, deliciously concupiscent bad girl and other more happy accidents—who pester overworked abstraction for the recipe to this heady, simmering stew, as the young Martin imagined it as a child playing in the kitchen as his mother cooked. An olla podrida populated by appetite, by fabulous dinosaurs that once or twice he got away with tracking over a steaming antediluvian plate—he reconstructed them from model kits contained in boxes with splendidly fearsome illustrations; he worshiped Tyrannosaurus Rex and who would blame him?—and old man God on high, predictably—but no harm in that—threatening just on the other side of a glowing storm cloud; there, outside the kitchen window.

Martin prays for the first time in so many years. In the first reflex, the extended instant tonight, as he straightens up in his chair blinking and biting the inside of his mouth, it is a spontaneous reaction to Thomas's voice; but this barely lasts through the salutation. Addressing God in a whisper his prayer falters. He tips himself slowly forward and slouches over the desk, leans his elbows on the uneven piles of text and covers his eyes with his palms.

This morning—what a morning it's been, Martin—the girl came. The weather, a pounding southwester, had been holding us down, mounted us before the dawn, climbed aboard and stayed on top till after noon. My island, even the ocean (I dare say the fish), my deer, my orchard, all things animate and inanimate, the very rocks, yes, we all resigned like nothing so much as a pinioned bitch; like atavistic kitty here, succumbing while still tensed, butt up and looking askance in compliant yet uneasy anticipation when I playfully wrestle her down and grab her by the scruff. My island covered, straddled and gripped by the neck in a battering, window-shaking chimney-howling rut, all of us pinned down by a massive gray sky, a heavy old Tom holding us fast until after midday. And we all poised. For what? Relief from such apparent purpose, this huffing resolution?

A last blow—I was standing at the door looking out, the fire crackling fragrant apple boughs, the cat scurrying behind me out of the draft, a passing, more tender shake of the pines and eucalyptus, a lighter touch on the now tangled wooden wind chimes and the weather rolled off us. The sky dropped, listless and indifferent. Tension loosed, it sprawled over the island in misty dissolution. We were released—kitty and I both hungry and a little tired—from the demands of atmosphere: the wind now fallen away, clouds hanging from bare branches. It was just weather again, raining steadily, and she appeared as, with something like primitive relief, yet while loving a storm, I was pouring myself a congratulatory whiskey and preparing to raise one to the tempest too. (I drink rather more now than before, Father.) She, rising up from behind the lip of the cliff from the shore below, concentrating in a long bright yellow slicker all the available light as she approached in the midst of the rain and prevailing gray, as in their golden shimmering foliage the now cloud obscured but gently rustling aspens had done the day before. Morpho betrayed by her walk. This Aphrodite, my nemesis?

Martin, meet my new neighbor; my only neighbor, actually, and a distant one at that. She tells me she is hiding at her parents' cottage, a sturdy Cape Cod backed up by several Gary oaks and fronted by a twisted old apple tree (this last a hoary old thing slouching with bright green fruit each September) all set back on a grassy knoll. The house, white with green trim, lights up the dark shore around the point opposite, just across the bay, but hidden from my island. Hiding from what? She hasn't said, exactly. Broad reaching and sensibly flying only the jib of a Dutchman—sleek, fast and low, Martin, you remember, hardly the craft to sail single-handed in a storm—she flew, she says, over the passage between us for a visit, to introduce herself, having wondered forever, she told me, who I might be, confessing to watching me for fascinated hours through a telescope since she arrived the day before yesterday. (And me and a woman years ago.) Fascinating hours, Martin; well, yes, so I should think; but made especially so by rumors, yes please, of my magic—Call me Prospero—from the water taxi man who, she says (not entirely unabashed), tried to get into her pants. Imagine: this made me indignant on her behalf; at least for a minute or two before I sorted through my feelings, gave myself a little pinch. All this as I unwisely—a potential victim of my own sexism, perhaps? Ask the ladies for me, Father—replaced the safety catch (on that old Browning 9mm you remember I fired over your head when you, training for Sports Day, jogged by one summer afternoon—what, twenty years ago?—and you crying like a baby and the police asking questions. The very same old gun, Martin, threatening to fall into my corduroys) and invited her in for tea—her eyes, Father—setting the kettle to boil, leaving the cat to vet her (burying her snout into a tangle of dark blonde hair, sniffing, sniffing), water continuing to pool on the floor beneath her slicker hanging on the coat rack as she calmly talked, damp jeans steaming some, as if we were old friends but for a little bite and nibble of the lip, a little extra tint of color on her cheeks, punctuations of shyness; she, Katya, an intrepid young woman who I might very well have shot (I am perhaps losing my grip and prepared to give up my vigilance; no, no, not yet) taking an engaging short cut through the usual preliminaries between strangers, charming me along the way.

How would you know, Martin (and please, leave your sociological formulae behind), but indulge me anyway: is it biology, is it glandular interest compelling a fertile woman's curiosity in the other women in a man's life? (Somehow it thrills me: Katya must have spent long periods of time staring through the glass that distant summer. I feel a familiar stirring.) Please pay attention, Father, and tell me what, for that matter, is the common impetus behind love? Stop. It couldn't be evolutionary perfection. Just look around you. Yes, consider the whole smelly business, Martin. What do you think, just the work of grubby appetite, a thoughtless parasitical accident of enduring strife for all things, all the selfish spawn…? In what occult genetic code, then, what chemical complementariness, do the preliminary secretions begin to effect that miracle of intoxication that makes poets out of dullards, fools out of poets, and couples out of seeming incompatibles?

In an accident of proximity a sudden wakening: catalysis between a man and a woman; and what appears a means to shared notions of happiness, a bridge by way of a log half-drowned in a choked and teeming pond over to the evident promise of the other shore, let's say, where fresh fragrant berries load the bee-loud glade and birds sing, is suddenly a raging crocodile and you are spending the remainder of your life crying out… Where was I, Martin? With a hard-on, Martin scribbles in the right hand margin, noisily exhaling through his nostrils. Is this curiosity of which I am writing a hormonal compulsion innocent of conscious intent, if of nothing else? Is there chemical competitiveness in a woman betrayed by the momentary dilation of pupils, the flashing of eyes; the adjustments to posture; the occasionally studied casualness in her precociously witty speech, its inadvertent hardening, the false objective tone occasionally punctuating her candor and diffidence, that charming, fine softness in her voice? In the boldness, the focused line of questioning which barely leaves unspoken an almost tangible criticism (biologically third world, where there is less confusion over these matters) along the lines of: Well, here I am, quite able to surround you with issue as she must not have been… And, indeed, no sound of pitter-pattering feet or mewling runs counter to this here, just rain on the roof top, sighs from the chimney, the fire burning and silence; silence after the storm underlining our voices, her sweet laughter which thrills me so. A telling silence, maybe, reverberating from within her fecund rosy womb? After all, how would she know of my children? And I can't understand it, Martin, how could my girls, Jane's babies, have married such dunces?

Do I speculate too wildly about the admiring interest Katya shows in me? Her attention occasionally seasoned with a childish reserve, not quite petulant, evincing competitiveness with my wife, my memory, trying to draw all my attention to herself and the others—oh, Jane—the other characters in my past evoked for contrast with her youthful ripeness, called on to signpost the immediacy of her being, measure her rising power in the world? Or is she just having fun? Think, Martin. Think. A clever, fetching, flirt? Or is that biological imperative at work again? (I may tell you something more; something apropos of Gaea soon.) Am I vainly imagining that her curiosity is another of Nature's tricks that this time I can see through, falsely reassuring myself that my reason will afford me free will? Clever, clever Nature. Katya and I both fooled. I by my self-regarding intelligence and a residue of self-love piqued by flattery, her curiosity, her smile and exchange of eyes, held just another moment longer, then another, before letting them drop; she in thinking there is something interesting in me, that she might put on my knowledge [Zeus now, are we? Martin scrawls above] and the experience be a diversion besides, that it might be a lark (what might she not have seen

through the telescope?). I don't know. The whole a biochemical accident intended now by crafty Nature to fill her belly? Heaven's sinister
plotting? Father? Father! What do you think?

The first thing Martin thinks, and he thought himself odd for
thinking it, is that Thomas is in mortal danger. (After fanning the
thick pile of paper remaining to be read, he resists the temptation to
flip ahead.) Martin jots in the right hand margin: First, flick the safety
catch off that fucking gun and don't take your eyes off the minx for
even an instant. A priestly suggestion? (Women: they bleed, as the
ludic Father Stephen was fond of saying. All of them, and I don't except
my own dear mother, God have mercy on her, all of them daughters
of Eve, wily agents of depravity, the Devil, man's perpetual falling…)
Or that of a captive reader? One might think both; but in the following
minutes, and while acknowledging a growing anxiety over the young
woman, about the improbable threat, the even more improbable value
of the Gaea formula and Heaven's wrath, he succumbs to practicality.
He shakes his head (play acting again), as if to rid himself of such ideas
and succeeds in activating his resident migraine. Thomas, he tells himself without conviction and while painfully tugging without success
on a long white hair that curls out of his right ear, is mad. Thus Martin
reasons with himself and searches his desk drawers for aspirin. His
headache spreads. Teary-eyed, indignant and anxious, his knees aching
with that helpless straining that with increasing regularity keeps him
from the sweet respite of dreamless sleep, he catches himself wishing
he could call Jane, telephone her, tell her what that bastard Thomas is
up to. He flips the page and reads on.

All this said, Martin, is there any good reason why I shouldn't have
some fun? (Wouldn't you like to tell on me, I'll bet? Does heresy tempt
you at such moments? Would you, Martin, be a necromancer if you
could, make the damned long-distance call and tell my dear Jane on
me? Fool, do you think she'd begrudge me this?) And I wonder, could

such a lovely young woman allow herself to effect such a contract with Heaven? Of course. Still prone to idealize, yes I am. If Katya is innocent of Heaven, she is herself in danger; can be made to play into Heaven's design, perhaps already a pawn moved close to force my hand. What would I be willing to do? They already have my Queen. Maybe, maybe.)

So, Father, maybe I'd not make such a good spy. Maybe my defenses are too easily penetrated. She's coming back tomorrow, weather permitting (the barometer's rising); we're going to go sailing together; a fall sail; a hint still of Indian summer. It's perfection here.

I just walked her down to the dock, she in her yellow slicker generously laughing at my foolishness. The wind is steady out of the west, the sea rippled, perfect for a broad reach back to her cottage. The cloud cover is high and there are chinks of blue in the west. I was reluctant, like a boy Martin, to cast off the Dutchman. The tide slowly took her out and she raised the main and jib both; with little fuss managed smartly to go about and in good trim sail toward her shore. I waved twice without her seeing. Then, just as my hand dropped to my side, she looked back over her shoulder, waved once, and quickly turned away.

Kitty batted my ankles and ran up the rock incline before me. (Now at my desk, she weaves herself between them and mews for her dinner; as if she hasn't eaten for days. You never much liked cats, did you Father.) It will soon be the happy hour. I think I'll move it up some, maybe the exigent cat's meal too, as soon as I finish this bit. Martin, the breeze is sweet with evergreen, rain and fallen apples. My back is only a little stiff. There is a hint in this delicious air of fermenting fruit, above all, the west wind fresh with scents of sea and sky playing me a sad melody on the chimes. It's a wonderful afternoon. Tomorrow should be fine. You know, Father, at times like this I am not sure I ever want to die. Tricked again.

Father Martin's cheeks burn. He is standing before his desk still wearing an oversized charcoal wool overcoat and a brown fedora with the rim turned up all around. With his good hand he continues to scrunch a thin brown paper bag that contains half a dozen scribblers he does not need; considers then that he might let them drop now that he is home again, for several minutes already. He kicks them under his desk as they hit the floor, and stares out the window at another foggy day. His bad hand, the bandage of which he ought to change every day just so as not to sully himself, the furniture, the once pristine manuscript with its endless suppuration, is especially ripe this afternoon. Even he feels queasy. It smells so that it might send Father Amaro into an ecstasy with no return. He resolves to experiment later. His eyes focus momentarily on a boy, running, clad in a blue duffel coat and gray flannels, chased by some phantom, a red knapsack bouncing on his back, running, slipping over the lawn in and out of the fog, finally disappearing. Martin looks with dull expectation to see who or what will follow. His eyes glaze over once again.

He shivers. A pair of middle-aged customers at Wu's did not conceal their disgust, practically ran from the shop normally smelling of incense and old cedar. That doesn't bother him. Martin glances down at his filthy bandaged hand and wonders if he will survive the reading of Thomas's confession and feels another rush of shame and fear. He is mumbling to himself. Father Amaro cannot make out a word of it.

An hour after his visit to Wu's shop, ostensibly to buy more oilskin notebooks he will never use, he remains flushed and nervous; still talking to himself; for the most part not aloud; and Father Amaro, his nostrils twitching, has snuck off in a sulk, given up his vigilance for the time being.

Martin has removed his coat and hat, and sits leaning on his elbows in his usual place behind the cluttered desk. He has switched on the goose-necked lamp and bent it over the pile of paper, but can't bring himself to read just yet. He still sees Wu in his mind's eye. Wu for the most part standing motionless, as is his manner, neatly dressed as ever, smoking a cigarette fixed in an amber holder, standing behind the tall ebony escritoire that doubles as a counter and from which—the moment the other customers, hissing indignant whispers, had closed the shop door, the green enameled door with a suggestive fissure running top to bottom behind them—he drew forth without being asked the no longer manufactured French cahiers that Martin has bought from him for so long.

Wu continued to stand still, moving only to draw on his cigarette. He looked past Martin, unnerving him as usual—a grown man and a priest, he reflected and flushed even more—without showing any signs of recognition beyond the sudden appearance of the cahiers. Other than an initial flaring of his nostrils, perhaps, and the greater frequency with which he inhaled from his perfumed cigarette, this was normal. But in fact he had a fuller range of relations, as Martin knew. His manner not limited to mysterious inscrutability, the aloofness of Cathay. Quite the opposite had been his way with Thomas, for example. Between Thomas and Wu there had been an engaging tension of nothing less than affection. Martin imagined a bond stretching between them, imagined even that, should he have tried to step or pass his hand between them, there would be a tangible resistance. This evokes an obscure jealousy in the hapless Martin who, whenever he had been cajoled into visiting the store with Thomas, had wanted nothing so much as to leave as soon as possible; and later, when on his own initiative he entered the shop, certainly as much for a test of strength as for the favored notebooks, he dared only the speediest of transactions, which without exception left him feeling foolish, clutching half a dozen in a brown paper bag and hurrying away through the crowded Chinatown, piggybacking some vague and nagging complicity. He had resolved, for his own peace of mind, to change all that today, imagining that he could dispose of the responsibility for taking Thomas seriously just like that.

He spoke of Thomas, a summation of what he had said of Wu, and concentrated on watching for a sign, desiring by this confrontation to elicit a reaction, anything to hang on to, that he might be better able to believe his friend. He willed himself not to shrink from the handsome old man's dark eyes, and never flinched. Only as Martin gathered up the bag of notebooks did Wu noticeably respond to something. With surprise and a touching rush of hope, Martin imagined that he had got through to him, saw that the hand in which the old man held his cigarette trembled, drew a little strength, stared with tactless curiosity and hope, but lost his imagined advantage and—as if it were any of his business—started looking around for an ashtray as Wu lay his cigarette onto the perfect enamel top; lying it down, moreover, without apparent concern as it slowly began to burn a lengthening matte finish hemisphere into the polish, the dullness appearing to spill from the lighted end like breath blown over glass, spreading across the shiny surface while the old man reached into his cardigan for a tiny cloisonné box. From it, the trembling but still dexterous Wu took a small white pill between his thumb and long forefinger and placed it under his tongue; Martin, increasingly helpless and spellbound by the unnerving metamorphosis: Wu's eyes wide, nostrils flared and mouth agape, an expression of ultimate horror. Martin would fuss with the door to his car ruing the recurring image of Wu picking up his cigarette after as if nothing had happened, with no apparent concern—and no wonder: the moment the holder was lifted from the black mirror surface, the growing genie retreated into the cigarette without leaving a trace—resuming his tolerant, serene gaze, quite himself again.

An hour later, with still burning cheeks, Martin sorts through his encounter. Wu's affectation, on direct questioning, of not understanding English sufficiently well, and Martin's subsequent deployment of a vaguely Chinese-sounding pidgin English. The shame, the shame! And if Thomas (the thought of whom has become inseparable from his conscience) were somehow to hear of it…

Father, I am having a restive night and poured myself whiskey, smoky, delicious; am at my desk again. On my island I am getting used to going to bed early. Typically I fall asleep by ten o'clock, make one or two concessions to my bladder and rise at dawn after a quick oneiric review. Tonight I started awake at one, and after an increasingly helpless half hour, have given up trying to sleep. Until this night I have found that my condition is at its least insistent here. Why do I imagine you looking daft and scratching your balding pate? My condition, Martin: the sensation that I am always dreaming (even now as I write, Father, accompanied by myself on this side of a dark night, looking back from the glass of the undrawn window, accompanied by the hoots of a pair of old Gray owls, the male with one crippled talon, hunting together still; and by the slightly stirring upper boughs of the fir trees.) I agree: one would think that after half a lifetime I, who, provided I'm not lying to you or simply stretching a hoary conceit, ought to accept the acknowledged difference between sleeping and waking reality.

People can have the same effect on me as place. When I was with Jane's mother, especially during that time we drove to Las Vegas together to play blackjack—and Jane recovering in Davos, insisting that she do so alone, having recurring dreams, she later told me, of wandering through the snow high in the mountains, wearing only her flannel night gown and my green gum boots, hearing my voice calling her from somewhere in the white—then, too, I experienced a diminished urgency to distinguish between waking and sleeping, to ask myself such questions. (The questions of idle minds, Father, the more I think of it.)

You never took the opportunity to enjoy Jane's mom. You might have learned something, Martin. While naturally candid about what did and did not bore her, something that could take getting used to, she would as readily accept the reality of the non-ordinary as the ordinary, the validity, if not the same pleasure, from a commonplace, wild or brilliant idea, tolerate the endless range of personality quirks and, depending on the degree of imposition or tactlessness, endure even the more obviously desperate lies from which we take our bearings. She would, with a somehow unmannered nonchalance, which yet did not preclude expressions of wonder, appreciation and silliness, as easily accept the sight of a young pterodactyl flying by, collared with a sixteenth century ruff, as acknowledge a common courtesy, a How are you? All things, however they might manifest themselves, were all right, everything was permitted (her sex life, as I was to learn on our trip to Las Vegas, had been particularly rich), as long as it did not overly impose itself on her, harm someone inordinately, or insist on its primacy. Not for her that certainty of the second rate.

So tonight it begins again in earnest. I pinch myself, am dreaming still: asleep, awake. Am I to have no easy rhythms, never be complacent, coaxed easefully along by sun and moon, tides, season, that larger measure so perfect this year, every year? Martin, listen, the migrating geese are passing overhead. Where you are too, I'm sure. They are a little late this year. (My father, dead so long now. His smile…) It must be almost morning.

So the young woman, this Katya, has spurred me out of any semblance of complacency. Into what? Surely not into a prolonged fit of idle questioning. I have other ideas, am not succumbing to obsession, I assure you; even should I dwell sometimes overly long on whether I wake or sleep, on the whys and wherefores of Gaea, or Heaven's malign persecution of me. Mine is a strange complacency from which to waken, what? One that includes murder, Father. Have you come to accept what I say? That I strive to hold out on Heaven, guard the Dead Souls, Gaea's secret, while Heaven continues to try to wound me, force my hand. I will take my revenge. Jane, with whom I should be growing old… Fortune keep me from killing more innocents.

I could have killed Katya, Father. What if she had been a boy? My genes are so territorial, so primitive. What if she had motored to my island, rather than—a splendid gesture, made to order for me—sailing over in fierce weather, and in a Flying Dutchman yet? Is there design here somewhere, do you think? What if she had not been so charming, so attractive? How much of what I have come to love and appreciate over the years will I see or imagine in her? But even so, I sit here now with a gun on the table, with the safety catch off, Father, my whiskey almost gone.

The loon is calling. I'm beginning to see color outside, beyond my tired reflection. I just looked down at my papers and for a moment had a rush of disorientation. Very much as strong as that time I ran from the family house, tripping out onto the boulevard on that windy afternoon; if now without a trace of the fear, disoriented all the same, so much so that I really must ask myself, am I dreaming? Of course I am, ninny. But I did write this; see for yourself; and the cat is stirring and I am tired, a little drunk and hungry, too.

I am surprised, Martin, surprised and admittedly happy (happy?) to be alive. I must have been more concerned than I let on, even to myself. How else explain my relief, my joy even, to be sitting at my desk and watching the sun go down with no hint, yet, of any murderous design on Katya's part. [Trumped by your dick, you fool, Martin scribbles in the margin.] Foolish is how I feel, and it seems right. It is foolish to feel so gay. Don't think I don't know what's happening; for all that I play the maumet jigging to Nature's tugs. I'll blame it on the day, at first, and later become more candid. Even you must see through me by now, Martin. I who extol solitude (to a point, to a point) must have been so lonely for company. Feminine company; and particularly for that delight told in laughter that has always meant so much to me.

Martin, as predicted, it was a fine autumn day. The good it might do you, you old fool. If only you knew: fermented apples, sweet-smelling broom, a fall marbled with unseasonal warmth. The inlet cat-pawed by playful zephyrs chasing this way and that; aspens scraping lightly, shimmering gold at the young Danae standing there. Warm and cold air interlard, I walked through alternate temperatures, down the trail toward the dock. A fog bank hung in the distant west. Katya hallooed and then looked out to sea, stood at attention almost, holding the bowline in one hand, the Dutchman's sails luffing, lightly keeping time as the hull gently beat against the tires on the dock. She watched me descend, smiling, looking away, shy at first (I was too; I'm not joking). She wore a man's heavy, cream-colored sweater and rolled up khakis; tapered, shapely ankles bare, blue boaters on her feet; hair tied back— hint of roots—with black ribbon. She stowed my picnic basket and we set out tentatively, talking about the day. I crewed at first; and by the time we were halfway into the inlet and pointing out to open water, my family of whales was accompanying us over the godly sea.

The orcas glistening black and white, snorting, squealing with what I wish to understand as pleasure (allow me a few pathetic fallacies, Father) as they broached a deep green sea, ploughing through a rolling furrow of kelp (and wasn't that a life jacket, and there, three familiar looking seat cushions, repeatedly tossed over in their wake?); the whales eying us again and again. Surely they can be allowed to experience pleasure, Martin. Why do you mistrust nature so? Was it something in your childhood? Your diet? [Piss off, you pagan shit-head. Drunk on vanity and hormones. Mid-life crisis. This in brown ink, directly over the text, followed by a note in the margin, illegible, and a pale spot of blood. What penitence, what bleak, doubtful and unfashionable theology, envy of Job or vision of Francis sucking lepers' pus, keeps him from seeing a doctor? He has even ignored a letter from his vacationing holiness the Bishop commanding him to see to it.] The pod of five, four adults and a calf, playing within a stone's throw as we sailed; the girl murmuring softly, her pony tail swaying from side to side over her shoulders, asking me to take the helm as she looked on, following them with her eyes until they broke away, disappeared in the glare of white sea and noonday sun.

I steered through the soft haze far into the open straight, beating into the warm west wind; jinked before a rusty, Orient-bound freighter that lifted us on its bow wave as its crew hollered; reaching for a small island on the lee of mine where finally we glided, sails barely luffing, into a mirror calm cove, scraped over pebbled shallows, gently coming to rest on the beach.

Somehow I caught myself, Father, becoming conscious of the changing nature of my relations with the girl, the tenor of our flirtation; and in simulation of long sought-for wakefulness, half woke, deflecting Nature before it was too late, dreaming still. I felt it in my belly, didn't much want to interfere. The movement toward wholeness, coercion of flesh, compulsive disregard for consequences. From teasing high spirits, that titillation of complimentary badinage and held glances, to the ineluctable embrace, I caught myself, Martin, deferred for just a little, I should like to think. This, as I was refilling our glasses, lean-ing into the charged air between us, smelling her, the sea, salty weed along the tidemark as it lay drying, Katya matching me glass for glass as we drank a fragrant Chinon. Considered restraint is worth some-thing after all, Martin, wouldn't you agree? Exactly. Years of regret for missed opportunities. Sweetly aching, I saw it in her eyes too (oh yes I did, Martin); saw that I could kiss her should I lean forward (how I wanted to tug her pony tail, taste her mouth), saw the acquiescence in the slight movements of her face tilting toward mine, trembling lips (full and rosy, without paint) about to speak (ask my age); more, heard the resonance of desire (unbelievers: there is such a thing) before she would say those words (she did not) from which there could be no simple avoidance, rather an honor-bound kiss—what else under the circumstances?—and another, and managed smoothly to lean over the roast chicken to carve her another side instead. I will kiss her. Don't be surprised, Father, but I should say that my decision was motivated not by any moral enlightenment; necessitated rather by the remains of my will to live. The sound of movement over the rocky beach coming from the other side of a small outcrop of stones, and the slipping down my pants of your favorite 9mm loosely jammed between my belt and coccyx, too low now for easy access. I looked past the girl, toward the sound, resisted pulling out the gun—can you imagine?—and then turned back to her. I thought—am becoming paranoid, Father [!!! in brown ink]—I thought I saw her slipping something into my wine.

It is now hours later—there goes the sun, Martin—and I feel well; a little tired but still quite alive. She is in the shower, and staying for dinner. Why not? She's alone, after all.

The intruder was an otter, not a Heaven-sent assassin after all. Long whiskered and slick, he peeked over the outcrop, only his sleek head visible, stretching his neck to take in the sight: the girl and I sitting on an old Moroccan blanket with our picnic spread between us: cold roast chicken, long green beans in vinaigrette and roasted potatoes prepared by me the night before. There was a smelly, melted Vacherin, green apples and two bottles of wine. He had little time for envy. Katya turned around and he was gone, to appear a quarter of an hour later swimming in our little bay, still curious, neck stretched far out of the water, until his mate swam up to him and the two, sinewy as water snakes, wrestled enviably.

Boldly, or in all innocence, Katya manages to slip by my body-guard, a detachment stationed around my life with Jane that I armor with generalities and ellipses, feigning candor with a few specifics and a friendly but matter-of-fact tone of voice. Somehow I feel less need to hoard special memories from her, protect myself from such a young woman. See how Nature fools me, sneaking past my scruples, gift-wrapped in youth and charm, sicking serpents on my Laocoön.

We had lain at odds on our sides, facing one another, resting on our elbows. Drinking from the second bottle of wine, we nibbled from browning wedges of tart apples and gobs of smelly cheese. Thus we loitered with intent and deepening affinities.

With wine-induced logic, I mention Heaven, watch for a sign. There is none. She wonders aloud if she's missed a joke. So I briefly explain this soubriquet for the Global Reach, wishing I hadn't started on it, tell her a little about the conglomerate's malign power, leaving out any other value judgments, for the most part, avoiding altogether any hint about murderous Heaven's responsibility for Jane's injury, her death, the theft of my life.

A vexed Martin can't help himself from scribbling over the manuscript: Yes, you self-pitying, delusional fool, you really lost your life, but not as you pretend. Now suffer, as I do your manipulated confession, the cheap irony of your situation. Good God: basking in the sun with a young woman, charged with shameless lust and the manipulation of your loss, both of which you boastfully exhibit here, imagining envy and sympathy as your due, both of which you feed on, and still blaming Heaven. And what, Thomas? The whole a pathetic waking dream, passing time as you suffer alone for your selfishness, imagining grand plots against you and that you possess a secret? Blasphemer. Quoting from the Psalms in your opening. In your hands the deep places of the earth, Thomas? No. Geomancy in a handful of dust, you fool? Then a large blot of brown ink. Vile stains tint the paper here, a shakily penciled "No" after all his contrary points.

Father Martin relieves himself of his fury and, with some contrition, has a little cry, sits by the window staring into the night until Amaro brings him dinner. Martin doesn't stir the whole time he is there, even when the latter kisses his repulsive bandage, instinctively flinching after from the expected blow, this time withheld. Martin pretends not to hear that two men had been to see him while he was out trying to provoke Wu and have promised to return the next day. Amaro places the card they left with him on the dinner tray (hanger steak, greens, and a carafe of Côtes du Rhône). That it has the name of a legal firm and an embossed solar system on it, with prominence of size by way of perspective given to the Earth—the international mark of Heaven, or the Global Reach—is not of itself significant. The Global Reach is what its name implies. There remains little not under its aegis (why hedge: nothing at all… maybe brats selling lemonade on suburban lawns) with one rumored exception—what is one to believe?—being the extraordinary, ruthless, ingenious, Shanghai Consortium. (Superlatives covering the whole amoral range of Du Yuesheng's operations come easily).

Even with conspiracy theories linking the Vatican to Heaven, Martin can think of no reason for the men's visit other than his unexpected contact with Thomas, the exigent confession pinning him down, he feels, like some leering incubus squatting on his chest, come as if from nowhere. I didn't want this, he says aloud. Amaro's ears prick up out in the hall. There is no freedom from the past. This when, after so many years trying to forget him, Martin's memory of Thomas and Jane had, for more than a decade now, finally subsided into a dull ache; and Martin expecting the odds-on inevitable (imagining his due for the two dollar bet of just carrying on) that he should be left to his small tasks, grow old and die. But no such luck. Thomas's nagging existence again, and the trouble it brings in its wake. Words are dangerous, as his Jewish friend, the unrealized cantor, never tired of reminding him; Martin thrilled and afraid some by the rich idea of this, not so much consciously understood but acceded to with the conviction of his instinct.

Martin will prepare for the visit. His hand is throbbing, the bandage repellent, stinking and soaked through in many places. He was going to change it tonight, but—smiling shyly—decides it may come in handy tomorrow. He trembles with excitement at his inadvertent entanglement with this story; considers if he isn't going mad. A manageable mental illness, he wrote in his notebook, contrived to attract with compulsive regularity the attention of one's friends, other people in general; of a potentially unmanageable kind was that which aspired to attract the attention of God. He was trying to do neither, he told himself with conviction, imagining Thomas japing at him for this. He ponders irrational things, mystic correspondences. Fevered and touched by his infection, he is feeling a devil-may-care courage. Dinner grows cold. He pours a glass of wine and drinks it down, feels exceptional that he has been trusted with this text, suspends for a few pleasant moments his doubts about Thomas. It feels good. There must be something more to it than confession, he imagines. He feels allied by tenderness, by friendship, considers, not for the first time, if he shouldn't flip forward. What a deontological dilemma he is in, Martin thinks, laughs and blushes at his self-conscious delirium. He ignores the ringing telephone that Amaro, rubbing his hands together out in the dark hallway, is beside himself wanting him to answer.

We packed up the picnic, and took a walk. As we were returning from exploring the south end of Little Darcy [Father Martin's skin prickles all over; he feels a rush of nausea; his bowels urge him away from the desk, but he is circling the name round and round, bleeding, ploughing into the surrounding words with brown ink...], Katya fingering a conch she had found, an Otter flew over us (a type of sea plane,

Martin) and then circled the little island repeatedly; too many times and too low. It disturbed the bald eagle that had gazed on us throughout lunch. He set off and glided back to my island after a few cranky flaps of his wings. I wished at the time that Katya hadn't waved. Two men in addition to the pilot. It is true that this haunted place is for sale. (Haunted by the ghost of an abandoned Chinese mariner, Wah Ling, a Pacific Northwest Philoctetes I've been told, a revenant who suffers a noisome and unhealable injury to some part of himself; wounded by the enraged captain of his merchant ship after having inspired, with some enchantment involving three ivory balls, the fascinated interest of the captain's young daughter who was en route to a convent in San Francisco). [Martin pauses here and rubs his eyes, flexes his nostrils.] For sale by a friend of mine, in fact, who has put his back out worrying that this story and a mysterious stink on the southeast side, occurring, he insists, only when he is showing the island to prospective buyers, will undo him. Nonetheless, Father, there was something not quite right about that airplane. If I'd had a Stinger missile I think I would have used it and done my best to explain things to Katya after.

An evil power; a worrisome airplane; a resisted embrace: what must she have thought? Either I have lasting reserves of charm or am marked with some purpose independent of my behavior and the girl's forbearance. I kept my eyes on the plane, Father, twice while she was speaking. I apologized, of course. She smiled. With expectation, with continued faith in something more? With better manners than mine?

The plane mercifully gone and my mouth bitter and dry. We reach for the wine bottle protruding from the packed basket together and both smile. I pour. She drinks first, looking into my eyes and then down. (Antidotes? Don't be silly. Well, maybe.) The wine is good; and I don't taste anything odd. My mouth is probably dry from nerves. The sound of the Otter's engine faded and a resonant silence, a palpable stillness, rushed in to take its place. This and the upbeat accompaniment of susurrant waves, sounding as if something new, somehow only just begun. There is anticipation in their rhythm. They lap at the shoreline, a percussion of stones drawn out after each lick. A line of Surf Scoters mournfully whistling and diving for fish on the tide. Terns crying, circling just beyond the Dutchman. I took her hand and squeezed; she squeezed back. She half turned to me, cheeks pink with wine, shapely brows full and arched. If there is art there I can't quite tell. The blue eyes are bold, the nose straight with a tiny hump on the bridge, nostrils flaring slightly. Her mouth opens then closes in a smile. She knows a secret; knows how to lead the dance with patience, with sustained good humor. Anywhere, I'm sure. It was getting late. There was a ring around the sun. We headed back to the Dutchman holding hands, crunching over the small pebbles and shell fragments.

We set sail. I am at the helm and Katya beside me. Before long, running wing and wing along the windward side of the island, we passed a deer, a young buck swimming toward the mainland, only his head showing, snout up, nostrils flared and huffing, a four point rack tilted above the water, desperately working legs beneath the surface chop. Suddenly the Otter was returning, the sound unmistakable, flying out of the sun, invisible until almost on top of us and I—fool—reached behind me to my belt and stayed fixed like that, gripping my gun (the good it would do me), straying off course which sent the boom swinging toward us. I apparently live to tell the story. I apologized, waived any flip comment on my interest in aviation, or lingering combat trauma. Did I detect impatience over what she may have considered an already full compliment of quirks and digressions? Something of a moue—so lovely—as she looked down at her hands? I wouldn't blame her. We reset the sails.

She sounds as though she should almost be finished in the bathroom. She will make herself quite at home; has borrowed a white dress shirt,

picked a custom Charvet yet. I can hear her brushing her teeth and—
listen to me going on, Father—I want to taste her, use the brush right
after. I just might, too, normally so fastidious that if someone even looks
at my toothbrush… I'm only half joking. She has insisted on cooking
tonight. It has been a long time since a woman prepared a meal for me;
but I am troubled. What sense is there in my becoming involved with
a young woman, with anyone? In my circumstances, Father… and yet
I am reluctant to send her away, to make those excuses betrayed from
the start by too earnest an attempt not to wound; and reluctant myself
to face the inevitable regret. If she is nothing other than a charming
and beautiful young woman with an adventurous disposition, she is
running the risk of being used against me. What will stop me from
letting things run on, Father? What has ever stopped me but inconve-
nience and even that not always. There is moral failure here. She is at
risk. It is not likely that I'll send her away.

It is late, nearly two in the morning. Through the dark stillness, from
the inlet a mile away, the fathoms deep resonance of slow turning
screws from a harbor-bound ship drums through the night. Otherwise
it is quiet, except for the occasional hissing and humming of tires from
passing cars, rarely the sound of their engines. They speed by along the
wet boulevard, heralded out of the distance, immediate for a moment,
then trailing an audible tail, sound traces diminishing into the silence.
It is so quiet that one can hear, well beyond the immediate evergreens
and oaks and the avenue of maples, even the regulated clicks of the
traffic lights administering the zebra crossing a block away. Mr. Walker
stalking on, stalking on, never free from the inevitable threat of Hand.

Martin sits at his desk for many hours now, long since having
stopped reading the manuscript and staring at the detailed chart,
unrolled and crumpled before him, torn some, and hanging over one
side. Propped up on an elbow, he slouches over the map, his head

held up, it seems, by a self-inflicted punch fixed to his right cheek. He appears to be looking at himself, the right side of his tired face pushed up into folds, in the viridescent reflection on the undrawn window. His other hand lies resting and leaking over the Gulf Islands. X marks the spot, a circle holds in Little Darcy.

In the hallway just outside, Father Amaro lies snoring, uncomfortably slumped against the door, apparently asleep; although against this evidence his oversized ear is still pressed to the keyhole as if listening for the telltale muttering from within that he has strained to hear throughout the night; Martin periodically talking to himself and to Thomas until an hour or so ago. Amaro is dreaming, certainly. His eyeballs ricochet beneath bulging lids like panic-stricken bugs. He has fallen asleep just knowing there is something happening on the other side.

Martin sleeps through the raucous early morning gathering of crows outside his window, through the matinals that he would not have attended anyway. Usually awake by at least the hour before dawn, like Thomas in fact, and no matter what the night before, this morning he sleeps on and on, lost in a deep and fevered sleep well into the morning, later than ever before, to be wakened by Amaro's tentative but unrelenting knocking at half past ten. There is an unscheduled visitor in the lounge waiting to see him.

Father Martin, Amaro hymns, there is someone here to see you. Amaro repeatedly calls out the words in his characteristically breathless, sing-song way between two sets of annoyingly regulated taps, three staccato knuckle raps to a set. He calls through the door against which he presses his nose and brushes his lips, tasting the varnish after each interval of knocking and next to which he had some few hours earlier been kicked awake by Father Stephen, who had himself evidently dozed off in the library. Amaro continues pleading news of the visitation until Martin staggers up fully clothed from his settee and lurches, coughing, toward the door. Amaro is certain he hears Martin say, in the moment before gasping for air and succumbing to a coughing fit, I have found you.

Father Amaro gasps theatrically, raises his hand to his mouth, affects surprise at the sudden opening of the door, genuinely aghast at the sight of Martin, sallow faced, disheveled, in a half-sleeping rage. As if to strike, Martin raises his good hand, by now almost a reflex action whenever confronted by Father Amaro. Inhaling deeply, Amaro closes his eyes and shivers, jumps when the door suddenly slams in his face. He's Chinese, Amaro special pleads through the door, unable to leave his curiosity unsatisfied without a struggle. A moment later he hears Martin grumble that he will see the visitor in fifteen minutes, as soon as he has washed up some. Delighted, Amaro scurries down the hallway to deliver the message and fix tea and biscuits. If I time it right, he thinks to himself, staring at his wristwatch, struggling with calculations for an opportune service.

Martin undresses and steps into the shower. Knocking his bad hand, a dying hand, against a chrome faucet as he turns into the rushing water, he stands within the blue tiled stall without moving, rigid, barrel-chested, the limbs handsome, traced beneath the sagging flesh with lineaments of former strength, the naturally athletic, with aging, somehow touching, masculine presence, anguish goading him to noble posture, modeling ten years before the walls of Troy, ten years getting home, ten more after that, this naked body performing agony, tensed, gasping in pain, a grimacing mouth cursing the world with a long groan. He promises himself to find some strong painkillers. No more senseless qualms. The codeine tablets are no longer effective. He starts to wake from the pain (thinking of Thomas's conceit), positions his head directly beneath the jet of hot water nervously speculating on the visitor waiting for him; imagining, then discounting, then imagining again that it could only be Wu himself. But how? He tries to think of any other Chinese who would call on him without an appointment. No one. His hand throbs. He unravels the yellow and pink stained bandage and stares at the jellied paw.

He manages to wrap it with fresh gauze; considered there to be no point in worrying about the smell. He doesn't bother shaving, but brushed his teeth and changed his linen and put on a fresh shirt and collar; gave in after a second thought and glance at the pile of stained and noisome clothing crumpled on the bathroom floor, and dressed in his other black suit. He stands up straight. What have you got me into, Thomas? he whispers, runs a comb through his thinning dark hair, examining himself for the first time in days, letting himself, for an instant, be moved by the handsome traces still visible beneath the patina of spreading infection and despair.

He shivers, remembers that he has left the manuscript and, more telling, the marked chart on his desk. He has no faith in these locked doors. The only privacy he can count on is within the one lockable drawer in the heavy blonde oak office desk to which he has the only key. To breach this drawer, emptied a week ago to accommodate the importunate pages, would require a bold commitment to snooping; a patience, a skill for picking locks, or the nerve for jimmying which he could not imagine Amaro, as devoted a busybody as he is, to possess. He shook away a feeling that locks were as nothing here, and Amaro of no account. Nothing to Heaven, he thinks, jingling the key in his good hand. His stomach ruffles with anxiety: that now he is actively party to Thomas's paranoia. But there is something stronger at work in him, something quickening the harried Martin to actively contend, to revive neglected and long-dormant skills. Martin steps round the corner into his study. There is Amaro, busily trimming the laurel hedge just outside the window.

There Amaro stands, vexed and muttering that the window proved to be securely fixed, startled by the sudden appearance of Martin now gesturing behind him at the sunshine, the first for many days, talking away as if there were no window between them. Martin is masked with a straight face, delighting, nonetheless, that Amaro can look so stupid. He stares through him now, ignores him altogether. First one half, then the other, he draws the heavy curtains and returns to his desk, passing through wine-dark shadows divided by a thin tendril of pale light frantic with motes. He locks away the chart and confession and stands looking at the beam of living sunshine. He is stirred: physically, he imagines, and mentally too. Which was first, he laughs to himself? Will, he calls it; eschewing further speculation lest he break the spell of this new life he feels, needs. It is what Thomas calls animal pride, he remembers, before walking back into the bathroom to stare at himself. He could not bear to go on, he thinks, if it left him now, this new life. He stands before the mirror, his back straight, and stares. He is quickened still. He will ask for leave. He will take it whether it is granted or not. He is taking a trip.

Martin will continue reading Thomas on the way. He will find this island just to the northwest of the ghost Wah Ling's Little Darcy, the unnamed mass half severed by a deep inlet and showing three steep elevations on the map that he calls his. He is going to find Thomas.

Martin sits alone by a window. He had shown no sign of deliberation, seemed to know of a certain bench in the lounge on the upper deck of the ferry and made straight for it even though he had never been on this or any other ferry before today. The lounge is almost empty, apart from a robust Native woman, handsome in a long green oilskin slicker, sitting opposite at some distance away on the starboard side, yawning and contentedly flipping backwards and forwards through a woman's magazine, a small sleeping child and a bag of groceries lying beside her, and toward the rear a small, wrinkled man in a red Mackinaw unbuttoned over oily white overalls smoking one cigarette after another and picking his finger nails. For his part, Martin hugs a battered Gladstone bag of coarsely textured bison hide that he keeps on his lap for the duration of his wait. Fastidious, he had early on moved as far as possible to one side of an unseemly tear in the center cushion of the bench. The moment he had sat down the red Leatherette upholstery had eructed its innards, a filthy, bile-colored foam stuffing. Earlier still, he had reached over to the arm rest, flipped shut the lid on a half full ashtray, then glanced at and examined the up-turned finger tips of his gloved hand. He remains quite motionless, moving only his head or right hand occasionally.

Martin is dressed as usual for the season. He wears his brown fedora pulled down low, rim turned up all around; and has securely wrapped himself in a large woolen overcoat, heavy and charcoal colored, collar up and buttoned to the top. He sits quietly, now and then clearing his throat, sometimes discreetly scratching his nose with a gloved knuckle, at others closing his eyes. The narcotics stolen from the dispensary are containing the pain rather nicely and making him feel unusually well.

He sits still and stares through a grimy window past his shadowy and fluorescent reflection, in particular drawn to a large, one-legged sea gull. It stands by itself on a piling in the near distance, no longer pestered by other gulls that had, unrelentingly, harassed the cripple for the catch of the day. A pallid-bellied sand dab grotesquely distends its captor's cheeks and gullet, protrudes from between the unhinged beak spread to a jaw-breaking 11:35. In the bird's red hooked yellow bill and rosy maw are concentrated all the available hues of this dull afternoon at the terminal bay. The promise of the sunny morning is no more now than a bright blue slit in the distant southwest, closing on itself by the minute. Martin continues to stare. Every half minute or so the bird will flex its sphincter and swallow. Fascinated and repulsed, he watches the muscle ripple down the bird's throat. To no avail. The fish won't budge. The still flapping tail of the tiny flounder continues to protrude from the gaping throat in which it is half stuck, staying to wave farewell to Martin whose ferry has several minutes yet before sailing; Martin compelled to watch, full of expectation, unable for long to focus on the naked maples and dark firs fringing the promontory, or that diminishing rent of bright blue sky in the west. Himself swallowing repeatedly, he has come to wishing the bird would get on with it.

A voice is welcoming all passengers. Martin thinks it must be recorded. It is that familiar broadcasting voice, a generic voice with industrial strength polish. Martin, with an aversion toward the speaker, his family and the ferry service, forces himself to listen to the names of the scheduled stops. He must disembark at the second to last and hire a water taxi to take him to another island not serviced by ferries; from there, if he is lucky in this off season, he must hire an independent boatman to take him to Thomas's island which, as if this all weren't trouble enough, has no name. At least not on the up-to-date chart Martin has consulted. And yet, though he has a four-and-a-half-hour trip before him, and though it will be growing dark before he leaves the ferry, Martin is little daunted thus far.

A raven caws from somewhere near. It is answered from a distance. Martin looks up, glimpses a black form blurring overhead and passing out of the frame. He looks down. The gull catches his eye again. It appears to be showing signs of worry. Martin is beginning to feel for it, a new sensation; sympathy for animals not being something he ever much indulged in; not like that fool Thomas who to amuse himself or show off his negative capability would talk aloud in the assumed voice of some creature, the full range of creation available to his prowess, any one of which would lend itself to deliver a poignant observation, hold forth on human failing, the basic challenges of life (the half swallowed sand dab must have a thing or two to say at this time, not to mention the hapless gull), a love affair, a scolding mate: Oh, it's not easy, I can tell you… The gull stands blinking, hopping around atop its piling on the one leg, turning to face out to sea, wings outstretched for balance. How doesn't it choke? Martin imagines that it must finally swallow its catch, allow it to be pulled out by another bird or die. It appears to blink at him. The ferry shudders as Martin blinks back. The terminal and its little town list; the promontory retreats; earth itself disengages from this vessel and is fast moving away. He hugs his bag as the pilings slip by. The fishtail waves farewell.

Adjusting his perspective, Martin settles down and watches the headland pass by. He has overcome nausea and an attack of hiccups; delivered himself of an Our Father for the latter. The distraction of prayer almost always helps in these cases, if in few others, he thinks, then formally abashed and in automatic reaction to his impiety asks, but as one might of an equal, for forgiveness. He closes his eyes, rubs his nose with the back of his gloved hand and sighs. He pictures Father Amaro running toward the end of the dock wildly waving his arms, stiff-limbed, prissy and helpless, exhaling noisily through his nostrils as the ferry sails away (much as he had done at noon today chasing after the withdrawing taxi); that he is standing, now, at the very edge, a long drop before him, watching the ferry disappear; sees the sight as if with his own eyes, having now left himself behind in Amaro's place to look after the boat, unraveling behind it a wide chunky macadam of cold froth over the sea; a speck now, and now vanishing at the end of the evanescent track.

Martin starts awake from his daydreams. That voice again. Irksome, but he feels just fine. Notwithstanding the nagging vision of that fool Amaro, and the disorientation from subsequent, and so very vivid, imaginings. He is on board after all. He opens his eyes and hugs the Gladstone, turns to look out the window. A small fishing boat is passing in the opposite direction. That voice again. It promises a tasty buffet being served in the forward cabin. The Native woman and her child have disappeared. The man in the Mackinaw passes down the aisle, finishes lighting a cigarette with the butt end of another. Coming abreast of Martin, he widens his eyes at him, in anticipation, one supposes, of their shared good fortune in the feast to come. Martin must unfortunately overcome an intrusive and unwonted vision of this passenger's underwear, unwholesome Y-briefs, incidentally, with a long history of truancy from the laundry, then an inevitable association of food with the unctuous Father Amaro, before sorting out whether he is hungry or not. He must for the time being remember how he could barely restrain himself from strangling the meddler during his unscheduled meeting this morning. Distracted this morning by Amaro's fussing from making the most of his redoubtable visitor's presence, Martin finally lost his temper, demanded that he leave the rectory lounge. Even so, it was Father Stephen, happening to be passing through with his favorite acolyte, who took it upon himself to pull the simpering Amaro away, gripping him by an ear. Amaro, who had been hovering about Martin and his visitor from the start, shivering with every word exchanged, offering refills of tea and extra biscuits with manic insistence before either of them had taken a sip or a bite, chatting about the sunshine the moment one or the other of the men paused to breathe. Ignoring Martin's demand that he leave them in peace and never one to give up without a fight, he busied himself with straightening furniture, first moving a chair out of place, then moving it back, reduced, finally, to picking invisible pieces of lint from the upholstery. Then it was that Father Stephen had come to the rescue, on whom it did not fail to register that Martin looked different, looked for his years rather handsome in fact, and that the Chinese gentleman had an extraordinary face and very large feet.

Throughout this awkward fuss, Du affected to notice nothing untoward, had long ago come to accept that not everyone could inspire the same respect he enjoyed. Nonetheless, as he didn't have all day, and

Martin was not showing enough resolve with this nuisance, he was about to suggest a little walk in the cloisters, of which he had heard wonderful things from his gardener, or if need be even a little drive in his waiting car, when, as Amaro was being led away, Martin himself suggested a walk through the cloisters.

In silence they entered, passing through sudden puffs of their own breath shot through by stray beams of sunlight, wan autumn rays angled under the west side arches to the garden cleared early this year, tied-up, well-turned, in stillness, the work of Father Floyd, tended by him with cultivated neglect, flourishing through spring, summer, and early fall, when it trembles with blooms, birds, and insects pressing to the four corners with perfume, color and vim, smelling now of humus, neatly bound and left to sleep.

There would be frost that night. Martin had not bothered to put on a coat. Du had not troubled to unbutton his. Slowly they strolled in the arcade. Neglected canvas curtains hung from the arches. Water and dung stained, some shivered or slapped in the occasional breeze, others were partially tied up or drawn to one side. Passing one drape that hung unfastened and trembled in the wind, the two men watched the shadow of a cat back-lit by sunshine stalking by on the other side, then the form of a starling flying over the same canvas.

Their footsteps resonate in the empty cloister. A starling sings. Neither man speaks. It seems like more to Martin, but little time has passed, and he feels an increasing confidence in himself; no longer feels afraid of Du, had seen his eyes soften, whether from the atmosphere itself or from some dear remembrance, it didn't matter, and Du himself appeared to acknowledge the change, shared a glance with him and carried on.

Staring now at the gray sea rushing past far below Martin remembers his excitement: see him sitting motionless, bundled up in black, framed in the fluorescent glow of the large window, dark head and shoulders alone amongst the otherwise empty squares, the glowing port side row like a length of film strip; seen from the outside a cutout of a man, a generic silhouette signposting something or other speeding by against the gray day, witnessed by a tall passenger wrapped in a long gabardine, an elderly man leaning on a stick and squinting into the wind, noticing the hatted urban figure, troubling to stare at this quaint sight of a man who at this distance, from the blustery promenade deck outside, is out of his element and even his time, before walking on, turning away to stare out to sea and disappear behind a bulkhead.

Martin sniffs, remembers his excitement—wariness had only caught up with him in the cloisters—which in the wasted quarter hour provided by Amaro's impositions had had time to settle to his advantage, against his almost overwhelming need to abandon courtesy, all caution, and demand answers. He rubs his nose with the knuckles of his right hand. Straining now to see the seam between sea and sky, a perfect match for eyes better even than his, Martin squints until he tears in an attempt to find the horizon. World without end. Elusive still. A distant freighter tips over the edge without betraying its element. He draws a folded linen handkerchief from a coat pocket and without unfolding it dabs at his eyes, blinks, shuts them and settles back into the chair, holding the cloth in his good hand.

It is warm in the lounge; heated air flows from the scuffed and dented radiator running past his feet, and yet Martin remains buttoned up, hatted, gloved; has given in to the schedule only in so far as having lifted the bag from his lap and, while possessively keeping his arm over it, placing it on top of the fissured seat next to him. He gently starts, opens his eyes, remembers how Du, as they continued their walk around the garden, had spoken first. It was at the moment when Martin had overcome his need to demand answers that Du spoke. He feels a retrospective relief. What right, after all, Thomas notwithstanding, did he have to ask anything of this man?

The manner in which Du spoke was straightforward, as if he were passing on a casual observation about the weather, say, or a football score, one man to another; and yet he said something unexpected, had so caught Martin off guard that he could not be sure of the exact words now, remembering as the Chinese gangster, tall, gaunt, and with not a measure less of the presence Thomas attributed to him, gestured at the garden and spoke of how nature demonstrates that what your faith offers is not impossible. Something like that. Not impossible here in our world, he had continued… And Martin was expecting Du, as if from out of the pages of Thomas's text, to confirm or deny his friend's paranoia—wasn't Du's very presence a denial?—to explain, as if to a stockholder, he now quips to himself in Thomas's imagined voice, how well in the last quarter the Shanghai Consortium was doing in its attempt to unbalance Heaven and other such matters as these, with perhaps something of Gaea, what with nature well-represented here… and they turned the corner, stepping into the eastern perimeter of the arcade without a word of Thomas; instead, Du quietly declaring that Buddha, and your Saint Paul, even mine, he then qualified, staring at the elaborate bird and water stains on a corner of delicately flapping canvas, say that the foolishness of God is greater than the wisdom of men… He could be talking of game scores or the weather, so natural was his delivery, and Martin full of anticipation, albeit with a new-found calm and confidence wondering how not even the archbishop could talk of, say, the Angelic Doctor without condescension, a hint of ironic distance from so far down that imagined road of progress, let alone of God, unspeakable Tetragrammaton… and Martin on tenterhooks, readying himself for revelation, the cornerstone to all his thoughts on Gaea perhaps, a hint on the development of the conspiracy against his old and perhaps both mad and sane friend, why not?

The whistle is blowing. Martin opens his eyes, flinches, wonders if he missed a stop, panics until he sees the clock before him palely glowing in the shadows between two vending machines, the one on the left quietly crepitating, stared at by a tall, skinny girl with shoulder-length brown hair. She suddenly turns an awkward circle, orbiting a brown smudge, a cigarette burn in the linoleum; overall her circumnavigation rather stiff, so much so as to qualify her, from a distance at least, as an innocent figure of fun, even to the preoccupied Father Martin. Look: her arms and legs so straight and long, their joints unrelenting. In a pique? She is very pretty, more than pretty, wears glasses, has a full mouth. On her way around she notices Martin and blushes, then faces the machine once more to agonize over its offerings.

Martin looks again at the clock, relaxes, feels a little foolish; somehow a not unpleasant awareness in this instance. The ferry sounds its horn. He feels a creaky sensation, a happy accident of reacquaintance with a forgotten thing, an alternative reality of time last experienced by the child Martin, as if tripped over today in musty attic shadows. And he wonders at this adjusted sensibility, so much time seeming to have passed already, so little evidence of distance traveled. He knows what it looks like on the map: a mere hiccup from the mainland. He closes his eyes again. Slow-moving images of gray-green waves roll by within the theatre-rosy glow of his closed eyes. Martin in and out of narcotic reverie this last hour, one only, an hour that weighed by its contents extends beyond the measure. He opens his eyes. The passing waves lit by a pale autumnal beam appear to be running on the spot. That voice again, announcing now that passengers with automobiles should descend to the car deck. What must it be like for the wife of that voice? Would she hear it ask just like that for second helpings of macaroni and cheese? Martin exhales loudly and looks around. He pulls a card out of his coat pocket, checks the itinerary scribbled in pencil that morning as he strained to understand the impatient accents of the ferry information operator, a young woman with other things on her mind who first gave him the summer schedule, ingenuously mentioning an extra sailing from the third week in August through Labor Day, until reminded by him, he thought politely, that summer had passed some weeks back, squinting now at his cross outs and scrawl covering the back of a mass schedule, scores of which he uses as one sided index cards for notes and reminders. Here was the first island being announced. Hours still to go. How the canned voice grated. A green and gray promontory, a granite outcrop iced in guano and topped with a beacon like some outsized failure of a dessert, passes slowly by. Here was time for a breather. He watched a gull hover alongside. They exchange eyes for a heartbeat. The ferry shudders; screws strain in reverse; audible above the diesel roar, the water froths. In a sudden silence they ease, almost imperceptibly, into the berth.

Father Martin, Du had started again, after politely listening to Martin's recommendations (how Thomas would have rolled his eyes to heaven, Martin reflects now as the ferry, rising in the water, debouches a truck and two cars. I don't care, he says aloud and shifts about in his seat. The girl still facing off with the vending machine looks around quickly, then back), Martin exhorting the boss man of the great Shanghai Consortium, rather enthusiastically for him, to take the time to look into the works of Meister Eckhart and Giordano Bruno; Martin rather taken by Du's seeming bent for metaphysics, a rare interest, rare even here, he had thought nostalgically, excepting the scholarly and mischievous Father Stephen who reads with youthful enthusiasm still, still moved by beauty, the ancient terror.... Father Martin, Du went on, you are highly recommended by an old friend. He spoke with chilling formality after checking his watch and without comment on Martin's heartfelt tip, doubtless having committed his suggestion to memory as, having walked the cloister's perimeter, they returned toward where they started from. Finally, Martin had thought to himself, anticipating the reason for Du's visit, thinking, too, how it would be to surprise Thomas on his island.

The sun beamed off and on, a faint diagonal from just above the southwest corner of the cloisters, for an instant spotting the men as they continued toward the door. No birds sing. A dark cloud moves into place. The chill settles, and Martin shivers in the cold. My good friend Wu, having known you since you were a boy, Du said, has told me that you are the man to talk to about an important, personal matter. Oh, finally, Martin had thought to himself again; and not only that, but how after years of penitence (and scored by Thomas's confession) for not having kept things to himself, he was to be trusted outside the confessional once more.

He shook off despondency, climbed out of the slough, progressing to and up the mountains delectable, one by one passing the tests, as he thought, one by one until it registers that he is to instruct Du's number one child, his beautiful daughter Mi-Ling, (Mimi), and her fiancé, Lee My, (Oscar), the latter a rising star in the Consortium, into the Catholic Church and then marry them. Martin had reeled with confusion, shame, and some distant sense of duty. This must have to do with Thomas, with "Dead Souls." How?

Du tactfully spared him witness to his confusion, apparently having taken an interest, as they approached the southern end of the cloisters, in a tawny cat stalking the silent and alerted starlings that had been pecking in the gravel on the other side of an authentic Restoration sundial (donated by a penitent steel magnate)—just as well his interest in the cat, for Martin in his confusion missed telling him the story of the antique— said to have kept time in the little private garden, shadowy sweet and musky with eglantine and fallen quince, of the delicious Nell Gwyn who, with John Wilmot, abandoning themselves to laughter and the blood rush more likely in a pair less sated and ill, more temperate and fresh, this one dark night and the King passed out from too much hock...

Only after Du had driven away did Martin think he understood how this encounter was a binding relationship with him, a keeping faith, a contract. He had flushed with anxiety. Oh, he had not asked for any of this, unless by his visit to Wu's infernal little shop. The thought nagged at him that there was nothing to any of this. How could there be, he'd whispered to himself? Thomas had duped him, he decided for all of an instant. God knows, he said aloud and sighed, walking back to his rooms, watching a squirrel bury, then disinter, a nut, deciding to hide it someplace else. But enough: he was certainly being trusted with something dear to this man who had stepped from his car as from the intrusion of Thomas's pages, and somehow urged belief in something more. And I have witnesses, Martin had said to himself, scowling over his shoulder at Amaro who was following several paces behind. I have committed myself to something. I am being trusted. Trusted and threatened, mind you.

Martin turns to the window. The landscape moves the other way now, the guano gateau and its one electric candle passing by. Oh, precious birthday tact to this old world, he thinks, imagining grandchildren and in-laws baby-talking granny, anxious for her health, too, you can be sure: she sees through you, he offers, and looks about. A car horn blares from the shore and echoes out to sea. Neither the Native woman and her child, nor the man in the red Mackinaw has returned to the lounge. Only the tall, skinny, girl remains; and she, having finally chosen from the many offerings, sits in the front row center of the lounge, busily devouring a chocolate bar as if in some dream too good to be true, as Martin looks on. Already she greedily chews the last bite. There may have been all of three bulging mouthfuls that she had been willing to concede to the sticky six-inch candy bar, after having noisily, or so it had seemed to sensitive Martin, torn back the wrapper to get at it. She, too, was suddenly aware they were moving, he couldn't help noticing, cocking her head and starting aback as if to illustrate in bold vaudevillian strokes the process of mental adjustment necessitated by the ferry's change in direction for the benefit of anyone who might be looking (and she had made it clear that she was aware of Martin's existence, theatrically widening her eyes and twisting her mouth in acknowledgment of his earlier exclamation out loud, that she was more than aware that he was an odd one as far as she was concerned), miming with a nod of approval her recognition of their return to the customary scheme of things when the ferry, having cleared the small bay and swung about, resumed its forward motion by the accepted terms of front and back, destination and schedule. The landscape, too, did its part, growing smaller as they passed through the milky swath of flotsam and jetsam that marked the hurrying tide, resuming its passage alongside, then further and further astern of the ferry, the dense evergreens crowding to the edges of granite cliffs, the narrow rocky beaches and cabins here and there passing by again from front to back. Martin closed his eyes, on his way once more.

He had walked Du to the waiting car, its engine running, exhausting the smell of fallen leaves and damp turf, past Father Amaro ineffectually raking, who simpered at them as they passed. With each step taken toward the close of this interview Martin agonized over his doubts, finally speaking, but only to repeat himself, for he had already agreed to what had been asked of him in the cloisters as they turned the final corner and headed for the door. In the quiet after the starlings had flown off, noisily scolding the tawny cat that had commanded Du's outward attention, both of whom continued to stare after the birds at an empty sky, Du spoke of his hope that Martin would accept his family's trust in this matter dear to them; that they might thus all be joined and enjoy a long relationship, that he should very much like another walk with him in the spring when the garden was beginning to bloom once more, and Martin finally saying again, for something had to be said, that he would meet with the young couple in the new year.

He opens his eyes. The girl is chewing on a thumbnail and flipping through a fashion magazine. Outside Martin's window three cormorants keep pace with the ferry, neatly breaking away toward the thin yellow band edging the horizon in the west. As he opens his bag and fusses with something inside, he reflects that his self-control during the meeting had not been provoked by fear, but was intuitively complimentary to the other's unspoken purpose. He was aware of how he must have looked, betraying his feelings, taken aback by his visitor's request, evidently disappointed and bemused as they walked around the garden while Du tactfully temporized with his confusion, drawn by the admittedly fascinating spectacle of the cat and the starlings. And yet Du's visit had effectively reassured Martin, added to his first blooming of confidence, his decision to act without guarantee, without expectation for the returns of purpose, the reassurance of design. This was something, he thought to himself, feeling rather well, removing his gloves, lightly touching, then rubbing his nose and cheeks, something he would dearly have liked to have known earlier in his life. Better late than never, a voice tells him, sounding much like his own, not noticeably glib. And with that he pulls Thomas's manuscript out of the Gladstone bag where it was folded with some clean linen and a considerable supply of morphine packed in a Saint John's Ambulance kit, opening it at the place where he had left off.

Father, it is so still tonight. I hear the ocean nudging the beach, tugging at the pebbled shore, slapping against the dock; now and again the owls from a distance, not just outside as is usual; otherwise, nothing remarkable: the fire crackling some, a beam or floor joint groaning. I thought I had grown so accustomed to dread as to deprive it of urgency. As a child it used to be moments like these, but while certifiably asleep (just for the sake of argument, Martin) and dreaming, that I could anticipate and signal the crescendo of fear in this favorite score, that I was about to be apprehended or given a good chase and scare by the witch who resided in the same oneiric neighborhood and who made a point of haunting me in the shadows, this witch, always the same, compelling me from her place in the darkness beneath the stairs on which I frequently climbed, racing up from the cellar on my way into what ought to have been either restful sleep or waking, an ordinary reality, but was nothing so certain, as I have taken pains for you to understand. Katya and the cat are asleep on the couch. I feel like writing to you some more before I go to bed.

There is something going on tonight. Katya cooked a good dinner: lamb chops, juicy and pink (from animals raised on a nearby island), with sautéed potatoes, a little underdone, and a salad of arugula from my own garden. She drinks well for her age, though the second Calvados, after a bottle of Medoc, got the better of her. I know what you must be thinking. How dare you?

She told me something odd, Martin. Just before curling up and pulling a blanket over herself—do you remember our old Lamont throw? Jane's… How many years? The same: cashmere fraying here and there—and sighing good night, her breath sweet and warm with Calvados and that something else that must be youth, she said that I was a very trusting man. Imagine that, Martin. It would have been unkind to laugh. She said that I should guard myself better. I asked her what she meant. I don't know, she slurred, shut her eyes and burped (I could barely refrain from kissing her then). I let her be, piqued though I was, imagining all sorts of things and straining to hear them too. It is so still. The safety catch stays off tonight.

I must have dozed, Father. In this time, no more than half an hour, the moon has come up. She shines on the inlet now; and while it is quiet here—there is no breeze I can see in the trees or hear from my desk by the window (the wind chimes, coaxed to sound at the mere thought of air, remain unmoved)—even so the passage is wide-awake, alive, silver-white with moon glow and the whole possessed by a saltant, frantic tide. I opened the window. Not a sound. The sight of the ocean dancing like this in the moonlight, and the air all the while so still, has the effect of making me doubt myself. Whatever state I may be in, I am witness, I swear (Father you would be reduced to prayer in my place), to an oceanic *Walpurgisnacht.*

The fire is low. Spasms of orange light and shadows animate the room. I ought to put on another log before it dies. I ought to close my eyes, and try to sleep. Not yet. I sit here and stare at my reflection in the window, at the dark silhouettes of firs and eucalyptus, the tenebrous loom of the mainland opposite, the moonlit chop in-between. I hear the cat snore, once, twice. The girl talks in her sleep. Little sibyl. I can't make out a thing she says, murmuring and sighing for the last five minutes. I should know all things then. Twice I have almost risen to draw near, twice lowered myself back down, let go the arms of the chair from which I intended to stand, reluctant to steal her mystery, to claim salvaging rights to words from the deep. Perhaps I am just too tired to move.

I have had such a fright, just now led Katya back to the couch and tucked her in next to kitty. Well out of range of the immediate, the cat continues sleeping, stretched out long, flying between two pillows and dreaming of being worshiped somewhere just this side of Bubastis. My nerves, Martin. Katya breathes deeply, apparently sound asleep. Warm with sleep, her smell, when I bent over her, concentrates the sweetest allure of her gender. There are these miracles, these imperatives of nature, Father. Attend. She is redolent with Gaea. Here is that Garden's fecund miracle, all the dark earth. Sow me here. Here is thematic rhyme with my secret, Martin, the blood experience for which I have come up with a representation in the neatness of an equation. The formula that for you is glimpsed at best through this tangle of words: a short-lived touch of late sun that through shadowy wood spots a tree with unlikely warmth. The fruit held out in silence. Martin, she is one of Nature's prime creatures. I could swoon from her special beauty, it draws me so. But I have had such a fright.

Father, Jesus, Martin, I was so startled. I wonder at the state of my senses. How was it I didn't hear her approach? I had put my pen down, was staring at the dancing lunatic tide lost in some remembrance; was thinking of you, Martin, a potentially dangerous barbiturate pastime, doped from the encounter, remembering that time when, coming into your rooms unexpectedly one afternoon, I heard you talking in your sleep, so clearly too, your elocution better than when you were awake, although somewhat stupider, a little like a mental defective in your slobbering emphasis between bites of spit-soaked pillow, holding forth on my perfidy, declaring your love for my wife, subsequently protesting with all the requisite pauses and acknowledgments to your interlocutor's points of view that I can only suppose you had a direct connection with your beloved, and mine. You beast. I was surprised, and for an instant—oh the greediness of human nature—even a tiny bit chafed. I remember being certain that I was the honored object of your affection. Moonraking from a distance, lost in reverie, and remembering how decent Jane was to you despite your moroseness and various betrayals (to criticize is not to condemn, Martin; this confession is no grudge, honest), I didn't hear her coming. Attuned to every creak of mortise and tenon in this fine house, to the sound of a fallen pine needle tickling the roof, to leaves touching down on earth from as far away as a stone's throw [You must have Dumbo's ears to be able to do that, Martin scrawls between the lines and rubs his nose], I heard nothing before seeing her in the window standing over me, her eyes fixed on mine in the dark reflection. How didn't I wake her, starting about as I did? How not perish from surprise? How did I stop short of shooting out the window, my first stupid impulse, actually taking aim at her reflection? If I don't get a better hold of myself, and Heaven ever finds me, I won't stand a chance.

Katya sleeps, a blanket gripped in one fist and pulled up to her nose. I rekindle the fire and make coffee without waking her, unless she's faking it, waiting for a chance to strike. Dawn is extravagant today. I wish you could see: color bleeds gouache-like from storm clouds as the sun rises, the russet east absorbed by thickening darkness, the whole now jaspé, a roiling ceiling of stormy gray veined in pink, rounding fast out of the north. The rosy veins are grown over; the first raindrops fall.

I'll be a wreck today. At my desk in a funk for another hour, I finally retreated, undressed, tucked myself into bed. A spider waited on one of my pillows. It ran away. I wasn't up to any squeamishness, to having to give up my bed, or to any gentle trapping with a whiskey glass and a postcard. The cat returned from Lower Egypt at about the same time as I finished examining the rest of the bed, and purring, stretched out alongside me. Things must have gone well; but she was tired from the journey. She fell off right away, ignoring me, sighing through her tiny nostrils. Only with the quilt up to my ears did I realize how unnerved I am, Martin. I am quite resigned to my odds in this haphazard game, but the girl has unsettled me with her somnambulant visit, taking me unawares with unnatural stealth.

Martin cannot concentrate on the text any longer, has been hiccupping for five minutes already after a powerful, extremely pleasurable, sneeze. For years he has kept a hanky in his coat pocket; since the funeral of his mother. It is one of hers. On that summer day, he took it from her dresser, turning away from a small photograph in brown leather frame of himself aged two, dressed in white shorts and white knitted tee shirt, lifting sunglasses from her young and pretty face and she gently laughing. Neatly pressed, and covered with lint, he cannot at first bring himself to use it to wipe the snot-splattered palm of his good hand. A faint scent of L'Heure Bleu recovers for him an afternoon nap in her arms from which he returns sorrowful, regretting that he has now soiled the neat linen square, missing her.

He is losing his patience, despite the experience of wellbeing enjoyed for most of the day. (His hand has not bothered him since morning.) These hiccups, these unholy spasms, interfere with his newly found narcotic pleasure.

He can't have known someone is thinking to help him; the skinny girl at the front of the lounge chewing on her thumbnail and reading a fashion magazine (an article on marriage), imagining various outcomes, giggling over some, blanching at others. Martin notices her chortling and nibbling at her fingers. He thinks—made less charitable since the hiccups—that she is an emaciated little fiend; a bone with hair, he thinks; admittedly very much more than pretty, he reluctantly gives in. She, meanwhile, weighs the potential consequences of her imagined charity, entertaining herself at the same time. What if she were to help the priest, sneak up behind him and give him a good scare, less likely to be lost on God than charity to a mere other, maybe? Her face takes on a pious look. She chances a glance back, peering through her round, black-framed glasses and past her bangs, tugging on a nail and making a face. She starts to giggle. Martin scowls. Mortified she jerks her head back around to face the vending machines, the one on the left still crackling. She will sulk. Horrible. Let him get over the hiccups on his own. She has a little cry, shoulders shaking noticeably, sniffs loudly every half minute or so. She wishes she could call her mom. Martin apparently doesn't notice, or care, unaware that his hiccups have stopped.

He stares through his reflection in the window, looking with some amazement. A fog mass, a miles-long phalanx of gray, is fast closing in on the ferry, stumbling over itself just above the waves, hurtling out of the west, speeding away from the early setting sun. Martin is not keen on this dark atmosphere overwhelming his sense of immediacy and place. Things were fine as they were. His nervous response surprises him. The long fingers of the cloudy vanguard, the sudden obscurity in its train, is more sinister to his imagination here at sea, more threatening than when he gazes at it from his study window, or reads about such things in Thomas's caroling evocations of Nature, or in those works tending with shadowy intent to a more literary bias. He struggles to trust the Captain.

The world shrinks with every blink; the gray rolls over the ship, slipstreaming against the windows. The close and compact island, a moment earlier passing abeam, is gone. He was admiring it, as against the encroaching fog, its deep green density so near he had caught his breath with concern, the island sailing past as if within reach from the rail, tree-covered, bird-possessed; hosting preening cormorants, devils decorating a dead fir that stood out against the sky, ornaments of a nether Christmas. Now, through the many layers of racing gray, not a trace of rock, tree, or bird remains; nor the lifeboats, ship's railing or promenade—all no more. The ferry lounge is all the solid world remaining, the rest metamorphosed, changed into fog fast moving with the dark, airily slipping by at the combined speed of ship and northwest wind. Odd conditions at sea, Martin thinks, and jumps in his seat as the whistle sounds.

The girl has stopped crying. She turns around to retrieve her fallen magazine, can't help herself, chances a look as she reaches for it, peeks through her bangs. Martin is grateful that she has got a hold of herself, tries out a smile. She blushes, and quickly looks away, may eventually find it in her heart to forgive him. He rubs his nose, sniffs and opens Thomas's bundle again, glancing warily out the window and at himself, before looking down and reading.

The rain is pouring down, Martin—the island socked in with this weather—nailing down the roof and making music just past the window before me. Not a savage sound in desperate need of missionaries, Father. No simple tom-tom this. An irregular overflow spurts rhythmically from above, from at least three different places along the needle-and leaf-filled eaves. Splashing onto the metal hood of a barbecue, a standing tin tray and a bucket, it beats a hollow percussion in an almost fixed if ostensibly erratic time, playing a resonant hocket to drive me mad. Like you used to, Martin. Never have I known anyone more prone to hiccups. Do you still eat as if at any moment someone may come along and steal your food?

A headline in a newspaper Katya brought with her announces that Pater has appointed a former K.G.B. officer to head the ecological arm of Heaven. His appointee has planted many a man, woman, and child, and promises his boss, I'll bet, that he will feed Gaea with my obstinacy.

I imagine blowing Pater's head into pink smithereens. I should like to be able to tell you how he looked in the moments before, how steady was my aim, to imagine asking that you not tell my old mother how I shattered his skull into fragments of dust and gore with the very gun with which you are personally familiar and that lies before me here; safety catch off, incidentally.

And Katya? Is she in Heaven's employ? Imagine such a precocious cynicism… (She is in the shower now and insists on making a breakfast of thickly-sliced bacon and baked eggs. This is some of what I have been missing. That someone should so want to please…) Here is a photo of Pater on the front page—good God—smiling in that fatherly way of his, one arm around the shoulders of his assassin who is grinning toothily, eyes magnified behind bottle-lens goggles, Moe coif (the cruel stooge, as you recall). Behold Pater himself—in the flesh, the photo would have us believe—glad handing the (his) press. I have work to do and more and more blood on my hands. Some of it innocent. Father, please, think, who is this handsome, smiling man who took my love and wants my secret? Loss, until it happens to you, never goes very much beyond numeration standing in for spilt blood, anguish, and sorrow. We live dangerously not because of the dare of some higher ideal, but by accident. In effect all of us housed, mutatis mutandis Fritz, on the slopes of Vesuvius that extend well into the flatlands of the suburban world. You tell me where the volcano stops, where the unfaulted flats begin.

Old man Pater needed to make sense to himself of the whole business, the grand scheme of things, Father, ever since it was put about and accepted on faith—and he wasn't about to disabuse anyone on this count—that he had everything under control with a purpose we could all trust in. Let's progress, he's been saying forever. God, Father, even you know… Of course I wouldn't have given him the time of day, and Shanghai got to me first and argued convincingly with hard cash and a certain probity about what the right thing to do might be under the circumstances. Heaven approached me soon after. I told them, politely, to get lost. It made them very angry. They in turn made me think about the scheme of things more than I am inclined to do. Not only while insomniac. I must look over my shoulder (yes, Martin, literally and figuratively both) all the time, attend to all my senses all the time just to stay a step ahead of them. To survive their pursuit of me I must always consider my position in this world—which place I have never begrudged, despite the handicap of consciously going about in my sleep—almost in the nagging manner of some spotty undergraduate agonizing over various imagined existential dilemmas, while no longer young enough to hope that I might ever grow out of such behavior. All this is not without its lighter side, mind you, these hungry metaphysics with their appetite for the earnest. There is humor even in Job's predicament, Father. I am blighted with the cankers and boils of these thoughts, jobbed with the business of existence. I who quite enjoy life, and yet, for not honoring the franchises of power… Extortion, Martin, nothing more than. I am still able to relax from time to time only because I no longer really care what happens. I've always been able to find oases of calm, grace and joy, and those more vibrant distractions, am able to enjoy, even now, my island, the seasons, food and drink, my dear cat, the garden, this young woman… but Jane gone. Stolen. To show me what? Not to count overly on myself? Not to get too carried away with notions of unauthorized free will? It will cost them some. I will make it difficult for Heaven: at the very least file this protest.

All those years ago, Jane and I thought to put off until tomorrow the niggling for certainty and other such understandable if unseemly notions. We enjoyed ourselves, grateful for our accident of complicity, believing we could extend with attitude the margin of credit between inevitability and us. We sent you post cards, Martin. Lots of them, as I recall. How we lived and traveled, Jane and I, especially after completing my deal with Du and the Shanghai Consortium. At first it was a vacation, the two of us running all over the world, making another child; but it was not very long before I realized that we were running for our lives.

Paranoia, she used to laugh (Jane's laugh, Martin…), teasing me, turning it to amusing account as I pointed out Moe haunting, squinting at us wherever we traveled, blighting from just beyond the Sarnath Buddha, hunkered like an anthropomorphic turd in the illuminated shadows of a camphor tree in the garden city Suzhou, sighted, between us and distant glimpses of hazy North Africa across the Strait of Sicily, diddling himself amongst the ruins in a fog bank on a flowering hillside of Erice in the spring, and I pestering Jane for her flesh, and then especially later, in Paris.

In her sixth month we took an apartment, soon becoming, Jane big-bellied, "with pretty and with swimming gait", favorites of the merchants who soon overcame their initial distance to the quarter's new foreigners, calling out and smiling in affectionate jest and encouragement at her sailing through the market; and I, who in the role of "wanton wind" had after all some part in this, deserving then of that timeless if questionable respect for fecundity, also enjoyed their smiles and salutes, choice produce raised aloft in gestures ripe with a full range of suggestion. Our favorite born then, in that last best time before Heaven caught up with us.

Moe was there from the beginning; and as it is with those who are mad or prescient or both, I felt his magnified eyes on us for quite some time before he, become a consummate haunter who always intended that I should sense him, let his guard down and I, pleasantly drunk after a good lunch, spotted him at the Metro Faidherbe-Chaligny, earning from Jane her usual amused and patient affection for my imagination when I tried to point him out, certainly visible for a good moment—there. There!—standing still on the opposite platform behind an increasing blur of passing yellow windows; on the other side of a departing train as if within an accelerating length of motion picture frames. Jane with her back to him, pressing her big belly to me, agreeing that yes, indeed, she can see him as clear as can be, straightening my scarf and kissing me: soft little kisses on my lips, the corners of my mouth, my cheeks, her breath heady, warm and delicious with garlic and crème caramel, her woolen coat smelling of rain. That was the first time in Paris.

I was carrying a gun everywhere. This concerned Jane at first. As she said without causing embarrassment or offense (her manner, Martin, her manner), she initially saw it as evidence that my so-called delusions were taking a serious turn. Especially when one rainy afternoon, as I was reaching for my gloves, I drew it out with them, the old Browning, and it fell from my coat pocket onto the sawdust floor of our favorite butcher. A little toy for my son, I toothily offered in an accent not everyone finds forgivable. Quick thinking, I thought, but not, I'm afraid, to anyone's evident relief. As I bent down to pick it up, its form and weight declaring me an obvious liar for most to see, I was somewhat angrily called an American by one stout woman who, if she hadn't started hiccupping, I knew would lay about her with a stirring verse or two from the Marseillaise, and, castigated overall in a general murmur of disapprobation, a sotto voce mob hum, a stomach grumble from the beast. The patron, a hunter and man's man, was happily more forgiving, but for a month after I had to accept his winks and, entre nous of course, exchange thoughts on stopping power, clip sizes, powder loads and whatnot. He had wonderful meat, Father.

Perhaps Moe lost patience with haunting us (just in time: Jane increasingly concerned that I might in fact not be so adorably mad after all, perhaps something a little more uncertain). Or maybe he was fed up with the French and Paris (as a surprising number of people will always be). In any event, something prompted him to actually confront Jane and her ripening child one cloudy afternoon, my loves sitting and waiting for me, sipping hot chocolate at the café just around the corner from our home. Moe (she insisted on just calling him this man) suddenly appeared as if out of nowhere, Jane said, not usually given to story-telling conventions. That's his way, that's his way, I hissed. He is consummate, a virtuoso ghoul, I said, my sibilants hardening into steel. He will appear as if out of thin air. Without warning. She waited patiently for me to finish, I remember. Not able to make enough out of a shadow in a doorway halfway down the street from where we sat, I stopped and let her go on. Her hand was trembling slightly. I also remember—I can see her now retying a scarf around her head, adjusting a pair of sunglasses, her lips trembling, too, just a little, as on occasion over the years I made them do, some words said, some thing done and she, knowing that my conscience had struck, trying to let me off the hook as she mastered her sorrow...—she said, "Just like you told me, Thomas..." Beating me to the draw, I dare say. Anyway, Martin, the monster held a spotted quail egg between his thumb and forefinger. He drew an orbit with it that corresponded to her ripening belly; then at just a little more than arm's length, he lined it up between her eyes and crushed it, letting the diminutive yolk depend from the straining ribbon of albumen for half its descent, free fall and splatter onto the ground. Being such a creep and noticeably disturbing Jane, who had stiffened in readiness and, as she told it, done no more than fix him with her eyes (his indeed goggled, magnified and froggy, she testified), a waiter possessed of that selective preternatural vision of the skilled serving professional who sees most everything going on before and behind him, witnessed the threat, came to her rescue and humiliated Moe, drew all eyes on him (Moe a somewhat shy man, Du has told me), and gripping his arm above the elbow, boldly ejected him—had the hero later known just how dangerous goggle-eyed Moe is, he would, for all his undoubted bravery, even now mess himself and swoon—, dragged him off the property with a curse and an appropriate gesture, returned wiping his hands on his long apron in workman-like fashion to see to it that Jane would be all right, offering calvados, another hot chocolate, before carrying on with a touching rendition of matter-of-factness, right in the face of all that existence might offer, all in a day's work.

I arrived minutes after the incident; genuinely sorry (with typical male vim; that mostly useless vivacity of manly revenge imaginings) not to have happened on it myself, blue-balled with vengeance, picturing myself in variations on the theme of rescue and violent justice in the manner of almost all men, men, men, but, mark well, Father, armed and quite prepared to effect it. Weren't you always looking for examples of my common humanity, Martin? Here you are.

I was reluctant to let Jane go out alone. Plaited as we were for so long, it was fortunate that we could maintain a comfortable sense of independence, without obligation to exhibit those assurances which I believe neither of us questioned, even at the worst of times, able to be alone while being together, together and alone without that sense of intrusion which one can feel from even the best of friends. The loneliness I know now is only the loneliness of being without Jane. I don't need others. Her absence is the original of incompletion. I am an amputee, Father. There are no substitutes, really; and yet, Katya stays on, prosthetic, and I am glad. How terrible that, like Jane, she is in danger by association.

Something is nagging. Again I have the sense that she is adding to my food and drink. It is not that I feel any different really; rather it is glimpses of certain movements she makes that in being deliberate deviate from her normal grace. A deliberate second, a moment's design, betrays her as an exile; not of Eden after all, Father; but this telling legerdemain, this moment of self-conscious action designed to escape notice piques my instinct, announces my destruction and defines her fall. Yet I can't bring myself to either believe or rationalize any of it with regard to her. I am neutralized, yet wouldn't doubt the threat for an instant if she were other; I have mistakenly killed with less reason, as you know. See how Nature is up to her tricks again and I blundering forward to spawn and what, Martin, swim back out to sea, or die? Is it Nature that has it in for me?

During this period in Paris my nervous energy, my magnetism, Father—let us, in a manner of speaking, step aside from dreams and the occult just this once—was playing havoc with time. [In a manner of speaking? Martin writes in pencil, sloppily covering the neatly typed text, feeling excited, exhilarated, high jinks even, at the prospect of seeing Thomas. After all these years, given the chance, I could slap your face until you woke, idle fool; stir you from this stubborn, slumbering conceit, he mumbles. Martin scratches his face and rubs his nose with newfound pleasure. He checks his wrist watch, avoids the window pressed against by the fog and considers if it is time yet for a booster of his rather delicious pain killer. His hand is not yet hurting exactly, but he has been periodically distracted these last few minutes—not minutes, a good half hour, as he now realizes, marveling at how time flies, or will drag its feet. He is having and enjoying both sensations today: hours passing in minutes; minutes seemingly lasting an hour—wondering when he ought to take another shot. He decides to wait, something of the Calvinist, he teases himself, rather than the sensual Roman, holding him back from the anticipated pleasure of his medicine.] In those days I possessed two wristwatches, one old Rolex and a newer Omega. The first my father gave to me when I was sixteen. I wear it still and it keeps good time. The other I inherited when he died. After the confrontation between Jane and that malevolent swine Moe, first one watch and then the other was running twenty minutes fast within a day, quite despite my adjustments over at least a week. The watchmaker around the corner from our home, from whom I sought arbitration, could find no mechanical fault with either. The watches were fine, he declared, with an emphasis on watches as he handed them back. He eyed me after examining them, peering over his half-glasses with the same professional scrutiny, if not quite the same affection, shown toward the perfect works he had just left off handling. Odd bird, I thought later, for I am not such a haphazard figure of a man, if not quite so regular and fine as a worm gear. I am a little pleased to say he was left with a taste more of the things there are in heaven and on earth. A coo-coo clock, then a gold leafed baroque mantle clock, started to sound thirteen minutes before the hour; to coo-coo and chime respectively; and as I turned to leave the old watchman was prying off the back of his own pinging pocket watch. A metronome unhinged itself to beat time to my exit as I closed the door behind me, escaping a cacophony of hurried hours; and when I walked past the little clock shop on the way back home from the newsstand its blinds were drawn. There was nothing for it but to stop worrying about what time it was, and I stopped wearing my watch for the time being.

The hateful voice announces tea in the forward lounge. Quite in spite of himself, Martin suddenly pictures the man's house, is compelled to tour room to room, glimpses the wretch's soiled Y-fronts turned inside out lying next to some crumpled tissue under the bathroom sink where he has left them for his wife, endures the disrespect, the high volume exuberance and greed of his uncomely children in their toy-littered playroom, the forlorn, put-upon resignation in the eyes of his wasted wife. Martin squeezes his own eyes shut for a long moment, then risks them on the opacus fog—a living thing with the vaporous elegance of an escaped story book djin—that seeks to find a way through the barrier of glass and bulkhead steel, a way to clutch at his heart. Better this than that other, this and the blind voyage, he thought, and dared himself to face the uncertainty.

Martin shivers, shortens his gaze to admire his reflection in the glass, reassured that his new self accompanies him still. He turns away to look around the cabin. The girl is still there, markedly concentrating, picking at her nails with those not yet so closely bitten of her other hand. The same fashion magazine lies open on her lap. Even from several rows away, the reek of a perfume strip intrudes. Martin flexes his nostrils and sneezes loudly, startling the girl who reacts visibly, as is her wont. He dabs at his hands with his handkerchief, and checks his watch, thinking of Thomas, more than ever reluctant to trust in time. He pulls out the schedule from a coat pocket. Two more stops, two and a half more hours at least, if the ferry is on schedule. Unlikely, he thinks, and again faces off against the fog, straining to see through it, find a weak spot, wondering at but soon losing interest in the state of technology that could preclude faith, the famous leap that Martin, laughing at himself a little, imagined he was making, taking a big run at it, he thinks, trusting not only in God and all his mystery, but that He should on a more personal level let him see his friend, not let him run aground because of the interference of a rogue radio wave on a delinquent rampage, sound energy tripping up with hooligan disregard the diligent heart-beat-sweep of the glowing green radar arm, or

as a result of the blood alcohol count of a tippling captain or first mate:
On the rocks, I said! And speaking of blood wasn't this as good a time
as any for another little shot and then he won't have to trouble with it
until much later? The question was where and how exactly—he being
fumble-fingered at the best of times—without drawing attention to
himself, or breaking an ampoule, or infecting his syringe, which last
for the hyper-fastidious Martin could mean uncapping it within the
same room as a fellow human being, for that matter, uncapping it at all.
He would read a little more.

Soon it was March. Jane did not labor long; half-howling squeezed
the girl into the world, her voice deep and triumphant, a plangent
moan in the last moments of her delivery. I heard from just outside,
Martin, pressing against the closed door, heard it as her victory cry,
imagined she howled her announcement for me and at the world.
One of the nurses told us how she had thrilled to the spectacle as if
for the first time. Later that day, a cloudy, windy, Ides of March, and
the city smelling of spring and the river running quick, she confessed
to her emotion: at Jane's voice, she stressed; the sight, too, of my love
commanding, neck straining forward, tendons bulging, head raised to
witness her issue, arrogant, fierce, she said; and the visceral charge she,
the nurse—a pretty brunette with husky voice and darling laugh —,
declared it sent through her. [Even at a time like this? Martin scribbles
in the margin, perhaps missing the point, as he thought after; but still
not bothering to erase his judgment, thinking that should Thomas ever
see it he might be amused; Martin almost drunk on anticipation of
seeing him.] I was absent from the delivery room, the enduring mysteries of the goddess et cetera. Jane had asked, smiling as I left her in
the delivery room, myself in surgical green, shower-capped and foolishly wearing on my fists—until a patient Vietnamese nurse snatched
them from me—the paper slippers obviously intended for my stocking

feet, that I leave this business to her. And we kissed (I tasted raw Gaea on her lips, smelled it on her breath; or call it baby if you'd rather; you can taste it, you know, I have isolated Gaea, licked the tellurian compound, savored its flavor) and I walked away, redundant now for nine months, and still not used to it, afraid of losing her, seeing Moe behind every surgical mask.

Her labor was wonderfully short, Martin. And I remember her then: hair slicked back with sweat and face aglow, mouth still uncurling from a sneer, that smile, those eyes. Join me, she had asked less than an hour before. Come in just after. As to any ecstasy she might have felt and which I enthusiastically suggested, she rolled her eyes at me, smiled patiently and said: it hurts. I have lost touch with my children, Father.

It is still raining. Kitty purrs loudly. She has put herself to sleep or, complex feline, perhaps hypnotized herself, not to some monotonous tick-tock, or rhythmic creaking from my rocking chair, but to the beat of endless variety, rain drops falling against the tin dinner tray standing outside the window just beyond the protection of the eves. We are alone. Katya has returned to her cottage to pack a bag. She insisted on going by herself, skillfully overcame my insistence to pilot her there. Her confidence disarmed me quickly, luckily, or I should have risked and probably shamed myself with the musty patronizing natural to my sex and greater years. She left before noon dressed the way she was when she first appeared in her oversized yellow foul weather gear, now topped with a black Northwester tied with a bow under her chin. I let her take my small motor boat; there is only a light swell; and from my window I look down from the bluff, watching her make her way across the inlet, the flushing wave parting behind her.

Something is up, Martin. I don't trust her; yet feel no resentment for the betrayal in the works. I follow the line of her wake, see a tiny yellow form against the gray, miss her already. Why do I want to find an excuse for her, for me? Fire-lighted shadows on the wall. Stolen comfort of fire. Stay a little, Father. [Martin rubs his nose anticipating Thomas's wild expository demands, deciding ahead of time not to crack his wits trying to sort the matter out. After years in the confessional, he prides himself at being able to determine sincerity in an instant, see the truth behind even the sincerely stupid, almost always. He promises to reward himself soon with a shot. Mind you, his hand still feels fine. But why suffer even momentary discomfort?] For all my self-consciousness I am not yet debilitated, am witness and participant, hymn the equation of her rule: Gaea in black taffeta lifts her skirts, hoists them scratching over stiffening thighs, urges my due and I comply, dressing my husbandry with purpose, accessorizing it with culture, whomsoever, whatsoever I can summon: no more than the antics of my kitty with a cornered spider… this equation sought after… and my love gone. Oh Martin… I must sort things out. I must fine-tune my instinct or risk terrible things, terrible, useless things.

Martin jerks awake and gasps. The ferry shudders; engines high-revving, her screws turn for forward motion once again. She churns debris and spume, breaks through a miles-long ribbon of tide, and distancing the mole, clears the harbor on course, on schedule despite the fog. Martin glimpses a headland and a small lighthouse through the cloud, hears a basso profundo hee-haw that echoes from the same vicinity, squeezes his eyes shut and rubs his face. When he opens them there is nothing to see outside but the fog once more. For all his opiate-induced calm and the confidence risen from his new-found sense of purpose, Martin is in a panic, his wan face flushing in alarm. He does not know where he is.

Having determined that he is actively engaged in the world, not dreaming in his study, not behind his desk (doubting himself and his eyes three times in the process), he groans, certain that he has missed his stop. Another miss, he insists to himself (Thomas's voice about to concur, lips parting, tongue rearing back). He looks around the deserted lounge for someone to confirm his sense of failure. Another missed opportunity, he whispers to himself in despair, though calming some to the narcotic's euphoric precedence that has already quashed the uprising by his anarchic, adrenal panic, if not yet put down his misery. He hadn't thought to look at his watch.

The girl walked in then, rather stumbled back to the lounge scattering crisps before her, catching one of the long upturned toes of her suede ankle boots on a metal strip that fixed the carpeting to the floor. As she caught her balance, as much as there was, and straightened her glasses, she saw Martin, that peculiar man, signaling to her. She squinted back, then quickly turned away, thought, actually said to herself, that she could die of shame and took her seat, pretending not to have seen him making that odd gesture, a hand up, the index finger lazily pointing upward, the whole trembling, something like a wave she acknowledged, but he was too weird and she too embarrassed and shy at the best of times, and so it was up to Father Martin to lift himself and make his way over. He swallowed back his rising gorge, steadied himself with a hand on the nearest bench back and, leaving his Gladstone to mark his place in the otherwise empty lounge, stalked over to the skittish girl with long strides, desperate for confirmation, of his failure, of chances still existing, anything. And yet, as he himself acknowledges, the urgency is already diminishing against the warmth and pleasure that he feels, and yet, and yet. She senses his approach and dares not look around.

In their combined fluster they deserve one another, at least for a moment or two. Thomas would have enjoyed the spectacle, Martin later reflects, having returned to his seat by the window, reassuringly embracing his bag with one arm, hoping that he won't later be called on by her to explain the ways of God to man in exchange for her informing him that he still has one stop to go before disembarking, the girl having had it established for her by Martin that he is a priest and not a pervert creep, which is what she actually called him as he had begged her pardon and permission and without waiting for it lowered himself next to her with a peppermint flavored sigh.

For a time she picked at her bangs with one free hand and at her thumb nail with the index finger of the other, quite full of remorse; for she was in fact a rather pious if not exactly devout Catholic, had once wanted (sometimes in an mood of excess sadness over the ways of the world still thought she wanted) to be a nun.

When Martin finally left the girl he had had to reassure her, was actually exhorted to promise, as he stood up and steadied his tentative balance by gripping the back of the Leatherette bench, that he would say a prayer for her. He had lied reassuringly that God was not angry with her (for actually he was fairly certain that He was angry with everyone), and went so far as to note his promise to pray for her down in his little blue leather day book, so moved was he by her confusion, beholden to assuage it (by nature more than the coincidence of vocation), perhaps extra-generous with relief that he had not thus far bungled his adventure.

Still hugging the Gladstone bag with one arm, Martin checks the time yet again. He looks up to catch the girl peeking over her shoulder at him from beneath her bangs. He smiles. She smiles back and blushes; then shyly but smoothly turns away and manages the rest of her trip without another serious fidget.

Jane's mother was always straightforward with me; never nonplused by my talk of ghoulish Moe's haunting, Heaven's malevolent reach, and other such things. She didn't react to my disclosures as though they were out of the ordinary, nor I particularly far out of my mind. Not that I think she ought to, Martin; but lesser things have been known to unsettle people. Jane's mother listened to my accounts without apparent doubt, smoking one cigarette after another, watching me, staring ahead or up through the open sunroof at the stars. I would say she trusted me even before her daughter's first wounding by Moe, from which she went to Davos to recover and I to Las Vegas in an attempt to draw and kill him there. Incidentally, Father, Jane's mother knew the inherent danger, if not exactly my plan for revenge. I think she would have insisted on accompanying me anyway (she loved to gamble), but I didn't share all that I knew about Heaven, assuming that it was enough for her to know what had happened to her daughter, and that she had lived long enough with both eyes open to know the ways of the world. Why should I have unnerved her more? The image of Jane, her heart bruised, hip dislocated, limping like brave Jacob after his wrestle, must have forced her mind's eye as often as it did mine. I tell you, Mother wanted to come with me. Still, people remain complacent only so long as the likes of Moe remain at the remove of a headline bogeyman, so long as they are not face to face with goggle eyes and rotting intestine breath. *Contrapasso.*

She insisted on being with me. I swear. [You protest too much, Martin scrawled; more and more carefree with his pencil as his confidence returns.] It was on the road to Las Vegas, on that same evening of which I have already written, when jack rabbits raced my high beams and coyotes sang, that I first confided to her in any detail; telling her of the years we had been dogged, our children threatened; hounded by uncertainty how best to protect them from the inherent harm in the world; and oh, Martin, after showing great promise they both married such dolts.

I was actively engaged with the rear view mirror as I spoke, mindful of the same pair of slant-eyed head lamps from a vintage E-type Jag that had appeared before, behind, and alongside us ever since we left Hollywood, periodically fingering my Browning, and punctuating the whole experience with a pint of Wild Turkey and a shared appreciation for the twilight as we sped through the desert.

Unlike you, Martin, Jane's mother was able to adapt to her imagination a broad range of human failing; generously allowing various madmen a little comfortable respite within her orbit without patronizing them in any obvious way. [Evidently, Martin scrawled.] I remember her allowing one such man (a lunatic as far as I was concerned, though of the gentler sort, the kind that always passes for normal) to flirt with her and offer his philosophy of life: "We live; we hope; we die…" in essence, but dressed in old rock lyrics, tales of alien spacemen amongst us, in government as a matter of fact, and television deals pending for already two decades then. He was sitting beside her at the hotel bar, we three in the early hours amongst all the dancers in mufti, the women unwinding after work, and Jane's mother letting this man regale her with all kinds of rather touching nonsense relating mostly to the second tenet of his philosophy, she managing to break away after the time it took to finish a cigarette and the rest of her whiskey without his or her embarrassment, in fact leaving him feeling rather good about himself from the look of his subsequent posture and expression, sitting up straight, chin up, a confident grimace if not exactly a smile, bold enough now, I would bet, to discommode with his world view (incorporating those ubiquitous aliens, fluoride conspiracy, a movie star brother, and that TV series under serious consideration) one of the tired dancers standing, leaning, and sitting along the bar on either side of him. She understood what he was getting at. Simple enough to see the shared line through most confusion, and nothing much else to do unless you believe that everyone really ought to agree on how to see things, how to do it. She didn't. She didn't care. And though insisting there was nothing like qualitative parity amongst them, found pathos and amusement, she said once, in every way of contending she had ever seen or heard of, except those involving cruelty, she added, and then admitted that from a distance, and in abstraction, having learned to swallow the misery of others as most will come to do over a lifetime, even some of these terrible last somehow funnily connect with all the others, the world a big family to her, a big, frequently embarrassing, often obscene, family. And, Martin, the way she listened to the madman was very like the way she listened to me, appearing to be taking it all in, trusting, offering the benefit of the doubt from the point of view of one for whom everything was possible, for whom it little mattered to insist on point of view. It is only now, really, that I appreciate that she wasn't just putting up the least resistance by her acceptance of all the linked disparity among the creatures of the world, but that she sincerely accepted the unskilled contenders along with the others, admittedly preferring the latter, she confessed, adding that I took more getting used to than most. Not right away did she believe in me, she said, calling me a difficult man to figure at first, for all my charm (honest, Martin), then going on to allude to our own intimate times together years before. Biology had made allowances, deferred our ethical problems, let us get on with things then. Martin, I feel a stirring, swell in remembrance of my embraces with her. [Is that any of my business? Martin wrote and then remembered that he was a confessor, after all.]

You don't want to hear about the blackjack we played, Father. Ann didn't do well, but had fun anyway. I left the table with about one hundred dollars more than I had brought. During my winning streak I did, however, witness strange behavior from the dealer. By the third hand he was staring at me in a manner of such significance that, were it not for his unmalefic earnestness, and that I was winning, I should have changed tables to escape his impudence. I affected impassivity, while he grew increasingly feverish. After losing many hands in a row to me he called for another dealer to replace him, all the while unable to stop staring at me and mopping at his brow with a disintegrating tissue sticking to the ends of his fingers. Before long, his forehead was punctuated with bits of stuck Kleenex, as if—like those unskilled wretches who leave home, their necks and chins spotted thus—he had had a little trouble shaving up there. Repeatedly his eyes implored me to understand, strained to tell me something, something very serious if one were to judge by the way they became increasingly teary and bloodshot, and by the hectic that flushed upwards from his collar and drew sweat from his brow. Able eventually to ignore him, at one point I felt—and oh Martin, I must tell you there is pleasure in this rare sensation—that I was about to wake. I still have it from time to time, this sweet expectation (what was it, I wonder, that God felt as he became man?); but now I know better than to expect anything from it beyond the pleasure of anticipation, the lingering allure of chance, a little enduring hope. Finally, I thought then. As you already know, no such luck, alas; but the rising anticipation... Martin, can you imagine this sensation? What is it most like? Like aphrodisia, a nexus of cerebral and physical, most like those moments before orgasm (should one still manage to take pleasure in this after a few years experience), or for some perhaps more like a daughter's graduation or wedding day, a favorite television show about to start, the delicious, fleeting pleasure that one begs to abide a while, stay a little more?

Anyway, Father, as I played another winning hand, I suddenly smelled Heaven's chief cudgel. I smelled Moe, that promise of decay, fecal comeuppance (and I stuck in this dream, with no real hope of waking, gambling in a crowded casino in Las Vegas with my mother-in-law). His is not a nostalgic stench, as you might want to suggest, like the sewer nose of Venice say, not just honest offal, barnyard stink or the anal bouquet from a fine wine; here was something more. Here was decay, intestinal rot without nourishment; unmistakably the agent of my nemesis, at the same time a living dead, a bag of noisome guts, a deadly pathetic fallacy, a flexing, impacted intestine full to bursting, out to coil about me, squeeze me like an anaconda, force my secrets from my soul. Not yet, not yet.

Nor was I yet going to give up my winning streak at the table. I may be fastidious, but am no sissy. Bad smell or not, I was going to play on between anodyne draughts of iced vodka. Unluckily the dealer did not have the same resolve as I, whispering to a supervisor without once taking his entreating eyes off mine, then handing the decks to another and, hapless lost spirit, casting one last and particularly baleful look at me before slouching off.

I started losing from the first hand dealt me by a buxom redhead possessed of a winning grin, smelling fresh and clean of cheap soap and woman; and so it was a little reluctantly, and with Jane's mother quipping knowingly about her pretty eyes, that I retreated after my fifth straight loss to try to exact a little revenge on Heaven, another of many tries.

It was a pity about the owner of the E-Type, and certainly his car. Admittedly, I was a little impulsive, what with Moe's smelt presence and thoughts of Jane maimed and so far away. So much for the notion of independent destiny: this poor fool's briefly but fatally towed along by mine. You might say—I lift myself off the hook—that we are all linked by sin and that all must pay the price for one another's inherent transgression. Really, though, I don't think I would, except to bait you in this instance, and you may, my friend, have grown resistant to this by now. I'll just shake off conscience like a drunken man's importuning hand. It won't be for the first time. You hang around if you like. Independent destiny: no man is an island, Father, what? But perhaps more to the point: these things happen. One can (most do, I think) play "What if?" for a lifetime. The more passionate, "If only…". The more compassionate (toward themselves, for this sense-making compulsion can be a brain twister, and toward those who might have to listen to such fruitless speculation) remain silent, along with the more knowing and those simply at a loss for words who are, so long as their jaws do not hang open and their eyes not bug out, indistinguishable from their betters. "So what?" is what I call this impulse now. It amounts to the same thing in the end.

Father, let's play a little: so what/what if instead of his repeatedly appearing to haunt Jane's mother and me on our drive to Las Vegas, I had earlier lost sight of this unfortunate, not have believed—anyone can make mistakes—that Moe was behind the wheel of the slinky roadster? Might the unfortunate's destiny have then remained clear of mine? Or was it written up there, Father, as the adorable fatalist Jacques would say; was it already entered in the future-perfect appointment book that no matter what (no matter what host of seemingly unrelated events), I would reduce him to a not altogether wholesome memory for his family and to a soon-forgotten dramatic subject for millions of television watchers around the world? Really, I think now that I was rather more than jumpy, perhaps much more so than usual. It was just that I sensed Moe's presence in Hollywood—my instinct, which I had learned too late not to ignore, too late to protect Jane from her first injury, remained on hyper-alert, an impure state when alloyed with my feelings of helplessness and guilt—and repeatedly noticed this showy car, a nostalgic favorite that followed us the whole way.

We were driving fast, the innocent and I playing a little with one another on the highway in much the same way as that ghoul and I used to play (yes, Martin, play; but without fun) on foot in the streets of Paris. But what if instead of suffering as an apparent consequence of my mistaking him for another—would you have it, Father, might it be, that God had it in for him long before that night? That I was a mere agent within a larger scheme? —, what if, instead of this case of mistaken identity, the poor fellow had had a flat tire in the desert, been luckier at craps, succeeded at his rendezvous at the casino with that pretty woman? After the accident she came forward to give a statement to the media, then to the police, and before the week was over, she had a fairly lucrative mini-series offer to consider. This pretty, young woman and the unfortunate had met a week earlier at their health club, become friendly and agreed to meet again in Vegas. With a week's anticipation behind them, they both fairly yearned for the adventure. But before the rum bubbas were brought flaming to their table on the first night, she had made her decision, promised (she didn't want to hurt his feelings, or at least see them hurt) that she'd be right back after a visit to the little girl's room, deciding to cut her losses and change hotels immediately, realizing that she (who—don't be daft, you can tell a great deal from a photograph, Martin—so delighted in having her lovely little breasts squeezed hard, harder, sissy, her fit little rump spanked) had landed a dud, a hormonally earnest old dude who would never leave his wife and children and who, instead of charming her with even a standard illusion, insisted on puncturing the balloon right away, going on and on about what a sensitive man he was, that he understood (and was misunderstood at home), why women were so up in arms about brute men, that he, for one, was different and what kind of little present would she like tomorrow? [Martin taps his foot impatiently, rubs his nose and thinks, "How does he know all this?"] Or—and I've almost had enough—what if he had simply not happened to park in the same lot as I had, been born in the same century, lived in the same world? It can be wearisome.

I knew (as did my nose) that noxious Moe was playing cat-and-mouse with me; unfortunately proximate to this hapless old fool going through his third mid-life crisis (cruel victim of nature): the Jag, and the jag, leather jacket, cologne, a senior executive on a fling, as it turned out—and with a patient, resigned wife, and three children at home too—when he should have been at an insurance sellers conference in Salt Lake City. Honest, Martin, it was in the papers. It's all so stupid. And I am sorry. It was gruesome. Watching it from a distance I flinched at the spectacle, a horrible, burning cold implosion, totally reductive in seconds—the car, the executive, his conscience, which last I am somehow certain was motivating him to drive back home that very evening —, all reduced to a powdery substance resembling "liquid paper" or "white out" after it has dried, smoking like a puddle of dry ice. (This the result of another of my secrets. Let's just say a potent and untraceable variation of the same chemistry found in ignes fatui, used here as a deadly tiger in the tank, a lethal gas additive along with a minute amount of a certain rare geological substance; a formula worth millions to the foul merchants of death and which, as far as I know, exists only in my mind, and of course in nature.) Incidentally, the paint finish on the automobiles parked in the adjacent stalls remained untouched.

That flash of white light, Father, and a sound most like an amplified gasp for air. Almost immediately—and the fiend must have timed it for effect—I realized my error, smelled Moe alive, alive-o, gagged and confronted the shadows: nothing more than a glimpse of movement from the corner of an eye and the lingering traces of his stench. My nerve gone and Moe in my nostrils I ran to fetch Ann, found her pulling the handle on a ten-dollar slot machine in the lobby of our hotel and hurried her away with me, she sweetly protesting, insisting that she was on a roll. She was a bit sore, eyes still glistening with the fever, having counted on a whole weekend of gambling; was sullen for all of a minute, and soon dozed off as I sped through the desert.

We drove all night to Los Angeles and reached home in the hills of Los Feliz by dawn, surprising my favorites, a handsome coyote couple swiving by the swimming pool. They recognized the car and did no more than modestly stagger into the shadows of an arbor fragrant with spring flowers in the night and early morning. That afternoon I flew to Davos, desperate for the only comfort I have known.

I remember it still, Martin, that telltale reek of Moe—so selfish, too greedy to shit, Du said of him once, surprising me, the only time I ever heard him say something coarse —, remember it even here on my island, even now, with the air fresh with rain, the apples left lying in the tall yellow grass to ferment in the orchard, the eucalyptus, pine, and salt air, even here gag at the memory of my tormentor. I hope Katya returns soon. I can smell her ever so slightly on the shawl she had been wearing and now wrapped around my shoulders. The rain is easing a little, but the ocean swell is still tooled all over with rain pricks, the percussion still beating the tin table, windows and roof top.

I can't help it, am smiling now as I write, imagining the questions I know you would feel compelled to ask, should you still be with me. Questions of such inconsequence: the age of the dead man, his religion, the color of his socks, how I should presume to know such things that I essay here, how commit murder (a slightly more consequential question within the context of the social contract, I admit). Oh, the list of unfortunates whose destinies have crossed mine. With eyes open and every imaginable contingency worked out, there remains the continuing arbitrariness of misfortune, or, (why be so glum?) arbitrary good fortune. Why does the latter so often seem even less deserved? Listen to me now, Father, myself stumbling into that rhetorical habit, that impulsive trap whereupon one reassures one's self (but is a sense of purpose from above or below really reassuring?), expects that there is rhyme and reason: good deeds, talent, hard work rewarded, bad deeds, ungiftedness, hack work, met with their due.

Just like you Martin, in the end, if with a different emphasis, like you I stumble into deeds, am tugged by rhetoric and wrestle with angels, but want nothing more for it now than your company through this text, that you might hear my story; while you have spent the better part of a lifetime wanting, praying for a receipt from God for yours.

Martin loads another lead into his mechanical pencil and sighs, turns the mechanism and watches the lead retract. True, true, he writes in the space after, looks up to watch the young woman turn the pages of her magazine, quickly looks down again when she sneezes and he scribbles with the fresh lead, But so what?

More than twenty-five years ago, he remembers, stretching the fingers of his bad hand under the gauze bandage, feeling no discomfort but catching a whiff of disinfectant and decay, Thomas had impatiently dismissed human expectation in much the same way, then gone on to qualify and buffer his impatience with japery and an unusually awkward sincerity. The foolishness was an ongoing variation on their private affection and long familiarity, personal jibes and jokes, already many years old by then. These old neighbors making ready exchanges with mothers and fathers as the protagonists and themes of dishonesty and perversion, macabre sexual proclivities, sparing not even the dead, each of them already having suffered death: the mother of one defrosting in the freezer to entertain secret visitors, the dead father of the other unspeakably maligned and, as if that weren't enough, duped before he died in a stock deal by the other's father who daily humps his raven haired, broad-butted gypsy secretary in the steaming compost, accompanied by the laughter these two had shared since they were children. This, then, and a paean to the day—Indian summer, geese in formation, a bald eagle in widening orbit around nothing in a deep blue sky, Martin and Thomas sailing together out in the straight between the mountains and the point with the steep and sandy cliffs towered over by old fir trees where the university was, both sides boldly swathed with maple, larch and poplar gold, both men full of joy for the moment, a couple of breaths in silence and soon wondering aloud, did their fathers behave this way? Decidedly not, and laughing more. This Martin remembers, and the heartfelt empathy which Thomas was then compelled to bestow on the world but which he cut short, hearing something in his own voice, his choice of words, which embarrassed him when he spoke of the common resilience inherent in all things, and his especial sympathy for the effective realization, the touching, broad success throughout the world of the common dream. This, he insisted (sensibly only once, and not managing to side-step an ironically expressed mock doubt from the not altogether humorless Martin), was not to be considered as patronizing (Martin rubs his nose and squeezes his eyes shut, ignores an announcement that if it weren't for the fog, passengers would likely see a pod of killer whales in this passage, felt touched by the memory of Thomas's face then, welkin eyes round and fixed on his, such eyes, really wanting some accord, only for a moment, his rare and manifest desire then to have his position confirmed), for it was a sympathy without any judgment whatsoever over merit. No quarter to mankind in the end, no, no, he wanted Martin to understand, returning more to type, eyes up, pulling in the main sheet, attending to the trim, distancing himself from his species; sympathy but no quarter, mercy here and there, yes, but no overall quarter, touching and remarkable this, he had emphasized: that no matter the great testaments over millennia, over and over again the lyrical, the trenchant expressions of despair ranging from the heroic package to the most abject, no matter the fashion, the conspiratorially changing hemline of what to expect, a solid core of life succeeded, succeeded at keeping at it.

Martin started, dragged rudely back from the golden day. The noisy vending machine's innards shifted again with an animal gurgle, another disconcerting crack, tempting the young woman with an illuminated pair of Hostess Snowballs: two pink boobs in a cellophane bra staring straight at her. Twice her hand reached for her purse; twice she let it drop. She really shouldn't: the bag of crisps, a hot dog and two candy bars already. She found and fingered a small pimple rising under her chin, glanced at a photograph of her favorite model, a fleeting gazelle arcing over the two pages spread on her lap. She believed she would be able to eat whatever she liked for only another year or so before it started to show in a dimple here and there and especially on her stomach which now was rounded slightly, a thing of beauty, but would, she was certain, come to lie in bed next to her if she didn't control herself. She decided to enjoy herself while she could do so with some impunity, stood up, stepped forward, skinny, long-legged and stiff, and fed the trembling machine that burped as it counted her coins. Martin pretended not to see. The girl anguished over what the Father must be thinking about gluttony, peered at him quickly from under her bangs. This almost spoiled the Snowballs for her. She wanted to blame him for this, was angry with Father Martin in fact. But she got over it. Another year only. Just another year before she had to think of such things as her weight, more school or a career, a boyfriend—boys didn't clean their ears so well and… marriage, a house, a baby…

Martin stretches, pleased by the sensation; squeezes his eyes shut, then opens them relaxed and unfocused on the manuscript lying on his lap. He lays his pencil onto the dense page. He looks comfortable, slouching some now, leaning a little to one side, propped over the Gladstone bag. He still wears his large, dark, woolen coat buttoned, is still topped by the hat pulled low, the brim turned up all around. He stares at the page over half-glasses without reading the words, feeling new, exhilarated by his resolve of this morning, pleased with himself without due consideration of the narcotic which is agreeing with him so. He is remembering that for most of his life he has given in to cir-cumstances, surrendered, either unthinkingly complicitous or quietly resentful, to whatever dominant state prevailed, in which latter case his face would tell all, tighten and color, until he became used to what-ever it was made him seethe, and he inevitably did, until whatever it was went away or wouldn't bear fretting over any longer and he would cease to care. He smiles now at the thought that he will break through the established barrier of confessional fret work, to find and engage the penitent Thomas at no remove.

Martin stares at the page and remembers. He saw the dear faces, the characteristic gestures, pictured rooms and furniture, a vase of drooping white tulips alone at the center of a pine table by the window. He hadn't forgotten the lighting, or the passing of the beloved cat through a wedge of golden afternoon sunshine, or the leaf-green sun-filled fullness, soft, green shade and fragrant air, the oak tree overwhelming just outside in the spring. He looked on instances of affection and kindness; saw and heard their laughter, grew sad. He swallows to loosen his tightening maw, determined not to surrender to the sweet ache of remembrances, nor to their overweening chaperon, that scolding prig, the ever-shadowing sense of failure that mercilessly nags him so; squeezes his eyes shut, blinks the tears away. He will not let himself drift out of this golden zone into that familiar sector of bleary-eyed despair. Not this time. He checks his watch. Soon. He reflects on the uncertainty of what he actively pursues, and thinks that it is in this active uncertainty, this pursuit, that salvation lies. Salvation, he laughs to himself. Salvation in purpose. How simple: virtue in necessity after all, of a kind. To seek is already to find, some faint echo whispers from long ago. He stretches (never had stretching felt so good, he thinks), pushes his glasses back up the slope of his nose, and focuses once again on the manuscript open on his lap, smiling a little, longing so to see Thomas.

She hasn't returned yet, Martin, and it is getting late. I thought I had put worrying behind me once and for all, hadn't anticipated this. I must say I used to overdo it some in the past: often anxious about my children; fretting over the welfare of cats and dogs, even plants; once receiving some beautiful live orchids and overwhelmed by the additional responsibility I had inherited for the lives of others. Jane was very good with such things. You probably remember, Martin.

I have just woken from a nap, jerked half-awake with a violent start. When the rain stopped, I think. It is very quiet, wind soughing in the upper boughs of the trees, the double bass groan from a swaying old trunk. I feel as though all my teeth are loose, am more constrained by my dream state than usual. Here is a moment of doubt, Father. Where is she?

That's better. I've showered and brushed my teeth. They are holding on now, ready to bite at my bidding. I'm ready for another round. It is teatime. I have put the water on and set service for two: a little sympathetic magic. The cat has finally woken, stretched, shuddered, yawned. She pesters me for her dinner. I'm a slave to her appetite. She is so greedy and selfish, her purring when I place her dinner before her dropping two octaves to a bass note of grunting contentment.

From my vantage by the window where I write to you, and as long as I do not look up and take my measure from the sky, it is as though the earth, my island and I, are visibly moving away, and the cliffs opposite as well. The inlet is flowing out to sea, the tide running smooth and fast. Katya will have to point the dingy well up above my property, or labor against the flow in a way that I still, after many years, find daunting: a puny foolishness in the implacable immensity, fathoms deep above and below, the sea-sky tugged. I have seen the sky coaxed, too, drawn back by the sea, no matter what they say. Three cormorants preen on the blasted boughs of a half-dead fir. Old wood, pale and gray, it intrudes like dry bone from the cliff side across the inlet. Something is up, Martin; and all the while everything is as it should be.

So I wait. In Paris once, some time after Jane's encounter with Moe, I waited in agony for her to return from the market where she had gone alone to buy flowers and food for dinner. We had been in all day. How well I remember, Martin. Let me show off after all these years and so many good meals [No one could ever stop you, Martin scrawls in the margin and swallows a burp]: carrot soup, roast chicken with herb and giblet stuffing, green beans, a gratin Savoyard and broiled tomatoes; green salad after. She cooked very well. A ready bottle of Chambolle-Musigny, or was it two? There are ample reasons to worry at the best of times, Martin, and she was gone for too long. I confess it almost always seemed that way to me, and we together so much of the time.

I sat next to the sleeping baby, watching the light fade. All matter of regrets, wrongdoing, and shame passed before me during the increasing agony of my wait. Panic lost the door, ushered in a stream of guests whom over half a lifetime I have known (they know my island address too), a never-ending line of memories, until finally I heard the door below, the familiar footsteps. But until that relief all of them intent to deliver their host his due. I showed them in as I feared for my love (here was a dark magic, Father), realizing what the loss would mean, exact in my prescience, weeping as they greeted me one by one, sometimes pushing and shoving, not all well-bred, some crowding impatiently to take me by the hand. The other tenants of memory, of the better kind, were out or preoccupied, while these, the concierge asleep somehow, were lining up all the way out the door of our flat, down the shadowy stairs and onto the twilit street, turning into a solid line—where are the police when you need them? Disgorging from a Black Maria, batons waving, to chase them all away?—of impatient remembrances queuing up to let me know of what I was made, stretching uninterrupted into the distance as I stared out the window listening for her footsteps, seeing far into the distance as the line darkened, burrowing into the dusky vanishing point. Within a queue of shame, Father, musing specters passing by, and I the host at the head of a receiving line of one. The din, Martin, a rising volume of dunning voices, revenants feasting on the well-laden table of my regrets. I bore it all—relive it now—and despised myself; and then, so as not to be too self indulgent, despised most of the rest of mankind, too. Sharing proved to be less of a relief than I had hoped, to be part of this species no consolation, no excuse.

I have fretted long enough, taken my tea alone. It is getting dark and Katya hasn't returned. I must go out and take a look around.

The public address chimes, announcing the imminent intrusion of the voice and Martin feels a pressure in his chest, is conscious of his heart beating fast. He looks up from the text. His focus taking some moments to readjust from the page, he squints through the window and watches the tall figure of that man who had earlier stood by the railing looking in. Tall and slim, his cropped silver hair brushed up and back, he passes now, hands deep in the pockets of a long gray gabardine, for a moment sharing eyes with Martin, smiling ever so slightly; and Martin actually smiles back, the dry skin pulling around his mouth and eyes, troubled to turn his head and watch him disappear into the fog. When he looked back into the lounge, he saw he was alone. The girl had left; and somehow in the time that had passed since he'd watched her devour the snowballs, someone had taped onto the noisy vending machine a hand-written OUT OF ORDER notice, black magic marker on green lined paper roughly torn from a spiral notebook. He felt the ferry changing course, and knew that soon he would have to disembark. He gathers the manuscript up and places a marker at his place near the end; not so long ago, he remembers, he had thumbed the bundle and was made tired only imagining the task that lay before him. He closes it and notices, as he holds the Gladstone bag open with his elbow, that there is very little left for him to read.

Martin stands lopsided on the dock alone, the weight of his bag pulling on one arm. The ferry had already drawn away from the island and disappeared. It is very still. Some crows chortle at one another on the rocky beach to one side of the dock; further on a small flock of widgeon wade and whistle in the diminutive surf, losing their balance now and again, or bobbing more easily atop the wavelets. A tan, shorthaired mutt cocks his leg along the fence opposite Martin, freshening his signature with a methodical sniff and squirt for every post. Besides Martin, only two others linger on the wharf: two employees of

the ferry company quietly joked, lighted cigarettes, glancing and nod-
ding in the direction of the stranger as they finally turned toward town
for a beer, the odd man in long dark clothing holding a bag and staring
at the cloud enveloped mountain. The two men and the mutt left him
behind, each taking a single glance back: Martin unmoving, uncertain
of what he should do next, staring beyond the little island town, head
tilted up at the slow motion roll and whirl of the fog shrouded mountain, the palpable mass of which rose above and seemed to lean toward
and unbalance him. He adjusted his footing, feeling rather fine nonetheless, all things considered.

Father. He didn't hear her the first time. Father, she said, and tugged
at his sleeve.

She had been watching him from in front of the fish and chip
stand, thinking how weird he is. Turning away only to shake more malt
vinegar onto her fish and potatoes, she watched, chewing without a
pause, as Father Martin stood staring up at the mountain; watched as
Jeff and Bill the ferry dock men gestured and laughed. She was a little
angry. At herself some, but mostly at Martin, for seeming to under-
mine the authority of adulthood, of belief itself. (She remembered how
her younger brother had been picked on for a congenital limp; how
angry she had been, not only at the cruel boys, but at him, the unhappy
boy, one foot turned inwards, visibly trembling but facing off against
them; angry that he should be at a disadvantage, that one could be
thus, that she should have to see and feel that all was not right in the
world.) And here she was at it again, let down by what she had taken for
granted: that doctors and teachers and parents, that all adults, almost
all, know best, confused that he should appear to be so simple-mind-
ed—a priest—as to make a spectacle of himself. Feeding awe-struck
on the dramatically obscured landscape, the vertiginous dark mass
glimpsed now and again, more a felt presence, Martin standing alone
on the dock, for minutes staring upwards, hatted, draped in a long dark

overcoat (What? Instead of a red plaid lumberman's jacket? he later said to her with a slight edge when she confessed her embarrassment over tea), having apparently set himself up as a figure of fun to the two ferry employees—and who knows who else? For the little community shared their eyes—whom she watched swaggering off the wharf, mocking him with various unambiguous gestures which she understood signified to them that he was a queer fellow in all the ways that they could imagine: not many.

She loaded her mouth with a last soggy chip and marched past the two snickering men, this young woman chewing and exhaling disappointment and vinegar at their behavior through her fine and pretty nostrils, her full mouth drawn tight and punctuated with an amber crumb of deep-fried batter above the swollen bow of her lips; leaving it to them to ponder what her problem must be and how they might like to cure it; they counted the ways and disappeared into the fog.

Father! She said again, flinching at the sound of her own voice, the assumed voice of adult authority that her family teased her about since childhood, with which she bossed the dog and her younger brother. She flushed and tried again with a more characteristic, almost childish reverence in her tone for this man of God (the same with which she spoke to and of the Blessed Mother), but still tugged impatiently at his coat sleeve until she realized what she was doing and left off, abashed, looking down at his shoes, picking at the cuticle of her right thumb with a finger.

Martin is glad, even relieved, to see the girl. My dear, I am quite hypnotized, I believe. He rubbed his nose and smiled. This mountain, this charming little town, he exaggerated a bit, wondered at the sound of his voice which seemed to his ears to drawl a little more urbanely than was usual, distracted for a moment, feeling a rush of displacement, really quite the alien, he considered; but also, in this suspended atmosphere, this darkling fog, a voice plangent with need. She heard it too, the weighted, active interest in her company, little different, oh, with too little difference, from the importuning boys she knew, after allowances were made for accent and grammar and hormones. She was needed; it seemed not to matter for what. She shivered at the subversive intuition. In an instant, she had seen through, and for the moment discarded, all the varietal dross of individuality. She had reduced it; it was all the same. She puffed a little at his need—only momentarily. This was new, this self-confidence in the face of authority; but it should not have come at the expense of the priest and all he stood for, and so it was short-lived and worse. In the end a malign soap bubble facsimile of forbidden fruit that quickly burst, its collapsed skin of rainbow sheen clinging to, corroding her faith in all human agency, emptiness undermining the little that remained of her trust. In whom now should she trust if a priest could need her? She was now suddenly more and less than before. Perhaps it was better when all he wanted of her was to know if he had missed his stop, so impatient, for all his effort to hide it, when she insisted on telling him that she was afraid of missing hers, of not going to Heaven. Where are you going, Father? she asked with just a hint now of childish piety in her tone, letting go of his sleeve.

She is a happy accident, he thinks. He needed to engage her, smiled, and fixed her with his eyes, blinking a few times in an attempt to focus. He is grateful for her presence and wants her to know it. He had already practiced buttressing her lack of self-importance during the half hour they had sat with one another. Here was a chance for mutual satisfaction. She was much in need of being valued—who not, after all?—but Martin, with his own particular need, was perhaps overdoing it; she had come to him, after all. He told himself to get a grip before he undermined his authority altogether. But his confidence was balking as he wondered how one might go about raising the dead, as it seemed to him (where was everyone?), and then once that miracle was got over (it was eerily quiet here), how to convince some such soul to take him, in this weather, to an island for which he hasn't even a name.

You know, I'm glad you're here. He is and it shows: smiles and attention, an overall solemn interest in marked contrast to the gentle detachment, if not aloofness, with which he kept himself from even learning the young woman's name when she confided her cosmic fears to him. By the way… He had to wait again as his eyes refocused on her worried face. She watched the glazed eyes sharpen and engage with hers with a sudden penetration from which she had to turn away. I am happy to see you. Lucky for me, really, for I'm looking… and he told her where he was headed, and how he had been instructed to hire a private ferryman to take him there. For all that he was prepared to seek out a boatman to take him to Thomas's island, he really didn't know where to begin. The town, shrouded in cloud, seemed oblivious to anything that might resemble agency for his concerns to find passage, or anything else. Even the fish and chip stand suddenly closed, a turquoise plywood awning dropping over the square yellow glow with a resounding slam from which Martin flinched.

She led him away from the dock. Stepping down from the reverberant boardwalk of the wharf, she pinched the thick fabric of his coat above one elbow, as if he needed to be steered or reassured to make the transition from the creaking planks to uneven macadam. Martin stiffened, and hoped she didn't notice. A crow, its wing beats audible, passed close overhead and settled on a tarred telephone pole to watch them pass. This odd pair, both taking long steps through the drifting fog, the bird especially attentive to the brass catches on the bag pulling down on the arm of the taller one. It blinked once, then again, puffed up and ruffled its plumage, cawed down to them, bobbing its head up and down. Martin looked up at it and thought of Thomas. A goosenecked metal street lamp with a verdigris glow clicked on with a pop a few feet below the bird. It croaked and leaped away, gliding down to the beach.

They pass before the fish and chips stand. A yellow band of light outlines the single closed turquoise shutter along the bottom and up its two sides, and from this thin, lighted interval steam escapes, curling into the cold dusky air. It is very quiet, but from somewhere close or far, Martin can't decide which, a cat cries. The girl murmurs something in a lugubrious tone about the animal whose cry seems to come from different directions for three or four more steps, and then calls out no more. Martin's stomach grumbles. He would be happier if he could carry on to Thomas's island without wasting time, but the promise of tea appeals to him, and he surrenders himself to the young woman now offering her home for the night.

With some difficulty she convinces him there are no hotels, motels, or hostels except, in the case of this last, for the locals; and Martin actually laughs, surprised at her joke. That there is no taxi on demand to where Thomas lives, and at this late hour to anywhere else is another matter. He cannot in all his excitement accept the supposed impossibility of finding passage, and all but whines throughout the walk to her family home, repeatedly soliciting with a different turn of phrase, each time as if it were the first, as if he has only to chance on the right combination of words for her resourcefulness to be engaged. There must be, can't not be, a service; or at least someone willing to make an honest extra dollar. Or even a dishonest one. The cause is that good, he insists. She calmly refused to repeat her explanation as to why he can't have his way, spoke a little about the island, shyly asked about the conversational abilities of the baby Jesus—which a preoccupied Martin unconvincingly answered was a holy mystery and which would later nag him as he tried to sleep—and finally introduced herself as Theresa. This was her confirmation name, she said. She refused to tell Martin her other one. He didn't insist.

Purposefully, she leads him along the deserted port, catching a pointed toe and tripping only once, urges him up an inclined street winding steeply around a wooded colline off the road of which here and there, through the cloying fog, lights and lighted windows shine from modest little houses. Small wooden houses, some with smoking chimneys, all of which are surrounded by evergreens and set back off the road at the end of unpaved, shadowy driveways from which invisible dogs barked. Remote foghorns: two notes, weary and morose. Martin, mindful of the elevation, giddy and displaced by the obscurity, is fatigued after climbing for half an hour. More and more desperately, he hopes the next barking dog will be hers, more frequently stops as if to admire a glimpse of quaintness here and there, a quality which Theresa is at a loss to see, inadvertently goading him to resume climbing by suggesting that he stop long enough to catch his breath, Martin insisting with a jagged delivery that he is fine, the air delicious, fragrant and fresh. How Thomas would have enjoyed this surfacing of Martin's residual male pride.

The house is out of plumb. Just a little. But enough so that Martin, when he finally catches his breath, has twice to take his bearings, find the vertical, squeezing his eyes shut to adjust the tilt from within. Looking again, he momentarily loses his balance, side stepping with the effort of his concentration, focusing first on an adjacent fir, from the lowest bough of which a bird house hangs (this helped some), then a seemingly upright lamp standard, and finally, but still without resolve, on the tall woman who stands on the wonky porch, holding open an angled screen door to let out first a projecting beam of yellow light (this propping the leaning clapboard structure, reddish brown with green trim), then a happily barking dog after whom she calls affectionate abuse. The dog skids past her. Blacky, the ever smiling, long-haired mutt, tripping and nail-scraping down the stairs, whose barks and lamb-like hopping welcome his young mistress, and from which exuberance he pauses only a heartbeat before trusting the stranger from whom, after an initial sniff, he stays away, dog-smiling only from a distance, flexing and wrinkling his long snout, and later beating the floor with his tail more tentatively whenever he looked his way. Martin exudes some of his newly found enthusiasm with a touching show of expectation: both brows raised, pouchy eyes momentarily just hatched and saucer-round, but with a glint of mischief, a hint of a smile at the role he will play for just a moment, the priest a boy again, face tilted up to mom as she, handsome, her every movement fluent with effectiveness, leans over to pour him more tea, he expressing his amazement that there is no available passage to his destination on demand.

Theresa sighs. Oh Father…

A shame and a pity, the mother answers, cutting for him another piece of apple pie. Such a pity and a shame, Father, that all of us on this island just live to chance our lives at sea on behalf of strangers who never come off season, but whom we nevertheless are always hoping will, and so we usually wait in readiness for such good fortune. Just finish your tea, though, and I'll row you through foggy night and riptide to wherever you're headed myself. Theresa blushes, indignant, and Martin laughs, while Mary, that was her name, smiles, enjoys her mischief, this chance at some social fun, a little daring coquetry, this almost thrilling disregard for the conventions called for by Martin's dog collar.

Relieved of his hat and heavy coat, and sitting at the kitchen table, there was a renascent charm in this priest, here and now a man, today not negotiating for grace on behalf of the unsettled laity, not tired out by disappointment, but a man keen with anticipation and comfortably relating his adventure and hopes to the beautiful Theresa and her handsome mother. Had Martin typically kept his professional distance she would not have fussed over him as she did with the dear men in her life, her fisherman husband and son, out at sea for another week, their mutual friends of many years and long ago the beaux of her brief youth, but kept her own distance, respectful, but with a reserve and attitude indicative of her own worth (a striking one), this mother and hard-living woman, this laughing companion of men. Hers a fine attitude lasting after these many years, Martin enthuses to himself, a natural charmer. And while the girl, Theresa, extra-sensitive still, picking at her cuticles and pulling her bangs, inwardly struggles with the realignment of what she expects from adults (her mother's charged womanliness here a challenge not for the first time, and the priest evoking anything but the sad and serious nature of the temporal, the imperiled condition of our souls), Martin offered intimacy and warmth as he had not for too many years, all the more eager as he became conscious of it to be able to make an offering of his new disposition to Thomas.

After tea and two whiskies each for Father Martin and Mary, dinner was served, a simple lamb stew with carrots and potatoes. Theresa ate two servings and managed a prolonged giggle when her mother answered Martin's comment that the island was charming (he regretted the word immediately). The Native People have a word for it, she said… a family joke he would come to see. Enjoying the attention, he laughs at Theresa's teasing description of himself standing on the ferry dock and staring at the hidden sheer face of the mountain for which the natives also have a name. Martin does not even think of his rotting hand, his medication, or his calling over dinner; he eats hungrily and accepts seconds, much to the satisfaction of the girl.

After he had finished enthusing over his voyage and the excitement he felt about his friend, Mary, pleasantly flush at his excess of emotion, talked the most, telling stories of her life on the island, of the few trips she had made over the years to Vancouver and Seattle and how the cities had changed so with each visit; and then, and it started easily enough, that she had always been possessed by a sense of belief, assumed, since she was a young woman—a peculiar and resolute thing, as she said, looking away for an instant—that something special, she couldn't say what, would happen to her, something along the lines of being swept away from here; something unknown, yet befitting a sense she had of her self. And now that she was old and, funny, it lingered still, this anticipation of what exactly she could not say. Martin could (and at first he wanted to) say something that would assure Mary that something special did happen; but of that she didn't need to be told. There was this something else; and Martin sat quietly, his eyes on hers for a long moment, grateful in the end that he had resisted any homily.

Both mother and daughter knew of Thomas's island, private and beautiful and odd, they said: the three elevations, the split, curious shape; but of him, little more than his existence, except that Mary had seen him and his wife on the port once, some years ago, and remembered how handsome they were, how special somehow; and she laughed affectionately, remembering how her husband had sulked on noticing his wife's fascination.

By nine o'clock, after teasing promises from both mother and daughter about a summer water taxi service and bingo on Saturday nights running through the autumn and winter, and after a mumbled question from Theresa about the great modesty of the Blessed Mother and what the Church had to say about her conjugal relations with old Joseph, the women were cleaning in the kitchen, and Martin, listening to the sound of their voices, of clattering plates and silver, creaking linoleum and running water, was lying on top of the bed in Theresa's brother's room, his head propped up with pillows, the manuscript open once more, resting against his raised and bent legs. He is reading again, no longer wondering about what life he had missed.

She is not returned. Where is she?

My back to a rock wall, I huddled on a bosky cliff top since tea, among gorse and granite, crippled fragrant pines that grow twisted from the buffetings of North and West winds, attentive to the inlet mostly, intermittently gazing down at the artful wrapping of owl dung at my feet; stiff in the knees and back from waiting, listening to deer forage in the orchard below and watching for Katya, staring through the dusk, looking out for the skiff, willing her to appear to no avail. Where is my magic now, Martin?

Why should I always fear the worst? With good reason, of course. It was characteristic of me to be in a helpless state of alert over Jane whenever we were apart; and although there was little to be concerned about here, for the tide had run and there was only a small chop, I stared and stared at a livid sea from atop the narrow wooded hump above the orchard, worried sick that I would witness, ineffectual from my perch, the skiff capsize and the girl drown, victim to a careless skipper at the helm of a trawler, a sudden blow, a malevolent whale and other such things. And still, now at my window at home and not wanting to eat alone, I am victim to improbable imaginings, and deprived by darkness of even the possibility of glimpsing the skiff, then find myself, for extended, foolish moments, afraid lest I do: the white hull rounding the promontory from the opposite shore, she a bright yellow form growing slowly larger as she nears me—then witness what I fear.

[Martin smiles and rubs his eyes, almost giddy with excitement at the prospect of seeing his old friend; himself anxious for a few moments lest he not find passage to the island tomorrow, that he be stranded here until summer playing bingo, that in the meantime something disastrous will happen to Thomas. He scratches his nose, asks God for a favor and carries on.]

Returning home from the hilltop, I was met by the cat at the front door, crying as though she'd not been fed for a week. Now she lies on the windowsill before me, legs folded neatly under her, purring, staring through half-lidded eyes into mine. How long can she intend to remain content? Can't she feel it yet? Something's up, Martin. I can smell it. For the record, there is someone on this island who shouldn't be, or shouldn't be hiding from me.

I haven't slept all night, Martin. I have been hunting the island, searching for the intruder, following my nose. Whoever it is must be consummate. There is not a trace of them that I have found so far; nothing to believe in; and yet I am certain in my faith. Isn't this just what you would wish for me, Father, if in a different context?

The sun is rising now, spilling over the peak behind me, a hostage wave of life stirring in its wake, moving the first breaths of sweet air and bird song, the aspen leaves shimmering on contact, the inlet, too, rising with the dawn. Look: a school of grilse (Martin I can see well; with little effort penetrate deep into the cold sea) flashing silver through the first fathoms-deep beams of day, turning this way and that through slanting light and life-rich motes, flinching as one, back into the still untouched darkness, followed by a marauding Coho. I should go fishing. It will be a wonderful day. I must get some sleep. Where is she?

For the past quarter hour I have been sitting outside in the sun, sipping coffee and staring dull-eyed at a gyre of tiny, late-hatching flies. They are spiraling in an unchanging pattern over a ripening tomato plant that has thrived on neglect, loading with fruit a burdened stock without support, bent over a clay pot pushed to one side of the front door. I think I'll eat the fruit for lunch. Winding above the plant, the flies will not stray from two ripe orbs that I will have as they are, halved and sprinkled with salt; won't break from their hypnotic worship, the tiny flies brought to life out of some late-laid larvae by this sun unseasonably warm after a day of storm, and certain to die tonight in the cold. There will be frost, I'm sure.

Enough. They are making me dizzy. I have taken to watching the sky instead. Some people have to work for a living, I know. This morning it moves at a stately pace, barred with clouds, ploughed with well-spaced furrows passing high overhead; here below, the richly fragrant autumn air, wet leaves, broom and seaweed, a half-drunk cup of dark coffee cooling askew on the mismatched saucer aloft in one hand. Immediacy passes to one remove and now another; fleeting remembrances of loved ones under this sky, the coffee barely warm, transition announced not by the red breast whose song (Father, a maddening twitter of worm-menacing stupidity) has never stopped, nor by the stretched notes of a starling, or a gull's triumphant screeching over a starfish pried off a mollusked rock surfaced above the low tide below, but by a hovering dragonfly, a luxurious blur catching my eye (I am keen on them, Martin). By means of self-consciousness, I am reengaged with a lesser involvement, the world's immensities reduced to a fading sensation in my belly, and in my mind's eye, a mere science room model of the earth spun according to the applied force and whims of school children, infinite darkness and orbiting planets no more than chalked ellipses round a blackboard sun, returned thus to a more practical scale by a ticking clock marking the convenient notion of passing time.

And so the shadows shorten toward noon and I sit outside sipping coffee, staring out at the inlet, wondering what to do. I managed, despite the hysterical red breast that may now be choking on a worm, to sleep a little, to dream after watching the dawn. My father, who sometimes comes to me sad—it is sad to be dead sometimes (Achilles doesn't much like it either)—stopped by, distinctly put out: I fear he is not pleased with me. This is the first time he has come to me like this (the visits always so tender before). It's not as if I can call him up or ask him back—just like that—in order to explain myself. Pray for him, Martin; he was so sad, because of me.

My destiny has been stolen… These words, an awful portent, and spoken by me. I awoke to them (or opened my eyes, if you prefer) after a dream, rich and dreadful, woke with kitty folded on my lap, staring at me green-eyed and purring, still hearing these words and they remain with me now after my coffee, musings, and sweet epiphany. As though

I haven't enough to contend with already. Implicit too was a sensation of oneiric mockery, a loitering suggestion that I am awake. I lounge here, sipping coffee and watching the sky move, augured unhappily by my dreams, deprived of the company of the girl, and haunted, stalked, unusually well. Let me tell you quickly what happened and then rouse myself to action. (How can you bear to fret so much?)

Martin. I am walking in a crowded market, drawn near a table around which the flow of shoppers and passers-by eddies before streaming on, a table at which, across from one another, two people sit. I stay near, listening as a magus tells a woman (my mother? I wonder with a sob, a dear lover?) many truths about herself, of a practical nature, not too profound, stirring in their accuracy rather than importance, the seer, this ancient, eying me as I move behind the young woman, he sitting on the other side of a small wooden table, turbaned, elaborately dressed in brocade robes, storybook-like, wise, of course, old and gray, noticing me, (of such importance as I am possessed in what is my dream after all, or so I'd like to think), as I remain near his table listening in, watching the young woman's responses to his knowledge, self-contained and measured. Then, with that liberty which he takes with anything so obvious as common expectation, to say nothing of teleological vanity, Morpheus the ringmaster plays a confidence trick. Suddenly possessed of an oracle shell or bone to hold like a ticket while I awaited my turn with the wise man—clutching this dear old thing in my right hand, rubbing it between thumb and forefinger, this chipped tortoise shell, scarab, or bone, thus equipped for scapulimancy, this one mine, significantly fissured with my destiny—I am just as suddenly relieved of it, hold it in my hand no more. I am anguished by my loss, witnessed by a short, malevolently smiling man in a gray suit and thinning oily hair as I search, despairing, the shattered stone ground. Twist with this Martin. Make something of it with your psychology. I have been deprived. I want my little chipped shell, a handsome well-worn thing of inherent beauty. I want my turn. I want my destiny back. What of it, Father?

There is a tentative knocking at the door just as Martin was addressing himself to the challenge.

Father? Theresa's pious voice whispers. Father! More an impatient hiss now.

Before he could stand up, she had let herself in, floating over, tented and inviolate under a floor length white nightgown with tiny pink flowers spotting it here and there, a large scalloped collar bordered in lace. A garment that even a surprised and distracted Martin couldn't help thinking positively about for representing the advanced modesty and moral high-mindedness of whoever wore it. With apparent familiarity of habit, the girl sat herself heavily onto the edge of her brother's bed, the better to twist her nail-bitten hands and stare at her knees. She busied herself thus and sighed. They might have been a couple already well used to one another, judging by her manner at least. She sat comfortably, then wriggled and adjusted her seat, blew away a strand of hair that tickled her face, and looked up at the priest while gathering the covers in one hand and smoothing them out with the other. This is not something she was likely ever to have considered, or by analysis wrung of its sincerity, but such was her unexamined feeling for the Church that Father Martin was by rights simply part of the great family, hers, and so her familiarity was natural, and he a guest in her home besides. She could sit easily for now. As if he were her husband, her father, her brother, not an odd man met only today, a strange priest with a decaying and stinking hand in search of a friend. This the girl understood only in the imagined light of Martin's vocation, to which she attributed as well the warmth with which he spoke of his adventure at dinner. She half-hoped there would be some warmth available for her troubled self; a thus far inarticulate trouble largely imagined, but aligned with instinct for inherent sorrow. She smiled shyly at Martin and looked at his bandaged, dying hand. If she was aware of its stench (Martin watched her lovely, tiny nostrils), she kept it very close to herself.

Her apparently chaste presence on the bed made Martin unaccountably self-conscious. Sex had never been a priority urge for him, and was something that he would not admit to having seriously troubled him in any of its various manifestations. But suddenly he was keenly and daftly imaginative. Not wanting to alarm her, touchingly alarmed himself, Martin remained lying as still as possible. The girl was not totally possessed by self-absorption. After an uncomfortable silence on his part and an increasing discomfort to his rigid body, sensations to his neck and the back of his head beginning to actually rival the narcotic, she came to the rescue. Oh, if Thomas had only been there to see the diffident Martin, who hadn't yet dared to move a suggestive muscle. Theresa looked up, and stood almost at the same time. She had assumed—a little like a child playing grown-up, or a movie director—a mother's manner: busy, a little stiff, authoritative. Not her mother's. She leaned over him, her breath smelling of tooth paste, her body of soap, to fix his pillow and scold him for his bad posture, slumping as he was against the wall, two ineffective pillows crushed beneath him. As he relaxed, abashed at his awkwardness, she, in all innocence, found herself staring down at the words of the open manuscript lying on his lap; and he started, inexplicably folded it close and laid his arms over the pile of paper. Piqued by his impulsive gesture and ashamed, too, he explained that it was a confession of sorts intended for his eyes only, adding, with the hope that with this confidence he could make up for his prissiness, that this writing was from the man whose island he was traveling to, these words the motivation for his adventure.

She had flinched at his gesture (much to Martin's continuing shame), straightened and stepped back from the bed, boxing reflexively, halfheartedly, at the air before her little chest. It could have been funny, this gesture, this little spasm of raised fists. Meanwhile, Martin lay still, talking freely, if a little desperately, about Thomas, his cadences more hurried than usual, trying to draw her back, rush her away from the trouble (what had he done?). As if his words might assuage by distraction, by his shared confidence, her evident hurt blooming, unfolding like time-lapsed film footage of a flower—the slight jerkiness between changes quite appropriate—he would later picture to himself bud through bloom to decay and back, she standing by the bed, fixed only two steps away. This hurt, which he did not understand as being commensurate with anything he had done; though he would doubt himself again and again. (Could he have imagined it, he later wondered as he settled into the tub after another shot, stronger than the last?) As it happened, his talk didn't seem to be working. He stops mid-sentence, something about Thomas laughing at him in front of Wu's, a place in Chinatown, he explained, how people gathered to feed, he said, on his discomfiture, the spectacle of his friend's hilarity. Thus he sought to identify with hurt feelings, although almost immediately found himself qualifying his experience and soon blundered into discounting the validity of her pain—Idiot! he later hissed at himself under water in the tub—when compared to his humiliation, which he re-experienced with a little anger then and there, just for an instant, before realizing where his words had led him, peering over his glasses, distracted by a thumb print on the right hand lens, distracted again for another moment, looking over his glasses, staring at her hands: both panicking, dodging, colliding with one another, white-knuckled, undecided.

Martin, his back against the wall, looked on quite helpless, aching and impatient at the same time. He babbled desperately about Thomas, unheard or not understood, as she stood just out of reach, standing at awkward attention by the side of the bed chewing on her lower lip.

She infuriated him standing there in expectation (turning her other cheek, Martin ruefully guessed), tall and skinny, somehow even more so under the ample gown; like nothing so much as an outsized and frightened child, he thought. Had he been so fierce as to compel her thus? She could be four years old, he said to himself in an attempt to reassure his conscience, before again being seized by self-reproach, as who would not before such an image of victimhood? he would later mumble as he prepared to inject himself while in the bath and change his dressing, unmoved by the ghastly decay of his hand, thinking of Thomas. She had stiffened more, standing there by the bed, a stick girl, joints apparently locked, thin bare arms extended downwards; seized in her fists and squeezed the cloth that hung over her thighs, gripping it and holding on, trembling for a moment.

She has refocused, her glazed reproach fading. She notices him again (he had hiccupped), been moved by apparent helplessness: Martin looking saucer-eyed, pale, painfully abashed, seeming to her almost as much a victim as she, as what sinner is not a victim? she boldly thought before going on to collect indemnity on her hurt feelings. Martin is not quite himself. Before such an emotional litigator and the world of feelings, he would normally have stood firm and reintroduced the world as he saw it, not altogether a gentler and kinder place. He now seems to ignore her, opens the manuscript and turns the pages toward his marker.

She returns to the bed, lowers herself onto its edge near his feet more tentatively than before, pausing once on the way down, remembering he was a priest and not exactly her father or brother to be manipulated thus, but still wearing an expression, noticeably self-conscious, as if to say: Just you look how you've terrorized me; yet I am trusting you again, letting go of the gathered cloth of her nightie, two crinkled pink bouquets, wondering out loud, quite in spite of herself, at the orthodoxy of written confessions.

Instead of caroling on about the modesty of the Blessed Mother, her initial impulse on coming to his room, she asks about Thomas and the woman, this pair her mother had seen and marveled at from a distance, asked that he tell her about them—were they Catholic? What did they look like?—while staring at a roughly bitten thumbnail through her bangs. She did not pay attention to Martin opening the manuscript, nor did she understand what she heard at first. Bemused, a little embarrassed at the unexpected narration, she had first to let go any misgivings as to his sanity, give in to the authority of his calling—easy for her—and try to sort through her initial misgivings at the propriety of listening to someone's confession. Privileged words, from what he had said only minutes earlier.

Without warning, Father Martin starts to read aloud. He reads well, taking pleasure in it. Theresa raises her head and pushes her hair to one side, confused, abashed at first, feeling her cheeks color; wishing for context as the words came, but for once too afraid to ask for any explanation. He was a priest, after all. One didn't interrupt. She overcame her doubts for the time being, listened as Martin read in a voice with intonations befitting a holy text, the Bible being the only book she had ever heard read with something like engagement, as if the words might matter, or could be made to. Theresa tucks up her legs, hugging them just under her knees, and listens. She spooks when he pauses to rub his nose and sip from a glass of water, but he smiles before continuing in his rich, slightly raspy voice, and she relaxes more, letting herself down onto her side at his feet, propping her head up with one hand. Still, before altogether giving in to the story, before striving to catch up with Thomas, she has two distracting thoughts: once again that Martin reads very well indeed—not that she has much to go by, but she at least had never heard anyone read quite like this—and then the thought that she is experiencing, tangibly aware of, something other than herself. It is exhilarating and frightening, and she would ask the priest about it, wanted now to ask him to go back and start again—could she believe her ears?—but didn't dare. He reads.

She is in the bath, back three days now; and the Indian summer extends well into this fine October.

We breakfast outside. Ruins of countless distant mornings: brown eggshells, yolk and pepper stained china, breadcrumbs fixed in honey, bees and stained linen. Moments of calm, a sustained pause, for the less anxious at least, before we stand up to do whatever it is we do, and I half expect to hear Jane speak, as her footsteps come from behind. But there is a telling silence, bordered on the one side by a scolding jay, on the other by droning bees drawing on the gorse. Audible from just beyond, wavelets lightly slap the rocks and dock, nudging, tugging at the narrow bit of loose pebble beach below. Expectation on hold, otherwise; some peace until I reflect. These last three days… Katya rediscovered, and the stalker on the island.

The midges are gone. They disappeared after the tomatoes, which I finished the other day, the fruit sweet and delicious; like that which my father once fed me when I was a child standing in the twilight of a semiarid landscape, dusty and shadowed in purple, we at the side of the quiet road across from a vegetable and fruit stand in the middle of nowhere, standing next to the car, smell of sage and night air, cool darkness rising out of the gullies, the two-lane highway still giving off heat, and my father and his older friend, who we called Uncle Gene, slicing September tomatoes with a jack knife, salting and eating them standing there by the car on the side of the road. Yesterday I ate mine like that, in the dusk, during the happy hour, cutting and salting them for Katya and me, drinking vodka. Anyway, I was wrong about the frost. It's glorious out again, and not yet all that cold at night. Soon. I wonder where the midges have gone?

Three mornings now we wake together, caked and stained; here and there swollen, raw and bruised, looking, smelling, like well-used voluptuaries out of Catullus—do you remember how keen we were on the poet, Martin?—with muscles sore, not used to the manner of exercise, compelled by haphazard lust to defy the logic of musculature, of generation, called upon nightly to take unnatural strain; and when, finally, one or the other of us stands from the bed we walk or limp with unconscious athletic swagger, that animal pride—Martin you could hardly forget—that I have spoken of for so long, since our years as students, spoken of with a lasting affection. Maybe you have experienced something like it yourself after some physical labor. Didn't you used to cut your parent's lawn?

What could have been her experience? Something in the eyes, Martin... Should we come to hanker for greater abandonment, a deeper trench to plumb, there is nothing left to do but dismember and devour one another once and for all. In the Japanese manner, Father. There is a calm, an established center to her depravity... in her eyes, Martin... something new with something old. There have been moments when—our bellies tumid with sensation sweet and strange— eyes heavy and dumb with animal impulse, knotted in thoughtless grappling, straining for and resisting dissolution, we are filled with knowing, strain to feed, untoward, gluttonous as if for hard-to-get-at delicacies, twisted in the manner of those tortured capital letters in an illuminated manuscript striving for the idea [Martin resists a glance at Theresa, continues to read aloud] only to fall apart in an arbitrary tangle. Here I struggle to seize that spectacular promise, to try to crown sensuality with understanding, a game for the overactive imagination, nature's carrot still held before, still fooling this ass; and she, without hesitation, with reflexive dexterity, will again and again give herself over to arcane virtuosity and desperate wildness made deftly familiar by need, by all appearances driven as I am, driven to coax us both through a variety of fuss and promise with the simple, most primitive end, to fill her womb. An end not in mind, accomplished with no conscious bother—unlike this rhapsody—but alive in myriad forms and with the roiling matter-of-factness of bugs busily foaming up from under a broken rotting stump.

Who worried about precautions? Not I. I have been leaving my gun in the pocket of a coat hanging in the closet (safety off, mind you) from the moment I almost shot Katya on her recent return, opened the door of my home to her again three days ago. Before she started in alarm with a catch of her cursing breath, flinching hard against the uncooperative door, seeing me poised to shoot, she had been struggling with a visible temper—the first I had seen of one—and a troublesome latch, believing herself to be unobserved. With a smile and a self-conscious huff she pushed past me and went inside. I didn't reflect on the danger. I was so glad; relieved that she was back, that I hadn't killed her (why am I stifling a laugh?). What does she want with me, Martin? Passion is articulate; has its own subtle language of unquestionable sincerity. [So you'd like to think, fool, Martin paused to scribble.] And while the counterfeit effectively blusters, puffs up a moment, it is always without the ineluctable tell, the truth in the eyes, the helplessness in the limbs. And if this is not so…? Martin, I confess, I feel again, since she has returned, as if worked on by some drug. She may in fact be poisoning me. If so, what a precocious cynicism. She must be a bit mad, at least, to be killing me… at her age.

Yet it was she who was in danger. She stood between the menace and me. It was Katya who was being threatened when I startled her trying the back door. (I can't tell you enough how happy I was to see her, Martin.) I was poised to fire, having tracked the stalker home, arriving just in time, I am certain. It just occurs to me that she never questioned me about the gun. What sang-froid. I wonder what her father does for a living?

I had returned mid-morning, under a humpbacked gibbous moon

still bright in the sky, the sky deep blue and fresh, swept by a gentle westerly shaking and picking at the trembling aspens as I write, roughing up the tide onto which the golden leaves fall and are carried away. She shines on us lately (do you ever look up, Martin?) through most of each morning, angled belly down and here above me now, today a little leaner, less gentle than on that beautiful morning three days ago when I returned from a bout of cat and mouse that kept me up all night. Father, I tell you, the threatening presence (this could not be mephitic Moe, for all his skill), magnificently stealthy, implicit, blending with the season and decay, mocking the anomaly of clumsy human agency. Still, I am not without my wiles, have not lost heart; but as it happened, it was she, Katya, who was in danger that morning as I chased the stalker home. No, Martin, not only from me.

She knew this, for all her startled impatience. It was clear: her stiffness, the way she was fighting with the door before she saw me, and I knew the stalker was near, even as she quipped, taking her gloved hand from her mouth, catching her breath with a curse, the reflexive anger in the wake of fear. Here a reproach of madness and paranoia directed at me from one taken unawares, surprised by my sudden appearance, gun primed, I must confess already squeezing the grip in anticipation of firing. There is so little time, so little time to think. How I tremble inside imagining having killed her. On the day before this, I came upon a deer, a beautiful young doe which must have cornered the cat against the shed out back, the two I imagine perfectly still and staring at one another before the row of loaded sun flowers growing hunched with seed along the salt-weathered cedar wall; and I almost shot her, the deer sensing me before I did her, leaping past me as I rounded the corner. I even aimed at the cat that dashed by me from the other side. Kitty regards me differently still. My nerves, Martin: the gun drawn in an instant, covering the young doe as she bounded between me and the raspberries, so near I smelled her. I believe as I write that I saw my reflection in the close passing of her moist, dark eye. She stopped once just inside the wood to look back. How I would have suffered. [And of the men you murdered in their boat? Martin wonders, pausing to sip some water. He shivers, a rush of anxiety succeeding in momentarily displacing the pleasure of the narcotic. He rubs his eyes, strains to see again a fleeting image of deep blue sky as seen by looking straight up, as seen from lying stretched out on the ground, as he hasn't done for more than forty years, which reflection does nothing to coax back the vision, instead returning him to his childhood: Martin stretched out on the lawn of his two-story family home with the fruit trees in the backyard and the raspberries along the fence that bordered the lane, mother and father murmuring nearby, and the dry grass prickling his back, seeming to grow through his shirt. A different experience, the latter: benign, tactile, fresh still after all the years, not like the new, unfamiliar one, fading now with every heartbeat, one altogether without feeling, allowing nothing of the moist earth textured with browning pine needles on which he imagined he lay to dampen and prick through his clothing, wholly visual: Martin lying motionless on his back and looking past wind-waving dark boughs to an early evening sky, to a single star and a lean crescent moon, lethal light sharp silver, the horns tilted down at him. Before the clouds come. He ached with sadness, and glanced at Theresa. Should I go on, he asks. She nods yes, is about to speak but sees his mouth grow hard in anticipation and thought better of it.]

The immediacy. I expect somehow that you should feel it too. What timing: the stalker here—a crow runs interference, scolds on and on —, Katya returned and more: she now bound to me in intimacy. I don't think I will be able to keep this up for much longer. Just a feeling, Martin. And tell me, Father, during deathbed ramblings over which you preside, do you listen? Do you sort through the discursions of fevered confession, or are you thinking of yourself, of meals overdue, a siesta foregone, of other things as you go through the motions of absolution, or as your eyes here go through the motions, travel these lines back and forth? I must confess, Martin, I hope you are with me still.

Oh Martin, here is remembrance again to hobble all action, with remorse in tow, charged with its own merciless dynamic. The door opens a little, and a host of marauding regrets and guilty emanations shoulder and shove to take possession of me, rush in to take the space of a guilty self in retreat. Oh Father, guns are dangerous (a mixed blessing). I'm dangerous.

One day in the fall years ago Du sent a messenger to our home. He was adorable, somehow. Shy and roly-poly, natty in a blue business suit, very polite, this young Chinese came to our door one foggy afternoon. A delicious autumn day, as it is here this morning, overcast suddenly with fog, the air moist and heady-sweet with decay and salt mist. Martin, I just stopped writing to watch a crow harass with swoops and caws a falcon from perch to perch. The falcon setting off from gable to treetop to fence post with avian languor: a couple of flaps, a short glide, a feint and quick turn, now fed up and disappeared. Lithe beauty. The handsome crow has returned to a fir bough to preen next to its mate. At the sound of the messenger's knocking I jerked violently awake where I lay. Couldn't whoever it was see the bell or knocker I remember crankily wondering from upstairs where I was intermittently napping and staring through the grid of leaded windows at the fog, trying to sort out a duet, the pattern of foghorn and horn of a freighter blindly and invisibly entering the bay. (Honestly, Martin, I remember. What a memory I have.) [It's true. He does, Martin says out loud, still staring at the page, reluctant to look up. Theresa is dying to ask some questions. Martin, in anticipation, hurries on.] This rapping, you see, on this so very still afternoon, was more a banging (my knuckles hurt for the boy): a knock, knock, knocking with theatrical portent or a dunning threat, and I felt the familiar dread, one that grips my guts whenever the phone rings or someone arrives unexpectedly at the door. Jane answered the knocking—she won't, she wouldn't wait for me to do it; no matter how often I pleaded with her—and on opening the door, was without warning presented, almost straight-armed, with a bouquet of white peonies (lucky on this occasion, as I later told her; more than once, I'm afraid); then handed a sealed, hand written invitation for me to meet Du for lunch.

In a separate, cloth-covered box wrapped in tissue and tied with silk that the messenger remembered was in his pocket only as he was about to leave, was an old, white jade prayer wheel that I had admired and first seen Du turning in one of his long, manicured hands when we negotiated (of course it was more like an offer I could not refuse) over the Dead Souls and Gaea so many years before. The poor boy's horror. The hapless young man's momentary oversight blanched his face with the implications of his near negligence, bleached away all its rosy bonhomie, all the flush of his friendliness and the relaxing warmth he had started to feel (as who did not with Jane?), relaxed enough so that in the two minutes that passed, his diffidence had lifted to show the mischief in his eyes (Du confirmed this of his nephew later), veiled once more by something little short of terror. Bowing—I had been watching from the landing above the entrance—the young man backed away, apologizing for almost being remiss and returned to his car, taking great care (and far too long as far as I was concerned as I impatiently worked the action on my gun) in negotiating the winding driveway back up to the gate, unless he had been pausing to admire the firs and turning leaves of the maples and dogwoods and wonder at the property. You remember that Eden, the garden estate above the seaside cliffs. If this business, this haunting, can ever be put at some greater distance from me, a compromise reached (for there's no victory) ending somehow in my favor if I can at least be given some respite, I will return there.

It was early October. The trees turning, the fresh chill layering parfait-like the lingering summer warmth, Snow Geese and Canadas clamoring for rest high overhead in passing formations day and night, old Russians mushroom hunting in the wood that surrounds the point, and the still living sense that the year is beginning anew, corresponding with the return to school, something that hasn't left me even now, even here on my island. How wonderful the fall is on God's own little acre. [Martin smiled at the schoolboy expression they had used for the area where they had grown up, explaining this to Theresa in a quick aside before carrying on. She shivers curled up at the end of the bed, asks him for a pillow and flips the bedspread over herself up to her knees, never taking her eyes off Martin.] I remember the day still: crisp and bright, a fog rolling off the bay that had been crowded with freighters held up at anchor by a dock strike, all pulled and turned to face the same way by the ruling tide, commanded this way and that, drilled into obedience for days, and crowded even the night before, the darkness lit by several constellations of the ships' many little lights and the bay become as if a crack in the world, an opening under the North Shore mountains opposite through which to glimpse another sky full of stars. By morning the bay was empty, suddenly empty for me who had fallen asleep, with Jane form-fitted behind me, staring through the undrawn windows at all the lights.

I had been contacted by Du's messenger three days before this particular morning—opening my eyes on the empty bay being only the first surprise—and asked to meet with him for lunch at a small French restaurant downtown which happened to be a favorite of Jane's and mine. Doubtless the thoughtful Du had taken this into consideration. He knows everything, Martin, even the secrets of Gaea; even my formula. Its mensal key especially, the "watery moon", was a favorite of his because of the correspondence he saw with his cherished Li Bai who tried to embrace the moon and drowned. Li Bai: poet, drunk, and god, as Du liked to say. I have come to think he had been aware of the secrets, Father, known them well before me. They have been here for all to see, been made much of from the beginning. You understand it only remained for me to reduce it all to a formula. Formula! Ineluctable Gaea reduced to a formula! The numbers, even for those who can read them, more, read behind them, are inherent with instability, purposeless, dangerous; and even this equation, I feel, remembering now sitting across from him, this courteous, soigné underworld king in a Saville Row suit, his extremely long and well polished shoes carefully placed under the restaurant table, even this I felt Du had already encountered elsewhere, the formula doubtless a household recipe from Shanghai. I am only half joking, Martin.

He claimed to be not very keen on French food, no matter how well prepared. Nor Italian, or even Chinese. His preference—although I can neither confirm or deny it, and come to wonder as I write if he weren't having a little fun—was for cereals of various sort, and usually a particular variety of rice morning and night. And yet I remember from the many meals we shared how he would order so well from whatever menu it was, with unerring taste choose and combine the simplest and most flavorful dishes and finest wines, eat and drink everything set before him, invariably declaim Confucius: "All men eat and drink; few distinguish flavors", and then promise that he would have to atone for the meal. I never knew if this was a demand of his intestine or a religious belief. He was a wonderful dining companion. As I recall, Martin, you were never all that comfortable in restaurants, could never get over having to pay, as I remember. [It's true, Martin mumbles, sips some water, then continuing.] Over time I could always assume from his arranging a meeting where I would be comfortable and likely to enjoy the meal that something was up; and yet he made it seem that we were meeting only for the pleasure of it, that anything other was incidental; and it is true we got on very well. [Martin paused to think back to his meeting with the redoubtable Du in the cloisters; tried to reconcile the austere yet evidently tender family man seeking to effect a traditional

Catholic wedding for his daughter with the unfolding image of a cosmopolitan gentleman of means, and not only, but also one of the most powerful men on earth. He felt, too, the tacit, the ever-so-quiet threat that had taken the place of the departing man; a noticeable vacancy quickly filled in the quiet atmosphere, he recalled, watching as Du was driven away.] He always left me feeling richer, Father. Du so ascetic and yet so sensually developed, so quietly melancholy and yet so gay. His wonderful eyes, refined schoolboy high jinks, as he would relate the actual or imagined folly of some colleague or public figure, or person within sight of us, and laugh hissing a little, his eyes filling. The sum of this blague is that Heaven was stalking me in earnest again.

Du's Shanghai Consortium follows closely the movements of the Global Reach, Father. By necessity they revolve one around the other, but the underworld is not, despite Heaven's comparative vastness, a submissive moon or companion star circling by virtue of the other's gravity, more a white dwarf sharing space with a larger sun. No submission by either, yet; rather both in wary orbits. However, in their intersecting ellipses, they are of such inevitable mutual interdependence, in the ineluctable attraction and repulsion of their physics (in this time of global reach, how not?), that should one move too far from the other, the sky will fall; or so Du claimed, saying, too, after a Chinese variation on Chicken Little, that the diminutive and maverick Shanghai Consortium, managing a form of free enterprise within the interstices of conglomeration, was the giant's worst nightmare.

Du wanted to see what kind of shape I was in, how susceptible to their threat should they take possession of me. After all, the word was out that Moe was about to be set loose again and someone else about whom Du claimed to know nothing. Understand Father, none of this was said outright. I gleaned it from the various elements in his conversation throughout lunch, a lunch during which I must confess I had extra-strong sensations of dreaming. Even as I ate my Dover sole, drank a charming Quincy and laughed, I was in thrall to the dream, and yet—this must come to some with practice—remained socially functional, in the grip of this sensation which lasted through a second iced Eau de Vie (Prunelle) which I sipped between bites of delicious tarte aux pommes. I didn't strive to wake, resisted the accompanying need, more, was actually concerned that I would awaken, (It is at times like this, full of resistance, that I believe I am genuinely close—my dream for all these years—to breaking free of oneiric bondage). Oh, the perversity of it: wishing instead to prolong where I was, snatch a few more winks. You do see what I mean, don't you, Father? The way I felt, so content to remain in this moment, cherishing the whole experience, this luncheon with my old friend on the autumn day, the sounds of cutlery played on china, conversation, bread crumbs on starched linen and yet always, almost always self-aware through all the pleasure of its passing, that I must carry on, carry on. Imagine this, after a lifetime trying to wake. My dream organ is a deformity and I am a humpback fleeing Heaven, running along, flailing behind myself, first with one arm, then the other, trying not to run into things, unable and yet always imagining it possible with a gesture, a lucky swipe, to rid myself of this cursed hump which suddenly is no hump at all, but mischievous Dame Gaea herself playing piggyback, straddling my torso, squeezing my sides, giddy-up, placing her long woman's hands over my eyes, riding me this way and that, whispering, tickling my ears with the most amazing words—I just can't stay mad at her. Try as I might can't keep from laughing with her—and she laughing and laughing her sweet, her sweet dirty laugh, her…

Of course you understand now that it was only because of Du's ethical sensibility, rather anachronistic you'll agree, that I am still alive. This apart from Heaven. It would have been better insurance for the Shanghai Consortium to kill me since I eschewed the death in life of conventional protection, the option of suburban burial. But I think—I know—he likes me. And so, by way of his courtesy, all I have been left over these many years to worry about is Heaven. For all my skill in the ways of contending I shouldn't have managed against them both.

Father...?

I don't know, Martin snapped, and closed the manuscript.

Lying in a hot bath an hour later, hearing the excited hum if not the actual words of the girl's endless narration coming from the mother's bedroom through the wall and conducted into the tub whenever he dipped his head under the water, Father Martin regretted having given his own mother's rosary to the girl, felt he had betrayed his mother and Theresa both. It was a fine piece, an old beauty from Rome, much cherished. He had as well as bought the girl off, he thought, and gnashed his teeth in the steaming tub. But having snapped at her, and again seen the effect of anger on the girl, feeling in fact as though he were Thomas, and not been so lucky with the deer, had squeezed the trigger and shot the poor thing dead, he felt positively damned, and worked overtime to assuage her with gentle words, and then the beads, amber threaded on gold. He pictured her looking down at her lap, knees pressed together; then looking up at him. Not angry but sad—sad for the world. She could have been posing for a religious painting, he thought, and then reviled himself more for his cynicism. He saw again now, sliding underwater and squeezing shut his eyes as he did so, squeezing them extra hard, how she, such a beauty, he thought despite himself, how she looked: the eyes, the little movement toward a smile of the gentle mouth trying, perhaps sincerely, he thought, to show him that she understood, and that he was not to feel bad about losing his temper with her again. A child, he thought, a little girl. She is a little girl. It didn't make him feel that much better to explain it to himself thus; but before long he had calmed himself somewhat, put away the syringe, and now more gently closed his eyes and thought of Thomas; how soon he should be seeing him. Tomorrow maybe.

Martin tickles, then rubs his face in the dark, imagines himself an egg suspended in the self-plucked down of his parents' nest. He blinks their old faces away. The bed is too soft, but comfortable and clean, the sheets crisp and smelling slightly, reassuringly, of bleach. He himself is clean and, moreover, well medicated. He is getting rather to enjoy the process, he reflects. So what? He challenges a shy reservation, a timorous, practical thought that quickly retreats. It's good to be alive, he says to himself, laughing at the idea; well, at least not absolutely unredeemable, he concedes, still pleased. He holds his bad hand up. It almost glows bright white in the dark, rewrapped in a fresh bandage (rather well-wrapped, he thought, after fumbling with it for a quarter of an hour, gagging only once) and the stench of decay is, for the time being anyway, only a nose-flexing hint.

Buttoned all the way up in laundered white pajamas (the bottoms of which he had taken off and draped over the back of a chair), Martin had dozed for a few minutes. Now he lies on his back sorting through dream images, images that could be refreshed, he discovered with some delight, should he will them back, by simply closing his eyes again and remembering. There is no straining with these as with that other seen for the first time earlier, when he was reading aloud: the sight of a dark sky looked on from the vantage of a forest floor, of fir boughs silently swaying above, no sound, a trembling stillness, no sensation but of the faintest dread.

Now the others replay at his bidding. He closes his eyes. Dark leaves fall over an orange-red background, metamorphose into bat-like creatures, all wings, winging nowhere in the safe middle distance; the process repeating between blinks. In the dark, he looks around at unfamiliar shapes. It is so still, Martin thinks. There are only a few punctuations in the silence: of joints creaking tongue in groove, the furnace shutting off, once, something scurrying over the roof. Far away, the foghorn sounds, with long intervals in between. Occasionally he hears the dog sigh, its tail thumping against the floor. He turns over, finds his father's old watch on the bedside table, and squints at the faint green glow, wondering that so little measured time has passed since he turned off the coral-colored gooseneck lamp on the wobbly table next to his bed; and finds, too, that he has bats in his belfry. He smiles at himself in the dark. It seems, as he gropes on the floor for the manuscript, that he has been dreaming for hours. He is feeling fine, conscious of it. Yet the manuscript's final pages will not wait. He finds the light switch and his glasses. Not long before, he had resisted continuing with the confession, shut the light off rather than confront what little remains, a mere pinch of Thomas's text left before the end.

So, Martin reads, the pursuit started in earnest again. Even before Du and I had shaken hands and embraced—an uncharacteristic display of affection from the stony-faced Chinese whose eyes glittered and filled, suddenly humid, I swear, in the moment before he turned away—I knew the haunting had started again. It was just there, there (feel me grip you by the arm), just out of sight in the fog and coming closer (then and now, as I stare out the window at the gray massing toward me, closing on the inlet from the open water), the familiar threat, the promise of harm moving in undercover from the sea. Don't you be shaking your head, Father. After a lifetime some few come to know with a different kind of knowing, and for these few, "just because" is more than just a frustrated answer to something that won't lend itself pat. [A knowing innocent of the meaning of murder "just because", scribbles Martin in the margin.] I hugged him in return, moved by friendship; unthinking then about what his display of emotion augured. A woman muttered as she passed around us, turning her head to sneer and stare.

We patted each other's backs. You, Martin (don't run), you were always undemonstrative; in receipt of affection, stiff and reluctantly beholden (even when nothing was expected from you in return), unwilling to part with any of your own, as I remember, as if you were saving it for a rainy day. Miser, how rich with affection you might be, as long as it's been stored properly. [Maybe tomorrow, Martin thinks, dismissing a sense he has of a wasted life, taking pleasure in the prodigality of his odyssey, soon to be a day old. Only a day, he thinks, reviewing his trip, his motivation so far, this braiding with another's life. He thinks (and the thought is accompanied by joy): a gesture, finally, my own, finally free (not considering just then the euphoria of the narcotic). As he expresses it to himself: to enjoy the pleasure of stepping aside from expectation, from what will happen no matter what, the succession of days and forgetting, unless he step aside. I am stepping out, Martin thinks, pleased, then emotionally seesawing, very sad suddenly, as if he knows it will not last. His old friend's life full of sharing, defined by it, an intensity of shared life; and his, Martin's, always removed by expectation, touched only for moments, never embraced as he had never embraced, never really squeezed back. Tomorrow, he says to himself and smiles. Tomorrow I will sit with him and stare out at his inlet and smile with him, partake in the richness of his nature, his surroundings and enthusiasms. He imagines the place, the three-layered heart-shaped island that Thomas calls his, sees the house and the view through the front window, and then remembers the girl. He looks back to the page full of anticipation, of excitement thinly edged in dread.] But anyway, back to business: this was an unexpected and touching surprise from Du. Martin, if you only knew what he is capable of. He is a force of nature, of Gaea, I almost said at first. I fear it begins to sound glib, this Gaea business; but I need my shorthand and trust you are still with me, will accept my coordinates and stand-ins which I need more and more now; for I know with that same knowing and some, that there is little time left to me to be scribbling, idly scribbling my confessions to you. Father, to return to Du, he is of a power that makes him more than just a man, as it were. With your permission, he giveth and he taketh away. [Still thrilling like a schoolboy to coy expressions of blasphemy. All this fuss over a gangster, Martin thinks, rubbing his right eye. Thomas gushes romance about being on the inside with a gangster. Like a bourgeois imagining he is living dangerously, unconstrained by normality, a rebel of his class who knows he can always go home. Really, Martin huffs to himself and looks around unsuccessfully for his pencil, that he might mark this passage and bring it up later with his friend. Then he remembers his own meeting with Du, and for a moment wonders that he should be so irked, so suddenly overcome with even more painful urgency to be on his way to Thomas's island.] For all that I knew he liked me, this was quite a surprise (don't be cynical, Martin: it was not a Sicilian kiss), this surfeit of emotion from Du, this formidable man; no, no longer just a man, remember, more than a man. I am still touched remembering. Like that, in each other's arms we stood: two tall figures in dark blue cashmere overcoats. We embraced. If one didn't look too carefully we might have appeared to be executives in love, working against common expectation. Pedestrians eddied around us, eying the spectacle. Holding open the door of the idling car, Du's driver quickly looked away, as if it were not meant for others' eyes, was maybe even dangerous to see: the boss man, there like that on the sidewalk hugging a round-eye on a busy afternoon in the city. I was moved, a little drunk too; and looking past his shoulder down the sidewalk into the fog I knew that my dream was never going to end, and then I stood alone.

Our waiter's face appeared above the green half-curtain hung across the window. He waved and turned away. Still standing outside the restaurant, I adjusted my scarf and fussed with my gloves, sunk my right hand deep into a pocket, and flicked the safety catch off my pistol, watching as Du's car, red tail lights blinking twice, disappeared into the fog, knowing that Moe was near.

Katya is up and about. The cat has sprung up and run away. My hackles are up. I am a dog.

I am back at my desk. The fog is over us now, and I hear the horn at distant Point O'Connor, a rather cynical and mock weary two notes, but friendly all the same. I am attached to this lighthouse, known as Tim by the fishermen, christened after an Irishman who almost succeeded in selling, to the country that already owned it, the small island on which it towers haphazardly blinking into the night. Haphazard to me anyway; for I have never, sailing in sight of it over these years, foolishly reaching up or running down on either side of its pine and moss covered rock in the night, managed to sort out any pattern from its yellow-beamed beacon. I feel a strange, whimsical gratitude for that—its large yellow lantern behaving less like a mariner's guide than an ignis fatuus. And yet it is one that has served its imagined purpose very well, despite, I don't know, perhaps because of, its seeming caprice. I have heard of no more than an average number of wrecks in its proximity; and yet the range of its unbound light, beaming skyward one moment, down into the sea the next, sometimes spinning like a fiery top only to stop and spot a point unwavering for hours, even tracking, as once it uncannily did, my sloop, marks a not very safe place either in the day or night. There is a folksy little moral trying to squeeze free. I'm too shy.

A Russian gentleman, who as a young man fled Petersburg during the October revolution, pursued by the Red Eyebrows (don't you know? Murderous Chinese gang members who coveted an ancient text in his possession), originally claimed to own the island. It was he who designed and built the lighthouse. I saw this man only once, at the General store. After he disappeared, the learned grocer, whose uncle had been a police inspector in Saint Petersburg, supplied me with bits and pieces of background. At the time I met him, this elderly Russian had sailed over to the supply island near here, come over from his lighthouse in an old and splendid black-hulled cutter with canvas the color of dried blood. She was a lovely thing to see—well trimmed and reaching into the gulf, or in port amongst the stolid white fish boats, a mythic predator in a hen house. I had admired her for years. Polytropoi she was called.

Her skipper was tall and distinguished, polite in a comfortable way, for all his eminence. He handled a fine, blonde wooden stick but it appeared more for affect or protection than support, for I never saw him lean on it. He must have been very old, impossibly old according to hearsay and my figures, of Old Testament senescence let's say, but he looked at most a fit sixty and appeared altogether vital. We exchanged observations on the weather and on oranges. And one other thing, all this within only minutes, standing together next to a display of salmon lures and crates of Japanese oranges. It was around Christmas, early December. There we stood, looking out the window and each peeling an orange. Here we had at least one thing in common to initiate some acknowledgment, enough of something to exchange amused smiles as both of us peeled our fruit, compliments of the grocer, cradling bags but lingering by the window as if waiting for something, not quite lingering with intent, just placing something of a caesura into the rhythm of the day, a short gray day, the low arching sun hidden behind snow clouds for a week now. This is slightly odd behavior from an urban point of view maybe, but without portent, nothing more, really, than island life. Anyway, after talk of prevailing winds, rain and snow, exchanging a shared appreciation of the oranges (he dexterously peeled his leaving the skin whole), he asked a most unexpected question. He wanted, without emphasis or any betrayal of eagerness, to know if, incidentally, I had happened to see three men, all Chinese, with purposeful and not altogether friendly expressions, anywhere about. I smiled and confessed I hadn't at the time. He smiled and nodded as if to confirm that he understood how I should find this amusing. But there is more to this; and I more than once considered sailing to him, chancing a visit to the lighthouse, curiosity piquing me over and over again, curious still, I confess, as I write to you of this matter with so many things of a more personal and urgent nature still to say. But stay a little; for the very day after our meeting, I spotted a forty-four foot Peterson floundering well ahead of me as I tacked around Little Darcy on my way home to my island. And I saw through my glasses what was undoubtedly the gentleman's malevolent triad. They appeared to be arguing fiercely; or rather the helmsman was hollering at two cowering crewman, apparent bunglers, the jib fluttering and the boom flying side to side. Three Chinese are not a common sight in these waters sailing in a handsome yacht, or any yacht for that matter, this one badly handled by the look of things. I never saw them again myself, but heard of repeated sightings of these three, all alike racially of course, but also in the detail that their yacht was handled as if by The Three Stooges. It is likely, don't you think, Father, that these were the three murderous fiends in search of the old Russian with the magic text, or whatever it was?

Before spring of the New Year, the old man is said to have disappeared. One day just up and gone as the grocer said. All traces of him vanished but his lighthouse. Make of it what you will, Father. Sightings of the Chinese continued for about three months after. I wonder what Du knows of the Red Eyebrows.

I am told the lantern atop the lighthouse is fixed on a gyroscope, tuned ages ago by its inventor to respond, by the varied movements of the water wheels and rudders at its base, sunk through a cavern into the sea, and the mirrors and reflective clock-like mechanism at its top, to the tides and phases of the moon. A lost key to its light semaphore is said to have been privately published by a Saint Petersburg press in

1916. Many years ago, I met another old Russian who claimed to have seen it in an antiquarian bookstore in Vancouver. He said, too, that it is a pornographic text, with illustrations drawn on some island in the South China Sea, disguised as a mechanical and philosophical manual. I don't doubt it. But this old fool also claimed, so long as I promised not to tell anyone, for the Reds were still everywhere in those days, to be Tsar Nicholas II, a substitute having been murdered in his place; as was done, he hastened to add in a whisper reeking of onions and chloroform, on behalf of our Savior, the Lord Jesus Christ, who also had a stunt man stand in for him at Calvary. There is at least a Gnostic text to support this last. Nick—Call me Nick, he said—Nick, on the other hand, claimed cosmetic surgery had altered all distinguishing features but—and this he offered as if it were the best known, irrefutable characteristic of his distinguished self —, but for the knotted royal vein that ran the length of his member; and would I like to see? I don't overly regret now not having taken a look. And ouch, Martin, even the thought... Don't you think? He has since died, I last heard, soon after being charged—in the wake of that media-spawned epidemic that suddenly ran amok throughout the western world—of molesting his grandson. He claimed only to enjoy telling him the facts of life while toweling down the little rascal after a soak. In the manner of Field Marshal Montgomery, Monty, he said to me and to an unsympathetic court when I last saw him in the little smoke shop we both frequented on the mainland. Well, anyway, the lighthouse: perhaps it just didn't catch on, this infernal machine that resists all efforts to tame its signal. There has long been talk of tearing it down; but with the help of the spell—Chinese, it's said—rumored to be written on rice paper and set into the foundation threatening endless variations on doom and unspeakable torment to the soul of whoever dares harm it, it is beaming still.

I love the fog; for all its shrouding of the enduring threat. I have poured myself a Calvados. The girl reads in bed. A succession of waves slaps at the dock below. From how near or far do they come? In the wake of what? I hear so well: the sough from fir trees' upper boughs; chafe of tremulous aspen leaves; wing beats of a passing crow. I am not afraid; anxious, rather, with expectation of trouble. This has come to tire me. I want to pack the gun away, spend my remaining time looking on and smiling like a wise old Chinese. I should rather have laughing crow's feet, I think, than a furrowed, frightened, puzzled brow, the first much more becoming after adolescence. I think I could do without philosophy, half-close my eyes and smile religiously instead. If I should wake and find respite, consolation in an imagined distinction between sleeping and waking, should be able to lull myself into the common dream, singing a cradle song of purpose and practical fictions which forgive me complicity in the nightmare and dismiss the substance of dreams; what if? Would there be some other rub, or would all be changed? Wouldn't I still know enough to worry, still attend to every sound and whispering breeze, the sight of a cat's paw delicately ruffling the inlet, a god's light footing over the forest floor, kitty's occult sight of unapparent danger? More, would I need to burden you so with words, words, words, hanker so after the girl as I have come to do, dwell on the lasting refrain here, the love I have lost? But enough. I have no complaints. [Martin rereads this last.] I am glad for this time to myself, glad to be able to write to you. I hear her sneeze.

I feel less jumpy when I can hear Katya moving about. I cannot hear her now. My instinct, Father, my instinct remains hyper-keen, and I'm afraid I feel ready as ever to pull the trigger. Her being here multiplies the approaches of danger to me. I am, after years of solitude and loss, encompassed by layers of menace, no longer able with assurance to track and dispose of perceived harm, am surrounded by stimuli, forced to choose between scores of possibilities. Oh, confusion,

Father. [Martin no longer knows what he believes, thinks back to his meeting with Du in search of support. A face to face meeting with Thomas, to talk, to converse a little less captive to the enchantments of language, to drink and laugh, that would sort the matter through, he thinks, and went on quite unwilling to commit his own instincts to thought. Ethical behavior on his part was journeying to his old friend, he believes, pleased with the idea, impressed with himself, the ethical aspect a happy accident of his own need, he readily concedes, rubbing his nose, drinking more water. The dog yawns noisily from the kitchen. Martin holds back a burp and hiccups. He is not tired, and thinks he ought not really to feel so good.] I'm like a porcupine, quilled with antennae on all sides, tender belly down, hunkered low. But no. That's not in the spirit of my sense of self, however well the image suits my prickly feeling. So I stand up and expose myself to the danger, vulnerable as any man. The girl is a danger to me. Isn't that the way though? The girl is a danger to practical matters. My survival. The girl is in danger. Oh, Martin, the end is near; and where will it end? But of Jane, the accident with the gun—where have I been towing you?

Jane became impatient with me one overcast afternoon, not long after my lunch with Du. We were walking in the garden, tracing two lines of tracks through the dew, moving through the tall grass and withered iris stalks, winding down past the fruit trees on the last bit of property before the cliffs. Can you recall our early trespass as children onto the grounds of the deserted garden estate, the cliffs falling off to the sea beyond the maples at the end of what became ours? As we stepped down from one of the terraces, Jane stooped to pick up out of the tall, yellow grass a purple-stained cork from a bottle of Barolo, its stenciled name still not weathered away. This one she seemed to remember. She smiled and raised a brow—I'm sorry for being coy, Martin; but I can neither remain altogether silent, nor bring myself to tell you what she evoked by her look and the accompanying epithet for me just then—holding the cork aloft that still August afternoon, fruit trees loaded, lilac pressing up to shade a single side of broken trellis-work smelling of warmed-over cedar, neglected floral rashes spreading many hued in this untended corner, bee-rich with lupines, broom, long-stemmed poppies… All this and the hay smell, hot grass with our smells combining and we, tensing half in, half out of the shade on the old kilim we used outdoors, the unraveling weave smelling strongly of must, wool, faded, but pungent dye, and whatnot revitalized in the sun. And the swallows and whirring dragonflies, and the raven looking on and purring. With us, the delicious dark wine, only a tiny puddle and dreg-flecked stain remaining in the bellies of two tipped-over glasses, on their sides amongst crumpled napkins, some few scattered grapes and picked-over stems, a squashed plum, smelly, melting cheese, and even a subsequently embarrassed voyeur (I know it wasn't you, Martin)—I swear we were unaware of him at the time—who fled when we stood to dress, crashing down into the ravine from where he had been kneeling behind an untended laurel bush cut away from elsewhere the year before and carelessly disposed of by the gardener, now rooted and flourishing on the edge of the grounds. Of many picnics, many wonderful times, of this one, Martin, I am especially fond, still aroused by it even, driven to recount it here, this imposition on you like a photo album indulgence forced on one whose image is absent from the pages, and plays no part in the reverie.

Jane held up the cork, squeezing it between a gloved thumb and forefinger. She pocketed it, and we carried on. Beyond and below, the tide was out, exposing the ocean floor. Rippled dunes, puddled here and there, showed gray through the trunks and thinning branches over which the mottle of remaining leaves blazed. Sewer wafted with sea tang. Near the edge, I felt the presence, smelled it: mephitic, a lesser fiend escaping the ravine from which the overripe odor of fall and run off and soil combine when trespassed to alert me to the presence of another. It is my property, after all. Familiarity had done nothing to blunt my keen senses.

It was nothing by then to draw my gun. We flushed a cock pheasant and three hens. After their fluster they sailed back the way we had come, passing over the dark meandering of our paths through the trampled grass, dodging the fruit trees, gliding up toward the house—sea, sand and sky reflected in its windows—to settle among poppies gone to seed. I had started at the sound of the cock pheasant's crowing, wheeled first toward the beating staccato racket of their wings as, almost at our feet, they leaped frantic with shame and surprise, a harem prurience: one cock, brilliant in the gray day; two colliding tawny hens; and the last, plump and startled beating off in the opposite direction from the others. I admit to being brutally surprised, turning with gun drawn toward the ravine in adrenal readiness for confrontation. I know it was there, Father, felt the pause of menace, a tangible hesitation by this presence, and my world was suspended for the duration of an expelled breath in the cold air rising up from the gorge beyond the tangled lip of briar and blackberry, the fruit long gone into jam, and birds' bellies. It was then that Jane took hold of it—Give me that thing, Thomas. For Christ's sake, she snapped—and pulled it toward herself. The gun fired twice, jerking before her face, missing her. By what? Martin, the lasting sickness, the panic. After the explosions a faint retreating percussion: leaves brushed against, crunched into the ground, squelch of mud, a presence fleeing almost silently, leaving us for now, its job done for the time being—I know the pattern well: coming and going over me, I am the floor beneath its tide, its ebb and flow of haunting, Father, perpetual haunting—it was running away, leaving only the lingering smell of humus trespassed upon, an intrusion on my private decay.

The accompanying stench of trespass lingered, violating me where I stood dying of shame and fear, inhaling, too, the immediate reek of shock, spent powder and metal. Here was the means to bring me down, known by Heaven. Scared and shamed I stood helpless. Isn't there something of each in the other, Father? I, terror-stricken by imagined loss, its nearness, and its eventuality. Oh, Martin, clumsy with emotion I had to work to return to the dance of all our years by laying down and stepping onto imagined cut outs, footing the unfolded pattern of our old steps, losing my balance by the self-consciousness of extra effort. Skilled and loving she helped lead, generously sympathized with my agony, reassured me for the remainder of the day and the next as I gazed on her until she would laugh or make a face, as she had when first I stared at her all those years ago and made her blush with awareness not so different after all the years. For some days I was extra-solicitous, foolish in every other move I made. After a week still carrying the terrible memory, but for the most part myself again, the gun, after a rest in the desk drawer, became my other constant companion once more.

Announced at the time of that last lunch with Du, the intensity of the haunting, the quality of its presence, changed. Almost always consummate, it became sublime. Untouchable, I fear. The transcendent transcended, to borrow from your old favorite, Eckhart. [Martin sighs self-consciously and looks up, admitting to himself that he no longer has the wind for such texts, stirring spells that kindle imaginings of brief certainty and certain, if fleeting, intoxication, enchantments untransferable, with which he ought to have been contented to remain silent and enjoy, which in his enthusiastic efforts to share crumbled into the debris of so many heartfelt but clumsy and embarrassing periods. And he wonders how it is not only with words that he no longer has the same relationship. The music that when he was a student would make him weep now left him dry-eyed, and while retaining its ability to touch, could do no more than make him frown with the pleasure of its sublime misery. All passion on a declining continuum with the body's, he decides. And yet he is making this trip, this pursuit. With what if not passion? The rest is like getting used to the death of someone dear, he concludes, and searches out where he left off, vigorously rubbing his nose with great satisfaction.] The haunting with which I am long accustomed hides behind everyday things that do not disappear in the camouflage of familiarity. I see them as if for the first time, glimpse what hides behind, see the stalker betray himself, spy his abiding threat in the visible flux. And here I sing like some distracted child wandering home alone in the dark, droning a mantra in a language sometimes shared, sometimes his own. (The comparison is in no way intended to evoke a touching notion on the lost world of childhood, innocence and other such vagaries. Of vulnerability, however, that is something else.)

Imagine singing, Father, singing after all that we know, with lasting wonder after all these years, having somehow resisted a complete dulling, the wearing away of keenness by habit and disappointment. [Martin felt only vaguely uncomfortable from this evident self-congratulation; couldn't help thinking it was little different from the trumpetings of aging fools insisting on their sexual vigor, then resumed, his tired eyes zigzagging back and forth across the page, allowing, without further examination, that all was permitted in the confessional, even lack of modesty, modesty not something Thomas ever appeared to see virtue in anyway, except from the point of view of good form. And to be fair, Martin reflects, Thomas had never been publicly immodest, saving it for the confessional, he decided; itself, he admitted, hardly a process to be called modest in any of its manifestations, even the apparently demure, to which he had spent a good part of his life attending to. Confession, self-importance in the outpouring of the nagging, importunate self's concern, was not modest. Human needs are not modest, he decides, anticipating the fun he would have with Thomas sorting through such matters, Martin smiling, lost in imaginings with his eyes closed until the dog whimpers and he starts awake from a vision of dark trees waving against the same orange sky enjoyed by those bat-like creatures earlier. He adjusts his glasses and reads on.]

The haunting accommodates, disguises the inherent rot. Noisome Moe loses points for the grave stink he carries, unwelcome reminder of our shared nature, we bags of guts, bacterial tenements, tectonic Gaea's fertilizer. We smelled him last—yes, Jane too—in Kyoto, but never even glimpsed him as we perned the spiral waves in a rock garden; heard the crunch of other feet, but never saw more than our own traces pressed into the stones as we wound back the way we had come. The only other person on that gray fall day, a young monk glimpsed when we first arrived, moving with a rake through a towering bamboo grove, shoveling slushy parts of a dead porcupine into a wheelbarrow when we left.

By now these hauntings will have come to seem all one and the same to you, Martin. Eventually all the dressed up differences may disappear altogether. Don't all the confessions to which you have attended, for all their penitents' insisted on differences, eventually begin to conflate? And yet you, you tired old fool, you will attach your sympathies to a voice, a way of mispronouncing a word, a glimpsed smile, a blush, the eager roundness to a pair of pretty eyes suddenly noticed through the grill, even to the sigh of an aged malcontent. The little differences in the hauntings give me my coordinates, but the other, vague and immense, sublimely threatens my perception of them all. I will finally be exposed with nothing from which to take a bearing.

No more show. No more distinction. Seemingly idiosyncratic wrigglings in the seething mass. Soon I shall be describing us all as porridge. But no, the other, the imminent threat, it will, this new presence not even smelling of ozone, it will not permit me to imagine that I am other than a configuration of cells—may I say at least a beauty mark?—on the derma of tectonic Gaea. Let me out. I could use a drink. A rather splendid ball it's been and now the morning after: clinquant debris in the mud, threat of aboulia. I really can't afford to lose any more volition, or be impaired by nostalgia. Lucky for me that I have the girl. I hope she stays away from my whiskey. [Facetious monster,

Martin mumbles aloud. The dog pads by his door, stops, continues down the hallway, nails click, click, clicking against the wooden floor. Dancing behind your cuirass of irony, Martin scribbles, looking up from the page, eyes wide for a moment, in a pique for no reason he would be likely to admit to. He has a terrible rush of anxiety, fends off its vagueness, a dark amorphous thing, with the sudden realization that he is equipped by his vocation to handle the universal, not the particular. Martin stares unfocused over the tops of his glasses toward the door in anticipation, imagines bantering with Thomas, just the two of them, sipping on whiskey (untainted), looking out at the inlet, imagines baiting him for a change, saying this: that you, Thomas, for all your childish irreverence and apparent freedom from religion, are nonetheless calling on me, a priest, and ought perhaps to thank me for still serving a lasting urgency in an increasingly temporal world. Thank you, he hears and smiles. Martin decides that he will pretend he has come purposely to draw him into the fold before it is too late, feels a rush of pleasure at his sense of humor, feels a new man. He continues to imagine sitting and staring out at the water, a table between himself and his friend. He imagines, shares the beloved trees, the mountains, and the sea. A luxury. All is calm and quiet, then suddenly no more. He starts with a shudder.]

Katya has been talking. Talking, crying, laughing. Something has happened. Oh, I hear you, Martin. Even here. The fire crackles, and is smoking some behind me. The inlet runs white-capped below, a cold running sea, bobbing with Surf Scoters. The black and white birds head into the wind whistling mournful tunes, dive for fish now and then, while in between us, the bare aspens, one or two coins left to shiver at their ends, and nearer by, the groaning fir, all composed against these clouds in well-dressed shades of gray. In this same window, Katya ghosts behind me, passing across the frame, speaking now: she should love to know what I busy myself with every day at this desk. There is an edge to her voice. Or do I imagine it? It is dangerous, I've found, not to trust in instinct. This one squats succubus-like on my chest, Father. No protesting, Martin! There is no time for it. [!] For your more valid if wearisome objections, even—the worrying of a newlywed over colors for a household appliance—no more likely to deflect my intent than zealous prayer. Poison will do that, I dare say. More later, if I am able.

I, who have been immune from headaches for most of my life, am feeling an increasing tightness around my temples, and butterflies in my stomach, since her return. Yesterday she left the gas on and the pilot light inexplicably extinguished. She has taken to insisting on a cocktail precisely at five every day, these last few. Could she have an antidote for herself? She daily brews a loose and unmarked tea for herself. She is a fine drinker, remains gay company, is as good-humored as ever, and there are other delights. Yesterday—we were quite tight, and rather involved—she slapped me three times and would have gone on, I think, but I caught her wrist and then orchestrated a variation on our accustomed pleasure, so that everything turned out all right. Of late, though, there have been incidents like this last, and others more aberrant. But of these more later. I don't know. [For Christ's sake, throw her out, Martin hisses.] Attend to this, Father. Not one hour ago she spoke of wanting to plant narcissus bulbs in my belly and tend them there. Because she loves me so. And then she made her fingers play the part of the white grasping roots, those little albino snakes rooting from out of the Gorgon bulb which her fingers became, probing my belly, then taking up the theme that they should do very well on a living body, those lovely paperwhites, a self-processing plot for fertilizer and nutrition. She then covered me with kisses and probed and… really I can't bring myself to tell you.

But of the other thing, the thing that has happened, maybe I can show you what is at the bottom of it all by way of what I am able to describe. Surely, Martin, there is entertainment value here in my misfortunes, a little curiosity and diversion for someone safely looking on from the outside. Can you tell I don't want you to go? [Martin smiles, but feels anxious, smells his rotting hand.] Entertainment at least of the sort that a snoop might derive from reading another's mail or diary. [Here we go again, Martin says to the page.] Are all readers snoops and all writers compulsive confessors, who when they make difficulties for the reader, do so only out of shyness: the diffident roots of modernism? And why should you expect answers here? [Because you have as much as marketed them, these secrets, held them up as bait all along, Martin answers aloud, which may have prompted the dog to bark and scramble to his feet with a painful arthritic groan, nails scraping the linoleum.] If you are with me, you will have to accept the provisional terms I have littered all along the way, accept a kind of shorthand from now on. There is not much time, Martin. The girl's carapace of identity has cracked, Gaea has hatched, raw, willful, the only power, the girl bound by the decree of her menarche, the blood pact. Meanwhile Gaea plays us both, but the guile inherent in her necessarily favors the girl. Guile is at the heart of the equation—I have the numbers, Martin, damn you, with all the seeming authority of strings of ciphers, numbers, and letters from Greek and Roman alphabets in unceasing combinations. Guile is the heart of the formula in which we are a mere integer. I shall read her as biology, yet ignore the threat and succumb. That must have been the intention—clever Heaven—all along. But how could she be party to it? It is an impossible cynicism. I won't believe it until I am fighting for my last breath; and even then… The agency of the girl is failsafe. Not all my grief and self-consciousness will save me from falling for it. What an extraordinary duping. How banal, finally, is the principle behind it all. Am I growing in her belly?

Three days have passed, gray and lowering. My pod of Orcas is more purposeful, less frolicsome, breaching the swell to one side of the skiff when I went fishing early this morning. No luck. There is no more Indian summer, are no more whorls of hapless midges lighter than air. There was frost last night, and the unkept promise of sun today. Good timing with those tomatoes. I saw a shooting star this morning, standing on a cliff edge on the other side of the island, offering myself as bait to Heaven, thrilling at the edge of a jutting granite top from which to be hurled headlong to perdition or, fancy footed, dance back from the edge and over to one side, glissade down a hidden scree to a dense pine wood, and live to contend another day.

I tried a concentrated pursuit and baiting, offering myself up and down the island, moving through endless combinations, stalking, feinting, in an attempt to draw some definition from the threat. (I have had no chance to write these last days. The tell is in my nerves.) The nearest solution was to fall from the granite face that fronts a long drop into a vicious gorge of turbulent sea and jagged rocks. Onto this rock face, above the ferocious chasm I had foolishly climbed, having edged out to the center, puzzled over from a tree top nest on the other side by a bald eagle that left off preparing his lunch to watch. A still living flounder, fixed by one talon, casually waved its tail at me as I shuffled into my predicament on the found scaffolding of an old fir bough weathered dry and sky-blasted into the shape of a large upturned beak, silhouette of Woody Woodpecker. Onto this I leaped for the first time ever in what I thought (without actually thinking, if you know what I mean) would be a bold maneuver that would afford me a little respite from the haunting, only to lose heart when it was too late to turn back to the questionable safety of the dead bough already some twenty feet below me; the only chance to survive was to continue clawing upwards, find toe and finger holds, straddle the rock face in the most unlikely postures. After all this, to end a crumpled bloody mass swept out to sea would scorn my idea of resolve.

How dependent I am on this confession. After three days of not writing I am less able than ever to deal with the threat which, even if I am at my very best, will come to outmaneuver me, for all that I imagine I am making it work especially hard. Of course it is I who am working hard. I have slept only fitfully. Kitty is keeping her distance, hiding most of the time, hissing whenever she sees Katya. She used to lavish her with attention. Meanwhile the ineffable—forgive me—and I are like two Toms poised for battle. It won't be a standoff. Keep up, Father, the presence is here to stay for some resolve. This is no mere reminder that I have displeased the powers that be. What has changed? Don't they need me anymore?

I am surrounded. The presence, Martin. Katya has been talking. She says peculiar things, has shown a moody and dangerous side of herself, a despair I have seen on three occasions now, each more intense than the last, each leading directly into a verbal and physical, barely managed... no, an uncontrolled frenzy. In her, a dangerous abandonment, a disregard for her own safety, a threat to mine, a madness surfaced in one whose demeanor was so controlled at the start, so mature, as one would be expected to say (maturity: I don't believe in it in the way that it is intended, approvingly, to describe a parochial behavior), occasions of madness that I have admittedly enjoyed, the derangement and accompanying richness of sensation full of meaning, Martin, full to the utmost degree, and despaired of as well. The last time, she was on all fours, making her way toward me over the glass of a broken drinking jar she had let slip, or willfully dropped, onto the bathroom tiles, crawled bleeding here and there, bleeding unimportantly, but blood has its own drama, crawling out I was saying, out over the tiles into the hallway and then toward me where I sat on the edge of the bed, masked with inscrutability, smiling slightly, actually working to keep up a front of impassivity, refusing to surrender to fear, talking wildly, obscenely, laughing as we embraced; and I find myself wanting her to leave my island, and fearing that she might.

Martin chokes on a sob. Woken by his sobbing he opens his eyes, squints and spills the pooling tears, straightens his glasses angled up over one brow, and fingerprints a lens, continues sniffling with a sorrow the source of which in an already forgotten dream he does not try to find, ignoring the fading dream images accompanying the proud soloist misery that will linger, but modestly keep to itself, skirting his mind's eye with vague forms, subdued shades of color and concern: there, the fading remembrance of his dear mother's face, while his right shoulder retains her parting touch. He sobs.

It is still dark outside, and quiet in the house, colder now, too. The shaded yellow light cast by the small bedside lamp hurts his tear-stung eyes. He turns it off, adjusts the bedding, which remains tightly in place around his feet, pulls it up, tucking it under his chin with the one good hand, the top sheet beneath weighty layers of white Afghan and Hudson's Bay blankets stiffly clean, smelling of outdoors. He reaches toward the small night table, good hand groping for his old wristwatch like a drunken amputee spider. It slides ahead of a clumsy thumb, and falls to the floor. With odd alacrity, and the aural precision of an owl, he reaches down blindly to snatch it up from where it lies. As if knowing he must race against some time-coveting presence lurking under this bed. Martin thrills in retrieving it without incident, retaining his hand, conscious that his heart pounds, remembering childhood ascents from the family basement, climbing the wooden stairs awake and in recurrent dreams, the mad rush up them prompted by imaginings of some dark amorphous thing in pursuit, just behind, only just. In his dreams he is sometimes caught, waking violently, a strangled scream finally freed from the choking grip of the oneiric sphinx that paralyzed a desperate call for mother as long as she could. He holds the watch up close before his face, squints at the radium glow. It is just after three. He carefully reaches over to the table and lays it down next to the lamp.

Martin sighs and rubs his face, feels about him, and lifts the manuscript onto his chest, where it lay turned over, the few pages remaining crying for his attention in the dark, propped up over the dark mesa of his blanket-covered form, the bed a dark plain. This too, the living geography of his form and that of the covered bed, these images return to him from long ago when he might metamorphose from mesa to mountain range, deepen, or close up completely a valley between his thighs, where godlike, he might picture a landscape populated from this selfsame source of imagination, or by the toys he had, or by both. Most often he would stare at the plain and the rising form and imagine an arid landscape, a southwestern desert; as likely as not because of the blue and green embroidery of cactus and desert range, a hint of bloom in white and yellow stitches here and there on his childhood bedspread, remembered now; and the years passing, running school year to school year, fall to fall and he clothed, fed, fostered, much loved, apparently a boy who could spend his time looking out windows, kneeling on the seat cushion of the rocker or divan to watch raindrops race down the pane; the one most certain to reach the bottom of the sill first free-falling ahead of the others, surrounded by trembling stragglers reluctant to let gravity have its way, his favored drop never, or so it seems now as he remembers far back, never knowing victory, some other drop reaching the finish line first.

Martin reaches over to the lamp, turns it on again, resolved to finish reading before dawn, perhaps to even sleep some before setting off for the other island. He doesn't remember having stopped reading, must have shut his eyes to soothe their itch—they prickle still—and nodded off. He blinks three times and sighs. Eyes water soothingly. He holds up the manuscript, brings up his knees to lean it against them, turns the page to find a blank, quickly turns again to find the text continuing, apparently with nothing missing, despite the stern white sheet, the division marked by a star.

Three days have passed, Martin. The girl is gone. But for the ache I feel, it is difficult for me to believe that she was ever here. And yet a record of her presence exists, is here on the page, isn't it? You, at least, shouldn't be having quite the same difficulty.

Today the deer and I happened on one another in a flooded meadow, a sudden storm raging down on us from over the mountains, the North Wind blowing hard in the late afternoon. Rain-pricked and blinking, we five meet coming around an islet of wood, a beech copse in the meadow, stop to stare, unmoving for an instant, then leaping as if together, retreating from something rushing upon us all, veering as one across the raging gust, flank to flank, nostrils flaring, smelling one another, damp musky deer, myself deer-like (almost), leaping at one point over a fallen birch only to land badly on my twisted foot, watching, curses and pain on hold as the buck, two does and a fawn leave me behind, splashing over the sky mirrored flood, arching over a rotting fence to disappear into the wood. And as suddenly as the Arctic bluster had rushed down on us, as certainly as the stalking presence had made urgent its threat, all was still. The wind no more; the rain falling straight down; and I limped back the way I had come, gun in hand hanging cocked by my side, making my way through the tall yellow grass that held the styling of the wind. I am resting less well now, not sleeping much at all, only in fits and starts, dreaming, always dreaming.

I smell the pillows, press my face to the sheets, search for a sign. Nothing. No stains on the bedding, hair, or familiar smell, so deeply delicious. She is gone, utterly gone, back into my head I don't doubt, my head split with pain. I do remember a laundry being done just the other day… nonetheless, something of her besides a memory, an idea… You believe me, don't you? Unthinkingly, I took to the whiskey. My worsening condition, my death, may be the only proof of her that I have. Worrisome, and ever more lonely for me, the cat is gone too. She at least left me the possibility of a hair's breadth of sanity, traces on several of the chairs, claw marks on the back of the couch.

I am sick with it all, yet must chase and be chased around my island (even as I write, it is as if I am out of breath) and have slightly turned one ankle. The presence remains. Yesterday I fired two rounds. At what? At a shadow, I suppose, pulling up my gun even as I did so with a rush of horror that the fast-passing form was hers. Yes, Father, you see it occurs to me too, but I want the girl, that self, the imagined, the cobbled thing. Immediacy is on to me, my story draws to an inevitable end, and I want the succor of her company, her talk, the laughter (her plump lips made crooked by hilarity), shared meals, the compulsion to which we are in thrall. I must say that I never would have imagined her to be so extraordinarily… athletic. Something has to give. There's nothing to it. It has to be me.

I exhort you, Father, if I should be found dead and you somehow hear of it, do not believe it to be by my own hand, as tempting to me as that option sometimes is. Besides, if that were what I had decided upon, I should have gone about it in the manner I wrote of at the start: a backward tip over the gunwales, with weighted pockets, to join the many fathomed secrets of the deep, never to be found. Unless I am transmigrated through the digestion of some fine, firm-fleshed fish, and discover myself served up to you one Friday supper, perhaps even commingling with the host in your belly. [Martin doesn't even flinch.] How delicious I am bound to be, Martin. Imagine. Mother always told me my flesh was sweet, that I was good enough to eat, and not only mother, by the way.

Are you prepared for martyrdom? I have tried to show you the fearsomeness and splendor of Gaea, Martin. And if I die, and the official verdict (should there be any official verdict. They could have me disappear just like that; snap your fingers to underline the effect), if their finding on my passing is suicide—make no mistake, Father, it will be murder, an assassination any day now I fear… Why don't they leave me alone?—if they so expertly tamper with the facts, please, you tell the world and make the actual secret of Gaea public. Why not stir things up? Let the Pope in on it. Give it to some young fool reporter. Tell it to the whole world. Find yourself on the covers of magazines (or maybe in an exclusive ward in Bedlam). Let them make of it what they will. I will send it to you. That's what I will do. I will get it to you under separate cover. Maybe. I must think this through. What mischief. And with your luck—or would it still be mine?—the momentous exposure of all time will be lost in an accident of programming, coincide with the Music Video Awards, or a celebrity divorce.

What a fever of identity had me in its grip. I'm happily rid of it for the time being. Really, as if it could make the slightest difference… unbecoming. Martin, I'm sorry. Still, you're not altogether off the hook. For all the shame in it, I may implicate you yet.

[Fool, if there were such a formula even I'd do nothing of the sort, Martin says to himself. He imagines Amaro holding up the envelope with the secret folded inside and, face puce and trembling, willing his vision through the paper, cursing the watermark in the way, putting the kettle on to boil in the manner of some shamus in order to steam the envelope open. He also imagines himself being chased around the cloisters by a band of balletic, sword-wielding Chinese. And he imagines Du, his face betraying no tracings of concern over cosmic, or even international, conspiracies, a father proudly looking on as he, Father Martin, marries his daughter. For an unpleasant instant, for which he takes rather too much of the blame, he imagines Thomas in a straight-jacket, struggling as best man to reach into his wrappings to extract and hand over the ring. Finally, and perhaps worst of all, he imagines a naked Father Amaro catching the bouquet, an unwholesome sight of white unworked flesh and yet the leap terribly accomplished, athletic for all that (then was this Gaea, too?), but then his face, Amaro's unctuous, now whey-colored face, smiling nose to nose with his, a most unwholesome stench settling on him, poor Martin unable to push Amaro away or himself retreat. He starts, winces in pain. The smell, not Father Amaro's breath after all, but very like, very like, he hisses under his breath, the smell from his rotting hand that he pulls from under the covers with more discomfort than he has felt for some time, the bandages soaked through with pus and watery blood. Without taking into account timing or dosage Martin fixes himself, rewraps his horrible hand which is showing a marked turn for the worse, a steady decay, Martin whispers to it, having turned himself out of his comfortable cocoon and shuffles over the cold floor to the bathroom. He returns to bed—something of an expert by now—after about five minutes of dressing and medication, feeling rather good and ready again to take on the text, the trip in the morning, the whole business. He might even share some morphine with his old friend. How delightful, he thinks, crawling under the covers again, how lovely, he considers, to lounge about with troubled old Thomas and look out at the world on their own terms, temporarily at least. He had meant to pick up the text. A half hour later he remembers his intent, startles himself yet again at the way time does or does not pass. No telling with time he concludes, and wills himself to read once more. Theresa coughs a second time from the hallway. A signal. Martin hopes that he will be left undisturbed for at least the remainder, just a few pages more.]

Martin, she is back. More, I surprised her reading my confession, bent over it, most of her hair pulled back and tied into a rough pony tail, a spit-wetted golden forelock in her mouth, my large black cardigan over her shoulders, covered, the beauty, neck to ankle, a picture of modesty in her flannel gown (a girl again, Martin; and I made almost helpless by it, by this oversized nightgown textured with sprouting pink blooms), Katya reading by candle light, picturesquely cupping the stub of the candle with one glowing hand like a George de la Tour saint. Of course saints wouldn't snoop, one would think. No canonization for you then, I suppose, unless the Old Man is overflowing with forgiveness these days, adjusting standards appropriately.

Around midnight I came upon the girl. She was startled and then, after directing toward me something of a defiant look, targeting me with her loveliness, and a slight and haughty little nod that hit dead on with anything but the effect one imagined as intended (absolutely adorable instead), shamelessly carried on as if it couldn't mean a thing to her what I might think of someone going through my papers without permission.

It appears that she started at the beginning. Well, there is a little time then, for this is not some clever conceptual piece to be started or stopped just anywhere. I still direct the scheme of things here. She started at the beginning, then, and I see that she hasn't reached the part where she comes into this thing, makes her lovely, beguiling entrance into my life. So long as she hasn't cheated and skipped about. But she will know that I am on to Heaven. Look out, she has to be on to you, too, Martin. If you see a beautiful girl eyeing you meaningfully through the latticework of the confessional… How can I go on like this; and laughing to myself too? I am smiling, Martin. Fool that I am.

She must not have reached the parts about herself yet. I know this. It's obvious, for she is not riveted to the text. Engaged, yes. She will read and sigh and look about her. Sometimes a little bemused, at others a little irked, I believe. She sees me sitting here in a soft chair in the corner by the fireplace, standing by the window or lying on the couch sipping whiskey or tea. I affect to be quite unconcerned. I doubt that I fool her all of the time. Periodically, she turns to look at me, sometimes in anger, sometimes so very thoughtful in expression, as though I've touched her somehow, meant something to her without her being named, without her and yet for her. But wait. She will read and reread anything that strikes her as having something rather more immediate to do with her. Here will be the distraction from the whole picture, telescoping, retracting back to the personal. Can't stay away too long, no matter who we are. And I see for a moment, even smiling, reclining, patrician Buddha, self-aware and rather pleased with the image, pleased with himself, this wonderful ability to partake in it all.

She is reading, concentrating. An owl is hooting; and another. My favorite pair, hunting just outside. Katya is studying something in the text. (Sometimes I can barely keep myself from walking up behind her and peering over her shoulder; perhaps to admire some fine phrase, share some moment.) Whether in anticipation of her own part in the story, or something else, the girl is busy reading. I genuinely hope that there will be some reward for her effort, for mine. To say nothing of when she reaches those parts about herself. Oh, she will be fixed to the paper then. What will she decide to do? I think it might unnerve her, flush her out, incite her to make a decisive move. For all her cool, she is not her own; no more than I. I won't let her get too far. I cannot afford to chance this bundle not reaching you, dear friend, dear for all that has gone by, for all my impatience sometimes directed at you. Father, I didn't realize quite how much before, but I am very tired after all.

Another day darkening already, and a good while yet before the Happy Hour. The days are becoming noticeably shorter.

More days have passed. It is a bit of a struggle to get anything done. The girl is at my desk, reading more intently now. I am letting her run with it. Her periodic gaze at me looks more and more one of challenge, as if to see if she can read any protest. I defy her expectation. She can see only some of how I feel. After all these years, I am not bad at disguise, but I do betray myself in little ways: an extra bit of color as a hectic rages to be released from my constraints, sometimes a tightening of lips; or a particularly high arch to one or the other of my brows. I don't know if she has determined that one rises in a manner more friendly than the other.

I do not want her reading all that I am trusting you with. It frightened me some in the beginning, and is still something of a strain. My feelings, their primitive demands, are costing me in the effort to keep them under cover. The people (imagine thus my feelings) are restless. The king waves and smiles from the balcony, picks faces here and there amongst them all and offers something of a special look. This works for a time. But for how long will this still their murmuring? And it is true, Martin, that to be natural is such a very difficult pose to keep up. But I am managing. More than managing so far; for I think my masquerade is undermining her confidence and expectations; her timing at least. Ordinarily I shouldn't do such a thing. Not to this extent, at least; but she, after all, she, is the aggressor. This is self-defense. Self again. But is it me?

She doesn't know, or at least is less certain, when to strike. Martin, I have now as good a chance as any to end this grand extortion. Any day now.

She has begun to ask me questions again. As she did when she first arrived on the island. Do you remember my record of that sweet time? She wants to hear all about my life. She wants to possess me, eat me up, digest me. I don't want it to be quite so simple. My text stimulates her interest more and more. She asked me, just a short time ago, what it was. What is this writing? I mean, what do you call it? A novel. Just something to pass the time, I said. But, she continued, I recognize all kinds of things about… All reworked, I answered. Something to amuse myself and pass the time when I am alone. She doesn't buy it. You can tell. Not altogether, anyway. I shouldn't insult her intelligence thus, perhaps. How touchy people can be about that. But you know, not Katya so much. Her confidence in herself, while sometimes exhausting—one can't let one's self become sloppy over it—has endurance and such allure. I am very careful in my answers, careful to tell her the truth. After all, she may have already encountered it in the text. The truth, Martin. Honestly.

There is, despite everything I know to the contrary, much to be keen about. Even now—but there is no time—now, for instance, on this dark afternoon, the illumined sea and lichen on the rocks, my island, my past, the girl, and I am glad she is back, even that the girl… so beautiful sitting by the window reading, inadvertently picking her lovely nose, then remembering that I am in the room, and pretending that her nose is itchy and rubbing it one or two times too many.

Katya is reverting to the young woman again, leaving off confrontation. The sweetness of her is more consistent just now. Earlier, she withheld the manuscript from me, and as much as dared me to try to take it back. Now that I do in fact have the whole bundle before me, I must get it into the post while I still have the chance. This cannot go on. But neither is it easy to say here, here is the end. Webster said somewhere—I can't remember everything—that the only concluding is on the edge of the grave. Soon enough, I'm afraid. I must say, I don't want to die, that, for all the rest, there is such joy in me still; I am astonished by inherent pleasure. I don't even think much of revenge anymore. That is not to say I won't take it. I have been thinking…

Here is the mail boat struggling against the tide, an old clinker with a low cabin. She hardly seems to be moving, her single stroke engine chugging at this quiet afternoon. Terns call, spiraling above spumy tidewater like my midges over the tomato plant, now gone… weeks, a month… I must rush off now. Katya is in the tub. Oh, she will be angry. I see her marker, an unmarked post card from the National Museum of Naples, a detail of Flora pinching a delicate white bloom that grows almost to her shoulders, picking it in an exquisite gesture of reaching back, having just passed it by, plucking the flower without stopping, the goddess betrayed by her walk, the marker just past where I surmise her intentions for me to be. So, she is playing my game, too.

This is the first chance I have had to gather the paper together. I hope you like these stamps, Martin. I will try to write again. I will try to let you know. There is something new, you see. No matter now. Remember me. I must run to catch the boat, signal to the Captain that I have something for him to take for me, trust it to the world.

Whether Martin wept over what he read, moved by the hasty scrawl, a blue-black smudge of last words promising resolve (of a kind he had not begun to imagine), from satisfaction at being delivered from confession, or because of pent-up emotion overall, is unclear. He blubbered and sniffed, had a good cry, and as before luxuriated in the process, the irrigation of his eyes feeling especially good, second in pleasure only to that of his total submission to the immediate feeling, abiding in the few seconds before self-consciousness made of it a thing at one remove, then another, and still counting.

Panting audibly, the dog is passing by with a pillow in his mouth embroidered with the name Carolina in cursive; he stops for a moment outside Martin's door, cocks his ears, tilts his head, sniffs and shuffles about, then carries on click, click, clicking toward the kitchen. Martin stares at the door and wipes his nose with the back of his good hand. The sound of the animal retreating down the hallway distances him yet further from his self-indulgence, takes the better part of it away with him, snatched and carried off like some table scrap. He finds his outsized hanky, blows his nose, listens to the dog circle about its spot in the corner by the stove, and hears it cautiously lowering itself, nails slipping over the linoleum, dropping its rheumatic hind quarters with a little whimper and thump to the floor.

Martin sniffs, dabs at his cheeks with the top border of the bed sheet, through clogged nostrils enjoys the scent of crisp linen, smelling still of childhood and summer holidays, followed by a wafting of disinfectant and underlying rot from the hand dying by his side under the covers. He smoothes the bedding down. There is no point trying to sleep, he decides, rereading the last page. He lets the manuscript down to rest on his stomach, enjoying its weight there, staring at the door before him, savoring still the fatalism accompanying sorrow, a lovely if fleeting taste of freedom—he should piss, only not just now—almost gone. Soon Martin will convince himself that his free will, if no one else's, is intact, something to be relied upon, necessary. He has something to do.

There is a tapping at the door. It has to be the girl. The insistence of it, as with her impossible questions and striving for theological certainty, mocks any suggestion of tact. The door opens before he can decide if he should pretend to be asleep.

She stands fully dressed, holding a black rubber slicker under one arm, hesitating in the hallway, finally tip-toeing inside, shutting the door gently behind her, the floor boards creaking despite her care.

Good Morning, Martin croaks, struggling to sit up in bed. She hushes him, green eyes emphatic and round behind her glasses. He shames at the smell of decay, reaches for the tin of mints lying open on the bedside table, managing to push one or two into his mouth.

Theresa stops by the side of the bed and stares for a moment at the closed manuscript resting on Martin's stomach, sneaks a glance at him, fusses with the rubber slicker, searching through its empty pockets. He offers her a mint in a whisper. She doesn't respond.

As before, she brought with herself a pleasing smell, of soap, of freshness, of youth (so Martin thought for want of anything better to call it. Wouldn't Thomas have the word for it, though, he sighs, and, satyr, a motivating conspiracy excusing all it might inspire...?) He rubs his nose and swallows, moved again by her beauty, so unlike the considerateness of please-everyone-prettiness, watching her deliberate over something or other as if for an acting class. This beauty something else, he imagines; beyond the features a promise, tangible insistence on the veracity of some ideal; no matter which. Yet instead of the resolute authority beauty can at least initially convey, here was something of the supplicant, child-like and helpless, consequently made almost manageable, he concluded. He recalled her persistent questions on the ferry and his impatience, how he was enervated by her unanswerable persistence, weakened and angry with himself from the realization that he was powerless, ultimately, to help her, cruelly tempted to disabuse her of the role of the eternal child of God that she sometimes assumed, then struck again by beauty in waves of sensation—in the manner, he reflects with a smile, tickled at the thought that he has become something of a connoisseur and sensualist (frowning then, with some doubt about himself), in the manner of Thomas who, surely, given the opportunity to explain, would make an awesome predator out of her, to which he would lend himself as spirited prey, and then, in their joining in sin, wax lyrical about the victims of Gaea. Martin winces and tells himself that he has in no way surrendered to Thomas's view of the scheme of things, despite, he insists to himself, his increasing tendency to consider in the manner he imagines Thomas might. Insidious, he says to himself.

She lets herself drop without hesitation onto the bed by his side. Oh Father, she whispers, seeing that he had been weeping. She looks down at her chewed fingernails, and then up, determined to get on with things. Who is Carolina, he asks? She starts. Theresa is my confirmation name, she says. Little flower of the Lord, you know. Her glasses are not sitting quite straight on her lovely nose.

After breakfast Father Martin bids the mother good-bye with many thanks. From the sink she looks over her shoulder at him, blows away a stray forelock, liking him, smiling with warmth and friendly irony as she scrubs a dish, wondering at his behavior. After all, he is going out with Theresa for a walk, not off to war. Thus she quips to herself, almost tries it aloud but thinks better of it, understanding the priest's diffidence in the face of her hospitality, at least in part. Martin continues his elaborate farewell (Theresa standing by the open kitchen door, letting in the cold, Blacky whining, beating his tail against a plastic trash bin, pushing his snout between her thighs until delivered a slap meant for Martin, the girl stiffening in fury at the thought of imminent disclosure of her plan. Father, she interrupts him, can't help herself; then more boldly, Father, you'll miss the boat. Thus she sang, laughing at her daring until humbled some by a quick and knowing look from her mother, who, she realizes, knows something is up. Oh, I'll pay for this one, the girl thought, but saw her sacrifice in the light of a self-less—if ennobling—ideal, imagines that she is doing something good for another, not just any other, either, but a priest; just as a saint might, she was sure, and had in fact prayed extra the night before for guidance in her venture. And it was, she admitted to herself, exciting besides).

Martin blanches, startled by her daring, not used to the requirements of this sort of pretense. He stands, his good hand traveling in and out of his coat pocket, pretending that Theresa is quite the little joker, directing a toothy grin in her direction, an understanding glance for mom at the sink. Anxiously he dallies, effuses over breakfast, the comfortable bed, risks a little joke about bingo, going on with genuine affection and much shame. Looking forward, he adds and almost chokes on it, looking forward to lunch, disgraced by the dissembling Theresa had urged on him and which he had barely resisted—hypocrite, he had already hissed at himself as he dressed, buttoning up another fresh shirt, troubling to groom himself, going only so far as to raise with her the doubtful probity of their behavior (and that was something like how, in an attempt to sanitize the whole business, very like how he expressed it, with a sprinkling of the carbolic of formality on his betrayal of hospitality and himself). The inherent sin of going against the wishes of one's mother (this wonderful woman especially. And he had remonstrated: she of all people would understand, approve, come along for the ride, even… No, the girl had answered, and that was that), letting the girl sway him, unable to restrain himself from spurring her on, prompting her to convince him that she alone should ferry him to the island. Everyone else, she said, was fishing. All right, he had decided, resolved to feel better about it. It would have to be her, then. There was no other way, nor time to dilly-dally (Theresa's expression, delivered in the way a child would imitate an adult). She had told him to get on with it, sitting on the bed, playing mother to a child reluctant, say, to rise and prepare for school, then commanded, hectored him to get dressed until she suddenly came to, heard herself talking to the priest in this way. Martin didn't even notice, so eager had he become at this final leg of his voyage. And he remembered (they were jokes, teases, but he restructured them to his own purpose, and shivered) the winter bingo, months long combinations of numbers and letters endless, arbitrary combinations. Trembling, he listened to her plan, listened to her, squeezing and releasing a handful of bedding with his one good hand.

He made a dash past his hypocrisy with this nominal, token, reservation about filial piety, simply by saying it out loud, albeit in a whisper, hating himself for so obviously not fooling the girl (who showed such pragmatism and perhaps a little scorn in affecting—did she?—not to have heard his little, his softly-breathed reservation), hating himself only so much, though, expression of such things, as he well knew, usually sufficient to assuage conscience, so that impulse may pick up where it left off, pick up and get on with things no longer burdened by moral niceties. He had to be practical here. He told Theresa that if he were to dress, she really ought to leave the room and let him get on with it.

She blushes, but always the thinker, asks to sneak his bag out with her so as not to arouse any suspicion. He decides he will leave his pajamas behind as a decoy. Stomach turning with anxiety and shame, he remembers the mother, her stories, her sad and cheerful manner. Here there was no space for the luxury of such things as moral qualms, he replies to himself again, the thrill of setting off, seeing Thomas today, pushing through the rest.

Conscience persists all the way down to the dock. Manic and fretting, he argues with himself, descending the winding road to the port. The two do not speak. Softly, the girl sings Christmas carols, which, if he hadn't been so preoccupied, would have driven him mad. He breathes fragrant sea air and haunts himself with arguments for and against his actions, heartfelt sighs steaming from his nose into the cold. If he does not act... not that that would be wrong, it could be argued, not that it would matter very much, but there was no time to argue. He carries on this discourse with himself even as he steps gingerly onboard, fearful of his balance, steadied by the matter-of-fact girl into the fisherman's seat of the twenty-foot fiberglass skiff.

Theresa lifts over her head a key threaded by string, fits it into the ignition on a mid-ship consul, and starts the inboard-outboard engine with a single turn. Before her, Martin sits erect and shivers, fusses with his scarf, pulls his hat further down onto his head, glances back at the port and up at the hills behind, stares at lines of smoke drifting upwards from various chimneys among the trees visible here and there, tries and fails to find the house where he was a guest, imagines how the mother will react to this betrayal (she who assured him that tomorrow she would ask an old friend to take him where he wanted to go. Just one more day, she had gently said, with evident care for his feelings, his eagerness to see his friend. She had listened well, been moved, was going to help him).

He is astonished by what is passing. Fato profugus, Martin

remembers, driven by fate like Virgil's Aeneas. Very like, he sighs, wondering at the safety of such a little boat in the wintry sea, pushed back suddenly into the molded fisherman's seat fixed before the consul, startled as Theresa, with unexpected authority and apparent recklessness, pushes the throttle forward. With a roar from the engine they speed away from the slip, racing past the ferry dock, ignoring the hollers, laughter and waving of the two young men who had been on the dock when Martin arrived yesterday, only yesterday, skimming past the breakwater. Martin swivels around in the chair, exhilarated, smiling. He stares at the girl. Aware of his eyes she sets her mouth with concentration, looks at him and smiles, then over his head returns her focus to the middle distance, her hair streaming behind her in a neat pony tail, black muffs over her ears, the wind coming across the bow, a pale yellow fissure slowly closing over the distant horizon, the fleet skiff beating over a small chop into the gulf.

The slit closes over the horizon, displacing the distant line of ocean, obscuring the pale light behind, extinguishing its lambent play over the waves. In each of the intervals during which Father Martin and the girl lost sight of the offing, a succession of islands coming between them, the sky gathered more mass; where the sky mixes with the sea eventually obscured altogether as the small boat enters the dense archipelago of small but hilly, even mountainous, islands, rock-faced and densely fringed with evergreen.

It had seemed it must rain from the time Martin and the girl left the harbor. There on the quay, two young men sat in the café, joked over eggs and bacon as the first drops beat against the plate glass; recounted—while betting dollars on which staggering drop would reach the bottom first—recounted the sight of the open skiff speeding into the gulf: the young woman at the wheel; before her, wrapped in a dark overcoat, hat pulled low, the city apparition, the vampire. They chortled: the man sitting upright in the molded plastic fisherman's seat, legs pressed together, the chair itself seeming—because of the skiff's low profile—to be speeding along with the motionless black figure held aloft, this wave-skimming apparition buffeted full in the face by cold salt air.

Martin and the girl have been at sea for the better part of the morning now; rapped over the spumy washboard tide racing in and out among a score of islands; bongo-beaten the hull over a back jarring chop; see-sawed over a Russian freighter's wake; now, finally, Thomas's island in sight. At first the girl doubted her own navigational skill. Thomas's island, its vague place in her memory, was indistinguishable from the whole landscape crowding the sky before them: a dark green mass consisting of low cloud, part of another island and the mainland, then coming into its own as the skiff rounded a promontory, leaving behind an incessant chop to glide suddenly with luxurious smoothness over a glass-calm passage.

The girl grips Martin's shoulder. He starts. She is pointing straight ahead, not watching where she is going, staring at him with a happy, relieved smile. She hollers over the engine: Father, look! They skim at full throttle over a perfect black calm, through a shadowy passage over which the air hunkers warm and freshly piscine, fertile, smelling too of the rain to come, passing now between the mainland and an islet.

Too close to the islet—Martin glancing down to his left (port, he thinks), gripping the sides of the seat, flinches from sudden brightness, paling of the shallows: gray reef rushing to seize them in their flight and he too astonished to cry out, twisting to see the girl stiffen and turn pale, mouth something—and slide on somehow safely past, the outcrop reeking guano, scores of cormorants crook-necked, waiting for something to happen.

Thomas's island, triple-tiered, rises above them, its sheer rock face on this eastern side overhung and fringed with fir and pine, hung with moss and ivy, the skiff skimming over the black water, air still and sky lowering.

The girl throttles down and their wake catches them up, lifts them gently from behind, passing on under, easing the skiff down to glide after it through a scattering of yellow and red leaves floating dead on the black water, tops dry and crisp, lately fallen, the wave carrying on to slap once against a rock, roll over and die. Martin looks up and sees the little maple from which the leaves had dropped. Almost completely bare, still ornamented here and there on its delicate boughs, it over-reached a granite ledge, alone of its kind between two pine shrubs.

Here is uneasy calm, the engine gurgling gently at idle, cawing of a crow from somewhere above. After hours of beating hull and engine roar, an eerie luxury in stillness. Neither moves. Exchanging eyes they realize, each with a smile, that they have been holding their breaths.

Martin stands on the end of the dock that floats out from the cliff below where the house would be, in sight of trees he knows already, before the familiar water. He is imagining details, straining to glimpse a school of grilse, quicksilver flashing in the black, willing the pod of whales to pass, expecting the sea otter to appear; he looks up to watch the girl speeding away, the long wake reaching back to him from across the inlet, a widening triangle dissipating slowly behind her as teary-eyed, but resolute, she races away.

He aches with guilt, overcomes an initial anger at its intrusion; at this of all times, he rages to himself, blaming her; and, curious, all this feeling, he thinks, remembering how she had irritated him. But there is no escaping it: he had behaved badly toward her and missed her already. He had sent her away after the long trip, a risky one in such a small boat, without more than a few minutes rest, he had forced on her a handful of money, for gas, he had insisted, though there was far more in the wad of bills than that. Whelmed by excitement over his arrival here, his betrayal of the girl's friendship, he had tried to buy her off. He is selfish, he said to himself. It would not have hurt to bring her up with him; but he had so wanted the moment for himself, a moment already gone wrong.

Blinking repeatedly, Martin removes his glasses, polishes them with his old black scarf, blows on them, both lenses spotted, rubbing the saltwater drops away. He sighs and searches the inlet again. Eyes wide, he looks about at the water, the mountains across the way, the sky, watches a single crow approach and disappear behind him. Still he does not turn to go up to the house, stands motionless holding his bag with the one good hand, staring up at the smoke undisturbed by any breeze it streams into the sky. He had not anticipated interference with his imagined reunion, and now stands motionless, staring at his feet. Turning to walk along the dock to the weathered wooden stairs that zigzag up the cliff he looks back over his shoulder, squints after the diminishing form, strains to hear the engine, something of hers. Nothing. He hears himself breathing through his nose, that, and the sloshing of water beneath his feet, and wishes the girl, his partner, he says to himself, was with him still.

She had wanted to disembark, had implored him to let her come along, to make sure everything was all right. Father, what if... she had asked, unable to finish; Martin pointed to the steady vertical line of chimney smoke seeming to issue from the top of the cliff, the rock overhung and yellow-fringed with fragrant broom above them, the smoke a steady pale gray smudge rising behind. Her lips had trembled.

Martin shudders; his hand aches. He was barely able to cope with his sudden anger, the responsibility he felt toward her, the sight of her sorrow; but this time, after so many years, he'd told himself, was his; this time he would shuck attendance on another's feelings. He'd wanted to bless her, but balked in time over the cheap gesture. She wouldn't look at him. Here was none of that posing for a religious portrait of a preternaturally put-upon saint, the understanding, forgiving smile at which she was so adept that he had found himself infuriated and amused, eventually smiling in response to it on so many occasions in just these twenty-four hours. Martin thought through his confusion, remaining uncomfortably resolute. She had risked much to help him.

Theresa did as she was told, seeming to accept his shabby treatment of her; already scheming, as she pushed off from the dock, already planning, as she swallowed her emotion, to come back. She, like the adult mother she sometimes played, knew what was best, even for a priest.

Eyes watering, Martin turns toward the cliff, tiptoes over the floating dock. He moves, a dark anomalous silhouette against the gray sky, as though concerned about unsettling the stillness lest he wake someone, and be noticed. At the stairway, he pauses to look up the first flight, struggles for balance, steps up, starting his ascent anxious, confused, out of breath, unable to use the handrail, gripping the Gladstone in his one good hand.

Theresa's stomach grumbles. She drifts, observing Martin through binoculars from the other side of the inlet, lifts on her own swell, her wake now caught up with the coasting skiff, sees him wobble as she rises and falls with the waves, watches him slowly making his way up the weathered stairs, stopping every few steps, seeming, eerily, to turn toward her after every other step, appearing to be looking back at her, then carrying on within the magnified circle, climbing with the tired deliberation of an old man. She had not yet thought to raise her glasses to the house; she focuses solely on him, the slowly ascending priest who, she decides, in order to account for certain lapses in what she considered acceptable priestly behavior, had abandoned his priestly authority for this quest that she had invested with inarticulate significance, of a kind that had certain correspondences, some unspoken coincidence, with Martin's own sense of resolve. It was—and she was conscious of the paradox but comfortable with it, let it be, did not strain to load her intuitive certainty with anything more definitive—it was as if in divesting himself of his symbolic authority he had become genuinely, significantly holy. She was partaking in it; even felt—and then blushed with humility—that she was like a guardian angel or, more likely, and she loved this idea, a handmaiden of the Blessed Mother herself, assigned to protect the priest on his quest. But with all this heartfelt imagining of a self-consciously fabulous nature—and she knew it was, but thrilled and teased herself with it still, did not discount it as unreal—she was driven by an unrealized sense of something like maternal instinct, in the womanly way of her mother. Now become less like the child playing, to which she was accustomed, she felt protective of this man in the way her formidable mother had for the men in her life, protective in her very being. She felt guilty, too, ashamed for the pain she caused Martin, had been conscious of effect after all, for all her distress and shame at not being allowed to accompany him.

She gasps self-consciously at what she sees, lowers the binoculars and realizes with a shudder that she is bleeding and has nothing with her to staunch the flow. She hurriedly buttons her black slicker all the way down to her knees, and sits down behind the stainless steel wheel, gripping then letting it go, picking at a thumb nail. She resolves to return to the island. With trembling hands, feeling the warm flow soaking her underwear, she raises the binoculars, finds the image of a tall figure leaving the house toward the wood behind, walking hurriedly, seeming at one time to stop and fix her from the distance, stare at her, before turning away and disappearing. She flinches from the imagined eyes. This was a second glimpse of activity above the cliff. In the first, she had watched this same form moving quickly and purposefully, as if pursued, from the front of the house. She found Martin again, too, still making his labored way up the stairs, stopping every few steps to catch his breath and look out to sea; she raises the glasses to spy on the other, now heading toward the wood. Again he stops, turning around as if to stare back at her; so boldly, she thought, standing there as if looking right at her, as if, for the magnification is not strong enough for anything beyond suggestion at this range. She lets the glasses, hanging from a rubber cord, drop to her chest, flinches from their painful impact, sits fixed and overcome by possibilities, uncomfortable, unable to act.

She shivers, staring through an unfocused blur at the distant island, watches a dark pointillist shade detach itself, a flock of crows rising above, then settling back onto the wooded crown near its center, just below the highest elevation, a cone of bare rock. She heard their cawing in the moment they took to the air; hears nothing from them now. It has to rain soon, she thinks, absentmindedly watching the lowering sky closing in from the open ocean to the west. She feels her mother worrying about her, sees that she is drifting toward some rocks. Fumbling with the key she restarts the engine, speeds back toward Thomas's island against a light chop and a tickling westerly cat-pawing round her as full throttle she races, goaded by dreadful imaginings.

At about the halfway point the engine, starving, but with very little fuss, died. Theresa, unwilling to think about her situation in too much detail, slid the oars out from under the thwart, fitted them in the gunwales and started to row.

Martin accepts more tea. He has not touched the first cup, already cold before him, a digestive biscuit leaning out over the saucer, also untouched; the saucer of a different pattern, he notices, from the cup. A young woman smiles, and refills an older woman's cup, and then her own. She takes away his existing tea , returns to pour him a fresh cup, and lays it before him, the cup and saucer again mismatched, from yet a different series, the cookie gone. She sits down and smiles back at Martin, who twice already has failed to stop himself from staring, marveling at the familiarity he feels toward her; disturbed by what he imagines he knows of her intimacy with Thomas, and also by something he cannot account for. She remains shadowy, soft light from a window framing her from behind. The older woman smiles at him too, a smile limned with amazement, affection, and some amusement. She does not appear to notice the young woman.

Jane: tall and gaunt, posture fine, hair completely gray, beautiful, as she should be, Martin thinks. Concentrating on a series of images accompanied by his own running commentary, he is conscious that he is at the same time missing most of what is being said, hearing only snatches of phrases, bits of words, beginnings, endings, partial sounds for things he desperately wants to know, this voice, then that, only just heard, never enough.

Something of a miracle has taken place, he feels, a happy accident at the least that they should all be suddenly together again. What a wonderful surprise, he wants to say, wants to say more, has something other than such exclamations to make; but this unsettling sensation, positively weird, he thinks, grows insistent, rhymes with an anxiety turning in his stomach. Eyes blinking, he continues to believe he is missing substantial parts of talk, whole conversations, must strain to find his place in this scheme of things but can't keep up. Keep up! as Thomas used impatiently to exhort him in conversation whenever he showed resistance to some improbable ordering of ideas.

Martin blinks. Here is Jane before him, close up, showing him her scars with that smile, those eyes, now the deeper sorrow that went so well with their riant glitter, he thinks, a thought resonating in the voice of some fashion commentator, he considers, missing more, whole periods of what have to be explanations of the most important kind. Here, though, at least, is that lasting trust, the familiar humor of a particular friendship, undiminished no matter what time has passed between the last and the latest meeting; and she is close to him, having made a joke that he has missed, smiling, her smile now half-crooked, half-beautiful, with a long tapered finger showing him where the bullet entered, taking his good hand and touching it where the bullet came out; and even as he does so, the sensation is of having missed touching it, not feeling her touch, not keeping up.

She is dressed in familiar men's clothes; her hair tied back in a ponytail. The young woman appears to be wearing only a man's white shirt and heavy woolen socks. She doesn't speak—if she did, he missed it altogether—and seems less distinct than Jane, moving slowly in the shadows, he never acknowledged by her, he realizes, blinking rapidly, unsuccessfully trying to clear his throat.

Martin wants to drink some tea, to take a bite from the biscuit no longer there, but cannot make the necessary movement. He wonders where the cookie has gone, curses himself for having missed more of what he knows are the answers to all his questions, thinks himself smiling, hopes he doesn't look too foolish, as he knows he must, wearing his bemusement on the outside, confusion dressed in a smile, the smile on the skin outside, he remembers Stendhal, sidetracked by increasingly inarticulate anxiety, self-conscious of his facial expression, feeling it numbly, yet distinctly, etched on his face, a frozen expression as the saying goes, he says to himself, conscious of his own lineaments. Bizarre sensation, he thinks, feeling these features of his that, despite the miracle of seeing Jane, the satisfied curiosity of seeing that girl, he knows to be a deep etching of despair. He does not wish to deal with this just now. Later. It is not new to him, but he hopes it's not too obvious. He doesn't want to give the impression that he isn't grateful to see Jane. He had thought… It wasn't as though he weren't delighted to see her. Maybe not delighted, he now considers, thinking he should be as happy as can be, nagged instead by some realization still distant, approaching… . In any event, he thinks to himself, they don't seem too bothered, and he manages to glance, with his eyes doing all the moving, head and neck not answering his desire to turn to one and then the other and smile, no, grimace, he thinks, feeling less well as the ticking of his wrist watch, the old stainless steel Rolex with the lizard strap that his father had given him when he graduated from the seminary, accompanied by the joke from the dear old man that it should return him safely from the eternal from time to time, ticking so loudly, reached him from all the way down by his bad hand, lying somewhere down by his side, and which didn't feel like anything at all just now. He glances up, and back and forth with even more difficulty. No one appears to be discomfited at all. No one is saying anything, just looking. No one had said anything, he realizes. He wants a breath of air, breaths deeply, tastes the freshness of outdoors that Thomas has written of: mixture of earth and tree and salt air; and now rain. He can smell the rain.

Curious, he thinks to himself, again focusing on the women, he has not been asked to account for being here. What for him has been an extraordinary adventure was, if their polite and normal behavior is anything to go by, as if it were nothing to talk about. It is as though it were perfectly natural that he should have passed by, dropped in and stayed for tea this afternoon; as if he had done so with enough regularity that there wouldn't be any urgency for him to account for himself; as if he'd just popped in from next door. He wants to rub his nose.

Both women are looking at him with what he thinks might be sympathy. Eyes straining, he looks back from one to the other, focusing on these faces that now anticipate his question, beseech him not to ask it, their faces increasingly horrible with knowledge of what he wants so much to know. His thoughts, he decides, are not independent of the others. What of his identity, then, he wonders? What of theirs? (Violently he blinks away a grotesque composite image, a single monster of conglomerate life, a grotesque and lonely organism trapped in senseless orbit around nowhere, lone sentient monster on which he is little more than a protrusion, a diminutive pathology, mole, wart, tumor, cyst. He squeezes his eyes shut again.)

To ask a simple question, the kind with a practical answer attached, nothing fancy, no straining for truth. That's all he wants now. I'll ask the obvious question, then explain myself at least a little, even if they do seem to already know, or not to care. He had come a long way, after all. He would have gestured to his Gladstone, perhaps even reached in and lifted from it the manuscript if he could have. He wills himself to ask them something, but by his effort finally wills them away, the two wearing the full compliment of regret on their faces, both women at first so lovely, now so frightening in their sorrow, metamorphosing into the embarrassment, the ugliness of powerless distress, vitiated of identity, reduced to mere matter before his eyes which he squeezes shut, seized by vertigo and a last sensation that travels the length of his body from head to toe, a sensation first of searing, then sweet pain that even—and even now he is embarrassed—makes tumid his prick; only for a moment, all sensation suddenly gone.

Martin is only eyes and ideas once more. He looks after the diminishing faces. They fade into the shadows that have overtaken the so-very-familiar-seeming house. He recognizes the desk by the window, the fireplace; thinks he sees the cat, her eyes catching light and flashing it back at him.

He closes his. He will rest a little before deciding what to do. He hears a voice from far away. Theresa is calling. Can't she see he is trying to rest? remembers that he wants to apologize to her, wills with all he has that she should know he is happy she is back. After many years of not having people near him whom he wanted there, it was the girl's companionship, for such a short time, too, that had made him feel something special. Father! He hears from far away.

He opens his eyes; doesn't know after how long, doesn't think to even try checking the time, no longer able to hear the ticking of his watch. Eyes open and lying on his back he sees the familiar, dreadful, sight of fir boughs waving above him, of tall swaying tree trunks all around, a dark gray sky beyond, which opens just then, pouring down on him, while the so very tall and deep green trees groan and motion above. He is playing his old game, willing to see beyond the clouds, through the atmosphere into outer space, and so he does. Through rain and dark, he sees the stars as he had sometimes done as a child, stretched out on his back, lying on the prickly grass in the yard, straining to glimpse them as not so far off in the background, kitchen sounds and smells conspiring with gravity, and the bees working the nearby row of raspberries to hold him down, have him stay a little longer among those that loved him so—lying there, feeling the grass grow, looking beyond the blue.

Everyone stands about, stands quietly, respectfully, just out of sight. The voice of the girl comes from far away, calling to him. Everyone he knows is here. Without exception. This can't be, he knows, yet doesn't trouble with it further, everyone miraculously fitted into a circle, standing around, looking down. He can't move, takes the rain drops, now the downpour, full on his face, can't turn away or even blink and the drops water and soothe his eyes once he accustoms himself to their impact, images carried over his eyes, parceled in ever-moving drops, sliding over his cornea one after another, passing forms of these figures standing round, closing in, the dark waving shapes above.

He lies quite still; only the odd glitter of raindrops falling over his eyes betrays now and again a slight, flinching life. It is almost dark. A squirrel deliberating in fits and starts advances, retreats, dithers in a frenzy of indecision and in a pique bites his good hand. Martin has no treats to offer. The deer downwind flex their snouts and snort, keeping a wary distance.

Rain pours down on Martin. Thomas stands over him. Finally Thomas, Martin thinks, contained within two rain drops, two of him, one on either eye; now stereoscopic, superimposed in depth on one another, balanced, staying in sight for a moment longer than the others, poised on top of his eyes. Martin, he says, the voice less confident than usual, his gun in his right hand hanging by his side, I will get that formula to you.

I am the presence! Martin screams, not, as he thinks, out loud. Martin filled with insight: how important it is not to let one's self be directed by another's bad conscience. He growls in rage at this moral, seeming ferocious to himself, making a little squeak. Sensation rushes through him. Father! The girl's voice implores. Can't she see he is busy? he thinks. And in another moment the temporary reanimation of his feeling fallen off, gone again, and Martin unbound, free of the universal bondage of sensation. But he wants it back badly, wants desperately to reach out and touch Thomas, get his hands on him; he struggles to reach out and grab at him, grab, pull down and squeeze the very life out of him. Again he feels his body prickle and surge, his being, his clothing, ground-and rain-soaked; he struggles to call out, tell him something, growls, screams, unbalances the two rain drops with all his effort, the delicate balance tipped and Thomas, bending over his eyeballs in a last distorted vision, blurs curving over his eyes and flows away.

The girl had done wonders, played the responsible adult to perfection. A few days later at Saint Paul's hospital she was sitting by his bedside devouring a Sweet Marie and watching the priest sleep, turning with less than her usual interest the pages of a fashion magazine that among other things promised on its front cover, just beneath the latest techniques on breast augmentation, to reveal the secrets of what men really want. Earlier, she had seemed to frighten away another priest whom she had surprised standing by the window, squinting, mumbling, holding up to the light an unopened letter addressed to Father Martin. He simpered, called her child in a tone that suggested he might not exactly like children, and asked only that she tell Martin that Father Amaro had been by. Then he had swished away mumbling what sounded to Theresa like nothing so much as curses.

Some days she surprised, and was surprised, by others. In between naps, there had been two Chinese gentlemen. One in particular impressed her with his somehow sinister beauty and elegance (he had especially long and narrow feet); while the other was quiet and pretended not to speak English until apologizing in a fine and resonant voice to a nurse who scolded him for smoking, thereafter returning to type, playing the inscrutable Chinaman once more, stubbing his cigarette into an ashtray, standing up to leave, and bowing slightly, his eyes sparkling and gay, silently sharing his ruse with the girl so that she had to forgive him his act. Her attitude was changing, she reflected to herself. Then, yes, there had been a wonderful priest called Father Stephen who had visited and made her laugh again and again after shooing that oddball Father Amaro away, whom they had both surprised peering into Martin's Gladstone where that same letter and the manuscript, part of its spine protruding, could been seen standing up.

Others had come, and made less of an impression, some leaving flowers, often tiptoeing away almost on arrival as if not to disturb Martin, who had not woken for days. Thus a week passed and one late afternoon Theresa grew tired watching raindrops course down the pane, tired of speculating whether Father Martin somehow knew, in his dreams at least, that he no longer had a left hand—for instance, would he in his dreams see himself with or without it? She wondered this intensely for a time, thinking that, after all, his brain knew that his hand was gone, even if he didn't, then grew dizzy speculating on who he was in relation to his brain, and finally decided she would like something to read. She looked about her and saw nothing, spied the Gladstone, then, and the manuscript, standing untouched with that same letter. She wasn't sure he wouldn't mind, but went over and lifted it out of the case all the same, then reached in after the letter. She returned to her seat by the window with both, picked at a cuticle, looked out the window feeling a little guilty, nothing unmanageable. It was quiet in the ward. The dinner trays had been removed, and visiting hour was over. She opened the bundle over her lap, tucked the letter between some later pages and started to read.

When Martin awoke three days later the head nurse spent more time telling him how the saintly girl had saved his life and, moreover, sat with him for over a week each and every day, and than commiserated with him over his missing hand. And oh, the lasting sensation of which people have remarked after losing a limb… How many times had he lifted his ghostly hand to scratch his nose or rub an itchy eye, swallowing back his panic and rising gorge, bursting into tears only after the first couple of times.

When the nurse had left him, promising to ask after the missing manuscript (and my hand, please Sister, he called after her), Martin lay looking out the window at the clearing southern sky. Under the heaping cumulus a pale yellow and robin's egg blue crack widened, a longitudinal gash across which a passenger jet slowly moved, descending toward the airport; he could see the whole picture by simply turning his head to the right, or his whole self onto his side as he did now, staring off past the grid of streets, the hills and houses and fall trees, into the distance. Thus he lay gazing out the window for sometime before falling off to sleep, and before dying without absolution, but with just the slightest of shudders and, actually, a very pleasant sensation, a stiffening in his legs that he likened, even as it happened, and despite himself, to the sexual spasms of women, of which he had read, to dream of the girl. The girl in her skiff speeding toward the island, the same widening crack in the sky before her now, increasingly obscured by the rising mass where she intends to find the perpetrator of this… this fiction that had killed him.

She knew he was dead. People just know sometimes. Besides, the nurse, who had tried every day to recruit her to the sisterhood of nurses (and Theresa would consider it, she promised), had herself said, confidentially of course, that his heart was too weak to last for very much longer. And there was something else. It was something that tingled in her belly, lingered there, her memory spurred by what she had read and richly imagined. Never absent for long, beside her crusading indignation, were images of the couple and the sulky girl just a couple of years older than herself, whom she had at first taken to be their daughter. Never absent for long… And the man, she would confront him—and she imagined variations on this theme over and over—she would bring to bear his responsibility in this matter with whatever indignation she could muster, remembering how Martin had struggled on his back like an overturned bug, how he had tried to reach his old friend, responsible for this dangerous ruse, the self-indulgence of leisure, this man who had lifted Martin—trembling, his fit subsided—and carried him into the house where Theresa found a telephone and called the Coast Guard. She remembered gazing at him in disbelief, staring at him as he stared at the priest, Thomas sitting by Martin's side on the sofa, speaking in a wonderful voice such words of encouragement, and some others she could not understand. She remembered how Martin had smiled, as if in spite of himself, before passing out. This, the girl imagined, as the looming island blocked out the sky.

With still half a mile to go, she pulled back on the throttle and let the skiff coast. Trembling within, she took a mirror from a large black leather bag and stared. Here was her self and something new. Understandably—here was what Martin had been stirred by, had to catch his breath over, before her own recognition—understandably she couldn't help herself; couldn't help but be drawn by the image, unable to do anything but feast on it, awed, seeing it for the first time, until the wind, gusting lightly from the west, stirred over her, drawing after a veil of hair. Released from the spell of her self, she brushes her hair repeatedly before tying it into a sloppy ponytail. For a time, she stares without focus at the water, wave after wave passing by, wave after wave as if staying in the same place, listening to the light chop slap at the hull, the whisper of the wind. She holds up the glass again, avoids looking into her eyes, paints her lips, and smoothes her handsome brows with a spit-wet fingertip. She did not see that the unopened envelope addressed to Father Martin in the familiar hand that had corrected the confession here and there, and with which she had marked her place in it, which she had carelessly pulled out with the makeup and left lying unsecured on top of the protruding manuscript, lifted just then, took off like a leaf, flew over the gunwales atop another, slightly stronger gust, a fast-passing murmur from the west. It flipped overboard and settled without a splash on top of the sea. For a moment only it stayed on the surface, darkened then with water and its running message, and sank, floating now just under the surface, carried away on the flow, sinking slowly, now wobbling off altogether into the depths, the ink bleeding and trailing off behind in a dark arabesque. She didn't notice, sighed, refocused her eyes and turned away from the waves. She put the mirror, brush, and lipstick back into the oversized bag and prayed… and lead us not into temptation, she said softly, tearing up, almost crying, first over the thought of Martin, then the familiar image of the deposition—oh, the Mother's grief—a habitual emotional accompaniment to the prayer, then her mother, and finally over the momentary realization of the impulse, this tickle of promise that was driving her so. Just for an instant, she thought she would turn back. She continued to waver; just for a moment or so; then pushing the throttle forward, thinking she couldn't, mustn't, had to, she carried on, headed into the wind.

P & P
2004-2022/2023

Acknowledgments

I am very grateful for the patience and excellent care of Marc Estrin and Donna Bister for making this book possible.

Fomite

Writing a review on social media sites for readers will help the progress of independent publishing. To submit a review, go to the book page on any of the sites and follow the links for reviews. Books from independent presses rely on reader-to-reader communications.

For more information or to order any of our books, visit:
http://www.fomitepress.com/our-books.html

More novels and novellas from Fomite...

Joshua Amses—*During This, Our Nadir*
Joshua Amses—*Ghats*
Joshua Amses—*Raven or Crow*
Joshua Amses—*The Moment Before an Injury*
Charles Bell—*The Married Land*
Charles Bell—*The Half Gods*
Jaysinh Birjepatel—*Nothing Beside Remains*
Jaysinh Birjepatel—*The Good Muslim of Jackson Heights*
David Borofka—*The End of Good Intnetions*
David Brizer—*The Secret Doctrine of V. H. Rand*
David Brizer—*Victor Rand*
L. M Brown—*Hinterland*
Paula Closson Buck—*Summer on the Cold War Planet*
L.enny Cavallaro—*Paganini Agitato*
Dan Chodorkoff—*Loisaida*
Dan Chodorkoff—*Sugaring Down*
David Adams Cleveland—*Time's Betrayal*
Paul Cody— *Sphyxia*
Jaimee Wriston Colbert—*Vanishing Acts*
Roger Coleman—*Skywreck Afternoons*
Stephen Downes—*The Hands of Pianists*
Marc Estrin—*Hyde*
Marc Estrin—*Kafka's Roach*
Marc Estrin—*Proceedings of the Hebrew Free Burial Society*
Marc Estrin—*Speckled Vanities*
Marc Estrin—*The Annotated Nose*
Marc Estrin—*The Penseés of Alan Krieger*
Zdravka Evtimova—*Asylum for Men and Dogs*
Zdravka Evtimova—*In the Town of Joy and Peace*
Zdravka Evtimova—*Sinfonia Bulgarica*
Zdravka Evtimova—*You Can Smile on Wednesdays*
Daniel Forbes—*Derail This Train Wreck*
Peter Fortunato— *Carnevale*
Greg Guma—*Dons of Time*
Ramsey Hanhan – *Fugitive Dreams*

Fomite

Richard Hawley—*The Three Lives of Jonathan Force*
Lamar Herrin—*Father Figure*
Michael Horner—*Damage Control*
Ron Jacobs—*All the Sinners Saints*
Ron Jacobs—*Short Order Frame Up*
Ron Jacobs—*The Co-conspirator's Tale*
Scott Archer Jones—*A Rising Tide of People Swept Away*
Scott Archer Jones—*And Throw Away the Skins*
Julie Justicz—*Conch Pearl*
Julie Justicz—*Degrees of Difficulty*
Maggie Kast—*A Free Unsullied Land*
Darrell Kastin—*Shadowboxing with Bukowski*
Coleen Kearon—*#triggerwarning*
Coleen Kearon—*Feminist on Fire*
Jan English Leary—*Thicker Than Blood*
Jan English Leary—*Town and Gown*
Diane Lefer—*Confessions of a Carnivore*
Diane Lefer—*Out of Place*
Rob Lenihan—*Born Speaking Lies*
Cynthia Newberry Martin—*The Art of Her Life*
Colin McGinnis—*Roadman*
Douglas W. Milliken—*Our Shadows' Voice*
Ilan Mochari—*Zinsky the Obscure*
Peter Nash—*In the Place Where We Thought We Stood*
Peter Nash—*Parsimony*
Peter Nash—*The Least of It*
Peter Nash—*The Perfection of Things*
George Ovitt—Stillpoint
George Ovitt—Tribunal
Gregory Papadoyiannis—*The Baby Jazz*
Pelham—*The Walking Poor*
Christopher Peterson—*Madman*
Andy Potok—*My Father's Keeper*
Frederick Ramey—*Comes A Time*
Howard Rappaport—*Arnold and Igor*
Joseph Rathgeber—*Mixedbloods*
Kathryn Roberts—*Companion Plants*
Robert Rosenberg—*Isles of the Blind*
Fred Russell—*Rafi's World*
Ron Savage—*Voyeur in Tangier*
David Schein—*The Adoption*
Charles Simpson—*Uncertain Harvest*
Lynn Sloan—*Midstream*
Lynn Sloan—*Principles of Navigation*
L.E. Smith—*The Consequence of Gesture*

Fomite

www.ingramcontent.com/pod-product-compliance
Lightning Source LLC
Chambersburg PA
CBHW022109310726
48972CB00007B/1950